FROM HERE TO OBSCURITY

"Shulem was born in the same year as Trotsky and Einstein.
Of the three, only Shulem could make a decent pair of trousers"

YS

"Hardest of all, the Luftwaffe will smash Stepney.
I know the East End!
Those dirty Jews and Cockneys will run like rabbits into their holes."

Lord Haw-Haw

FROM HERE TO OBSCURITY

A Novel By

Yoel Sheridan

TENTERBOOKS

2001

FROM HERE TO OBSCURITY

First Published by Tenterbooks

BM Tenterbooks
London   WC1N 3XX
www.tenterbooks.com

A catalogue record for this book is available from the British Library.

ISBN 0-9540811-0-2 Paperback
ISBN 0-9540811-1-0 Hardback

Cover design by Kevin Sheridan

Printed in the United Kingdom

Preface

Some years ago, when watching television, I saw Joseph Burg, the then Israeli Justice Minister, on a visit to his one-time home town in Germany, pointing to an undamaged building and saying that that was where he had lived prior to being forced to leave Germany due to the rise of Nazism. I turned to my wife Tova and said how strange. Why strange? She asked. Well, I said, I cannot visit my previous abode in the East End of London, because it was totally destroyed by the German bombers in world war two. Not only was my house destroyed, but the whole street. Destroyed too, were my infant and senior schools, the Synagogue in which I had my barmitzvah and the infrastructure of the thriving Jewish Yiddish speaking community that lived there prior to the outbreak of the war.

I decided that I would read whatever had been written about the plight of that now non-existent Yiddish speaking community and found that very little, if anything had been written, certainly not regarding the war years 1939 to 1945. There seemed to be an erroneous consensus that Jews of London had not suffered in the war and that they had all been emancipated in the nineteen twenties when the history of British East-European immigrant Jewry came to a halt. This opinion was exemplified in the catalogue to the 1984 exhibition held at the Museum of the Jewish Diaspora in Israel entitled "World of Yesterday - Jews in England 1870 - 1920. The catalogue stated "the exhibition portrays the integration of the immigrants with the older established Anglo-Jewish community, *a process which was essentially completed after World War 1*" (my italics). This statement ignores that, in September 1939, there were about one hundred thousand Jews (forty per cent of London Jewry) still living in the East End London enclave, some thirty thousand of whom were Yiddish speaking immigrants.

I took up this point with the well-known London historian, Professor William J. Fishman, at one of his lectures, and he agreed that the post 1920 period had been mostly neglected by historians and he encouraged me to write about it. Hence this book, which in the Professor's words "brings to life those characters that made up the majority of East European Jewish immigrants who settled in the East End, with style and perception that makes for an exciting and moving fusion of history and literature." I thank Bill Fishman for both his encouragement and (I hope deserved) praise.

I was but a person of tender age when Hitler came into power in Germany and the events recounted in this book occurred during my formative and youthful years. I had no wish to rely on my own memory when recording those events, as the result would have been a narrow parochial view of the earth shattering dramatic events of that tragic twelve year period 1933 -1945. Hitler's rise to power heralded the rise of anti-Semitic fascism in England that led to aggressive attacks on Jews in the East End of London. It led to the outbreak of war in 1939 and to the vicious and deliberate bombing of the borough of Stepney that housed most of the Yiddish speaking Jews of London. Many questions arose. What happened in that period and why and what was the reaction of the local and wider Jewish community? These were questions that my limited personal memory could not possibly answer and so began my extensive research.

I took year-long refresher courses in Yiddish at the Bar Ilan University in Tel-Aviv to enable me to read the London Yiddish newspapers of the time. I have to thank the University and the two lecturers, Rivka Reich and Aviva Tal, in particular, who persevered pleasantly and polished up the rusty Yiddish I had not used since my youth. The Hebrew University Library in Jerusalem provided microfilm copies of *Die Zeit*, the main London Yiddish daily newspaper of the period and the facilities for me to pore over them for hours on end. They also provided microfilm of the London Jewish Chronicle. Later I was able to continue my research in the archives of that newspaper's London offices.

I had no intention to write a simple biographical essay on my own early life and that of my family, but rather to use the personal and family knowledge to describe the life and times of the Yiddish speaking Jews who lived in the East End of London and to give them voice. Here was a vibrant community that suffered untold misery during world war two, that was forcibly scattered into oblivion with no one prepared to tell their story. That in itself was a mystery to which there appear to be two answers. The first stems from the tendency of emancipated British Jews to disassociate themselves from their foreign immigrant roots. The whole Jewish educational system established by the emancipated Jews, was designed to alienate children of immigrant Jewish families from their East European environment. Unlike the USA, Britain was not an immigrant society and it was necessary for immigrants to shed their foreign traits and to become "more English than the English" if they wished to advance within British society. The young were taught to be good Jews, which had a two faceted meaning. One was to follow the Anglicised Jewish religious practices and the other was to behave like an English gentleman and not antagonise the local Christian society by exhibiting foreign mannerisms in speech or gestures. The second and more telling reason stems from the fact that the London Yiddish speaking Jews considered their own suffering as nothing compared to the tragic plight of their European brethren who suffered the true horrors of the Nazi concentration camps.

East London Jewry was never parochial. The community always recognised that anti-Semitic events occurring abroad were likely to have their local repercussions. Although disenfranchised because of their alien immigrant status and poverty, Yiddish speaking Jews were nevertheless in the forefront of the movement for the boycott of German goods in retaliation of the 1933 German decree boycotting Jewish goods and services. Many volunteers for the International Brigade that went to Spain to fight Franco's fascist onslaught on the legitimate democratic Spanish government, came from the ranks of East London Jewry. The Yiddish speakers reacted sharply to the growth of British fascism, economically by boycotting local stores and food suppliers that were supporting the fascists and physically by demonstrating publicly and participating in the famous Battle of Cable Street, that stopped the Mosley fascist march through their enclave and resulted in the government ban on provocative political parades in uniform. They took such action even though the British Jewish leadership called for restraint in fear that open demonstration would annoy the establishment. This was a policy known as "*Sha Sha the Goyim*" (keep a low profile, do not annoy the Gentiles). In the wartime years, their concern for the fate of their brethren and relatives in Europe and Palestine was patently obvious.

My personal knowledge of the events related in this book was more than supplemented by information from my elder brothers and sisters, by eyewitness reports, and books and articles in newspapers and magazines. My uncles and cousins in Israel told me of their immigration experiences into Palestine and deportation to Mauritius, which were supported by press and UK parliamentary reports and records, kept at the Illegal Immigration Museum in Israel. Before and while writing this book, I read extensively whatever material I could find that might be remotely related to the subject. I revisited the East End of London several times, walking the streets, talking to people and retracing steps to schools, *talmud torahs* (Hebrew bible classes), Synagogues, public baths, libraries, theatres, art galleries, museums, the docks, the Tower of London, and the speakers' corners in Hyde Park and Tower Hill. The many weeks that I spent in the Tower Hamlets Reference Library were especially productive and the librarian Chris Lloyd was more than helpful.

I also rediscovered the village of Soham in Cambridgeshire to which I had been evacuated during the war together with my schoolmates at The Jews Free Central School. I was pleased to find that many residents remembered the Jewish "vaccees" or "furriners" who descended upon their village from distant London. So much so that the local Resource Centre under the direction of Michael Rouse, mounted a Holocaust exhibition in 1997 and then published emotionally charged poems written by children of the Soham Village College who attended the exhibition.

I wish to record my appreciation and thanks to all those who gave me encouragement and helped me in the production of this book. I give particular thanks to my wife Tova and our two sons, Mark and Kevin. Tova read every word of the original manuscript and corrected errors and drew attention to omissions. Mark was always encouraging and urging completion. Kevin edited the book, questioned facts, asked for proof and/or collateral sources and requested immediate translations of Yiddish expressions. Any remaining errors are mine alone. Kevin arranged for the publication of this book.

Yoel Sheridan

To my loving parents,
and their lost generation, who once filled the Yiddish speaking
East End of London with vibrancy and *menchlechkeit*.

Chapter 1

Rivka gently pushed open further the partially open door to the front parlour where Shulem was just completing his morning prayers. Rivka's timing was, as usual, immaculate. She knew that Shulem would now be winding the straps of his phylacteries around the edges of the leather boxes before placing them carefully into their blue velvet gold embossed bag. Those boxes contained the religious text that exhorted devotees to keep the word of the Lord close to heart and brain. He would also carefully fold up his prayer shawl, along the obvious foldmarks that appear from extended use, and place it in its bag. He would then carefully place the two blue velvet bags, together with his prayer book, on the shelf reserved for his prayer books, in the right hand cupboard of the mock-mahogany sideboard that filled most of the length of one of the walls of the parlour.

Shulem, she said, your sandwiches are all prepared. He nodded approval. And please Shulem, try to eat something substantial at lunchtime. How else will you keep up your strength through the long hours you have to work? He knew it was not really a question, but rather an admonition. Somehow she knew that many times he had not eaten lunch at all, even though he had never divulged this fact to her. But she sensed it when he came home tired, pale and drawn. Shulem, she said again even more earnestly, Shulem, don't forget that there is something else you must do today. You really cannot delay any more. You must ask for that loan.

Shulem emerged from his house into the greyness of the early morning autumn London atmosphere. He turned right to the corner of the street and then left into St. Mark Street which was more commercial than residential. He crossed Great Alie Street where the Workers' Circle and his local synagogue were located and walked through Half Moon Passage to Whitechapel High Street where it joined with Aldgate High Street. He crossed the main thoroughfare into Middlesex Street which is popularly known as 'Petticoat Lane' and then on to Strype Street where the clothing factory in which he worked was situated. The journey could take him between fifteen and thirty minutes, depending on the weather and his attitude of mind. On colder days he would walk more briskly. On wet slippery days he would walk with care. On miserable days, such as this, he would walk at a steady pace, looking within himself, oblivious to the grey surroundings. He must, as Rivka had said, ask for that loan.

But how had he come to this pass? he asked himself. Not so long ago, his economic position had been much better. Why, only five years previously, he had saved enough to be able to pay the key money required to enter and rent his present home in Newnham Street. More than that, he had put down lino in all the rooms. He had furnished the front parlour with a sofa and a 'mahogany' sideboard, a table and a set of nice looking chairs. He had purchased two new beds that were placed together side by side in the front bedroom where four of his sons slept. Likewise he had provided two new beds for his three daughters, two of whom slept in one bed under the window of the mezzanine room at the top of the first flight of stairs. The other girl had a bed to herself at the other end of the room. He and his wife had shared the upstairs back bedroom with their youngest son who was now five years old and who slept in a blue enamelled iron cot decorated with Dutch children wearing traditional clothes and clogs.

Shulem was an honest man and somewhat naive in that he believed that others were as straightforward as he. This had cost him dear in the past as the few partnerships into which he had entered, had collapsed. He still kept the picture of himself and another, standing in the doorway of a small factory in a street that he could not now remember. One could recognise him as the working partner. He stood there in his shirt sleeves, hands by his side, like a man restless to return to work. The other man is wearing a jacket over his patterned waistcoat. Shulem's work-a-day waistcoat is plain. The chain of his fob watch is showing. He was always conscious of time. The other is wearing a bowler hat while he is wearing a trilby. Being religious, his head was always covered. At home he wore a cap or a yarmulke. He would even sleep with his head covered. For work, he wore a trilby. His bowler, that he brushed with care and kept in a hat box on top of his wardrobe in his bedroom, he kept for Sabbath and high holy day attendances at synagogue, or for weddings. He was meticulously clean and tidy. His clothes were always well brushed and his shoes were always shining bright whatever the day and whatever the occasion. He kept one black jacket, waistcoat and trousers for Sabbath and festival wear. For weddings, he would convert this suit into a tuxedo outfit by attaching silk facings to the lapels of the jacket and silk braid down the outside legs of his well pressed trousers. The attachments would be removed on returning home from the function and stored away for future use. Shulem always stood upright and also sat upright except when working with his back bent all day over a sewing machine. He was not tall, but made most of his five feet six inches by his natural upright stature. In the picture, his hair was black and he wore a short clipped King Edward beard. Now he was going grey, he had shaved off his beard but kept his full moustache. He did not shave every day, but allowed himself the luxury of going to the barber's every Friday where he had a shave and his hair and mustache trimmed. Shulem did not work on the Sabbath or other Jewish Holy Days.

He kept the picture as a reminder of one of his unsuccessful attempts to escape from poverty and the London East End self-appointed Jewish ghetto in which he lived. He was not alone in this situation. Mass Jewish emigration from Eastern Europe began in the 1880's. It resulted from the violent and widespread pogroms that swept through that region following the assassination of Czar Alexander ll. Many Jews then found their way into Britain. Ten to twenty times as many went to the United States of America. Many members of the relatively small, but well established mainly middle class and professional anglicised British Jewish community were not too happy about this influx of foreign Jews. They were concerned to maintain the position that they had so painstakingly built up for themselves over the previous hundred or more years. The mainly Yiddish speaking, mainly poor immigrants who looked and dressed so differently from them, were likely to erode their position and give rise to yet further bouts of endemic British anti-Semitism. The East End of London was already overcrowded with the indigenous poor and this influx of immigrants could only make a bad situation worse. Attempts were made to dissuade more immigrants from coming, but the politico-economic situation in Eastern Europe was so bad that the flow of refugees could not easily be stemmed. British Jewry raised funds to finance onward travel to the United States and even to help immigrants to return to their countries of origin.

The British government introduced the Immigration Restriction Act in 1905, after which East European Jewish immigration began to dwindle and effectively came to a halt with the outbreak of the First World War in 1914.

Those East European Jews who came to London in the 1880's located themselves in the Whitechapel area in the borough of Stepney. This was an impoverished area where housing was of inferior quality and rents were relatively low yet outrageously high for the miserable quality of accommodation provided. It was a traditional area for reception of immigrants. The Huguenots had settled there some two hundred years earlier and then departed. Their church in Brick Lane was later converted into a synagogue for the 'Keepers of the Faith' where a *minyon*, the Jewish religious quorum, could always be found at any hour of the day or night. Jews coming home from, or making their way to, work at unusual hours could call in to say *Kaddish*, the special prayer of remembrance for their dead relatives, that always requires a *minyon*. Many Irish made their homes in Stepney in the nineteenth century, when most of London's bridges, tunnels and docks were being built. The Irish stayed. Their songs of home were legion and one that perhaps, best reflected their hopes and plight could often be heard through the walls of the many public houses in the area.

Oh Mary, this London's a wonderful sight
Where the people are working by day and by night
They don't grow potatoes nor barley nor wheat
But there are gangs of them digging for gold in the street
But dig as I may, I might just as well be
Where the mountains of Mourne sweep down to the sea

The East End of London stretches from Wapping in the south, where the St. Katherine's Dock was situated on the north bank of the river Thames just east of the Tower of London, through the constituencies of St.George's in the East, Whitechapel, Bethnal Green, Hoxton and Shoreditch to Hackney in the north. It begins on the very eastern borders of the City of London and stretches eastwards from Aldgate, Houndsditch and Bishopsgate through Whitechapel, Mile End to Limehouse and Poplar where the West India Dock was located. Much of this area was previously called Tower Hamlets, a name since re-adopted in the mid-twentieth century. In the 1880's the area was occupied by the indigenous English poor. They spoke cockney, an East and South London dialect that is characterised by dropping aitches at beginning of words that normally require the 'H' to be pronounced or adding aitches where not required to some words that begin with vowels. Also 'Th' becomes an 'F' if it appears at the beginning of certain words and a 'V' if it appears in the middle or at the end. Thus 'She is firty years old and lives in 'er 'ouse hover there wiv 'er bruvver.' They also make use of a cockney rhyming slang where the second unspoken word of a pair of words, rhymes with the intended word. Thus 'Apples' means stairs because the unspoken 'and pears' completes the rhyme. True cockneys are born within the sound of the bells of St. Mary-le-Bow church situated just inside the boundaries of the City of London.

The East End was overcrowded and parts of it were the refuge for prostitutes and criminals. The famous unsolved Jack the Ripper murders that took place in 1888 dramatically brought the monstrous deprivation and overcrowding in the area to the attention of the public at large and were major contributors to the movement to improve housing conditions for the working poor. Parliament introduced unprecedented legislation for the total demolition of a large area of slum housing in Stepney. Unfortunately Parliament did not also make provision for alternative accommodation and so, when part of the area was cleared of housing, the tenants merely moved into adjoining districts, aggravating still further the poor conditions prevailing there. It was in this atmosphere that the mass immigration of East European Jews was taking place, adding to the already overloaded labour and housing markets.

4

Charitable and not so charitable Trusts soon entered the scene and began constructing tenement buildings on the low priced vacated sites, for rental to the working poor, many of whom were employed in the tailoring and bootmaking sweatshops.

The immigrant Jews were mainly Yiddish speaking and while many were anxious to learn English others were too busy trying to earn enough to maintain themselves. Husbands often came first by themselves to find work and accommodation before sending for their wives and children. The established Jewish community was more than eager to educate the new arrivals in the ways and mores of English life. If they could not change the ways of the adults, they were determined to instruct the younger generation in the proper ways of English behaviour. Schools were established and existing ones expanded. The Jews Free School that was established in 1732, became the largest school in the world with over four thousand students at the end of the nineteenth century.

The East European Jews who comprised the first wave that descended on the East End of London were first employed in the existing small factories and sweatshops. Some soon established small businesses of their own. As their own economic position improved they tended to move out of the East End, first moving northwards to Hackney and Stamford Hill and then further to the northern suburbs of London. Others moved west or further east and some crossed the river to south London. The whole East End of London was hustle and bustle. When Sholem Aleichem, the great Yiddish writer visited London during this period, he wrote that he had not, in his entire life, seen such excitement, clatter and activity, or hubbub. As he put it, the place was crowded like poppy seeds (in a *Hooman Taschen* - a Purim festival ear-shaped pastry) and the people were running to and fro like ants. There was no elbow room and one had to aggressively elbow one's way through the apparent pandemonium.

Each wave of immigrants tried to leapfrog out of the Ghetto over the backs of the next wave of newcomers. Those Jews who came to London after the 1905 Immigration Restriction Act had very few backs over which to jump. Their many efforts to set up businesses were defeated by the economic recession of the twenties and the deep depression of the thirties. Shulem was among the latter, having arrived in London in 1912 at the age of thirty three.

Shulem was now fifty four and had reluctantly accepted the fact that he was no businessman. He knew well enough how to conduct a business, but as Rivka often reminded him, he was too intellectual, too soft hearted and not sufficiently hard headed for that barbaric jungle. That is what Rivka had said, and she was right. The clothing industry had been boosted by military requirements during the Great War. But any savings he had managed to accumulate during the war years had since been dissipated in his unfortunate business ventures, or utilised to furnish the rented house in Newnham Street. He was thankful that at least his home was decent and intact. There were many others much less fortunate than he.

This house was so much better than the previous overcrowded two room apartment that he had rented in the tenement buildings in Bacon Street, off Brick Lane, where toilet facilities had to be shared with other families living on the same floor. Now that he was living in a six roomed house with its own private toilet, he could not imagine how they had managed to live in those terribly cramped conditions. Only Rivka knew how she had organised feeding, washing and sleeping arrangements in such a way as to keep the family of nine intact while maintaining the essential privacy of growing teenage boys and girls. But when number ten was due to come on the scene, even Rivka realised that all limits had been crossed. And so, Yulus, the last born, was both a burden and a blessing. A burden that the crowded Bacon Street apartment could not carry, and a blessing in that a move to better housing conditions became inevitable. Now, at least, in Newnham Street, the family could breathe and the girls had the privacy of their own room.

Times had since become harder and he had agreed with Rivka to take in a lodger. They had moved their bedroom downstairs to the back room that had a window that looked out onto the back yard. The room was divided from the front parlour by large wooden double doors that were usually kept closed, as the back room also housed a foot treadle operated Singer's sewing machine. This machine was an essential investment. He would use it to make the children's clothes from remnant materials that he purchased cheaply in the markets or that he honestly gleaned from work. The upper back bedroom was to be converted to accommodate the lodger. A new bed and bedding had to be purchased together with a wardrobe and a gas hob for cooking and jugs and bowls for washing and this that and the other and a chamber pot for nighttime use. This latter was absolutely necessary. The only toilet in the house was situated in the back yard, in a small outhouse. Access to the yard was through a door in the scullery that adjoined the kitchen. Access to the scullery was through the kitchen which was also the main living room where the family would congregate for meals, listen to the newly acquired wireless set, meet, discuss, quarrel, reconcile, laugh and, in the summer months, count the number of flies that had come to a sticky end on the fly paper hanging from the central light fitting.

Rivka had already found a lodger and had committed herself to buying all the necessities to accommodate him. *Rosh Hashanah*, the Jewish New Year, was in the offing. The younger children were growing and required new clothes and shoes. He had never failed to outfit them anew each year as the winter approached or again in the spring before the Passover festival. Hard times or not he was determined to continue this practice. That was why he needed the loan.

Chapter 2

Rivka watched Shulem walk with his steady gait down the street until she saw his upright silhouette disappear around the corner into St. Mark street. She was astonished that he still had such an upright stature after working so many hours each day with his back bent over a sewing machine. And often, when he came home at night, he would bring a bundle of material to make up into some garment or other, either for work or for her or one or other of the children. Rarely for himself. One of his favourite sayings came into her mind. *Allus fur di vibe und di kinder*, everything for the wife and the children, he would exclaim in Yiddish, his deep black eyes atwinkle.

Rivka's own working day had started much earlier. She had already been to the baker's in St. Mark Street to buy fresh bread and platsels, circular rolls with a halfway deep hole in the centre into which sliced or chopped onions had been placed before baking. This baker did not bake beigels which were also round but with a full hole in the centre. She will have already prepared breakfast, and in the winter months, have cleared the grate of ashes from the coal fired 'Kitchener' situated in the kitchen.

The Kitchener, made of black wrought iron, stretched across an alcove in the kitchen. To the right side of this device was the fire place that was fed with coal through a hole in the top, the iron cover of which often got red hot. The centre of the cover had a circular indent with a small crossbar designed so that it could be lifted by use of a metal bar with a curved forked tongue at its end that fitted under the bar. The front of the fire had a vertical iron-barred grating through which the burning coals could be seen and through which heat radiated into the room. To the left was an oven which was heated through an adjoining side wall. In some houses, a boiler was installed at the back of the fire so that the device provided economical heating, cooking and hot water. Smoke from the fire escaped up the chimney, that had to be cleared of soot from time to time by black-faced chimney sweeps.

Coal for the fire was kept in a cupboard under the stairs, access to which was through a door in the kitchen immediately to the left of the entrance to the kitchen. Some houses in the district had coal cellars, access to which was through a metal covered coal hole in the street. Some kept coal boxes in the yard. The coalman would download a large canvas sack of coal from his horse-drawn cart onto his back. Holding the sack by its ears, he would trundle down the narrow passage that led from the front street door, down three stairs, manoeuvre skillfully through the kitchen door by ducking under the lintel, make a sharp left turn, and empty the sack of its dusty contents into the cupboard under the stairs. Rivka, or one other of the family, would have already opened the cupboard door and removed any possible obstruction in the path of the trundling giant who miraculously avoided damaging or even marking any walls or doorjambs on his trek through the house. The cupboard door would quickly be closed to prevent swirling coal dust from permeating the kitchen. The falling coal would rumble like thunder into the cupboard. On stormy nights, when one or other of the younger children would be frightened by thunder, Rivka would calm the child by saying that it was only the coalman delivering his heavy load. The coalman would carefully fold the now empty canvas bag in such a way as to minimise any leakage of coal dust, collect the price of the coal delivered and return to his horse and cart.

These rough, tough coalmen seemed to have a deep rapport with their hardworked but wellgroomed and patient horses that daily dragged their heavy loads through the cobbled streets of London.

There were many jokes told about the mighty strength of coalmen who wore one-piece leather skull caps attached to capes that fitted tightly over their heads and draped over their shoulders to protect their necks and backs. They often wore sleeveless jackets that revealed thick, hairy and bulging muscular arms. One story told was that of a coalman who, tired and worn, had reached the last call of the day, which was to deliver a sack of coal to a customer on the fifth floor of one of the tenement buildings. The load on his back seemed to get heavier and heavier as he ascended the stairs. When he reached the third floor, he discovered, to his sorrow, that instead of lifting the coal sack, he had lifted the horse up by its ears! Another story was told of a husband who explained to his friend that one day he came home only to find the formidable figure of a coalman in bed with his wife. What did you do? asked the sympathetic friend. What do you think I did? retorted the deceived husband' I went downstairs and kicked his horse! What else should I have done?

Rivka now had the task of waking the children, who without her cajoling, were unlikely to get to work or school on time. That is, those who were in work. Times were very hard in 1933 and unemployment was rife. She had hoped that the three eldest children (Ha! she thought, one could hardly call them children), who had been born in Poland and who came to England with her in 1913, would have been married by now and set up homes of their own. But despite the fact that the eldest was now twenty eight years of age and the youngest of the three was twenty three, there were no immediate signs of any of them getting married. Friends they had galore. But serious relationships? That was something else. One of the reasons for furnishing the front parlour so nicely when they came to Newnham Street, was so that suitors for the two girls could be received in style. They could then tell their parents how well they had been treated. Likewise, the eldest son could entertain his potential bride and Rivka and Shulem could entertain the potential in-laws with pride. The front parlour had not been used too many times for these purposes. But Rivka continued to hope.

Rivka always called the girls first in the mornings to give them the opportunity to wash and dress first in privacy, before the boys descended on the scullery for their ablutions. There was no bathroom in the house and personal hygiene had to be conducted in the scullery which had the only water source. Hot water was provided from a kettle on the gas stove or kettles that were forever boiling on the Kitchener fire. The kettles had to be refilled from the tap in the scullery by the person who took the last of the hot water from one of the kettles. Who has taken all the hot water? was a common cry from those who arrived late at the scullery sink that served many purposes. Clothes and linen to be washed in the adjoining coal fired clothes boiler were often first scrubbed with a yellow stiff fibred brush or with experienced knuckles and stain removing soap, on a corrugated galvanised scrubbing board in this sink. The washing would be rinsed in the sink before being rung out thoroughly with the expert twisting of wrists, or it would be pulled through a hand operated mangle before being hung out on the clothes line extending from wall to wall in the little yard where the toilet was situated. In bad weather, washing was hung on a framed stand set before the kitchen fire.

Enamel bowls proliferated. Babies and toddlers were bathed in an enamel bowl placed in the sink. Crockery was washed in enamel bowls placed in the sink. Separate bowls were used for *fleishedik* and *milchedik* crockery and cutlery, as meat and milk products and the utensils used for them, had to be kept separately in accordance with Jewish dietary laws. Similarly separate tea cloths were kept for drying meat and milk utensils. The girls shampooed their hair by using enamel jugs and bowls placed in the sink, usually on a Thursday night or a Saturday night after the Jewish Sabbath had ended, even though Friday night was claimed by the wireless advertising broadcasts to be the national hair washing night. The jingle of the popular brand of shampoo kept repeating that 'Friday Night is Amami Night.' Often one sister would help another or they would call for their mother's assistance.

How does a person keep clean in such circumstances? Rivka instructed her children with the maxim she had learned from a friend who had since moved to South London. What you have to do, she would say, is wash down as far as possible, then wash up as far as possible, and then if possible - wash possible.

Adults washed fully at least once a week by visiting the Public Baths called 'Slipper Baths' apparently due to the shape of the baths. The younger children would be bathed in a large oval-shaped galvanised iron bath, a *vunner* in Yiddish, until they were old enough to attend the Public Baths. The *vunner* would be brought into the kitchen and placed before the fire which would be blazing in winter time. It would be filled to the correct level and temperature from jugs of hot and cold water filled in turn from kettles and the taps in the scullery. When empty, it would hang on a hook on the wall of the yard next to the smaller circular shaped bath that was used for boiling clothes and handkerchiefs as an alternative to the boiler. Later, linen and towels were taken to the laundry in St. Mark Street as 'Bag Wash.' This was the cheapest form of laundering because the items sent were never taken out of the rough woven bag that was marked clearly and indelibly with the customer number. Rivka's number was H 11. The dirty linen was washed in the same bag in which it was delivered. The clean bag would be collected with the now clean linen inside and kept for the next wash. Cheap is sometimes dear. The strong detergents and bleach used in the laundering process would damage the linens and towels that sometimes arrived home 'more holey than righteous.'

The shortage of bathing facilities in East End homes made both the local slipper baths and Russian vapour baths popular. Schevzik's Russian Vapour Baths were located in Brick Lane on the corner of Fournier Street, only three minutes from Liverpool Street and Aldgate underground train stations. The vapour baths were open daily for gentlemen, but Wednesdays were for, Ladies Only. A placard by the entrance proudly offered 'The best massage in London and valuable relief from rheumatism, gout, sciatica, neuritis, lumbago and allied complaints.' If one could not bathe each day then it was essential to thoroughly cleanse one's body at least once a week. Orthodox Jews, in particular, would frequent the baths on Friday afternoons so that they could greet the Sabbath without the grime of the working week. Others went to Nevill's Turkish Baths that promised to make a new man of you, to banish all your aches and pains, make you feel years younger and give you extra keenness for business or pleasure. The Turkish Baths claimed to quickly bring relief to all sufferers from rheumatism and kindred troubles. More adventurous souls would go to the Turkish Baths in the Imperial Hotel in the salubrious area of Bloomsbury, where the baths remained open all night.

For Rivka and many of her contemporaries, 'cleanliness was next to godliness.' Much of the waking day was spent in the battle against dirt, insect and rodent infestation that was an intrinsic part of life in the East End of London. Although she had more rooms to clean in her present house, Rivka was grateful that she did not have to deal with the near to impossible conditions she had left behind in Bacon Street. There, the bare wooden floorboards had to be continuously scrubbed with the help of carbolic soap until they were a greyish white. But all attempts to eradicate the blood red wall and bed bugs were doomed to failure. Yiddisher cynical humour was the only real weapon that allowed the defensive human population to survive the persistent onslaughts of the indigenous obnoxious bugs. After the Communist revolution in Russia, the cynics would refer to the bugs and say, With each spring, the Red Army marches. The Yiddish word for a bed bug is a *vunce* and the plural is *vuncen* and so with their typical play on words tenants would proclaim that the slogan of the Bacon Street Tenement Buildings was '*Vuncen* (once and) for All.'

Likewise, it was claimed, that when a Jewish schoolboy was asked to write a sentence with the words once and twice, in it, he wrote, Twice I saw a *vunce*.

One neighbour would say to another, I killed a *vunce* yesterday. So, you should be pleased, the other would reply. I should be pleased, the first retorts, but, you should have seen the size of the funeral!

The house in Newnham Street was not devoid of *vuncen*. Each spring, Shulem joined in the fight against them. The crevices in walls, joins and edges of the wallpaper, the edges of the picture rails that circled most rooms a foot or so below the ceilings, the edges of the skirting boards that ran around the rooms at floor level, all these were brushed with paraffin, while bed legs were stood in cans of paraffin to prevent the bugs from invading the beds and pestering sleepers. The smell of paraffin vapour that permeated the house for weeks, was a small price to pay for keeping the 'Red Army' at bay.

Rivka would prepare breakfasts for all the older children who were working, seeking work or on work training classes and provide them with sandwiches or rolls for their midday meal breaks. Then she would feed her nine year old boy and send him on his way to the Jews' Free School in Bell Lane with admonitions in Yiddish to take care crossing the busy thoroughfares and to come straight home for lunch. Rivka understood, but did not speak English. Sometimes she would ask him to accompany his five year old brother to the Infants' School, which he was often reluctant to do, as it required a small detour from the way he preferred to go. Sometimes Rivka persisted and when she did, she invariably got her way. If one of her smaller sons misbehaved in any way when out walking or visiting with her, she had a clever way of surreptitiously pinching momentarily but sharply the flesh of his arm at her side. She did not pinch with her fingertips but caught the fleshy part of the arm between the upper joints of the knuckles of the index and second fingers. She would give a quick twist. A shriek would emanate from the mouth of the offending boy or his face would flinch to the astonishment of bystanders who could not decipher the cause of the outcry or grimace. Gentle Rivka, whose knuckles had been hardened on the galvanised iron scrubbing board, used this, her only weapon, known as the *Yiddisher Knip*, to good effect. It mattered not on which side of her the unfortunate boy was standing. In this matter, she was ambidextrous. No words needed to be spoken and often just the threat of the *Knip* by word or by gesture was enough to ensure swift compliance with her wishes.

Generally, she would accompany Yulus, the youngest, to the Buckle Street Jews' Infants School as she had done with the older boy until she felt secure enough in herself to let the boy walk to school by himself.

Although the incident had happened so many years back in another town in another country, the fears attached to it still lingered with her. What a trauma that was. Her eyes filled with tears at the thought and her heart would always beat a little faster. She did not relate these fears to anyone, not even to Shulem. He would only say that 'that' was what had happened 'there' and it would not, could not, happen in London. Indeed, one of the impelling reasons for him to suggest that they move to London, was to calm her fears in this matter. The girl, her second born, was only four when she went missing in the little town of Mlawa which was some fifty miles north of Warsaw the capital of Poland. Oh what a panic! One minute she was playing outside their house in Warsawa Street and in the next, she was nowhere to be found. Rivka ran frantically round the streets. She called in at her neighbours. She called Shulem home from work They called again on the neighbours. They enlisted the help of relatives, neighbours, friends and even strangers to search gardens, sheds, everywhere. They went to the police. But days passed and they were distraught.

They went to the Rabbi to ask advice. Prayers were offered up in the Synagogue. They even went to the Catholic Priest, a most unusual thing for religious Jews to do and begged him to ask among his congregation for news of their child. Their beautiful, black haired, black eyed, little girl. Perhaps the Gypsies have taken her. Perhaps...... She would not contemplate any perhaps. We must find her she said.

Three whole days and nights passed. No! They did not pass. They stayed in Rivka's heart those three days and nights. And on the morning of the fourth day, Rivka, distraught, stood leaning against the framework of her front door. She had not eaten, nor slept and hardly had the strength to stay upright, and then, miracle upon miracle, who was that hopskipping down the street? Her eyes were blurred from tears. It could not be. It must be. Pray O Lord it is. She summoned up strength that could only come from deep set hope. She started to run and call out in a voice without words. Neighbours opened windows and doors. What is it? they cried and they too could not believe what they saw.

It was Rivka's little darling black-haired, black-eyed girl. Rivka lifted her, cuddled her, kissed her, wet her with her tears. Baby mine, where have you been? Are you all right. Have you been hurt? Where have you been? The girl was overwhelmed by this reception. She clung to her mother, cried a little, cried a lot. They examined her closely. Physically she appeared no worse for wear. She was still wearing the same clothes. They were a little dirtier but not torn. Through the tears they asked again and again. Where have you been?

Who were you with? But they could get no comprehensible reply from the girl. I don't know, she would answer to all the questions. Leave her alone for now, Rivka said collapsing onto a chair still clutching her found-again child. Later she will tell us.

But she never did. And no one knows to this day exactly what happened. The girl returned safe and sound, but Rivka never fully recovered from the trauma. Who could have done this to us? she had asked over and over in her sleeplessness as she grudgingly lost part of her faith We must leave this place, she whispered to Shulem that night. And he readily agreed. We will go to London, he said. His emotions were not as visible, but deep down, she knew that he too, had cried inwardly for those three days and nights.

From that time on, she watched her babes like a hawk or rather a hen. They were either with her, or with someone she could trust, until that fateful age of four had well and truly passed. Her youngest was now five and she could relax a little if not completely and even entrust him, from time to time, to the care of his elder school-aged sibling.

But today, she would as usual, take and collect the boy from the Infant School herself.

Chapter 3

Shulem arrived at his place of work. He climbed the stone stairs to the factory floor. As usual, he was the first to arrive after the maintenance man who had unlocked the doors and opened the top hinged halves of the high windows with the aid of a hooked pole that fitted into a ring attached to the window latches. The upper halves of the windows hung down at an angle of about forty five degrees They were supposed to provide daylight and fresh air, but as they were never cleaned, the electric lights had to be kept on continuously and East End London air could hardly be called clean. The maintenance man was wearing his blue overalls. He looked at the clock hung high on the far wall, nodded a welcome to Shulem, lit the gas hobs on which stood the heavy irons, pulled the main electric power switch and then the subsidiary switches to start the motors that operated the sewing machines and lit the gas jets that heated the steam boiler for the Hoffman steam irons. The noise of machinery that now filled the room would soon be complemented by the chatter of the girls sitting at their machines and the men standing at their ironing boards and steam ironing machines. This floor did not house the cutting table which was on the floor above, where the noise was a little more subdued.

Shulem clocked in and then removed his jacket which he hung on the lower half of the double hook on the wall reserved for him. He took off his trilby hat and simultaneously replaced it with a cloth cap that he wore while at work. He carried out the reverse procedure when leaving work. In accordance with Jewish religious custom, his head was always covered. He adjusted the armbands that kept his shirtsleeves at the right length. Shulem was not tall, and when he bought shirts that would fit over his broad shoulders he found that the sleeves were too long. He could, and sometimes did, tack up the sleeves to his required length, but sometimes this was not worthwhile and then he resorted to using the metal-ringed elasticated bands which could be bought cheaply enough in Woolworth or some other haberdashers.

By this time, other workers had begun to arrive and take up their places after clocking in. He noticed that the office light was on, a sign that the boss had also arrived. Normally, he did not come in quite so early. Shulem pondered as to whether he should approach him now for the loan, or wait until the tea break. He decided to wait. Who knows out of which side of the bed the volatile boss had arisen? Leave it, he thought. Wait for the best opportunity.

He took up his position at the head of the line of machines. He was the top machinist in this trouser making factory. The rush and bustle started. Every day

14

was a rush. No! Every minute was a rush. Nothing could wait. The boss was gesticulating. This order should have been out yesterday he shouted at some unfortunate. What do you want? that I should go bankrupt already? And where will you be then? He reproached the ironers. You are supposed to press creases into the fronts of trousers. His voice would rise. Is that the front? I ask you. Is that the front? The workers would shrug and grimace when he had gone away. Confrontation would gain you nothing, except perhaps the sack in these times of high unemployment.

Shulem looked down the line of machinists. The girls had their heads down with their eyes on the work in front of them, following the material as it was pulled past the steel needle that rose and fell at such a speed that often the eye could not see the movement. The machines were operating all the time whilst the needle could be disengaged by a latch on the side of the machine. The machines pulled the material through the engaged needle while the machinists tugged the material with one hand and guided it with the other to obtain the correct tension and ensure straight and uninterrupted stitching. When a thread snapped, or a cotton reel emptied, or a colour change was called for, the machinist would disengage and speedily rethread the needle, wetting the end of the cotton thread between the lips to get a pointed end that would pass through the eye of the needle. The author of the saying that complained of the difficulty of passing a camel through the eye of a needle, had clearly not seen these expert machinists at work.

The machinists sat in rows opposite each other at their machines that were separated by a U-shaped well into which the stitched material would fall. An electric motor was located at the end of the row of machines. A circular drive shaft ran from the motor, under the centre well, to the end of the row. A spoked wheel, grooved to receive a drive belt, was fixed at intervals to the drive shaft. Each sewing machine was driven by a leather drive belt looped around the grooved wheel and connected to a smaller grooved pulley that was connected by a smaller belt to yet another pulley. Each machine had a knee clutch mechanism that would isolate the machine from the central drive shaft, in the event of mechanical problems. The clutch mechanism allowed individual broken leather belts to be repaired without stopping the rest of the line from operating. The mechanic would crawl under the bench with a new drive belt and screwdriver in hand to replace the offending belt. Often as not he would be scolded by the girls who suspected that he took the opportunity, while under the bench, to steal a look up their skirts. Sex lessons cost extra! Some would shout to the embarrassment of the mechanic and the giggling pleasure of the other girls.

If work problems arose, Shulem would be called upon to sort out the difficulties. Everyone knew that there was hardly a tailoring problem that

Shulem could not solve. What this intellectual was doing in this place no-one ever knew. Well, they did know, as Shulem himself would say, that economics was the great dictator. But for all that, here was an intelligent man, so well versed in the Torah, that he often acted as lay reader in some *steibels*, little rooms converted into synagogues, where he had been given the honorary title of Reb. He was also well read in secular matters, having read through all the books worth reading of the five hundred or so volumes in the Yiddish section of the Whitechapel Public Library. What? the librarian would remark. Are you reading Upton Sinclair's Oil again? Until you get in some new titles in Yiddish, what else can I do, but re-read some of the earlier books? would be his sad reply.

I was born in the same year as Einstein and Trotsky, he would say when his friends chaffed him about his daily activities, but of the three of us, I am the only one who can make a decent pair of trousers. Tell me, he would continue, how could Einstein get to school and how would Trotsky have engineered the Russian revolution without a decent pair of trousers? They may work with their brains, but who keeps their behinds covered? When it comes to the bottom line, he would add enjoying the pun that applies equally in Yiddish, who is the more important?

Shulem returned to the thoughts that had occupied him on his walk to work. Here he was, fifty four years of age. He had worked hard all his life and what had he to show for it? He was beginning to become cynical. Money in the bank? That in itself was a joke. He had never seen the inside of a bank let alone have any money deposited there. Even when he was in business on his own, or in partnership, he did not operate a bank account, rather he would cash any cheques he did receive with friendly tradesmen. Recently he had opened a Post Office Bank Account in an attempt to save for a rainy day, but so far it contained only a few measly pounds to be touched only in the direst emergency. He had never previously borrowed money, this was the first time. Although he did not approve of it, Rivka did buy items on credit from the local grocers when necessity so dictated. She also bought furnishings on credit from Blundells, the door to door sales company, and who could blame her. She had to feed the family and she wanted the house to look nice.

Who wants windows without curtains? Rivka would say, repeating the smooth sales talk of the door to door salesman. Look, they would say, you don't have to make up your mind now. Keep the curtains for a week. Hang them up. Try them. If you don't like them I'll take them back when I call next week. She, like many of her neighbours would hang the curtains, just to see. And who could resist buying them on easy terms? Not many people. Rivka only bought sensibly, not like some others who overspent and then had to hide away from the debt collectors. Many times, lately, it was not a question of overspending, but rather the result of unfortunate circumstances that overtook a family when the breadwinner suddenly found himself out of work and with little prospect of finding a new job. That is why Shulem did not intend to ask for too big a loan, no more than a week's wages. He did not want to dig himself into too deep a hole.

What else was there in his personal balance sheet? He owned the contents of his home, but not the home itself. That looked way out of his reach. He had a fine family. The elder children contributed to the family income when working, but this current recession was a disaster. Even the eldest son, who was a master tailor could not find work at the moment, and he would not take a lesser position because that would damage his prospects in life. He had great dreams of living in a fine house in a good district. The saying that clothes maketh a person must have been based on one such as him. Any person putting on a jacket hand-tailored by him was immediately transformed into a smart well groomed individual. Now comb your hair this way, clean and polish your fingernails and shoes and I will guarantee that no-one, I say no-one, will know that you live in the East End. Better still he would say, change your name, sharpen up your accent, move, find yourself a good address, and no-one will guess that you came out of the Jewish ghetto. Then you will be able to get on in life. When you consider that he came to England at the age of eight speaking only Polish and Yiddish, he had certainly come a long way. His English was impeccable and he had developed a drawl that fully disguised his ethnic origins. He would dress smartly and sometimes shave twice a day to avoid the five-o-clock shadow that might appear on his smooth cheeks after too few hours had passed since last applying a perfumed astringent. His black wavy hair was cut in the style of the times and held in place by the latest in hair creams and conditioners. We should try to save together, he would say, and put down a deposit on a house in the suburbs.

Shulem was always in two minds about moving out of the East End of London. He had improved his position when moving from the two-room flat in the tenement buildings in Bacon Street to the six-roomed terrace house in Newnham Street. But since his arrival in London, a *greener* from Poland, in 1912, he had not had the time to learn English and as time went by he found that he could survive with the little English he knew. Here in the close environs of the East End ghetto, Yiddish was the lingua franca. The Yiddish daily paper kept him up to date with the news which, as a politically interested person, was essential for him. In the Yiddish discussion forum of his close friends or cronies as his sons called them, he was dubbed the Foreign Secretary, because of his knowledge of international affairs. His peculiar combination of religious and worldly knowledge made him a respected member of his community. This, to a greater or lesser extent, was also true of other Jews living in the area who now considered that local improvements in their standard of living were more important and acceptable than migrating to suburbs of London where anglicised Jews and his eldest son, were encouraging him to live. Besides, once the elder children married and set up homes of their own, the house would become less crowded and much more comfortable and he could then maybe even buy the house or at least introduce improvements The area in which he lived was friendly and *Haimish*, homely. Young children could play in the streets without fear. If anything untoward were to happen, neighbours were always ready to assist. *Shuls* and *Steibels* were nearby. Those other districts may be more salubrious, but socially? What would he have in common? No. Despite the inconveniences, he preferred to stay put.

Anyhow, in these difficult times, such thoughts were pipe dreams. At the present time, his weekly wages were the only real income he had to maintain Rivka and the eight children. The eldest daughter was always in and out of work. She too, was a machinist, but worked in ladies' wear, which was a very volatile branch of the clothing industry. She was six years old when she came to London from Poland with her elder brother and younger sister. Since the 'kidnapping' Rivka and he had spoiled her. It took her a little while to learn the English language which somewhat impeded her schooling and even now she preferred to listen to the wireless rather than read. But she had a wondrous mastery of the vernacular and could hold her own in any argument. She remembered words of many Yiddish and English songs which she would sing on any occasion. She was the only one in the family with a melodic voice. He had taught her to use the Singers sewing machine and armed with that knowledge she would get low paid jobs in appalling conditions which she could not tolerate for too long. She had grown into a beautiful girl and attracted many boyfriends, none of whom suited her taste for any length of time. She had become totally irreligious, would never attend *Shul* nor even attempt to fast on *Yom Kippur*, the holiest of days in the Jewish calendar. She knew how to dress smartly and make up stories that belied her humble origins. She would go dancing at the fashionable Astoria but would rarely bring her boyfriends home. Often she gave them a false name, using the surname of the family along the street who ran a business and so was the proud owner of a telephone, the only one in the street. On a Sunday morning after one of her late Saturday night dancing escapades, there would be loud knockings on the front door. The owner of the telephone would be at the door shouting that, again, again, there is a telephone call for your daughter. Tell her to stop giving our number to her boyfriends, he would shout, but when she came to the door, even he could not deny her those moments of impetuosity. And so they would both run down the street, she the slim lithe one following behind the plump trundling telephone owner, to make her social arrangements for the day or next week.

Then there was her younger sister who was only three years of age when she arrived in London and so language was no problem for her. She soon became an avid reader, reading everything in sight, including sauce bottles but with a strong preference for romantic novels. She too learned to sew on the Singers treadle machine but soon became an expert seamstress and a proficient dressmaker. She was less flamboyant and more determined to better herself through hard work. She tried to save and who could blame her when she begrudged parting with some of her hard-earned money to contribute to the stretched family purse. She too was an attractive girl and although she had fewer boyfriends, the likelihood of her being the first to marry was the greater. She made her own clothes copying the latest fashions and made dresses for her sisters. She was always in work despite the volatility of the rag trade that sported five seasons. Summer, Autumn, Winter, Spring and the Slack season when work was indeed difficult to find. The slack season was said to follow the Lord Mayor's show each spring, an expression that had a double tragi-humorous meaning. One chronological, while the other referred to the fact that a team of road cleaners, humorously called brush and pan artists, always followed the procession led by the Lord Mayor's horse-drawn carriage, in order to clean up the inevitable trail of horses' dung.

Shulem, Shulem, an urgent voice whispered in his ear as a friendly hand shook his shoulder and brought him back to reality. Shulem, tea break. Are you all right? Where were you? Where was I? If I told you, you wouldn't believe me. And so he dismissed the question. Shulem is not himself today, he heard someone whisper. That's true he thought as he took out the platsel that Rivka had prepared for him and then put it back in its brown paper bag. I can't eat now. First I must do what I must do. He stood up, straightened his shirt sleeves, brushed the front of his waistcoat and trousers with the back of his hands, adjusted his tie and walked firmly towards the boss's office. The clean-shaven self-satisfied looking man was sitting on the edge of his cluttered desk examining a sample wadge of suiting materials that he held in one hand while sifting through each sample, feeling the quality of the material with his thumb and forefinger. He looked up as the door opened. He could see the determination in Shulem's face. Shulem, he said, is anything wrong? No, came the answer. Good, he said, so now that you are here, perhaps you can help me. You are a man of taste. Which pattern do you think I should choose for my new suit? Shulem thought to himself, I have come in here for a loan, and he's asking me to choose material for a new suit for him? The one you are holding in your hand looks good, he said aloud. You really think so? I think I prefer this blue herringbone. That too looks good, replied Shulem, thinking in Yiddish *foor voos is er hucking mir oon a chanug*, why is he driving me mad, about suiting materials?

OK, OK, he said shifting aside papers, samples of lining materials, zips, buttons, tailor's chalk and other bric-a-brac of a trouser making factory, to make room on the desk for his suiting samples. What can I do for you? He asked, still smiling at the blue herringbone. I need a loan, said Shulem firmly. There, he had asked. No-one could know how much effort that had taken for this proud man to make such a request. The smile had gone from the boss's face. How much? Well, I'd like the equivalent of my week's wages now. There was a pause. Should I ask him why he needs a loan? The thought flickered through the boss's mind. What for should I get involved in everybody's private business. I've got enough trouble running this business without worrying about his domestic problems, and in any case, Shulem is unlikely to tell me the real reason. Nobody ever does when asking favours. I hope he doesn't ask me why, thought Shulem. Why should I have to explain to him about my personal affairs? Shulem felt the tension rising within himself but kept a calm but firm expression on his face. A full week's wages, eh? The boss asked rhetorically. OK, OK, he said, in the manner of many Jews in the East End. He would invariably repeat such words as OK, OK, yea, yea, soon, soon, sure, sure, in their suitable context. I'll tell you what I'll do, he continued, I'll give you, that is lend you, ninety percent. Is that OK? Sure, sure, replied Shulem, relieved that the ordeal was so short-lived.

Chapter 4

A week had gone by and Rivka was, as usual, waiting for Yulus as he came out of infants' school. While waiting she had been looking at the grey unattractive edifice of the Buckle Street tenement buildings located opposite the school. Once again she thought how pleased she was that she had moved out of Bacon Street where her friend still lived in those old tenement buildings. She had little Yulus to thank for the move. When he was first conceived, she had thought Oh no, not another child. Seven children were not enough? But then she realised that this extra burden was actually a blessing in disguise, because the already overcrowded two roomed flat could not possibly accommodate another living soul, however small. And so they would have to move. Her friend had said to her, Rivka, another one? And she had replied, God decides. Yes, said her friend, who had stopped at five. But who provides? She knew the answer to that only too well. Poor Shulem. He had worked and worked to improve their status and he was still working unnaturally long hours and yet still remained part of the working poor. Perhaps it was a good thing that he would not work on *Shabbas*, the Sabbath or on *Yom Toivim*, the Jewish High Holy days. Otherwise he would most likely have worked a full seven days a week. As it was the hours he worked were sufficient to fill a full seven day week. What other time would he have to sit and read and think and discuss with his family and friends?

Perhaps she should not have been in such a hurry to join him in London. Perhaps she should have waited a little longer for him to have found his feet before making for the Polish port, destination London, with her three children in tow. She had thought to wait, but the influence of gossips in her home town had been too great. A young handsome man in London on his own, they would say, where many young girls were looking for husbands, is a dangerous thing. In any event she longed for him. Although their marriage had been arranged through their parents, as was the Jewish custom in Poland, she had been acquainted with Shulem for some time before they were married in February 1904. They had both already developed a fondness for each other that had soon blossomed into true love. He was not an over demonstrative man but even so he had written many letters that indicated how much he missed her. And how happy he was, when she arrived in London in 1913. They fell into each other's arms, and the first Englishman in the family was born the following year. A child of passion, he called himself. She and Shulem often jokingly referred to him and the second son born in England as the *Englisher menschen*, Englishmen.

As fate would have it, the first World War broke out the year he was born and East European Jewish immigration into England was effectively halted. So, she argued with herself, what would have been the alternative? No, in the final analysis - she had learned this expression from her radical *Englisher mensch*, who was now nineteen - in the final analysis, she had made the right decision. Problems they had and problems they would struggle against, together.

Shulem had managed to retain a large measure of his faith and continued to practice all the tenets of the Jewish religion. She maintained a fully kosher house although her own faith had been somewhat eroded, first by the kidnapping episode and then by the death in 1917, of her eighteen month old baby, the first girl to be born in England. It had been another trauma. She had run away from Poland because she had nearly lost one daughter and here in England, the dreaded flu had claimed her baby daughter in this so-called safe haven. The doctor tried to save her. She had nursed her poor baby, bathed her and prayed for her, but acute bronchitis took her.

Her second Englishman, who was born in 1916, was also sickly and had to be nursed and protected from that deadly flu epidemic, Spanish flu, they called it, that struck the whole of England in the following year. Fortunately the two *Englisher menschen* had grown up to be strong, healthy and intelligent youths. They had both excelled in school. The elder one had won several prizes at the Jews' Free School on various academic subjects before he left school at fourteen. He was also a fine student at *Cheder*, the Hebrew classes, that he attended every weekday evening. So much so, that Shulem wanted him to continue with his religious studies at a local *Yeshiva*. The boy objected but Shulem insisted that he attend some classes after he reached his *Barmitzvah*, his thirteenth birthday, when Jewish youth become adult members of the community and participate in religious ceremonies. On the evening of Guy Fawkes day, when the *Goyim*, Christians, light fires and burn effigies of another *Goy*, the Barmitzvah boy placed a firework under the chair of the teacher and was duly expelled. Even at that age the boy had begun to read radical books and soon knew Karl Marx's philosophy by heart. Recently he had joined the Socialist Party of Great Britain, the SPGB, which was considered by many to be Trotskyist and politically left of the Communist party. At the moment he was out of work. Numbered as one of the unemployed, was the way he would express his condition.

One day Shulem showed him an advertisement in the Yiddish daily newspaper, *Die Zeit*. The advertisement was of the North London Academy of Cutting in Clapton Common, London N.16. - For Day and Evening Gowns. This academy, it stated in grand terms, is the best place to learn designing and cutting with afternoon and evening classes by specialist teachers. Write or telephone to enrol, it said. Listen, said Shulem, you are unemployed and the

22

only real chance you have of getting a new job with some sort of prospects is for you to be an expert in your trade. You are artistic. You are always drawing faces and even cartoons. Why not design dresses? On this matter there was agreement. But why that academy when there is the Parisian closer to home in Whitechapel, that does the same and even more? Look, it also teaches cutting and designing of mantles and costumes. Maybe, said Shulem, but the North London Academy is run by a distant cousin of ours. You remember, through him we got this house in Newnham Street. Oh yes, I do remember, didn't you complain that he took too much key-money and that the rent you are paying is too high? Maybe, Shulem said again, but that was the state of the market at the time, and I was not looking for charity. I also remember how happy you were when you came into this house and found that it had been fully wired for electricity and you ran through the house into every room switching the lights on and off. So we may have paid a bit too much, we may still be paying too much rent, but we are much more comfortable now than we were before we came here. Again there was agreement. We are not looking for charity this time either, just speak to him, you'll see, he'll give you easy terms. And so in the mornings the first Englishman in the family signed on at the Labour Exchange and in the afternoons he started learning his new profession. In the evenings, he attended political meetings. *Shul*, he avoided.

The younger Englishman brought home a certificate proclaiming that he was 'Top Boy' of the Jews' Free School in the year that he left. Then he was fourteen. That is the age they send most of them out into the world to earn a living and learn how to be men. They look so young. True, in the Jewish religion, thirteen is the accepted age to join in adult religious practices, but that is different. The boy is not competing. He is cooperating and contributing to his society with the full support of adults around him. But to send fourteen year old boys out to work, to compete with experienced men or to be exploited by them. This, thought Rivka, was wrong. But what was the alternative when their meagre earnings were an important contribution to maintaining some semblance of decent family life. Mind you, when you hear of the deprivation elsewhere, even here in the centre of the empire, things could be worse. That's what Shulem the optimist always says. After what happened this week, I am not so sure. She must tell her friend about it. Now the boy was seventeen and he too was in and out of work even though he had been apprenticed to become a diamond mounter. The jewelry trade, it was thought, would have better prospects than the tailoring or dressmaking trades. But in these hard times, it mattered not what was the trade. Unemployment was rife and everyone was adversely affected.

The school's double doors opened and out streamed the children, laughing, talking, some running, some dawdling. But where was Yulus? He is usually one of the first out. Oh. Here he comes with the teacher. No, it's not the teacher, it's the nurse. Oy Vey! His hand is bandaged. What has happened? She asked anxiously of both the nurse and the boy. They both began to answer together then stopped. He is a bit of a hero, you know, said the nurse. He really didn't make a fuss. Why? What happened? Rivka asked again and perhaps again while bending down to embrace her son and examine him all over to see whether he was hurt elsewhere. Does it hurt? Where does it hurt? It is only his hand, the nurse said. It is only my hand, the boy repeated. But what happened? It was an accident, the nurse continued, an accident that should not have happened. Yulus was not at fault and the other boy has been reprimanded and his mother told that an eight year old should not be allowed to carry a pen-knife or a knife of any sort. The Headmistress also assembled the whole school and told them all the same thing. What same thing? Rivka's voice was now an octave higher. Her boy's hand is in bandages and this nurse is talking about assemblies and Headmistresses? Yulus, the nurse said, tell your mother what happened. Yulus took a deep breath. I was coming down the stairs in the school and when I got to the landing a boy cut my hand with his knife. What? exclaimed Rivka, her voice yet another octave higher. A boy attacked you with a knife? She could hardly get the last word out. No. No. said the nurse, taking Rivka by the arm in an attempt to calm her. It was an accident. The boy did not do it deliberately. What then? What then? asked Rivka incredulously. It was an accident. The boy was standing on the landing sharpening a pencil with the new knife some stupid adult had given him as a present. The knife was very sharp, and as he cut the wood of the pencil, the knife slipped and shot through the air just as Yulus was passing. It cut him on the back of his hand. I treated the wound immediately and I think it will be all right now. Rivka heard the words, knife, hand and wound and her head was pounding. Can I look at it? She asked and without a pause, she said to Yulus, here let me look at it. The nurse became firm. Please, don't touch the bandage. Bring him to me each day and I will re-dress the wound. You hear, please don't touch the bandage, just bring him to me each day.

Yulus walked alongside his mother. He walked on her left side so that he could hold her left hand with his undamaged right hand. Where are we going? He asked as they turned right onto Leman Street. Homewards was in the opposite direction. We are going to visit our old neighbours in Bacon Street, she said. Tell me, he asked in Yiddish, why did the nurse talk to me in English and to you in Yiddish? Such difficult questions this five year old is always asking, she thought. Why did you ask me in Yiddish? She countered. Because, he said, pausing before continuing, because you don't speak English? His answer changed into a question. Exactly, she said. Why don't you speak English? Why? Why? Everything is Why with you, she said with a little chuckle in her naturally gentle voice. Yes, but why? he persisted. I don't have time to learn, that's why. You and your brothers and sisters are lucky. You all go, or have been, to school, where they teach you to speak English properly and to behave like Englishmen. You are luckiest of all, because you have older brothers and sisters to help you speak grammatically. Your father had to go to work as soon as he arrived in London. And he works long hours. And I am too busy looking after the house and the children and getting meals and cleaning. So that is why your father and I speak Yiddish and not English. Why don't you speak Polish? Another question! Because we don't like Polish. OK? Fine? Yes, but you do understand English, don't you? You know very well that I do. But you don't read English. No, I do not. But you do read Yiddish. Yes I do. But you don't write English. No I don't. And Papa? The same. But..... Rivka, stopped him in mid sentence. Enough for now. We have this main road to cross. Hold my hand tightly.

The two of them had reached Gardiner's corner, so called because of the big store that formed the corners of both Commercial Road and Whitechapel High Street at the point where the roads converged at an angle of forty five degrees. This was also the junction where Leman Street, to the south, and Commercial Street to the north met Whitechapel High Street and Commercial Road. This was indeed a busy junction. Tram lines ran down the centre of Commercial Road and Whitechapel High Street that was a continuation of Aldgate High Street. It is said that these two high streets were by intention, among the widest in London. There had once been a plan to run a four-lane tramway system, east, west, through London. The idea being that the two inner tracks would be for express trams, while the outer tracks would be for local trams with more frequent stops. This grand idea, that would have solved much of London's transport problems, came to a halt at Aldgate, on the eastern borders of the City of London. No-one would give up land in the City of London itself to allow for such a tramway. All westbound trams terminated at Aldgate. There the drivers would stop their trams, disengage and secure their brass driving handles and march in their blue serge uniforms to the opposite end of the tram where they would release and engage their duplicate brass driving handles, clang their bells and begin their eastward journeys. Trams could travel in both directions. Cartoonists would illustrate the inconsistencies of government' and trades union' policies with an imaginary tram as the vehicle of management sporting two drivers operating at opposite ends, attempting to take the tram in both directions at the same time.

Once we have crossed this road, we have to turn right into Whitechapel High Street, walk along until we turn left into Osborne Street which shortly becomes Brick Lane. Then we have to walk down almost the length of Brick Lane, under the railway bridge, past Hare Street, where the *Shul* to which your father belongs is situated, until we reach Bacon Street. It's a long walk and we mustn't dawdle. I know you are curious and like to look into every nook and cranny, but we do not have much time today. You hear? No dawdling. Yulus nodded. But can I ask a question? Yes of course. Why is father's *Shul* so far away from home? Well, when we lived around here it wasn't far away and when we moved your father still wanted to keep up his connections with the people as many of them came from the same town in Poland as we did. But, the boy persisted, he doesn't always go to that *Shul*, does he? No. Because it's too far away? Yes. She answered. The full answer was somewhat more complicated, but she did not want to burden the young head with all the details. Synagogues in England are not supported by the State and so depend on contributions from members. The United Workman's and Wlodowa and Mlawa Synagogue was a very modest institution located between residential housing in Hare Street. It was independent and did not belong to the general Federation of Synagogues which had access to better funding. One of the essential reasons, other than religious, for belonging to a Synagogue, was the necessity to belong to the attached Burial Society. Members generally stayed with their original Synagogues through basic loyalties, but another consideration was the avoidance of administrative problems associated with change. Shulem was now also a member of the Great Alie Street Synagogue, which he attended regularly and where his younger sons would conduct their Barmitzvah ceremonies. Apart from that he would actually take services at local *Steibels*. He could read the Holy Torah scrolls without error and so found himself in demand on occasions when the regular reader was unavailable, and being Shulem, he could rarely, if ever, refuse.

Here, we've arrived, said Rivka. Now let's find number forty six. Did we live in number forty six? Asked Yulus. No. We lived in number forty two. And who lived in number forty four? came the inevitable question. This boy is sure to be an accountant when he grows up, thought Rivka, he is only five and yet he can count to one hundred already. No-one lives in number forty four. Why not? Is it empty. No. What then? It's not there. Is there a space? No. There is no space. So where is it? Listen, that's your last question for now, because we've arrived. But mama? OK, OK, the truth is, it's a mystery. No-one knows why the two adjoining buildings were not numbered consecutively. No-one? No-one!

Rivka! What a nice surprise. Her friend greeted her with open arms and a grand smile. And you've brought Yulus. What a fine boy he is growing up to be. He already looks a *mensch*. But what's happened to his hand? Words flowed out of her friend, non-stop. Don't ask. Replied Rivka. What happens in schools these days, is not worth talking about. Rivka, Rivka! It's so nice seeing you. Sit down. Have a cup of tea. The kettle's already boiling. And you, young one?

Would you like a glass of milk? The friend did not wait for an answer. She was already busying herself in the kitchen, pouring out the tea and the milk. Here, she said to Yulus, sit here by the table and drink. He climbed on to a wooden chair that had been scrubbed white and sat by the wooden table that was covered by an oil cloth, a *serutta*, the one time pretty pattern on which had more or less disappeared after a myriad of scrubbings. He looked down on to the plain floor boards which too were a greyish white, like the chairs. The clean smell of carbolic soap, permeated the air. Rivka, her friend continued. You look so pale. Your hair looks nice, but your face is so thin. I am so pleased to see you, but tell me why have you come? Tell me all the news. Before Rivka could answer, the friend turned to Yulus. Finish your milk and I'll get my son to take you around the corner to see the cow in the dairy. That's where we got the milk that you are now drinking. You'd like that wouldn't you? As usual, she did not wait for an answer. She called to her son who was in the other room of her two-roomed apartment. Take our young visitor to see the cow in the dairy. You remember Rivka, don't you. She used to live next door. This is her youngest. Her son came into the room, nodded a welcome, and stretched out his hand to take Yulus's hand. What happened to your hand? He asked in a friendly tone. Tell him on the way, Rivka said.

Her friend turned to Rivka as the two boys left the room. Like almost everyone else, he's also out of work. It will relieve his monotony to take Yulus to the dairy. Also, she continued, I could see the look on your face, when you came in, that you needed to talk. So now that they have gone, tell me. *Voos hot bershared?* What has happened? But first, drink your tea. Would you like a biscuit? She brought out a jar of broken biscuits. I too, have been buying broken biscuits, said Rivka. You too? Well, they are so much cheaper. So now tell me all, persisted the friend. Where shall I start? Asked Rivka. Start with the nice things. Your hair is looking so nice. What have you done to it?

Shortly after we moved, I decided to give up the *sheitel*, the obligatory wig worn by orthodox married Jewish women in Poland and by very orthodox women in more enlightened societies. The original purpose of the wig was to make the bride unattractive to other men. A purpose that has since been made obsolete by the fact that many of the modern wigs worn are even more attractive than the bride's own hair. At first, Rivka continued, I found that my hair had gone thin by being deprived of air, but slowly, with gentle washing and the application of some patent creams, it has come back into its own even though, it is clearly going grey.

And why is your face so thin? asked the friend. That's because of my teeth, said Rivka, or more correctly the lack of teeth. All my children, God bless them, drained too much calcium out of my body and so my teeth started to decay and

27

shrink and move about in my mouth. I had neglected them. Not always because I wanted to, but dentists are too expensive and my teeth had the lowest of priorities. When Yulus was born, I was already forty four and now I'm nearly fifty. The dentist, that I visited at last, said it was too late to save my teeth without extensive treatment that he could do at a price that was way outside of our means. So, like so many others, I agreed that he take them all out. It may look bad, but I feel a lot better. I have tried false teeth, but I don't know, they're uncomfortable and I haven't the patience these days to persevere. But that isn't the worst of our troubles.

Tears welled up in Rivka's dark gentle eyes. She held them back as she continued. As you know, it will soon be *Rosh Hashanah*, the Jewish New Year and every year we make sure that the children have new clothes and shoes. This past year has been very difficult. The older boys have been in and out of work, mainly out. The same with the eldest girl. The nineteen-year old boy is now learning cutting and design and the seventeen-year old is apprenticed to learn diamond mounting. The youngest girl has just now reached her fourteenth year and she has gone to work with her older sister to learn dressmaking from top to bottom. We have all learned that to get a job and to stay in it you need to be proficient. But while almost every one of the children is learning or entirely unemployed, the income of Shulem and one of the girls is not sufficient to make ends meet. And who wants to take money from the hard working girl who is trying to save for her trousseau? Not that there are any signs of marriage yet. But she is of age. So, we decided to take in a lodger.

Shulem and I have moved out of our bedroom to the back room downstairs and we have furnished what is now the lodger's room, sparsely, but for all that, it costs money and you can't take rent for nothing. We used most of the little savings we had and we bought some things on the never, never. The lodger will be moving in next week. Rivka paused. Her friend saw her distress and refrained from interjecting, as was her wont but waited for Rivka to continue. I urged Shulem to obtain a loan from work and last Monday he came home with cash. He had managed to borrow most of his weekly wages. I was so pleased. I paid off some of the debts I had accumulated at the grocers. I bought shoes for the two young boys and the youngest girl. I really felt good for a change, despite the general situation. You know. The pressure was off and we could start the new year in style. And then. The tears came to her throat. And then..... She was not sure she could continue. Yes? Encouraged her friend. Here drink some more tea. Rivka waved the cup away with her hands. She began again. And then on Friday, Shulem came home, white as a sheet. I have never seen him in such a state. What is it? I asked him. He could hardly talk. You know what that so and so did? Even now he could not bring himself to use a blasphemous word. It

28

simply isn't in his lexicon. Do you know what he did? Do you know? He wasn't expecting an answer, he was exploding a little. What? What? I asked. He deducted the loan from my wages today. The whole loan! I said to him. What's this. What's what? The so and so answered. Why have you paid me so little? What do you mean so little? I have paid you your full wages and I just deducted the advance I gave you at the beginning of the week. Advance? Advance? Shulem actually shouted at him. I asked you for a loan, surely you don't have to take it all back in one go? Why not? He said. What do you think I am, a bank? Don't you realise, said Shulem, that I can't get through a whole week on this pittance? Surely you must understand that. Understand! Understand! shouted the boss. Did you think of me when you and the others took a day off in the middle of the week, last month to go on that silly march to boycott German goods? Shulem was flabbergasted. What has one thing to do with the other? Shulem asked, but got no answer. Shulem felt faint. He thought of what I might say when I heard. He thought of how he could get through the next week. He knew he could not argue with the boss who, the coward he was, could no longer face Shulem, but had already turned to deal with other matters. Shulem felt like giving in his notice there and then but was sensible to the difficulties of finding another job and could see no reason to cut his own nose to spite his own face. So, he just left the office, hid his humiliation, collected his hat and coat and clocked out. He went back to work today. How he has the strength to do that I do not know. He'll start looking for other work, but that won't be easy to find.

Rivka started to cry. I feel so responsible. I pushed him, I urged him to take that loan and I overspent on the strength of it. Rivka, Rivka, her friend empathised. You couldn't have known. How could you have known that the boss would act in such a way? Do you know what rankled Shulem over the week end? Rivka asked rhetorically. That selfish man had referred to the boycott march as though it were Shulem's own personal parade. Shulem said that the man had no idea what was happening in the world. He is so taken up with his own selfish affairs that he could not, or would not, see the terrible dangers confronting, not only the Jews of Germany, but also the Jews of the world, including England. If it could happen in Germany, then it could happen here.

One of Shulem's brothers had written to him from Berlin and another from Hamburg, detailing the anti-Semitic activities of the German government since the Nazis had come into power. And not only the government. There were also the Nazi Storm Troopers and paramilitaries. But there was no need for personal verification. There were reports in both the Yiddish and English press about Goebbels' lies, that Jews had heaped up millions by blackmail, trickery and swindling. The papers reported that it had become commonplace to see groups of Storm Troopers roaming the streets looking for Jews to beat up. The Yiddish newspaper reported the Nazi declaration to boycott Jewish goods and services. This had also appeared in the Jewish Chronicle and in the English newspapers that were also reporting the outrages against the German Jews. My sons showed me pictures of Nazis harassing Jews in the streets of Berlin. Jewish shop windows were being smashed. Thousands of bank accounts, including that of Albert Einstein had been seized by the Nazis. Oswald Mosley and his Fascists were mimicking the Nazis, dressing themselves in black, attacking Jews and distributing anti-Semitic literature here in London. What were we supposed to do, ignore it, turn our eyes away?

Shulem did not always agree with Moshe Meyer, the editor of *Die Zeit*, but on this issue he was in full agreement. That Thursday, it was the twentieth of July, the paper wrote that Today Is A Protest Day and added that a Rabbi and his *Hassidim, Shoykhetim* (ritual slaughterers), men and women, shopkeepers, skilled and unskilled workers, all are marching together against the persecution of German Jewry. A few days before, Shulem took a notice to his workplace that was going to be displayed in shop windows and factory doors. It read, National Jewish Day of Mourning and Protest. This establishment will be closed on July 20th 1933 as a mark of protest against Hitlerism. Join the Jewish procession to Hyde Park. The boss wouldn't put it on his door. Nevertheless, most of the workers joined the march. Fifty thousand Jews marched that day. On a weekday! It's really quite amazing, in these difficult times, with two and a half million people unemployed, for workers to take time off from work and shopkeepers and factory owners to close their enterprises. It just shows the height of feeling that the London Jews had. In the past, in Eastern Europe from where most of them or their parents had come, they had bowed to oppression or run away. But that day, we were holding our heads high. Rivka surprised herself at the vehemence with which she related these events to her friend, who generally was less interested in politics. But Rivka's emotions were high as she felt and recalled the extent of Shulem's dismay when he realised that he could not walk out of his job, which he would otherwise have done if the economic situation had not been so dire. As usual he had put his family first.

It was quite a long march, you know, she continued. It started at Stepney Green and proceeded through Whitechapel High Street, Commercial Street, City Road, Pentonville Road, Euston Road, Seymour Street and Marble Arch to Hyde Park. There were three platforms and many speakers who called for a boycott of German goods. They argued that in the poor economic state of Germany, if the Jews led the way, and could encourage the English people to join with them, then Hitler's regime would fall. They felt that there was a good chance that the English people would join with them, because they had no love for the Nazis, especially after the Germans had used gas against the allies in the Great War and because a weak Germany was considered to be in the interest of the British.

Did you go on the march? asked her friend. No, I wanted to, but I couldn't as I had to look after the young ones. Then how do you know so much about it? All the rest of the family went and each one told me every detail in turn. And of course I read all about it in the paper the following day.

Yulus returned, chatting away to his new found friend who was carrying a jug of fresh warm milk. Does he ever stop asking questions? Asked the boy. No. Said Rivka. *Er tomid vill vissen fon vunnet die feese vuchsen*, he always wants to know from where the feet grow. The boy laughed at Rivka's accurate if untranslatable description of her son's insatiable curiosity. Come Yulus, it's time to make our way home. They said their good-byes and began the long walk home. Mama, said Yulus, the dairy has a real cow and I saw the milkman take milk from the cow. The man I went with, what's his name, said that the dairy would not be there much longer because the world was changing. Is the world changing? I hope so. Said Rivka. I certainly hope so. How can the world change? That my son, is something you will have to learn for yourself.

That evening, Yulus's hand was the centre of discussion. Each member of the family on returning home from the day's activities, asked in turn what had happened to his hand and he had to explain over and over. Only eight times over, as he and Mama already knew the gory details. How does he get into so many scrapes?

When they were all assembled in the kitchen for the evening meal, they discussed his recent exploits. Only last year, he decided to see if he could balance on one of the kitchen chairs. He had stood awkwardly on the chair. It toppled. He also toppled, and in order to save himself from falling on his face, he stretched out his arms and both his hands, palms down, came into contact with the top of the hot Kitchener. Fortunately the fire had only been lit a little while before he fell and so the burns on his hands were relatively light. One of the next-door neighbours came running into the house on hearing the ensuing commotion and suggested the quaint remedy of putting butter on the palms of his hands. To oil the skin, she said. Rivka in her distress, did as suggested and to her horror watched the butter sizzle. She fried his hands! Now there was laughter. You can laugh now, said Rivka, but at the time I was terrified. The peculiar thing is, that the remedy worked. Maybe, but it is not to be recommended.

Later in that year, on the eve of Guy Fawkes Day, many fireworks were being set-off and children and adults were standing around the bonfire that was burning brightly at the end of the street on the junction with West Tenter Street. Children were dancing around the fire, some adding bits of wood they had scrummaged from somewhere or other, while others threw crackerjack fireworks into the fire and laughed and shouted as the fire crackled and sparks flew in all directions. In the midst of all this melee, someone lit a squid firework that snaked along the ground spitting fire from its rear. People jumped out of its way. Children backed away. Yulus turned his back and the squid caught him on the back of his ankle. He screamed. Adults screamed. What a stupid thing to do, directing a firework towards a crowd of people. The culprit could not be found. A neighbour took Yulus into her house and applied her East European remedy. She immersed his foot in a bag of flour. To exclude the air, she said. The peculiar thing is, the family said in chorus, the peculiar thing is, the remedy worked. Again laughter. Yulus too joined in the laughter while adding. It wasn't funny at the time.

After Guy Fawkes Day, he and his friend from West Tenter Street, decided that if adults and bigger youths could light bonfires in the street, they too could participate in that practice. Yulus found a matchbox and his friend acquired a match. The Stanton's warehouse, that is located in St. Mark Street just opposite the entrance into Newnham Street, had two sets of high wooden doors inset in alcoves, where tramps occasionally would spend the night. The two boys piled up some boxes and straw, that they had collected from the adjoining unsuspecting greengrocers, into the corner of one of the alcoves against one of the doors. One of the boys struck the match against the rough glasspaper on the side of the matchbox that was held by the other and put the lighted match to the dry straw. Surprised by the consequent sudden speedy conflagration, and the shouts of passers-by, the boys turned on their heels and ran hell-for-leather homewards. The friend who was wiry and lithe soon escaped out of sight but plump Yulus was recognised. The fire, that was soon put out, left scorch marks on one of the warehouse doors. A little later, Rivka, unaware of what had happened, opened her front door to the loud knocking of a burly policeman. Does Yulus live here? He asked, and can I speak to him? Yulus appeared from behind his mother's skirts clutching them tightly. That's him? said the policeman greatly surprised to see a plump bright-eyed four year old. Did you light that fire? Yes, came the mumbled reply, but we didn't mean to burn anything. We were playing Guy Fawkes. Nonplussed by such logic coming from the mouth of this shame-faced knee-high recalcitrant, the policeman, wrote a few words in his notebook, and tried hard to overcome his natural tendency to laugh. He forced a stern look onto his face and said gravely. That was very naughty. Don't you dare do that again or you will be in real trouble my lad. He then departed. Rivka was not sure whether he was coughing or laughing as walked away.

Rivka turned to Yulus. So that's why you came running back into the house and said, Nothing. When I asked what was the matter. You heard what the policeman said. Stay away from fires. I don't know, every time you get near a fire, some calamity seems to happen. Yulus was then reprimanded by each member of the family as they heard of this latest dare-devil exploit. This evening they all laughed. For a short while, he was given the title of the young arsonist. The family, led by Shulem, indulged in using honorary titles when referring to family members, friends and strangers following incidents or successes of note. This practice sometimes made light of disabilities and reflected a warm relationship. And in contrast the mirthful granting of a title could also act like a pin bursting the bubble of assumed pomposity.

One minute, one minute, cried out the dressmaker above the general clamor. There was one other incident concerning firewood which we should not omit, if we want to keep the record straight., and that happened only last week, or was it the week before. A youth came around the street as usual selling bunches of about ten ready cut pieces of wood suitable for lighting fires. Usually, the firewood sticks are made from rough old pieces of wood. This time, they were nicely cut and must have come from one of the cabinet makers' shops dotted around the area. I was at home at the time, and bought a few bunches from him. Later that afternoon, Yulus came to me and said. Look what I've got. He had five penny pieces in his hand. Where did you get those from? I asked. The ladies gave them to me. He answered. Gave them to you? I queried. Why? Well, because I sold them some wood. I went to the cupboard to see whether the bunches of wood were still there and noticed that one was not there, although the string that tied them together was lying on the shelf. What wood did you sell for fivepence? I asked. You know, he said, those in the bunches that you bought from that boy. The one you said was clever to collect the wood and sell it in bunches. I was curious. To whom did you sell the wood? I asked. I don't know their names, some Ladies in the street. Come with me, I said and show me who. We went down the street and called at the houses. Did you give Yulus a penny today? I asked, and for what? Well, they all replied, he came to the door, offering one piece of wood for a penny. Who could refuse such a sweet salesman. Yulus. I said sternly. Take the wood back and give the penny back. He must learn to give value for money. I explained. And so, reluctantly, he retrieved all the pieces of wood, one after the other. And came home penniless! rejoined the designer and cutter, enjoying the pun. The master tailor said, I think you may have ruined his entrepreneurial acumen. His mother said, enough laughing at the poor boy. He was only mimicking his elders.

You know. She continued. He even gets into scrapes when he is trying to be helpful. In the summer, when it was very hot. When was that? interjected the diamond mounter. Family discussions were always full of interjections and digressions. When was that? On Madame Butterfly's Day? What is he talking about? asked Rivka. He's talking about an opera, mama. An opera? What has an

33

opera to do with a hot summer's day? Well, there is an aria in that opera called One Fine Day and that is often the extent of an English summer. You understand? No. But never mind. I believe you. Now where was I? Oh yes. One day in the summer, when it was hot, Yulus came home with blood running down his face, carrying a block of ice. Look what I have brought for you. He said. Never mind what you brought. I said. Why are you bleeding? Oh. I hit my head. He said. But look, I've brought you some ice to put in the food safe, you know, the cupboard in the yard with wire netting on the door to let in air and keep out the flies. You said that the you needed ice to keep butter from melting. It was such a hot day that the block of ice itself was melting in his hands and dripping water everywhere. And it was too cold for him to hold so he was tossing it precariously from hand to hand. Let me look at your head. I said. How did you cut your head? The ice, he said. Take the ice quickly. I took the block and put it in the sink. It's for the food safe. He said again. I know, I know, I said. But first I must deal with your head and then I will wash the ice and then I will put it in the food safe. Rivka and cleanliness always went hand in hand. How did it happen? Asked the eldest brother. How is it that I haven't heard of this incident? He asked, not expecting an answer and feigning hurt that he had been excluded from an important piece of information concerning his youngest brother. He always reminded Yulus as to how embarrassed he was when he was twenty three and had to ask for some time off from work because his young brother was ill. How old is your brother? His boss asked. Three months. He said turning bright red. His fellow workers teased him about that enormous difference in age for weeks on end Anyhow. How did he manage to cut his head and what has it to do with a block of ice? Wall's Ice Cream has a warehouse in West Tenter Street. Lorries come with frozen ice cream in crates surrounded by blocks of ice. The edge of one the blocks chipped off and slid under the lorry. Bright-eyed Yulus espied the prize and darted under the lorry to retrieve the ice. He then backed out, so he said, head bent, until he saw, or thought he saw, that he was out from under the lorry. Then he stood up and hit his head on the bolt that closes the tailboard of the lorry, that was hanging down from the corner of the tailboard. Why were you there in the first instance? I asked him. I heard you say that the butter was melting so I went to see if I could get some ice for you. That was his sweet reply. He hears everything except when he chooses not to. Could you reprimand such a child? So I told him not to go crawling under lorries. What would have happened if the vehicle moved? Who would have seen you? I told him a thousand times while I bathed his head. What else could I do? She asked, also not expecting a reply. You should have put the ice on his head, said the nine-year old. Laughter. See how young my children become clever? said Rivka sardonically.

Hard times had to be tempered by humour.

Chapter 5

If one stopped almost any inhabitant of the East End of London and asked for directions on how to find Newnham Street, the chances are that the otherwise knowledgeable person would be unlikely to have even heard of the street, let alone point in its direction. Yet, Newnham Street was a real street. The lives and fortunes of its inhabitants and surrounding streets that formed a larger Jewish enclave, reflected the trials, tribulations and triumphs of the whole of the mainly Yiddish speaking, changing, Jewish East End.

If however, when standing in Aldgate High Street, one asked for the Tenter Streets, then faces would light up. People would become knowledgeable and ask. Do you mean the Tenter Streets or the Tenter Grounds? This is because the former is to the south, close to the Minories, while the latter is to the north, close to Bell Lane. The former please, because there, in the centre of the North, East, South and West Tenter Streets, Newnham Street could be found. There, Shulem lived until the German bombers in the second world war totally obliterated the Street from the map. Today, it is no longer a street and its name no longer appears on a modern map of London. In its stead, stands a Catholic School that occupies the whole of what was once the living accommodation of a thriving, industrious, diverse, community. Yulus, as an adult, visited the school. One of the senior Nuns asked him whether he had lived in the area. No. Said Yulus. No? said the Sister querulously, then what is your interest? I lived on here, said Yulus emphasizing the word on. He then pointed to the very spot where the house of his childhood once stood. It is a pity, said the Sister in her strong Irish accent, that the Jews left this area. They were so clean. It was a pleasure to hear her lyrical voice rising at the end of the last sentence. This sentiment was so different from the cries of 'dirty Jew' emanating from the mouths of Christian adults and youths, that he could remember from the pre-war days.

London has a great history. The area in which the Tenter Streets are situated is also known as Goodman's Fields. Even today, at the eastern end of Alie Street, in the midst of all the bricks and mortar of built-up London, a street sign announces that one has reached Goodman's Stile. The imagination can, with difficulty, conjure up the once-upon-a-time set of wooden steps that provided the facility to climb over a fence from a well-trodden path into those green well-kept fields. The London Historian, John Stow wrote of the area in his quaint English, that in 1599, 'Near adjoining to this Abbey (Minories) on the south side thereof, was sometime a farm belonging to the said Nunnery at which farm,

I myself in my youth, have fetched many a halfpenny of milk, and never had less than three ale pints for a halfpenny in the summer, nor less than one ale quart for a halfpenny in the winter, always hot from the kine (cow), as the same was milked and strained. One Trolop and afterwards Goodman, were farmers there and had 30 - 40 kine to the pail (30 - 40 milking cows).' He also recorded that the fields were later used as tenter grounds where frames were placed for stretching and drying fabrics woven in the neighbourhood by poor cloth workers. He wrote of the Goodman's Fields' Theatre that was founded in 1725 and operated successfully for some years. He also explained that the four streets which encompassed the area in which Goodman's Fields was located, Prescot, Alie, Leman and Mansell Streets were named after four families who were allied by marriage. Sir John Leman, Bart. was Lord Mayor of London in 1616.

Commercial and residential building in the mid-nineteenth century so encroached upon Goodman's fields that not a single blade of grass remained. Those persons wishing to enjoy recreation in green surroundings would have to take a tram or bus ride or cycle to Victoria Park in the adjoining borough of Hackney. They could also visit the Tower of London, which was within walking distance, and wander about Tower Hill Gardens, provided they did not walk on the grass. One of the main functions of the Beefeaters at the Tower appeared to be chasing children off the grass. The once luxurious mansion houses of the rich whose windows overlooked the green fields, were either demolished over the years to make way for commercial buildings or became multi-residential, providing accommodation for a number of families. The rich moved out and immigrants moved in. Firstly the Irish, who established a Catholic Church in Prescot Street. Their descendants continue to live there and that street formed the southern border of the Jewish East End ghetto. Later, Dutch Jews moved into the area, occupying the houses that were built in the mid-nineteenth century. They established a small Synagogue in nearby Sandys Row. This group should not be confused with the much older Spanish and Portuguese Jewish community, who had established themselves in England over many hundreds of years and whose magnificent Synagogue still stands in Bevis Marks, inside the borders of the City of London. In due course, most, but not all, of the Dutch Jews moved out of the area and were replaced by the East European Jewish immigrants who formed the bulk of East End Jewish population.

The Jewish enclave of Goodman's Fields was socially similar to, if physically different from, other Jewish enclaves in the East End ghetto. The four to five storey tenement buildings in East Tenter Street and Buckle Street were not as high or as formidable as the seven storey Rothschild Buildings in Thrawl Street. Nor were they spread over such a large area as the Brunswick Buildings in Goulston Street and Hughes Mansions in Vallance Road, all to the north of

Whitechapel. They did not have the enclosed courtyards of those other 'grander' buildings, which acted as playgrounds for children and meeting places for adults. The surrounding streets were the playgrounds and meeting places. Important facilities that existed in the enclave were utilised by the whole East End community, such as the Workers' Circle building in Alie Street that was both a political and cultural centre. Monickedam's wedding reception hall was also in that street. Camperdown House that housed the headquarters of the Jewish Lads Brigade and the Hutchinson House Youth Club, was located in Half Moon Passage. Leman Street boasted the headquarters of the Cooperative Wholesale Society (CWS), the central Police Station for the area, and, at one time, the Temporary Jewish Refugee Centre that later moved to Mansell Street with a back entrance in West Tenter Street. The various enclaves within the ghetto preserved their own character and yet because of the common origins and social, political and ethnic struggles, there was a continuous interaction that made the Jewish East End of London one complete whole. The experiences and stories of one enclave were too similar to those of another for a distinction to be made. The one hundred thousand Jews or fifteen thousand Jewish families, that lived in the East End of London up to and during the second World War made an homogenous whole. They represented one third of the entire population of the three boroughs of Stepney, Bethnal Green and Poplar.

The parents generally spoke Yiddish. Some also spoke English while others had only a sprinkling of English words in their vocabulary that enabled them to communicate when required, albeit with thick accents, for the essential activities of normal life. They generally understood English and it was common for the parents to address their children in Yiddish and receive replies in English. The thirty thousand parents were mainly immigrants who had received their education abroad in their countries of origin. East European immigration virtually ceased with the outbreak of the first World War in 1914. By the nineteen thirties, most of the children, even if born abroad and now adult, received their education in Jewish Day Schools whose overall social purpose, as distinct from teaching the normal pedagogical subjects, was to inculcate English manners and mores into their young pupils. They were to become good English gentlemen or gentle ladies. Yiddish was forbidden in those schools.

There is a myth, supported by such rich humorous and tragic stories as those written by Sholem Aleichem, that all the East European Jews came from *steitels*, small towns or even *steitelech*, small villages, and brought with them their peasant attitudes to the great metropolis. In truth, many of the immigrants came from the capitals and other large towns of Eastern Europe. The *steitel* people, as Jewish inhabitants of the small towns and villages came to be called, remained in those small towns and villages. Those who wrote about them or

37

painted images of them, left those places to live in the larger towns of Eastern Europe and subsequently emigrated to the capitals of Western Europe, Great Britain and the Americas. From these ivory towers, they looked down upon the people of the small towns and villages that gave them birth and inspiration. There was, and still is, an erroneous tendency for many Jews, often the progeny of the so-called *steitel* Jews who had received a western education, to apply the term *steitel* Jews, in a derogatory manner, to the Yiddish speaking Jews of the East End of London. This tendency, to call those Yiddish speakers, peasants, comes from a pompous belief that an ability to read and write English bestowed upon such scholars a greater intelligence and intellectual ability, than their elders who carried out their intellectual discourses in what had become an alien language associated with poverty and one that was unsuitable for social and economic advancement in a western society. Peculiar peasants, these, who had the get-up-and-go to get up and go away from their impoverished surroundings and to work their fingers to the bone to ensure that their children got an education in an alien western society. An education that enabled them to become doctors, lawyers, accountants, engineers and writers. Peasants usually want their offspring to remain on the farm and continue their traditional agrarian occupations. The Yiddish section of the Whitechapel Public Library was always busy and the librarian reported that Jews represented two thirds of the readers at the library (English and Yiddish), although they accounted for only one third of the total constituency.

There is yet another myth that needs exploding. There are those who believe that all the English Jews were more or less emancipated by the nineteen twenties after which they had joined the Jewish middle classes. Thus relatively little has been written about the activities of the Yiddish speaking enclave that was thriving in the East End of London up to and during the second World War. When histories or comparative studies have been written concerning English Jews and their brethren abroad, the story seems to cease with the aftermath of the first World War. The historical period between the two world wars could not be totally ignored because of the momentous events of the time, including the successful fight against Fascism. The terrible destruction of that part of London during and after the blitz also could not be overlooked. But the suffering and destruction of the infrastructure of the Yiddish speaking community has been virtually ignored.

There are two main and complex reasons for this. One is the nature of the English society which on the one hand always allowed limited immigration but then insisted that the immigrants, either kept to themselves in their specific enclaves, or completely adopted the manners and mores of the host country. Unlike America, England is not an immigrant country, it is rather a country of tradition. Until the nineteen twenties, English type anti-Semitism was mainly of a passive nature. It excluded Jews from, or made it very difficult for them to enter, clubs and institutions of higher learning. And so in defense and in the pursuit of advancement in society, English Jews tried to become "even more English than the English". The Jewish schools set up in the East End emphasised at every stage that this is England, the centre of the Empire, and that the Jewish religion and ideals were not incompatible with English manners and modes of behaviour. It was essential to behave as English gentlemen or ladies when in English, as distinct from Jewish, society. This meant that Yiddish words had to be excluded from the vocabulary when speaking to Gentiles, and one did not shake hands so readily and certainly one did not speak with hands gesticulating in all directions. Hands should be at one's side when speaking. The first essentials were to discard the London cockney or foreign accents in speech and then the foreign sounding first names and surnames. Elocution lessons were given in school and prizes awarded to successful pupils. The second was to obtain a better address if possible and in any event to disguise one's humble or foreign origins. The third was to dedicate oneself to the tasks in hand, whether educational or professional to ensure success and advance economically and socially in the English society. And if successful, and many justifiably were, why jeopardise one's position by talking or writing publicly about life in the Yiddisher East End as though it still existed even if or especially if, it still represented some forty percent of the total London Jewish population?

The second more compelling and more commendable reason that the story of the destruction of the infrastructure of the Jewish East End has not been told, is the advent of the Holocaust and the terrible suffering of the European Jews in the Nazi concentration camps. Most of the East London Jews originated from Poland, Belarus, Russia, the Ukraine, Rumania and the Baltic States of Latvia, Lithuania and Estonia. Almost all had relatives that were eliminated in the Holocaust and they considered their own suffering to be minor when compared to the suffering of their fellow Jews on the continent. The Jewish lives lost in London were few compared to the millions lost in Europe. The deliberate destruction by the German bombers of the Jewish East End of London was as nothing compared to the wholesale elimination of complete Jewish communities in Europe. And so the story of the demise and suffering of the East London Yiddish community, immediately prior to, and during, the second world war, has not been told.

Some would have it, that as with the case of the Jews of East Side New York, socio-economic developments would have, in any event, resulted in the Jews leaving the East End of London. But London was not New York. Conditions in the East End were beginning to improve in the late thirties and the Yiddish speakers had no real motivation to leave the Yiddish social and religious infrastructure that they had built up over the years. They would have preferred to stay and to have invested yet further to modernise their living accommodation. The location of the district was really most convenient. It adjoins the City of London and public transport was available to take them to any part of the capital or its suburbs with ease. But the war came and as promised by Lord Haw Haw (William Joyce) in his broadcasts from Germany on behalf of the Nazi regime, the borough of Stepney, where the bulk of the Jews lived, would be hit hardest by the German bombs and rockets. And it was. A third of all housing was destroyed or made uninhabitable. Forty thousand bombs fell on Stepney during the war. Synagogues and Jewish schools were destroyed and the Yiddish speakers had no choice but to move out of the area leaving behind a derelict Yiddish infrastructure that was never to be rebuilt. It is ironic and tragic to note that even after Jews were being released from Auschwitz and other dreadful death camps in Europe, Jews were being killed in the East End by German rockets. The last V2 rocket to fall on London, fell on Hughes Mansions in Vallance Road on March 27, 1945 and killed one hundred and thirty one people most of them Jews, including twenty one members of the Jewish Brady Boys' and Girls' Clubs.

There are those who contend that the bombing of the Jewish quarter of the East End of London was not deliberate, but the consequence of the area being so close to the London Docks. The docks nestled in the bend of the river Thames and because of its natural proximity to the river, was the easiest of targets to identify. The Tower of London that is also on the river adjacent to the docks, stands out as a clear identifying landmark. It was hardly bombed at all. There is plenty of evidence to show that the concentrated East London Jewish community was not excluded from the Nazi's perverse preoccupation with the destruction of world Jewry. Here the Germans had the opportunity and here they sadly succeeded in totally destroying the infrastructure of a once thriving Yiddish community. Luckily, most of the London Yiddish speaking Jews survived but their community was dispersed and never reconstituted.

Chapter 6

It was now 1935. More than two years have passed since Shulem's loan episode. Economic conditions in the south of the country were showing the first signs of improvement and this was also reflected in the family's situation. Shulem had looked for, but could not find, other employment. However, the business for which he was working changed hands. The new boss was a more pleasant character although no more liberal in economic terms. The anger in Shulem subsided and he was now more composed as he settled down to his daily tasks of ensuring that the population of England and perhaps the world did not walk about with bare behinds. His son the master tailor was now in full employment and the cutter and designer had completed his course and had also found employment. The diamond mounter was not too sure that his future life should be devoted to poring over precious stones and placing them into gold or silver settings, especially for the miserable wage he was earning as an apprentice. He wanted to write. Writers earn better money? Asked Shulem. The diamond mounter gave a shrug of indifference. Some do. He replied.

Rivka now had something to be pleased about. Her front parlour was being used more and more frequently. The master tailor had brought home a very presentable girl. She had a ready smile, was pretty and her blond hair contrasted with the jet black hair of her chosen one. They seem to be very serious said Rivka one day. Does that mean that they will get married? Asked Yulus. Yes, came the positive answer. And does that mean that I will not have to sleep in the cot any longer? Yes. Yippee!

When Yulus next spoke to his eldest brother he urged him to get married as soon as possible so that he, Yulus, could then be promoted to number four in the bed in the upstairs front bedroom where all his four brothers currently slept. We have only just got engaged, said his brother. You'll have to wait a while. But my legs are already sticking out through the bars of my cot! Be patient Rivka remonstrated, hardly restraining a smile. Just think. When your big brother will be happy, you too will be happy. Will you also be happy mama? Yes dear. I will also be happy for you to move out of our bedroom.

Rivka had yet more pleasure in store. The dressmaker had brought home a beau. A smart looking young man, a furrier by profession, who assured Shulem that he could set up a fine home for his daughter. Don't they make a handsome pair? said Rivka with her kindly face beaming. *Sheinkeit is narishkeit*, the cult of beauty is the cult of nonsense, came Shulem's quick response. This was an expression he often used when anyone suggested that beauty or vanity had some intrinsic value. His alternative expression that he used when anyone remarked that he had beautiful children was *Shenerer kinder vee meiner can mir nisht in die ganzer velt gefinnen*, more beautiful children than mine you could not find in the whole wide world. The tinge of sarcasm increased when one of the children referred to himself or herself as handsome or pretty. Then the upward inflection on the word *ganzer*, whole, would increase and the first syllable would be elongated to show clearly his own disbelief in such a nonsensical conception.

But what of the eldest daughter? She had plenty of boyfriends, but where was the serious one? Don't worry. Said Shulem to Rivka. With God's help, all will be well. And the cutter and designer? He's too busy with politics. And if it's not politics, then he is too busy gambling. If he is not playing cards then he is down at the dog track. But he is right to worry about the political situation. Life in the East End is not as safe as it once was. Mosley and his Fascists are aping Hitler and his Nazis. Jews are being attacked in the streets, here in London. And the world news? The world is preparing for war. And while the world is preparing for war, said Rivka, I and the whole of the Jewish East End are preparing for *Pesach*, the annual eight day Passover feast.

As family members were growing older and they felt the jingle of some spare coins in their pockets, they pursued their own interests more and more. Rarely these days were all the family together on a weekday, other than in the early mornings. And even then, their work and school requirements varied and they would breakfast at different times with Rivka always busily in attendance. You may be late, but you cannot go out without something in your stomach, she would say while placing a cup of tea and rolls and butter on the table. Sit down, she would command as one or other of the children supped the hot, always hot, tea while standing up and making for the door. No time. No time. They would reply. This was not only true of the mornings. It often happened at other mealtimes when the urgency of a social engagement of one or other of the family took precedence over stopping to eat in a civilised manner, *vee a mensch*, as Rivka would put it. But on *Seder* night, the first night of *Pesach* everyone, but everyone, attended.

Pesach and the period immediately prior, was always a ritual for the orthodox and also for the not-so-orthodox Jews. Jewish religious practice required the complete separation of normal daily food and the utensils used in its preparation or storage, from the specially kosher nature of Passover food. The main essential was the exclusion of leavened food such as bread and flour. This meant that the house had to be cleared of yeast and yeast products by the noon of the eve of the *Seder* and substituted by matzos (pronounced motzas), unleavened bread, and other unleavened food. Trouser and jacket pockets had to be turned inside out and brushed to ensure that there were no traces of *humatzdicker*, that is unkosher for Passover, dust particles. Food cupboards were emptied, thoroughly cleaned and re-lined and the everyday crockery was replaced with *Pesachdicker geface* that was extracted from a cupboard where it had been stored from the previous year. Utensils were cleansed by immersing in boiling water. Those who were too poor to have separate crockery for the Passover, would treat their crockery in a similar way.

Mothers would deliberately place a few bread crumbs in strategic corners of food cupboards so that these could be found by fathers, accompanied by their youngest children, who would comb the house with lighted candle in hand to search for any remnants of *humatz* which, when 'miraculously' found, would be brushed on to a wooden spoon with the use of a feather. The spoon and feather would then be wrapped in paper and burned. To be absolutely sure that no trace of *humatz* whatsoever remained in the house, the wrapped package of spoon, crumbs and feather were sold to a friendly sheigetz, a Gentile boy, who by pre-arrangement would travel the streets of the Jewish quarter with a coal fire on a wheel barrow, calling out in his cockney accent 'Oomaits, Oomaits.' The *sheigetz* would be given a sum of money for his services out of which he would pay the purchase price of the carefully wrapped parcel that he immediately placed in the open fire. Thus the *sheigetz* ensured that Jewish religious rites were preserved while carrying out what was for him a quaint but profitable annual practice.

The Passover festival celebrates the exodus of the Israelites from bondage in Egypt. Rivka set the table with the help of daughters, while her sons re-arranged the furniture to make room in the kitchen for added guests. At the end of the table where Shulem sits, she placed the three matzos in a special white cloth cover that separates each matzo from the other. Wine glasses are placed on the table for each participant plus an extra goblet which is filled with wine and set aside for the prophet Elijah who is believed to be the messenger designated by God to bring news of the coming of the Messiah. On a ceremonial plate are placed bitter herbs, often horseradish, to symbolise the bitterness of bondage, charoseth which is a mixture of chopped apples, nuts, raisins and cinnamon and wine, to represent the mortar used for building the Egyptian cities or pyramids, a roasted egg in its shell to represent the festival sacrifice in the days of the Temple in Jerusalem, the shank bone of a lamb to remind one of the blood of the lamb that was used to mark the door posts of the Jewish houses so that the angel of death would not visit, some parsley or celery leaves said to represent the simple meals in the desert and the springtime of new hope as the Israelites neared the promised land, and a dish of salt water to recall the tears shed during captivity. Matzos are eaten throughout the meal and for the full eight days of the festival. They represent the hurried departure from Egypt when the Israelites did not have time to add yeast, or to knead their mixture of bread dough, that they carried on their backs and which baked without rising, in the hot desert sun.

Rivka, in the presence of her daughters, lights the candles as dusk begins to fall, with a prayer for the festival. Soon after, the males arrive from *Shul* ready for the festive ceremony and supper. The story of the exodus is told and re-told every year by the reading of the Haggadah. The ceremony begins with a prayer and the drinking of the first glass of wine. It is mandatory to drink four glasses of wine throughout the evening. Shulem ceremoniously washes his hands, dips the parsley in salt water and distributes portions to each guest. He then breaks the middle matzo in two and places one half aside to be eaten at the very end of the proceedings. This half is called the Afikoman and by tradition it is hidden, not too well, for the young children to find and to receive a nominal prize when successful. Then the narrative begins. Firstly, Shulem sends one of the children to unlatch the front door and then all those near enough raise the ceremonial plate previously described, and extend an invitation in Aramaic to 'all those who are hungry' to enter and participate in the Seder together with the declamation that this year we are here but next year we will be in Jerusalem. Legend has it that prior to the Spanish inquisition the plate would be carried out into the street, a practice that could hardly be followed during the Inquisition. Since then the front door is symbolically left ajar to allow the prophet Elijah to enter. The elder participants would whisper to the children to watch Elijah's goblet to see whether any of its wine is being drunk. Every now and then one would shake the table and as the wine rippled in the cup, say, See! He's drinking now. Shortly afterwards, the children would catch on and shake the table themselves and make the same remark. Legend also has it that children must not fall asleep during the ceremony or else the prophet may come and snatch them away.

The highlight of the ceremony is when the youngest child asks the four questions. Yulus asked them in sing-song fashion in three languages. In Hebrew according to the Haggadah text. In Yiddish and in English, to the applause of all present and with Rivka's ample bosom swelling with pride. Why is this night different from all other nights? Why may we only eat unleavened bread? Why do we dip the parsley in salt water and the bitter herbs in the charoseth? And why can we lean while eating? The answers are many and varied because the Haggadah details the discussions of many a learned Rabbi. It tells the tale of the four sons and the correct attitude to be taken towards the wise, wicked and simple sons and the one that cannot as yet ask questions. It tells the story of slavery in Egypt and of the ten plagues wrought by God upon the Egyptians in order to persuade them to let the Israelites go and about the parting of the Red Sea. It tells of the trek across the desert and the handing down of the Law from

Mount Sinai. And it entreats all that hear the story to hand it down through the generations. The long story has to be completed before the repast. The male participants all take part in reading, in Hebrew, sections of the Haggadah which helps to liven the proceedings. Any errors in Hebrew pronunciation are corrected by Shulem, if not already preempted by others. Guests who are not so well versed in reading Hebrew are allocated shorter paragraphs and are prompted by the more experienced.

The traditional meal starts with a small portion of hard boiled egg in salt water followed by chicken soup and *knaidlech*, delicious matzo meal balls, and then the main course of boiled chicken and potatoes and finally a compote of stewed fruit after which Russian tea is served. Rivka and the girls continually run backwards and forwards from scullery to table or vice versa to bring food or to take crockery. Meanwhile they join in the lively discussion that develops on a wide range of topics relating to family matters, Jewish history and inevitably to the current political situation in the country and in the world.

Pesach epitomises the Jewish religion and the lot of the Jew over the ages. It forms the magical link between the ancient past and the worrying present. The festival, by its nature, encourages family unity. It makes demands and yet at the same time makes allowances. Members need to participate but they are not called upon to believe literally everything that is written. It encourages the asking of questions, but refrains from questioning God. As Shulem was apt to say, *Fin Gott freigt mir nisht*, one does not question God. The central theme of the festival emphasises how separate Jewish life is from that of the Gentiles in whose midst the Jews live. The general Jewish dietary laws form the first barrier to full assimilation and the special Passover dietary laws fortify the fences around Jewish life. Even when the general dietary laws are broken as acculturation to the host country's way of life takes hold, *Pesach* comes as a strong reminder each year that the Jews have a need for family ties and have a distinct history and position in society, and a history that has the habit of repeating itself. Thus *Pesach* is not merely a religious festival, it also represents the struggle through the ages for freedom from bondage. All elements in Jewish society from the ultra-orthodox to the completely secular can associate themselves with this festival and participate on equal terms.

Yulus enjoyed *Pesach* as it was celebrated in the East End of London. It was spring and the cold, cold winter had receded. The streets were full of children as Jewish schools were closed for the eight days of the festival that often coincided with Easter, whereupon the Gentile schools would also be closed. Special games were played in that week, particularly with cob or hazel nuts that were plentiful and used as substitutes for marbles. As nuts were not perfectly round, different games and methods had to be devised in their use. They could be, and often had to be, thrown more strongly if they were to reach the intended targets as they would not roll so smoothly and often moved in the wrong direction by their own volition. The games were mainly competitive. Two or more children would line up their nuts in equal numbers on the line delineated by the square paving stones nearest to the wall on the pavement. The competitors would stand in the kerb at the edge of the pavement and aim their larger nuts, in turn, at the tidily arranged row of nuts with the purpose of knocking them off the line. The ones so disturbed became the property of the successful thrower. An alternative arrangement would be for the nuts to be placed within the square paving stone and the thrower had to dislodge them from the square. Some enterprising children would cut five square holes of differing sizes in the top of a matzo box and give each hole a numbered value. The smaller the hole, the higher the value. The box would be placed against the wall, holes uppermost, and competitors would throw their nuts with a view to entering the holes in the box. Nuts that fell outside of the box became the property of the box owner who had to pay out in nuts the number value of the hole into which nuts successfully fell. Adults would lean a halfpenny against the wall and invite children to knock it down with nuts thrown from the kerb. Knock down the coin and it was yours. More generous adults would place a sixpenny bit instead. It was all the fun of the fair with the advantage that losses could always be made up from the bank of nuts generally available in mothers' cupboards. No-one was ever a real loser and the nuts could be eaten during and after the games. What fun!

Yulus had reached the significant age of eight. Shortly he would leave the infants' school and go to the Jews' Free Junior School. The headmistress of the Buckle Street School had presented him with an autograph book for being top boy in the school. Yulus proudly showed everyone her first entry which said that she hoped he will always come out on top. This comment in itself opened up some discussion. First place should not always be one's aim. Why not? What's wrong with being successful? And if one is not, what should one do? Grin and bear it. You will find Junior School quite a different place from the infants. Ask your brother, he moved from there to the Senior School only last year. He's not doing too badly either. He keeps coming home with prizes, especially for Hebrew. And look, he has been chosen to be the Station Master in this miniature railway that the schoolchildren are building themselves. You know, said the eldest brother in his acquired drawl, that school is quite amazing. All of us have attended it and yet it continues to function. Whether that illustrious institution will survive the latest onslaught is another question. He continued among laughter. I think he will have to stop getting into his usual scrapes when he goes up to that school. Why? What is his latest? Shall I tell them? asked Rivka of her youngest. If you want. Yes. Yes. Let's hear!

A couple of weeks ago I sent him to buy a bottle of fruit sauce. He likes it with his chips. What do you mean he likes it. We all do. Anyhow, I gave him the money and a brown carrier bag with strong handles for him to carry the bottle home. Come straight home. I said. He did come home, eventually, but instead of the bottle being in the brown carrier bag, it was in a white bag. What happened to the bag? I asked. You mean he lost the bag? No. No, she replied, it is no good guessing, his life is much more complicated than that. So what did happen? Shoosh! If you don't interrupt, you will soon hear. The other day on the wireless there was a discussion on the different types of hair in differing ethnic groups and even in families. What has that got to do with Yulus and the bag? Wait. Wait. You will soon see. Yulus heard the program and asked his usual questions. Is my hair strong? Yes dear. Stronger than yours? Maybe. And we left it at that. Where is the brown carrier bag I gave you? I asked him. I dropped it. He said. So. All you had to do is pick it up. No? No. Why not? Because it had the bottle of sauce in it. So? Well, the bottle broke and the sauce ran all over the inside. So how did he get another bottle? And how did he pay for it? Wait! I haven't finished. The grocer replaced the bottle and gave him a clean bag after she learned how it happened. And how did it happen? The tension is killing us. He decided to test the strength of his hair by threading some strands through the handle of the carrier bag. He held the end of his hair like this, demonstrated Rivka, and then let go of the bag. His hair wasn't strong enough? suggested one of the listeners. Wrong again! It hurt. So he let go of his hair and...... The rest was drowned in laughter. You can laugh. Said Yulus. But it really did hurt. And did you have to pay for the second bottle. No. The grocer wouldn't take any money. She said the entertainment value was worth every penny and she has been living on that story ever since. Every time I go in there she says. No more hair tricks?

The discussion turned to more serious matters. Marriage plans for the two pairs of lovebirds. The weddings would take place at the end of the following year. Seems a long time to me, said Yulus, dreaming of his own exodus from the cot in which he still slept. Not so long. Not so long. Rivka said knowingly and reassuringly. The Diaspora had two Seder nights with the procedures at the second Seder closely following those of the first. This arrangement was said to have arisen from the difficulty of informing Jewish communities that were distant from the Temple in ancient times of the exact time that the festival should start. It also, however, enabled a married son to attend, with his wife, the first night's festivities at his parents' house and the second night at his wife's parents' house. This practice also applied to betrothed couples prior to their marriage and so the dressmaker spent this evening at the furriers house while the

47

piano player, who was also a seamstress, attended her first Seder at Rivka's and Shulem's table. Bringing an intended to a Seder was a true expression of seriousness and Yulus felt assured that his own cot bondage would soon be over.

Shulem said that he had received letters from his youngest brother who had left Berlin in 1933 as soon as Hitler came to power. He had returned to Palestine which he had left ten years earlier, to join another brother in Berlin. He was now back again in Tel-Aviv. The situation for the Jews in Palestine was not easy and the Arabs were becoming violent, but he preferred that to the situation in Germany where two of his brothers had decided to remain, the one in Berlin and the other in Hamburg. The Nazis were in full control. The swastika appears everywhere and Himmler has been appointed to set up concentration camps. Hitler says that the Third Reich will last a thousand years.

Here we are, said Shulem, anticipating weddings while the Nuremberg laws are depriving Jews of German citizenship and making their life a total misery. All our protests to boycott German goods have come to naught because the Jewish Agency entered into a transfer agreement with Nazi Germany. German Jews who wished to emigrate to Palestine, could deposit money in a German Jewish Trust Company for the purpose of buying German goods to be exported to Palestine and sold there. The proceeds are paid over to the Jewish immigrants in Palestine at a ridiculously low rate of exchange so that the German Jews were being cheated in all directions. Most Jews can't get into Palestine without showing that they had enough cash to qualify for the capitalist, youth, student and artisan immigration certificates that are issued by the British Mandatory Authority. Any Jewish opposition to the transfer agreement was defeated at the 1935 Zionist Congress in Lucerne. You see. It's always the same. Money comes before people. Why shouldn't people who are being persecuted be allowed to go somewhere else? What of the poor Jews in Germany? Where can they go? All these immigration restrictions are so wrong. And the Jewish leadership is also wrong to undercut the German goods boycott. If they had supported us when we marched, when was it? Two years ago? If they had supported the boycott movement and worked hard we could have mobilised British opinion to support the boycott. The British people haven't forgotten that the Germans used gas in the first World War. We could have mustered their support. Then Hitler's regime may not have lasted a hundred days, let alone a thousand years. It is all very discouraging.

Everyone added their concerns about the current situation. The drums of war are beating everywhere. Mussolini's Fascist army has already marched into Abyssinia. The Germans have ordered conscription and have reoccupied the Rhineland. The Poles have also ordered conscription. The Japanese have taken over Manchuria from the Chinese and called it Manchukuo. We here in

Britain are re-arming. The Fascists are pushing on every front. Mao Tse-Tung is in trouble, despite his six-thousand-mile-long march and Spain is on the verge of a civil war.

And here, on our own doorstep, Mosley and the British Union of Fascists are getting more audacious every day and they seem to get police protection when anyone protests. That's what happened at the BUF meeting in Olympia in June last year, no not last year, the year before, and now look what happened at the Albert Hall just a few months ago in February. The hall was full of Fascist supporters and when some people stood up to protest, Mosley's thugs beat them up and threw them out into the street. Some had to be taken away in stretchers. The police refused to intervene. Some three thousand of us, no, not all Socialists, but people concerned about the growth of Fascism, some three thousand of us held an anti-Fascist demonstration nearby in Thurloe Street. The police came in large numbers and violently dispersed the peaceful, if vociferous crowd. Mounted police made baton charges. It is only a miracle, I suppose on Seder night, one can speak of miracles, it is only a miracle that I am here in one piece, said the Socialist. The horses came charging down the street. I ran for my life. I have never run so fast. I turned down a side street and to my horror discovered that it was cul-de-sac. I could hear the horses' hooves and the swishing of the policeman's baton behind me. I ran up some steps and turned towards the horseman with my arms crossed above my head for protection. I was sure that at any second the baton would come crashing down on my head. But I had *mazel*, luck, the policeman waved his baton and turned his horse back to chase some other unfortunates. That's really terrible, it really is, came the chorus. So much for your pacifism, was one comment. Maybe. But pacifism does not mean that one should not protest. In fact that is what it is all about. One has to protest against violence. Not use it. I don't know, said the bridegroom-to-be, I prefer to stay away from those meetings. There must be better ways of protesting without having to fear for one's life. You don't have to go to meetings to be attacked in the streets nowadays, contributed the diamond mounter. Even Yulus complained that the kids in Prescott Street shouted after him dirty Jew, you killed Christ. Poor Yulus, he didn't even know who Christ was. Our Jewish schools don't teach Christian history. Anyhow, he certainly knows now. For myself, I have been doing athletics and getting fit at the Hutchinson House Club for a couple of years now. I reckon that we have to be physically as well as mentally prepared to defend ourselves. Let one of them try to attack me! Unfortunately, Shulem said, it's not just one against one. And what of the older and weaker ones? We have to protest, but we have to do it wisely.

Enough of this, let's talk of happier things, said the eldest. What about the budding Barmitzvah boy? Tell my fiancee, now that's a nice word he said smiling at his intended, tell my fiancee, he repeated the word with relish, when you will be Barmitzvah. It's a long time yet, came the reply. June of next year. *Shavuos* added Shulem who knew all his children's birthdays by the Jewish festival or Holyday closest to the day they were born. My fiancee, he enjoyed the repetition of this word, is new to this district because she lives in the *hoicher fensters*, which literally translates to the high windows but means a posh area. Jewish East Enders applied this term to any district outside of the immediate boundaries of the East End where the houses had their own bathrooms. She needs to get the low down on our family matters. And where are you learning? asked the newcomer a little embarrassed by this introduction. In Christian Street Talmud Torah came the reply amid laughter. What street? she enquired. Christian Street. He repeated. Hardly a name for a place of Jewish learning. She said. That's nothing said the boy. We used to live in a kosher house in Bacon Street. Quite incongruous she said a little perplexed. We Jews only live here. Said the youngest sister. Our own names we can change, but street names, we just have to live with.

Shoin said Shulem, re-opening his wine-stained Haggadah and tapping the table authoritatively. We must now finish eating because I want to distribute the Afikoman and as you know, after that, no-one can eat any more this night All turned to the page for Grace after Meals in their own Haggadah while Shulem went with deliberation to the place where he had hidden the half matzo that he had broken at the start of the service. All were expectant. Where is the Afikoman? cried Shulem with feigned surprise. Why? everyone chorused. Isn't it there? No. He said. I wonder where it can be. This ritual was followed year after year. I've got it, called the budding Barmitzvah boy. It was his turn this year to find it. He held the matzo wrapped in its white napkin high for all to see. And here is your prize, said Shulem handing him a shining silver sixpenny bit to the applause of all present.

Just as Grace was being completed, the sound of loud singing came wafting through the kitchen window. The family next door had finished Grace and had started to sing the traditional songs that always concluded the Seder. The song *Adir Hoo* that related to the rebuilding of the Temple has eight verses. The song *Achud Me Yodaya* is a madrigal of numbers that sets out in thirteen verses the various numbers applicable to certain facts in the Jewish and for that matter world's books of knowledge, such as the twelve tribes, the ten commandments and the one God. The third song *Chad Gad Yah* is the well know worldly tale whose ninth verse reads "And there came the Holy one, blessed be He, and smote the angel of death, who slew the slaughterer, who slaughtered the ox, which drank the water, which quenched the fire, which burnt the stick, which beat the dog, which bit the cat, which ate the kid, which my father bought for two zuzim, one kid, one kid."

We always compete with them, the fiancee was informed. We are eight children and they are eleven, but we try our best to out-sing them. The window was opened wide and the singing match began. As the family sang louder, the neighbours raised their voices an octave to another level and each to another level and so on until everyone was hoarse with singing and laughing and calling. Louder! Louder! from both sides of the yard that separated the two kitchens. This same or similar process was being conducted in house after house in the street and the whole district. The whole area was alive with song and laughter. You know, said Shulem over the din, Jews all over the world are doing what we are doing now. My mother and sister in Poland, my brothers in Germany and Palestine, your mother's sister and brothers in America. Everywhere. Everywhere in the world. Sadly, very sadly, they are not all able to sing so loudly.

Chapter 7

Rivka was always busy. If, for any reason however unlikely, there was a gap in her work schedule, then she would find something else to do rather than sit down and relax. The black fire grate which she had just polished could always do with another polish. The whitened square at the entry to the front door, must have at least one foot mark that should be removed. The windows, yes the windows could well do with another wipe. There must be some dirt somewhere she had missed even though apparent to no-one but her. Surely the children's clothes must need brushing, or a button replaced. If friends of hers or of her children called at the house, as they often did, she would insist that they sat down and had a cup of tea. The kettle on the stove was never off the boil. What a question, she would exclaim. Someone visits and you don't offer a cup of tea?

If Rivka was busy on weekdays, then on Fridays, she was doubly busy. Preparations had to be made for *Shabbas*, the Sabbath. The two youngest boys both went to the Jews Free School that operated what was called a double session day. The lunch-time break was halved to one hour and the afternoon session, while being a full session, ended an hour earlier than usual to allow teachers and pupils to get home prior to the onset of *Shabbas*. Instead of coming home for lunch, the boys were each given a fresh crispy, nicely wrapped roll, already cut but not buttered because of the dietary laws, and sufficient money to buy a saveloy sausage and pickled cucumber, commonly called a wally, at the Bloom's or Freshwater's delicatessen near to the school. Elsewhere, for a farthing, they could each buy a lemonade drink that consisted of a bottle of water into which was placed a purple or other coloured lozenge which fizzed on contact with the water and finally changed the still clear liquid into an opaque bubbling mixture.

When school ended, the boys often left separately because Yulus attended the junior school while his brother was in the seniors and each was usually accompanied by his own friends who with a four year gap in age had little in common. They each had certain things to do on their way home. They both had to attend the Goulston Street Public Baths every Friday. This was an experience in itself and the first visit by a young boy is rather daunting.

Yulus was escorted, on his first visit, by his eldest brother who had the appearance of an expert bather. He always looked immaculate. His plump smiling face, always closely shaven, was topped by a full crop of carefully brushed black wavy hair, kept in position by perfumed hair cream. The lapels of the master tailor's jackets were never crumpled and the creases that extended down the full length of his trousers always looked newly pressed. His appearance belied his humble background and his smile denied the chronic shortage of money which he tried to remedy at the dog tracks. He sometimes placed horse racing bets with a bookmaker with a Scottish name that with his innate humour he transliterated into the Yiddish as *mach mir lachen*, meaning make me laugh. On this theme he would often sing a song at parties that required the audience to sing Far, Far Away, at the right juncture to get the best effect.

> I went to the races last July - Far, far away
> I put my money on Pudden and Pie - Far, far away
> The horse came first, I laughed with glee
> And went to get my L S D (Pounds, Shillings and Pence)
> But where was the bookie, where was he?
> Far, far away.

He smoked cheap cigarettes to the last shred of tobacco. His work involved the use of both hands and he learned to keep the cigarette constantly in his mouth, alight or not. Once he forgot that he had a cigarette stub still attached to his lips when he ventured to give one of his younger brothers an affectionate kiss on the cheek. Although no fun at the time, it was always remembered with laughter, as he would jest, Shall I give you a burning kiss?

Having paid on entry Yulus was given a ticket that he handed to an attendant in exchange for a clean neatly folded white towel and a bar of soap. Yulus sat with his brother on a bench against the wall of a clinical white-tiled ante-room that had a strong smell of chlorine. Next! Shouted another attendant who wore white overalls over white trousers and white canvas shoes. He carried a long handled-broom with a bright yellow soft fibre head. Yulus was ushered through swinging doors, his brother at his side, into a long, wide corridor flanked on either side by cubicles, all but one, with their doors closed. The doors were not full sized, there being a large gap between the bottom and the floor and of such a height that the attendant, by stretching, could see over. There was a clock on every door, each showing a different time. On the outside walls of each cubicle were hot and cold water taps that were operated by a large removable key handle, presently attached to the tap of the open cubicle. The attendant swung the door open further to reveal a white bath that in Yulus's eyes was enormous, big enough for a swim. The bath was half full of water. Clean looking but yellowish in colour. Test it, said the attendant as Yulus stared at the bath in bewilderment. It's his first time, said his brother. Put yer 'and in and see if it's too 'ot, said the cockney attendant standing at the open door, broom in hand. Yulus touched the water gingerly and said Ouch! Too 'ot? Fought so, said the attendant as he moved the key from the hot to the cold tap and swung it round. A strong gush of cold water streamed out of the elephant-sized tap outlet for a few seconds and then stopped as he swung the key handle back. Try it now. He ordered. Go on, stick yer 'and in. Be"er? (the "t's of better and other words were not pronounced) he asked. Yulus nodded. Fought so, said the attendant as he adjusted the clock face on the door. You'f go' twen'y mini's, tha's till 'alf pas' the 'our, like the clock sez and not a mini' more. Unnerstan'? How will I know, if the clock is on the other side of the door? Cos there's a real clock up there, ain't there? He said pointing upwards with his broom to a large clock hanging from the ceiling that could be seen from every cubicle.

Ask him now, said his brother, nudging Yulus to instill confidence. Yulus had been told that it was more private to bathe in the public baths than at home. If that's the case, said Yulus, then why don't they call them private baths? You'll have to ask at the baths, he was told. Whadge wanna know? Asked the attendant with a momentary show of kindness. Why are the baths called public when each cubicle is private and why are they called slipper baths? Ventured Yulus, never short of adding a question. Wha' a bloody question!. How should I know? I only work 'ere. Retorted the attendant as he turned to the master tailor. You 'is bruvver? 'E looks like you. You're next. We ain't go' all day yer know. Nah you! He said turning to Yulus. Ge' yer clothes orf, ge' in and ge' washed. Every bi' of yer nah. There ain't much of yer, so i' shoodden take long. The master tailor added, I'm just over there, call me if you want anything. 'E's a bright un, the attendant could be heard muttering. Why is public private? What a bloody question!

The water that had felt comfortable to the touch was too hot for the body, but Yulus was too embarrassed to call for more cold water having said it was OK. He got in, turned pink all over and washed and dried within five minutes. He wanted to get out as soon as possible but was afraid that they would suggest that he hadn't washed at all, so he stood by the bath splashing the water and said everything was OK again when asked. After a couple of visits he soon got used to the atmosphere and learned to call out like the rest of the bathers for more hot or cold water or joined the communal singing that would break out from time to time. One song that was sung to the tune of the Volga Boatman contained the lines. Hot water number forty four repeated three times and followed by Ooh Ooh and a long drawn out Aaaah and shouts of laughter. Quiet! The attendant would shout above the din. Carn 'ear myself wash ou' the barvs! Which he did dexterously with his long-handled yellow broom after each bather and before the next.

Yulus heard somewhere that it was not healthy to dry oneself with a towel. By far the best thing to do was to massage oneself dry after a bath. In this way the muscles and skin tissues were improved as excess fat was removed. That's why in films, fat gangsters who were in the money, were always being massaged. Yulus was often told he was too fat. Now an experienced bather, he tried to refuse the towel, but the attendant insisted he take it, saying 'Ow can yer dry yerself wivvout a tow'l? Yulus took the towel and placed it on the side. Having bathed he began massaging himself dry with little success especially because of the steam and condensation in the tiled cubicle. Slapping must be the answer, he thought as he began slapping his thighs. Slap, slap, slap was a novel sound for this establishment. Wha's goin' on in there, asked the attendant. Nothing came the reply as the slapping continued apace. The attendant's head appeared above the door. Wha' yer doin' son? He queried. You'll never ge' dry that way. You 'ad be'er use yer tow'l. Tha's wha' i's for and cos yer time's nearly up. I will, said Yulus continuing to slap desperately, still without success. He was determined that the attendant should not see that he had failed, so he wiped his face and knees with his vest, dressed and handed the dry folded towel to the attendant on his way out. Blimey, said the attendant, you'll catch yer death. No I won't, retorted the defiant Yulus, knowing full well that the man was right. He resolved not to believe everything he heard in the future. If it had worked, he thought, I'd have called this place the slapper baths and not the slipper baths.

It is easy enough to leave the baths looking clean, but remaining clean during the fifteen-minute walk home, or half hour saunter home was a much more difficult matter. One had to exercise an extraordinary amount of restraint not to pick up some new dirt on the way. Life is much too exciting for a young schoolboy with curiosity for him to remember not to kneel occasionally while playing some physical contact game with friends. That expanse of exposed leg between sagging short trousers and sagging socks acted as a magnet to all the dirt in the neighbourhood by the time he arrived home. Rivka, already prepared, with soapy flannel in hand would take one look at the *lobos*, urchin, and say. Your hair is still wet, so I suppose you have been to the baths, but just look at your knees. Her expert wrist action was already operating on the right knee which miraculously turned pinkish from her professional application, while the left knee appeared even blacker by contrast. Next time you have a bath, she would say, please go in feet first!. Perhaps the best way to describe a *lobos* is through two little burning deck poems.

The boy stood on the burning deck
His mother called him *lobos*
Because he wouldn't wash his neck
And go to *Shul* on *Shabbos*

The boy stood on the burning deck
His mother was frying *lutkas* (potato pancakes)
And every time she turned her back
He stuck one down his *gutkas* (long-johns)

Sometimes Yulus looked back with nostalgia to the Fridays when he was younger and when he enjoyed bathing in the galvanised iron *vunner* in front of the fire in the kitchen, especially in the winter. His mother would stoke up the fire until the flames roared up the chimney and the iron lid on the kitchen fire turned bright red. She would open the slats on the front so that the gleaming coals could be seen and the comforting warmth would waft out and envelop him as he sat in the soapy water and listened to the dance bands on the wireless playing the popular tunes of the day. Often, he was so busy observing the varied pictures in the fire and examining the myriad patterns that could be made from soap bubbles, that he would forget that soap should also be used for the removal of dirt from the person. On these occasions, Rivka, flannel in hand, would use her expert dirt-removing wrist movement to remedy any omissions. Objections were useless because her swift application of the soapy flannel was faster than the rebellious outcry that nevertheless found expression. I've already washed that part. So it's twice washed, she would reply flicking the flannel to yet another area of his plump body.

Some Fridays, it was Yulus's turn to buy the *schmaltz* or Dutch salted matjes herring that formed the hors d'oeuvres of the evening meal. The large bosomed herring seller sat on a chair next to the large brown barrel, the wooden slats of which were held together by several steel bands. One could always find her at her permanent site on the pavement opposite the entrance to the public baths in Goulston Street. As a customer approached, she would stand up, adjust her thick blue linen apron and wipe her hands on the towel hanging over the back of her chair. Everyone asked for a good quality herring. What, she would say, You think I sell anything but good quality? There was no answer to her booming question. Nevertheless when her favourite regular customers came, she would say. For you, I will pick out the best. And with this, she would roll up the already rolled-up sleeve of her blouse or jacket and dip her right hand and arm deep into the brine in the barrel. The higher she rolled her sleeve, the deeper she would dip and out would come an oily fish clasped firmly in her hand. With her left hand she would take a sheet of newspaper from the pile on the adjoining table, place it on the tray of her scales, place a smaller sheet of waxed paper on top and then plop the fish onto the scale wiping her right arm with her already greasy towel and adjusting the metal weights on the other side of the scale, almost in one movement. The best herring you've ever had. She would say as she lifted the fish by way of the newspaper to place it on the pile of papers and complete the wrapping by adding sufficient sheets of paper to prevent any oily leakage. She only parted with the package on receipt of the price that she had announced when weighing. Her right hand held the package, while her left was outstretched to receive the coins. Here, *Boobela*, she would say to Yulus and any other young customer, take it straight home.

Newnham Street was busy preparing for *Shabbas*. Rivka was not alone in whitening the square area outside the front door. When Yulus arrived home with the well-wrapped *schmaltz* herring the street had an air of festivity. All the pavements had been washed and the white squares outside each household looked like a bouquet waiting to be presented to the *Shabbas* bride. People were hurrying home in their work clothes.

There was the rotund occupant of the house at one end of the street, whom children naughtily called fat belly because of his rotundity and because he always tried to confiscate their tennis balls that disturbed his peace on rest days. He worked at the ritual chicken slaughterhouse as a feather-plucker. The remnants of his daily work could be seen on the front of his apron which he sometimes did not take off until arriving home, and on his shoes. And yet, when a little later he emerged to go to *Shul* for the Friday eve-of-*Shabbas* service, he will have changed into his *Shabbas* clothes and none could guess his occupation from his new appearance. The wholesale green grocer made sure that all the empty cartons that sometimes piled up outside his house were discreetly taken inside and stacked in his back yard. The barber, whose shop was some distance away, was always home a little later than the others, as he always had yet another customer who required the full treatment, just at the last moment. A shampoo and haircut, short back and sides or just the back with the sideboards left a little longer. A shave, except for the mustache or the sideburns. A hot towel. Not for me! Thought Yulus when witnessing the steaming towels wrapped around a helpless customer's face. He didn't even like to have his hair cut at all. In fact he refused to go again to the Dutch barber in Half Moon passage, frequented by Shulem, who relieved him, on his first ever visit to a barber, of his full crop of curly hair. Instead he reluctantly took his custom to the barber shop in St. Mark Street where the barber placed a wooden plank over the arms of the chair so that he could sit up high and joked with him and the rest of his customers.

There was the musician who practiced his violin on weekdays, with his window wide open, because, according to the local wit, he couldn't bear to hear the caterwauling alone. In fact he was a fine musician and played in many a popular band. His elderly father was a bad tempered man who attempted to chase away children who played outside his house. While running, he would unfasten his belt and wave it threateningly at the fast retreating children. By the time he

57

came to a stop, he would be having difficulty breathing and also difficulty holding up his trousers which started to fall, having lost the support of the thick silver-buckled strap. The children would titter in the distance, out of harm's way.

The wholesale merchant closed his doors for *Shabbas* and took his telephone off the hook from Friday eve until after dark on Saturday. The stevedore also came home on Friday afternoons. A Jew working as a stevedore? Visitors to the street would remark with surprise. It certainly was unusual. His house too was unusual. He had painted the outside green. He had an arrangement whereby he would work on Sundays instead of *Shabbas*. The plumber would stride down the street towards his home in his working clothes as though he were marching with his troops in full uniform in the Jewish Lads' Brigade of which he was an officer and a founding member. The ladies, next door, would take in the chairs on which they normally sat during dry days patiently making button holes by hand in men's bespoke tailored jackets. They worked with great precision, first marking the correct places and then sewing the edges of the proposed holes with silk thread before expertly cutting the material between the stitches with a razor blade. No gap or wobbly line would ever show, not even when examined with a magnifying glass. False, that is uncut, buttonholes were made on the lapels for decorative purposes.

The cobbler worked from home. He too would close up shop for *Shabbas*. He was a small man who bore an amazing likeness to King George the Fifth. His face was adorned with the same type of beard trimmed in exactly the same way. He spoke no English. Legend has it that one Sunday, shortly after the Aldgate East Metropolitan Underground Station was opened, the cobbler was on his way to a wedding. He wore his best clothes. His bowler hat was well brushed. His shoes shone as befitted a man of his profession and he wore spats. He also wore his newly cleaned pin-striped trousers and a black tailored overcoat with a black velvet collar, the very same type of coat worn by the King. Unintentionally, he looked an exact replica of His Majesty. His son, tall and somewhat eccentric in his dress, was wearing a burgundy red waistcoat under his jacket. Both father and son were wearing white shirts and black bow ties.

They arrived at the underground station. The father stood aside, upright and aloof. His son, an English speaker who had passed his elocution lessons with honour, approached the ticket office. It suddenly came into the mind of the clerk, who had seen the two enter the station, that the bowler-hatted gentleman must be the King himself and this other lanky gentleman must be his aide. Obviously they had come in mufti to see the new station. The older man did not talk, nor did he make any attempt to approach the booking office. As would be expected, he left it to his aide. What to do? Certainly he couldn't announce the 'monarch's' presence without permission, nor could he possibly accept money for a ticket. He came out of his office, made a short embarrassed bow in the direction of the 'king' and said to the aide who had already made his destination known. Come this way sir. He led the submissive pair to the platform where he asked them to please wait a moment. He then addressed the platform porter, who by the way he glanced sideways at the silent couple and nodded his head, could be seen to agree with the clerk's analysis of the position. The porter spoke to a colleague who also glanced and nodded. The first porter aware of the importance of the occasion, then straightened his ruffled jacket and stood near the edge of the platform at a point where he knew a set of doors of the train would open on arrival. His colleague waited at the end of the platform to inform the train driver of the quality of his passengers. When the train arrived, the first porter politely asked all the occupants of the carriage to disembark, without explanation, and to board the adjoining carriage. He then signalled to the clerk who escorted the still bewildered pair into the empty carriage. Take your seat, your Majesty. He said, backing out with another embarrassed short bow. Only then did the meaning of the clerk's behaviour dawn upon the son. There are no records at the London Transport Museum to verify this account of that legendary hilarious incident of mistaken identity.

Other people of a variety of professions were making their way home before the Sabbath. Carpenters, furriers, shopkeepers and assistants, office workers, dressmakers, jewellers, taxi drivers and market workers were all hurrying home. The person who lived in the house that had the nicest front door in the street, gave it an extra clean. This door would often be used as the background when photographs were taken of any members of other families in the street. The house of the *shammas* of the *Shul*, the Synagogue beadle, was also located in this street. It was always ready for *Shabbas* and yet his wife found some extra things to do before saying the customary prayer while lighting the *Shabbas* candles. The whole street was abustle because, as the general saying went, *Shabbas* is *Shabbas*.

Food had to be prepared before *Shabbas* as no active cooking could be done on that day. Nevertheless, in the winter months, it was important to have hot food available for the family. This problem was solved in an efficient and systematic way. Fires were stoked up prior to the Sabbath and Gentile boys, known as *Shabbas Goys* would come and re-stoke the fires the following day, having been paid in advance. Food was cooked in enamel pots that were left to stand on the fires or in the ovens attached to the Kitcheners, to keep hot. Not all food was suitable for this treatment and so the most popular and traditional recipe was *cholent*. This concoction contains meat, potatoes, beans, barley, browning and any other variety of food, dependent on the whim or purse of the cook. Dumplings too could be added. The larger pots belonging to the larger families were too big to go into the family ovens and so an arrangement was made with the local Jewish baker for the *cholent* to be cooked overnight in his oven. An arrangement that was both economical and energy saving. The baker damped down the fire in his oven after the Thursday night's bake that included *challahs* which are braided loaves for the Friday night *Shabbas* eve table. No active baking could take place on the Sabbath. On Friday afternoons Yulus and his elder brother would take the family *cholent* in its big two-handled brown enamel pot to the bakers located in St. Mark Street next to the Scarborough Arms Pub on the corner of Scarborough Street. Other youngsters from other families would do likewise. The baker would place an identifying mark on the pot with chalk and place it deep into his oven with a long-handled loaf paddle which he also used to remove the pot the following noon when the two boys came to collect it and carry it back home using *shmutters*, rags, to wrap around the handles for insulation against the heat. The heavy well-cooked *Cholent* meal was held responsible for the necessary Saturday afternoon siestas before walking leisurely to *Shul* for the afternoon and evening *Shabbas* services.

If all the family did not attend the Eve of Sabbath services, everyone came home to the evening meal. The Sabbath candles would already have been lit by Rivka while saying the relevant prayers just before the beginning of the Sabbath. Shulem would tear one of the two *challahs*, traditional loaves, saying the customary prayer for eating bread, sprinkle some salt on the pieces that were offered to one and all to eat. Two *challahs* are placed on the Friday evening table to symbolise the double portion of manna that was received by the Israelites in the desert on Fridays as no manna fell on the Sabbath. The Friday *challah* is torn rather than cut, in memory of Abraham not using the knife on his son Isaac and of the prophet Isaiah's hope that swords would be beaten into ploughshares. *Kiddush*, the traditional prayer over wine, would be said to welcome in the Sabbath. Then the meal would be eaten along with the usual discussions and ended with Grace. Shulem sat at the head of the table in the kitchen on an armchair made of natural wood, varnished to give a light yellow finish. He sat on a cushion under which he would place the Yiddish newspaper after he had finished reading the daily news and stories. Consequently his stature rose day by day, as the pile of papers increased. Every now and then, as the pile grew too high, or on *Yom Toivim*, High Holydays, the papers would be cleared away and Shulem would resume his usual height much to Rivka's amusement.

Shulem, like most of his generation, was losing religious control of his adult children in this fast moving modern world. He still retained moral control. Swearing or the use of any bad language picked up in the street, at work or at school, could not be used within his earshot. If such a word did slip out within his hearing he would remonstrate with the simple sentence, *duff zech shamen*, you should be ashamed of yourself. Sometimes a frown would be enough to stop the flow. He rarely if ever raised his voice or used his hands to chastise his young children. When they complained, or whined over some shortage or unfairness that they considered had been meted out to them, he would quiet them by saying *sha, sha, Ich gay dir mitnemen*, Shush, I'll take you with me, not meaning it literally, but indicating how small the problem really was. On Friday evenings and Saturdays, he and his two younger sons, would attend *Shul* regularly. There, the two boys would sit on either side of him, with Yulus at his left side, nearer the aisle. Yulus and his brother, being pre-Barmitvah boys, would be called up to the *Bima*, the Dais from which the *Torah* is read, for a communal blessing. Yulus was often reluctant to go and had to be encouraged to stand under the large outspread white *tallas*, prayer shawl, with blue stripes, with other young boys, while the Rabbi or the Cantor said the blessing and sipped the wine and one of the *Gabbais*, Wardens, drank the rest of the wine from a silver goblet. On one occasion Yulus refused point blank to go. *Gay shoin* said Shulem several times. *Ich vill nisht*, retorted Yulus in Yiddish, holding firmly on to the hinged rail in front of the bench seat. This rail would open to hold the prayer books and would be closed to allow access to the seats. After much useless cajoling, the *Shammas*, the Sexton, came down from the *Bima* and holding Yulus by one ear, led him up the steps of the dais to take part in the ceremony. *Du mainst doos hot gevehen shein?* You think that was nice? asked Shulem sternly, when Yulus returned to his seat. No, was the shamefaced reply, I won't do it again.

Shulem kept an eye on his youngest son to make sure that he was following the service and reading the prayers together with the congregation. The elder boy always knew the place in the service, but Yulus's attention often wandered and he would find he was several pages behind, or he had not turned to the section of the psalms. In those instances, Shulem would, with his left arm stretched out, flick over the pages of Yulus's prayer book with his index finger and point authoritatively to the correct place in the proceedings. This he was able to do without interrupting his own prayers, that he knew by heart.

An important prayer in all the morning, afternoon and evening services, was the *Amida* or *Shemona Essreh*, the eighteen-verse prayer that was said standing and during which no one spoke. Prayers in the Federation Synagogues were not said in unison. They might be led by the *Chazen*, the Cantor or Reader, but each member of the congregation read at his own pace. Some finished earlier, others later. The *Chazen* would wait for the slower readers before proceeding to the next prayer. Latecomers would start at the beginning and try to catch up with the rest of the congregation. Rarely was there absolute quiet in the *Shul*. Sometimes, in Alie Street *Shul*, when the ladies, who sat up in the gallery separately from the men, chattered too loudly during the service or between prayers, the *Shammas* would slap the top of the rostrum with the palm of his hand, and looking up, would shout in a remonstrative voice. Ladies! Ladies! A short-lived quiet would follow. When the noise again grew too loud, the process was repeated. The *Amida* was said first by the whole congregation and then repeated, this time led by the *Chazen*. There were certain sections where the Reader said his piece and the congregation responded and other sections that were said together in unison which was possible in the second reading.

The *Shema*, the universal prayer that begins, Hear O- Israel is recited before the *Amida*. The end of this prayer is denoted during the service by the word *Emes*, the truth, that is the first word of the next prayer. This word is said aloud by each in turn when reaching that point. Children who wanted to prove their ability at reading Hebrew fast, would attempt to finish that section before the *Shammas* of whom it was said, that if there had been an Olympic competition for the fastest *duvvener*, reciter, of prayers, in the world, he would qualify for the gold medal. He always managed to finish first even though, at the very beginning, when he came to the word *achad* meaning one, where the prayer states that the Lord is One, he would throw back his head, raise his voice to heaven and intone an elongated *Achaaaaaaaaad* until one thought the veins in his neck would burst. Yulus and others would meanwhile race through the section. Skipping words was not allowed, but sometimes the competitors would apply a handicap by starting well before the *Shammas*, but never could anyone reach that word *emes* before the champion's booming voice resounded throughout the Synagogue.

That is a nice new pair of trousers you are wearing today, said his sister to Yulus. What! Another new pair? said his brother. Every week he seems to get a new pair, while mine last for months. Don't exaggerate. Said Rivka. It's not every week, although I admit it's too often. It's a good thing your father is a trouser maker, otherwise you'd be running about without *hoisen*, trousers. How did he do it this time? Came the question from another brother. The family often talked about the exploits of Yulus in the third person to each other even when he was present. Ask him yourself. OK then Yulus. What happened this time? This time said Yulus you can blame the CWS. Come on now, how can the Cooperative Wholesale Society be responsible for your torn trousers? Because they import tea. You tore your trousers on a packet of tea? No. They don't import packets, they import tea leaves. On tea leaves you tore your trousers?

The conversation would carry on in this vein for quite a while until the actual event was fully described. *Mema Rechel*, an elderly cousin, who was given the respectful title of *Mema* meaning aunt, collected silver foil for a hospital. The foil when accumulated in quantity had a sale value, the proceeds of which went into the coffers of the hospital. Some cigarettes were packaged in silver foil lined with tissue paper and Yulus would save the wrappings for her. But the quantities were all too small to be of any value. He discovered that the CWS whose headquarters

62

were in Leman Street, had import warehouses in nearby streets and one of these imported and repackaged loose tea that arrived in wooden tea chests, the lids of which were sealed by way of spring steel bands secured by long thin sharp steel nails. The empty tea chests, that still retained their thick silver foil linings, were put into the warehouse yard for collection and disposal elsewhere. The steel bands that had been cut and prised away from the wooden chests hung haphazardly from the sides of the chests. Yulus had to climb in and about these boxes to collect the silver treasure that he brought home with great pride. The anti-social spring steel bands and their protruding sharp steel nails counter attacked as Yulus proceeded with his raid and made ribbons out of his trousers. He thought he was doing the right thing, said Rivka in his defense.

After the Friday evening meal, Shulem would often stand with his back to the Kitchener, enjoying the warmth of the fire that had by then reduced in strength because it could not be stoked up on the Sabbath. He could relax a little on Friday nights knowing that he did not have to get up quite so early the next morning to go to work, nor did he have to lay *tefillin* phylacteries, on *Shabbas*. Instead, he would put on his *Shabbas* clothes and walk leisurely with his two sons to Alie Street *Shul* where he had a permanent seat. On his way home, he would call in to the nearby Temporary Shelter for Jewish Refugees. There he would talk to people who had come from the *Haim*, the old country, sometimes from his home town, and get first hand news of his mother and sister and her family who were still living there.

Each year life was getting more difficult. Anti-Semitism was growing increasingly violent, yet many, nay most, were hopeful that times would get better. On what they based those hopes the refugees could not say. They had seen the writing on the wall and were determined to get out of Eastern Europe. Britain and the America would not take them and so they were making their way to South America, not that it was easy to get visas to enter the countries in that continent. Britain allowed them right of passage and so they arrived in London from a European port, stayed a few days in the shelter and then made their way to South America by ship via the port of Liverpool. Shulem would sometimes pray with the religious refugees in the shelter's synagogue. Occasionally, he would take Yulus with him. Once, on *Yom Kippur*, the Day of Atonement when all religious and not-so-religious Jews over the age of thirteen fast for twenty five hours, one of the old sages in the shelter who had prayed throughout the previous night, asked Yulus, who was all of nine years of age, whether he too was fasting. *Host ge'essen?* Have you eaten? asked the old man. Yulus shook his head as if to say no, hoping that his fib would be accepted. *Az, loz mir zehen die tzung*, then let me see your tongue. Yulus submissively pushed out his pink tongue whereupon the sage waved his forefinger and with a twinkle

63

in his old eyes said *Noo, noo, noo!* Indicating that he had discovered the falsehood, because the tongues of those who fast are white.

Tutta, said one of the children to Shulem, the backs of your trousers are scorching again. Shulem took a half step forward from the fire. *Es is gournisht,* it is nothing, was his regular reply as he brushed the backs of the legs of his now warm trousers. Coal fires were pleasant to watch but they tended to give off either too much or too little heat. One had to be expert to regulate them. They were not always easy to light. Both Rivka and Shulem were experts and while this chore was routine for Rivka, Shulem always took a delight in seeing the flames start to roar up the chimney. If there was insufficient draft, he would take a sheet of newspaper and hold it against the front grating to encourage the draft. Sometimes, the paper itself would catch alight whereupon he would quickly stamp it out and add it to the now blazing fire. *Ven Ich mach a fire, mach Ich a fire,* he would proclaim with a smile. When I make a fire, I make a fire, the emphasis being on the last word. The fire was the centre piece of the kitchen, particularly in the winter months. On it stood the perpetually boiling kettle. Slices of bread could be toasted through the front grating by the use of a telescopic toasting fork. When not sitting round the table, the family sat around the fire place discussing the issues of the day, the events of the week or the year and, it seemed to Yulus, the exploits of Yulus.

How is the new school? Are you still top? No. I am no longer top. I went straight into the second grade and so I am the youngest in the class of forty three boys. But I am holding my own. No. I am not late for this school. I know, I was always late for infants, but that was because the school was too near and so I couldn't make up time when I started out late. Here, because the school is further away, if I start out late, I can always run to catch up. That's a good story. You get to Junior school earlier because you know that the discipline is stricter and because you leave home when I do, said the senior schoolboy. Is that true? I am afraid so. Tell them what the master said on your first day at school. You know. Tell them about Uncle Abie. Oh. That. What? What Uncle? Well, the master came into the room, sat down at his desk, told us all to sit quietly and then said that before you all introduce yourselves, I will explain something to you. You may look around the room and think that apart from yourselves, only I am in this room with you. If so you will be mistaken because there is always Uncle Abie. With this, he opened the drawer of his desk and brought out a cane. This, he said, is Uncle Abie, and what I can't do Uncle Abie can. What an introduction. Does he use the cane often? As it happens, he doesn't, but there are other masters who use it more frequently. One day, two boys got the cane publicly from the headmaster. They had been caught stealing and brought disgrace to the school. What do you mean publicly?

Well, now that the headmaster has had a microphone installed in the main playground. A microphone? Yes, he's a very modern headmaster, full of innovations. What innovations? Let him finish the caning story first. OK. We were all assembled there. What, just the Juniors? No, all of us. Juniors and Seniors. They were Senior boys. How many of you were there. I don't know, a thousand or more. No wonder he needs a microphone, though in my day, the teachers could bellow way above the din. If they didn't, they couldn't teach. Well, today things are different. Yes well, you were all assembled. What then? The headmaster explained that this was an unusual occasion, but he said that what these two boys had done was so bad, that he felt that they should be punished publicly as a lesson to all of us. He then gave each of them six of the best on their behinds. On their bare behinds? No. He wouldn't do a thing like that. What other innovations? Well. He has a moving picture camera and he takes films of us on outings and we can see how we enjoyed ourselves when he puts on a picture show in the main hall. He also travels during the holidays and brings back travel pictures for us to see. He says he is going to introduce a model railway soon and he has already had a complete model house built in the school.

What outings have you been on? The first one was a joke. A joke? Why? Well, The teacher said we were going to visit the historic Tower of London. Yes. So? Well, I thought the Tower of London was somewhere far away, especially as we were going in coaches. I thought it must be somewhere up the West End. Instead, the coach brought me home. Well, not exactly home. But I always play in the Tower. I always knew it simply as the Tower. My friends and I would play in the Tower gardens and in the forecourt. We would be chased off the grass by the Beefeaters and then stopped by them from clambering up on the guns lined up along the river. We would duck under the arms of the Beefeaters and make our way down into the dungeons and study the steps of the Bloody Tower looking for the bloodstains of the nephews who were murdered there by King Richard the third and laying in wait for Anne Boleyn to walk past with her head tucked underneath her arm. And then there is the bowling green. I could stand there for hours watching the soldiers playing bowls on that green grass. Boy. Is that grass green! Anyhow. You can imagine my disappointment when I found that the coach had brought me to my own playground.

Tell them what else you do at the Tower. What, watch the bridge open up to let the ships come through? No. You know. What, watch the lorries come with loads of sand to make a beach along the river bank? No. You know, how you follow the soldiers. Oh that. Why should I tell them that. Well, you've told them everything else. Yes what's all this about following soldiers? Do I have to tell? We're afraid so. You won't be angry? What is there to be angry about. Well, the Beefeaters stop us from playing on the grass and on the guns and they even

65

stop us from watching the bowls, so sometimes we march mockingly like the Dead End Kids, behind the sentries, as they march between sentry posts. At other times, we make funny faces at them and remark at the sweat pouring down their faces on hot days. They swear at us through the corners of their mouths because they are not allowed to speak when on sentry duty. They have to stand there like statues. *Doos is nisht shein*, That is not nice, said Shulem, whom everyone had thought had fallen asleep leaning back in his armchair. Family members were often caught out by his semi-somnolent cat-naps. *Duff zech shayman*, he added in remonstration. See I told you I'd get into trouble. And don't the rest of you encourage him with your laughter added Rivka.

And the other outing? Now that was good. We went to Crystal Palace. So what can you tell us about that? Well, it's a gigantic building. It's made of glass and iron. It was originally erected in Hyde Park for the Great Exhibition of 1851. The building was transferred to Sydenham the following year where it has been standing there for over eighty years. Together with the lovely gardens, it covers over two hundred acres. It's as big as that? That's what the guide said. There are gardens inside and outside the buildings. It was a nice warm June day and after touring the building and being told something about the 1851 exhibition and how the building was reconstructed, we then had a cream tea. Scones, butter, strawberry jam and cream. Scrumptious! There was only one problem. The windows had to be kept open because of the hot weather and so hundreds of wasps came flying in to join us in the feast. We tried to fight them off and managed to kill a few by squashing them with fruit cake, but they won out in the end and we left them to enjoy the remains. Afterwards, we were offered a sixpence if we would come forward, stand on the steps, and recite a poem. A few boys did so. They seemed to know such long, long poems. What about you? Did you recite. Oh, Yes, but my poem was much, much shorter. It was about the fly. Laughter. Tell it to us again now.

Poor little fly upon the wall
Ain't you got no clothes at all?
Ain't you got no shimmy shirt?
Ain't you cold?
Poor little fly upon the wall.

That's it? Said the teacher. Yes, said I. It's very short, he said, and it's full of double negatives. Surely there must be more lines? Not that I know, I said. OK then, he said as he gave me the sixpence. That was the easiest money I have ever earned, said Yulus earnestly. The easiest money you'll ever earn, came the family chorus.

Chapter 8

The year nineteen thirty six was not a good year for the world and it certainly was not a good year for the Jews. It started badly with violence and got progressively worse as the year wore on. The Fascist and Nazi concepts were permeating the political atmosphere and the Fascists of many countries, backed by the Germans and Italians, were becoming more and more arrogant. The London Yiddish daily newspaper, *Die Zeit* reported outrages against the Jews in all parts of the world as well as the growth of violent anti-Semitism in Britain, particularly in London. British anti-Semitism could at one time be distinguished from its European counterpart. Anti-Semitism in Britain had been mainly passive or negative. Jews were excluded from certain clubs and other social gatherings and they had difficulty in entering the professions and universities. They needed to be more capable than their Gentile colleagues or students to gain admission. There seemed to be unpublished quotas to keep down the number of Jewish entrants. But Jews could go about their daily life without undue hindrance in the Jewish quarters in which they lived. British anti-Semitism was subtle, it was clothed in coded language. The British anti-Semite did not have to use the word "Jew", he could say instead 'those people' or 'you people' or 'people like you' for any listener to understand the underlying meaning and yet be able to deny the implication of the statement should it be challenged. The difference between European and British anti-Semitism might be seen as the difference between openly sticking a knife into the side and surreptitiously applying a screwdriver. That is how it used to be before Fascism began to grow in strength.

Prior to the Nazi era, violence against the British Jews was marginal and generally took place on the periphery of their enclaves, where Jews rubbed shoulders with Gentiles. With the advent of Hitler's rise to power, the Fascist anti-Semites became aggressive. They started to invade the Jewish quarters to physically attack Jews, old and young alike, and to disrupt their businesses and way of life.

Fascists were holding public meetings at which they were openly inciting people against the Jews. Protests to the British government and the police were not only ignored on the basis of the principle of freedom of speech, but the police gave the Fascists protection and dealt harshly with any anti-Fascist demonstrators, often arresting them for breaking the peace. They did not mete out the same treatment to violent Fascist demonstrators who came to Communist or Socialist meetings. Instead, they would often arrest peaceful demonstrators who were objecting to the violent Fascist hecklers. The police would even break up peaceful anti-Fascist meetings. In other words, the freedom of speech principle seemed to work in one direction only. Fascists and anti-Semites could incite freely, but anti-Fascists and Jews could not protest so freely. No wonder that many rank and file Jews, such as one of Yulus's brothers, felt that their best protection was solidarity with other anti-Fascists and so became attracted to the Communist and Socialist parties who appeared to be their only allies in the fight against British Fascism and anti-Semitism.

The self appointed Jewish leadership had other views. The leaders took the peculiar view that anti-Semitism could be separated from the political arena. They argued that the British Jews should fight anti-Semitism but not Fascism. Thus they said that Jews should stay away from anti-Fascist demonstrations otherwise the Jewish community would be tarred with the red Communist brush. The British Jewish leadership was divorced from the view of the Jewish population as a whole and particularly from those Jews who lived in the East End of London and had to take the brunt of the violent and invasive Fascist anti-Semitic attacks.

The emancipated Jewish leaders seemed to believe in acculturation to such a degree that it almost appeared to be assimilation. They were basically anti-Yiddish and did not allow Yiddish to be spoken in their institutional forums. Indeed, even in the Federation of Synagogues, where the majority of fee paying members lived in the East End and were Yiddish speakers, it was not until November 1925 that participants were allowed to address meetings in Yiddish. They were also, in the main, anti-Zionist. They felt that without a Jewish State, they were undeniably Englishmen, or better still English gentlemen of the Jewish faith, whereas with a Jewish State, their loyalty to Great Britain, the country of their birth, could be questioned. They seemed to ignore the fact, that their loyalty was always being questioned in one way or another. So much so, that they, as Jews, always had to act in a way to indicate quite clearly that they were loyal citizens of the realm and to educate the children of immigrants to act as English ladies and gentlemen. Most if not all those emancipated Jews who had come from Yiddish speaking parents, would unconsciously, or subconsciously, exclude Yiddish words or expressions when Gentiles were present. They would change what are called 'Cohen the spy' jokes to say 'Murphy the spy' jokes, so as to avoid any Semitic or anti-Semitic connotations. Their first action when leaving a synagogue would be to remove their *kupples*, skullcaps, from their heads and place them in their pockets. Their outward appearance had to resemble the British norm. Why invite anti-Semitism? And if not personally experienced, maybe it did not exist at all.

The German Jews, who were the most emancipated and assimilated Jews in the world, had found that acculturation was no safeguard against virulent anti-Semitism. But Britain was not Germany and so what was happening there did not necessarily apply to Britain. Noisy, vociferous demonstrations were to be avoided. Any behaviour that could be considered Jewish as distinct from British, was to be avoided. *Sha. Sha. The Goyim*, do not antagonise the Gentiles, was their motto. This attitude was in direct contrast to that of most of East End Jewry, who as early as nineteen thirty three, when Hitler came to power in Germany, could see the writing on the wall, and knew that if they did not make a stand at the very first signs of violent anti-Semitism, then the situation could only go from bad to worse.

Shulem was among those who believed that anti-Semitism was universal and endemic throughout the world. He accepted that the ferocity of anti-Semitism varied from country to country and that some countries, Britain included, were more benevolent than others towards its Jewish minority. But he also felt sure that it was indigenous and dormant everywhere, even if sometimes disguised as anti-alien He knew, for example, that the 1905 British Alien Restriction Act was mainly directed towards preventing East European Jews from entering Britain and that it had indeed been successful, because virtually no such Jews had been given residential entry permits since the outbreak of the Great War in 1914. That was why the Temporary Shelter for Jewish Refugees in Mansell Street was always full of Jews on their way to the South American continent, having gained British transit permits. Yulus would often come home to report that he had spoken to some refugees who were leaning out of the upper windows of the Shelter that overlooked Newnham Street. *Fin vunnet kimmen zie?* Yulus would ask in Yiddish. From where have you come? *Fin Polin*, from Poland, most of them answered. *Unt vo geyen sie?* And where are you going? To Argentina, they would cry, using the hard "g".

January the first nineteen thirty seven was a Friday. That night, after the Sabbath meal, the family sat around the fire for the usual discussion of current affairs. Friends had joined them this evening as on many other evenings. There was a particular atmosphere of earnestness in the crowded room where the flickering flames from the fire competed with the flickering light of the two *Shabbas* candles that stood in the centre of the table fixed firmly in their shining bright brass candlesticks. Warm candle wax was clinging to their sides and building up on their bases like stalactites and stalagmites in ancient caves. *Shabbas* candles were ceremonial. They were never extinguished, but allowed to burn themselves out and they were never used for lighting a room. The wireless was quiet. Neither of the two stations, regional or national, could be listened to, as it was *Shabbas* and on *Shabbas* one had to find forms of entertainment that did not involve work, writing, or the switching on and off of electrical appliances. One rested, walked, read or talked. Even the less religious members of the family, respected the long-held views of religious parents when it came to behaviour within the household on Friday nights. The less religious would often leave the house after the Sabbath meal to find their entertainment elsewhere, outside the orbit of religious restriction.

But on most Friday nights, one talked. Someone suggested that in view of the experiences of the past year, the gathering should review the year, to put it into perspective and "to see where we go from here". To this there was general agreement, but where to start? Let's each deal with a particular subject, suggested another. Good idea said many others as they all started to talk at the same time. Shulem said that he could see that it was Friday night as usual. One suggestion was finally adopted. Foreign affairs would be dealt with first and then local politics and domestic matters.

Tell us Shulem, said one of the friends, what you have heard from your brothers in Europe and Palestine. The news was not good. Germany was continuing to introduce anti-Jewish laws. The Nazis have gone completely mad. Their latest law bans Jews from employing women under thirty five. Can you believe that? When there were some international protests, Hitler told the League of Nations that Germany's treatment of the Jews was its own business. And what about Jewry worldwide? Was it not their business? The Nazis' anti-Jewish terror tactics have been extended outside of Germany. They are harassing the Danzig Jews. My brother who lives there with his wife and two children tells me that his son can no longer attend a German school but has to go to a Polish school. The boy speaks only German. My brother there, once wrote to say that he and my other brothers in Germany had thought that I was foolish to live in such poor conditions in London, when their own economic situation was so much better, but now they were having second thoughts and perhaps I was not so foolish after all. But now that violent Fascism has raised its ugly head here, who knows? At least it's not the government here. That's true, that's very true.

My brothers don't understand why, internationally, no one is even tying to restrain Germany from flexing its muscles. It has marched into the Rhineland without any significant objections from the French or the British. They say, and they are probably right, that it is due to the fear of Bolshevism. But who is to say that the German, Italian and Japanese Axis alliance will only be directed against what they called the Bolshevik menace? Many Jews were planning to leave Germany, indeed several had already left, including my youngest brother who had gone back to Palestine, but the others were still hoping that things would get better. My brother in Berlin is not too well and so won't contemplate moving. There are also violent anti-Semitic outbreaks in Poland. Not that that is new. Is anyone fighting it there? Who knows? There, they seem to be relying on God. They had special prayers against pogroms in all the *Shuls*. The Yiddish paper here writes about Yiddish blood pouring in Poland, but my mother and my sister and her family still do not want to leave Poland. Why not? I suppose because my mother is now much too set in her ways. And what about your brother in Palestine? He tells me that the situation there is also very difficult with Arabs and Jews fighting each other while the British were fighting both. Jews were also being murdered in Baghdad in neighbouring Iraq. Who knows where it is safe. Even here, despite the victory in October when Mosley was stopped from marching through our district, anti-Semitism is getting worse.

OK popsky, that's a later subject, said the eldest son to Shulem. The master tailor had taken the position as chairman for the evening, otherwise, as he put it, we might be here all night! The term popsky was an endearing term developed from the word papa that had been given a Polish suffix. Shulem had many titles. The children would call him *tutta*, which was Yiddish, or dad or pop or popsky or father, depending on the current mood of both father and child.

What other nasty things are happening in the world? asked the self-appointed chairman. Hitler wasn't the only one who is defying the League of Nations, someone said. Mussolini has done the same and he has also ignored the sanctions that were voted against him. Not that they were properly implemented. Look what he has done. What? What has he done? He has demonstrated to the world, the importance of air power. How? By bombing Abyssinian towns which helped him to win the war and make Abyssinia part of the Italian empire And he used mustard gas on the poor defenceless Ethiopians. That was disgusting. What about international Fascism? It's spreading throughout the world. Look, Austria and Rumania in Europe have turned Fascist and also Paraguay in South America. Paraguay? Yes why not? People also live there you know. And what about South Africa? A Native Repression Act has been enacted there against the blacks, and if that is not Fascism I don't know what is. The Fascist party also obtained a good vote in the Belgian general election and Leon Blum, the leader of the French Socialists, was attacked in Paris by Fascist thugs.

Zennen zie nisht farshtik? Are you not thirsty? intervened Rivka, *ver vilt noch ein cuppatea?* Who would like another cup of tea? The phrase 'cup of tea" that is pronounced by the Cockney as 'cupertea' (one word) has also entered the East End London Yiddish language. All hands were raised without interrupting the earnest discussion, more earnest at this time than on past occasions because of the worrying political situation. Each participant was anxious to raise a point or express another view. Sometimes it seemed to Yulus that that everyone was speaking at once, while at other times, side arguments or discussions would develop while others were holding the floor. He sat quietly next to Shulem and marvelled how his eldest brother, the chairman, managed to regain control of the discussion from time to time. The rattle of tea cups did not stop the argumentative flow of words, some in Yiddish, some in broken English, some in the vernacular and others in perfect grammatical form that would have honoured any self respecting debating society.

The civil war in Spain and Spanish Morocco was started by Fascists who want to overthrow the Republican government. Franco won't be able to win without external support. Well, he's getting it isn't he? True. Hitler ignored the call for non-intervention that came from the international conference in London, and sent his Condor legion to Spain. The Italians too are giving Franco military support. Meanwhile the British Government is trying to prevent Britons from volunteering for the International Brigade. Volunteers have to go through France to get to Spain. The Labour party supported the call for the supply of arms to the Spanish Republican government, but the British and French governments are blocking any such sales. All the world knows that the 1936 Olympics were staged in Berlin last year. So? What has that to do with Spain? Just a minute and I'll tell you. What they don't know, or want to know, is that German and Austrian Jewish athletes of Olympic standard were excluded from the Games. Yes. But what has that to do with Spain? Well, a rival anti-Fascist Olympiad was to be held in Barcelona. But it was frustrated by the outbreak of the Spanish Civil War. And what about those three London Jews who were on a cycling tour of France at the time? They crossed over into Spain and became the first British international volunteers to fight against Franco's Fascists. Aren't they members of the Communist party? Yes they are, but so what? Who else is fighting the Fascists? Other Jews soon joined with them in the fight against Franco whom they consider is the surrogate for Hitler. In fact, about ten percent of the two thousand British volunteers in the International Brigade are Jews. Where did you get those figures? I can't remember, but they were published somewhere. Most of them come from the East End of London. The Workers' Circle Ladies' Guild has voted in support the civil war against Franco. The Spanish nationalists claim that they are not anti-Semitic but when the people of Catalonia supported the Republic the phalangists referred to them as Judeo-Catalanes and called some of their leaders secret Jews. General Mola who is one of Franco's generals praises Hitler's anti-Jewish policies. And all this, despite the fact that there are very few Jews in Spain. There are even fewer now, because many left the country as soon as the civil war broke out. It's funny, isn't it, funny peculiar that is, while resident Jews are leaving the country, other foreign Jews are rushing to fight there. Well, that's always the case. Jews as a people are made up of various factions. Even the religious have their own. Why the Jews should be considered as being one homogenous whole, I don't know. Some of us are religious while others are atheists. Some are Communists and some are capitalists. Yes, but for all that, we are all Jews, and anti-Semites will only make a distinction when it suits their purpose. That's true, they tell the Gentile capitalists that we are all revolutionaries and the Gentile workers that we are all capitalists. Shame that we too, can't have our cake and eat it. And look what the Russians are doing. They may be against Franco but that doesn't stop them executing sixteen staunch Communists including Zinoviev and Kamenev, both Jews, after forcing them all to confess to supporting a Trotskyist plot to overthrow Stalin. There are Communists, Jews among them, who think that anti-Semitism is the result of the class war. Remove the class struggle, they say, and pronto, out goes the need for anti-Semitism. So, why are the Jews being hounded in the Soviet Union? Well, they say, they are being prosecuted for their political beliefs, not specifically because they are Jews. So, how come the majority being charged as counter-revolutionaries are Jews? You may well ask. And is there an answer? Socialism in theory should be the answer, but it is yet to be practiced. That sounds too much like one of the answers the Reverend Donald Soper likes to give about Christianity. He says, Christianity hasn't failed. It simply hasn't been tried. Anyhow, the unfortunate fact is, that here in England, the British Labour party vacillates and the only party truly fighting Fascism, which for us also means anti-Semitism, is the Communist party and of course the SPGB (Socialist Party of Great Britain) and the ILP (Independent Labour Party) both of which are vociferous but short of membership. Then you should all join, declared the lone SPGB member. Jews do not always vote for Jews. Last year, the Liberal party thought, that if it put up a Jewish candidate in the general election, the majority of Jews would vote for him. But the Jews in this district are almost all working class and the majority voted for the Labour candidate even though he is a Gentile. What has his religion to do with it? It is his policy that counts. I see we have arrived on home ground now. Does that mean we have finished with foreign affairs? No. Not yet. We should mention a few other wars. Such as? Well, Moslems and Hindus are killing each other in India and there is the Sino-Japanese war which may have seemed a long way off until the Japanese joined the German-Italian axis. Nothing is a long way off, if it affects fellow Jews. Do you know that the Board of Deputies of British Jews actually asked the Japanese ambassador in London to intervene on behalf of the Jews of Harbin, in Manchuria, or Manchukuo, as it is now called, who were being ill treated by some White Russians there? Where on earth did you hear that? If only the Board of deputies were more active here.

Yulus, said Rivka, it's time for bed. But mama, all this talk is interesting. Can't I stay up just this once? Just this once? How many times have I heard that one? It is the new year mama. Let him stay up. Consider it part of his education. OK, said Rivka. Just this once. Who wants more tea? Who doesn't? How can we talk without tea?

Have you noticed? We British too have started to re-arm. Anthony Eden is now advocating peace through strength. The Royal Air Force has introduced a new fighter plane called the Spitfire. Perhaps that is why the economy is improving. Wages have actually started to go up where there is work. That may be true in the south, but in other places the economic situation had deteriorated beyond measure. Look at Jarrow, two hundred workers from there marched three hundred miles to London to publicise their miserable condition and to petition for work. And they marched in vain, because the Prime Minister refused to see them. There was a recent survey of the nation's health. It revealed that the diet of forty percent of the population was below the standard set by the British Medical Association. Many children were suffering from Rickets through lack of vitamin D in their diet which results in a shortage of calcium and a consequent weakness and deformity in bone structure. What is the name of that doctor who does his rounds in this district? Is it really Doctor Rickets or is that his nickname because he often diagnoses Rickets when he examines the kids in this area?

Many children are not eating properly and if they are, then their mothers are probably going without. Only now have the Local Authorities succeeded in re-introducing free meals at school. They were first authorised under the 1921 Education Act but one of the cut backs in the recession restricted this benefit and only children who had definite symptoms of malnutrition, as certified by a doctor, could qualify for such meals. There is a subsidised scheme in operation for the supply of cheap milk in schools and free milk for poorer children. The Jews' Free School provided free milk for all its pupils. In the winter, Yulus, with others, would place his bottle of milk on the hot radiators to warm the milk which was drunk during the morning break. Health Insurance has become compulsory for all workers, but it doesn't cover other members of the family. Some people joined the Hospital Savings Association scheme to provide for times of sickness. Dental care was much too expensive and many, like Rivka, neglected their teeth and attended a dentist only when in severe pain. The result was that many had all their teeth removed. False teeth were common and the loss of them when eating or swimming had become a subject for cartoonists and seaside picture postcard artists.

That modern economist, John Maynard Keynes has just published his general economic theory. It states that the way to get out of the economic depression was to increase the money supply by government spending on national projects and social welfare. And will that make a difference? Sure it will. Past governments had contributed to the downward spiral of the depression by cutting social welfare benefits so that even fewer people could afford to buy manufactured goods which in turn led to further unemployment. Now at last, Keynes has suggested that the policy be reversed. More money in the system. More demand for goods. More demand for workers to manufacture. Better economic conditions. Is it Socialism? Don't be daft. This is a liberal attempt to restart the capitalist system which had ground to a stop. The armament's industry is being revitalised and that will help to boost the economy. Even the Socialists have to admit that. True. It is a real paradox. The production of waste makes for work in the short term even though it does not add to the wealth of the nation, but only to the manufacturers. Why not manufacture useful products that will benefit us all, rather than armaments which in due course will encourage those countries that think they have the military edge to rush us into war?

It is a shame that the current technical revolution may be used for the wrong purposes both in war and in industry. Why in industry? Have you seen Charlie Chaplin's great new film, Modern Times? It's worth seeing. It's still a silent film, but it is a real parody of the technological age and the belt system and how management can use machines to dictate work schedules. Do you know that there are now two and one half million cars on the roads of Britain? And Hitler has just introduced the peoples car supposedly to compete with Henry Ford. And look what is happening in the air and on the sea. The German airship Hindenburg crossed the Atlantic. So did Britain's latest passenger liner, the Queen Mary. Amy Johnson flew from London to Cape Town and back in record time. And here in London, the BBC has made its first Television and sound broadcast. Who can afford that? Never mind that. We have to admit that technology is advancing by leaps and bounds. True. Not so long ago we were listening in on crystal sets and cats' whiskers. Soon our wireless sets will have more than two stations, regional and national. And the agreement with the newspapers that the BBC can only make news' broadcasts after six o'clock in the evening will also come to an end. Did you hear, they say that electrically propelled Trolley buses are going to be introduced into London instead of trams? They will be less noisy.

Before we get on to the local political situation, what else of importance happened this last year? There was the Crystal Palace fire. Oh, boy! And what a fire! The flames shot up hundreds of feet into the sky. Some newspapers called it the best show in town. Better than the usual fireworks display. But what a shame, such a fantastic building and in hours it was just a shell. Yulus was there on an outing from school, just a few weeks before. Not guilty said Yulus with a wry smile, at last he had got a word in edgewise. He was always being chaffed about the fire he had started in the doorway of the local warehouse some years before, when he was just a four year old. But no one would let him forget it. The Crystal Palace fire lasted quite a few hours and there were three great explosions. People came from all over the place to see the fire. Really? Yes, and extra trains were even put on to take people there. Unbelievable! The fire could be seen from as far away as the coast and yet further, from an airplane. We could see the red sky from here. One of the sad things was that the aviary also caught fire and although people tried to save the birds by releasing them, they still got caught up in the flames and thousands of them died. There is one consolation. There is? Yes, the Peoples Palace in Mile End has been rebuilt. Wasn't that also destroyed by fire? Yes, some five years ago. It is due to reopen very soon. Do you think they will rebuild Crystal Palace? Who knows!

One other very important thing. We now have a new king, King George VI. Three kings in one year! Yes, that's right, but one of them has not been crowned. His father King George V died at the beginning of the year. Many of us thought that that in itself was a bad omen. Why? Because his natural successor, Edward VIII, was known to have anti-Semitic friends. It was somewhat of a relief when he abdicated at the end of the year in favour of his brother who seems to be more solid, like his father. The old King had established himself as a figure of stability even though his reign had covered the Great War and the terrible depression years that followed. He was not too modern, although he was the first king to speak on the wireless. Neither did he like to follow foreign practices. He was once reported to have said "I don't like abroad, I've been there". Who told you that? No one told me, I read it in the newspaper.

OK now, let's deal with the battle of Cable Street in October 1936 and all its implications. Yes, let's. One thing is clear, the Fascists didn't just simply decide to march through our part of the East End of London without prior preparation. They knew that the Jews and the Communists would oppose them, but they thought that they would have sufficient police protection to get them through. The Fascists also thought that the law was on their side. What made them think that? Well first of all there were the earlier incidents such as the Fascist meeting in the Albert Hall in February when the police did nothing to protect the anti-Fascist protesters who were manhandled and bodily thrown out of the hall. Then the police violently broke up the anti-Fascist meeting in Thurloe Street. Then there were a number of smaller incidents throughout the year when Jews were attacked in the streets. Did you know that Jewish wholesale traders have had to agree to operate a six day week to avoid what was called unfair trading? What has that to do with the Fascist march? Nothing really, but it all adds to the general atmosphere. More to the point was the dismissal of the case against Raven Thomson, one of Mosley's chief supporters and public speakers. Oh yes. I've heard him speak. He's really vituperative. The judge didn't seem to think so. He said that there was no evidence that what he said was a general insult against the Jews. Can you believe that? The man makes the most slanderous statements against the Jews at every opportunity, and the judge says that there is no evidence of a general insult against the Jews? So whom was he insulting?

The Fascists are not just anti-Semitic, they also throw stones at non-Jews. Such as? Well, there was that time, last August, when James Hall, the Labour MP for Whitechapel and Sylvia Pankhurst were in a procession of ex-servicemen and Labour supporters, when the Fascists threw stones at them. The Mayor of Bethnal Green complained about the lack of police protection and said that it was not safe to walk in the East End. He also said that the Jewish question, had been introduced by the blackshirts, and was being used by them as a smokescreen for attacking the rest of the working class movement. It's interesting and also good that he spoke about the rest of the working class, acknowledging that most if not all of the Jews living in this area are also working class. The Fascists were getting more and more arrogant. What do you mean, were, they still are! Yes, but we are talking about what happened before the march aren't we. I am not sure you can make such a clear separation. They were, alright, are, getting publicity and encouraging their supporters to attend public meetings, while the Jewish press and leadership are still telling Jews to keep away from those meetings. Barnett Janner has suggested that Jewish speakers should hold meetings at the same corners, but at different times, in order to combat peacefully the tide of poisonous anti-Semitic propaganda. Who does he think will attend those anti-Fascist meetings? The Fascists? If they did come they certainly wouldn't come to listen. That's for sure. And then there was the letter to the press by a leading Jewish personality, begging the Jews to exercise restraint in what he called the tradition of orderly citizenship and leave the defense of the Jews to its leadership. We are being hit, spat at, vilified, beaten up in the streets by Fascists who have abandoned all traditions of orderly citizenship and yet we are supposed to stand by and wait for something to be done to stop it, when we know full well that nothing effective is being done? At least the Jewish Peoples Council (the JPC) is on our side. They have berated the Board of Deputies for not doing enough. There are also non-Jews on our side. At the beginning of October the five Mayors from Bethnal Green, Hackney, Poplar, Stepney and Shoreditch together petitioned the Home Secretary to stop the Fascist march planned for the fourth of October, but to no avail. Also the National Council for Civil Liberties has complained about Fascist behaviour. The JPC organised a written petition against the Fascist march. They actually collected over one hundred thousand signatures, also to no avail. Even though scores of people were injured and twelve people were taken to hospital at a Fascist meeting in Leeds at the end of September, the Home Office still considered that the obviously provocative march in London should take place even though there would have to be two policemen present for every three Fascists. What do you mean, even though? That is exactly why they thought the march could take place. But they underestimated the strength of feeling of the local population. And how!

What a day that fourth of October 1936 was. Full of tension and expectation. All of us were there. Everyone was there. Not everyone. No? Then who wasn't? Well, the Jewish newspaper editors for one, and the Jewish Board of Deputies for another. They are so afraid of being tarred with the Communist brush that they keep insisting that Jews should keep away from Fascist meetings or demonstrations. Who else didn't come? Well, the editors of the News Chronicle and Daily Herald, they too made calls to stay away. The Labour Party was having its conference in Edinburgh. From that safe distance they condemned the rise of Fascism. Bravo! Well, apart from them, everyone from this area was there. Members of the ILP (Independent Labour Party) were there. And so were we SPGB'ers. I thought you were supposed to be pacifists? We are, but that doesn't obviate our right to protest against violence, does it? I suppose not. I suppose you could be defined as aggressive pacifists. That's not a bad title. Each and all of us there were determined to stop the Fascists from marching along their pre-selected route. There were over one hundred thousand people crowding the route. The Communists claimed that they organised the protest, but in reality it was a spontaneous demonstration of the people of the area. When you think about it, you realise that almost every able-bodied anti-Fascist in the district came out. There were Communists, religious and secular Jews, London dockers and many others from all walks of life. All had a common interest to stop Fascism in its tracks. The dockers were far from being Communists, but they agreed with the assessment that the Fascists were using the Jewish question as a smoke screen to attack the rest of the working class movement. In addition they have an innate dislike for Fascists who try to emulate their German or Italian counterparts and they remember only too well the use of gas by the Germans in the Great War and they also despise the Italians for using gas against the helpless Abbysinians. The black shirted Fascist thugs are anathema to decent minded British citizens.

It was amazing to see how the streets became crowded. Slowly but surely from early morning people began to congregate along the route. Some were carrying banners saying the Fascists or Mosley shall not pass. The people were quiet at first, but the excitement increased and slogans were being shouted as more and more people poured into the streets. Young and old, men and women. The Fascist march was due to start at two o'clock from Royal Mint Street which is near to the Tower of London and just outside the Jewish enclave. Mosley arrived with his henchmen. He was wearing a black military type jacket with a red armband, grey riding breeches and, would you believe it, jackboots. He also wore a black peaked cap. He looked like a replica of a German Nazi in the cinema newsreels. The black-shirted Fascists started to march up Royal Mint Street which leads into Cable Street, shouting "The Yids, The Yids, we're going to get rid of the Yids". They intended to turn left into Leman Street and continue to Gardiner's Corner. There, they were going to turn right into Commercial Road and march on right through the Jewish quarter to Limehouse. Then Mosley, William Joyce and Raven Thomson and others were going to address their Fascist supporters. That's what they intended, but the reality was something else. The cross roads at Gardiner's corner were not only crowded with people, two tram drivers had parked their trams on the crossroads to help block the roads through to Commercial Road and Whitechapel. In any event, the Fascists didn't get that far. They, and the police protecting them, soon found that they couldn't turn into Leman Street because it was packed chock-full of people and the police could not make a way through them. They then decided to continue up Cable Street, but there, barricades had been erected. A lorry had been overturned and cobblestones in the road were dug up. Mounted police attempted to charge the barricades to make way for the Fascists to march. But marbles were sent rolling down the road under the horses' hooves. Many stumbled and their riders were thrown to the ground. It was a real battleground.

I saw a lot of the police action, said Yulus, surprising the adult debaters by his sudden intervention. How can that be when you were not allowed to join the demonstration? Well, I saw things happening from the window of my friend's flat in East Tenter Street. His window looks out onto the back of Leman Street police station. First we saw hundreds of policemen waiting in their vans before the march started and then we saw them drive away in a hurry. The mounted police followed them and then later we saw lots of them looking dusty and untidy. You mean dishevelled. Yes, if that's the word. They were walking their horses back to the police station yard. Others brought in people who were arrested, some of them still struggling with the policemen. That could hardly be called the centre of action. May be, but it was the headquarters of the police on the day and they say that over one hundred people were arrested. The boy's right. He had a bird's eye view. He probably saw more than many of us caught up in the crowds. Not everyone waited for the Fascists to march. Some of us went straight to Royal Mint Street to confront them. There were many scuffles,

79

mainly with the police who were there to protect the Fascists. The police made baton charges against the demonstrators. I saw several of them hurt. Some had had to be treated in hospital. Several others were arrested for disturbing the peace and assaulting police officers. Some of the police were hurt. Other protesters in other streets were also arrested. The Commissioner of Police came to Royal Mint Street. Yea, and it didn't take him too long to realise that it would be impossible to get past us. When he saw those aggressive and dense opposing crowds, he called off the march. Apart from the crowds, there were women shouting and screaming from the upper windows of the buildings along the route. Some of them threw pots and pans down onto the heads of the Fascist marchers who had to change their route to get away. When we heard that the march had been called off, we were all elated. Crowds of us danced and sung in the streets and even joked with the police who also seemed pleased now that the tension had eased. There was a rumour that Mosley was in any case going to speak in Victoria Park Square in Bethnal Green. Thousands of us made our way there. But Mosley did not appear.

So what did the newspapers have to say about the march and our demonstration that stopped it. First of all they dubbed it the Battle of Cable Street, as though that was the only place where the battle was fought. And, of course, they had to justify their previous attitude. God forbid that they might change their opinion. I've kept a copy of the Jewish Chronicle and *Die Zeit* (the Yiddish daily). So read what they say. Just a minute, let me find it. OK. The JC says 'da, da, da, much as we detest the campaign that is being waged by the Fascists in this district, we cannot pretend to any feeling of satisfaction with this result.' What? Wait a minute , there's more. 'Its chief effect is to enable Mosley to pose as a martyr in the cause of civic liberty, da,da,da' Can you believe that? That editor is completely divorced from the masses. Wait, wait, there is still more. Here it is 'Jews who assembled in the streets were vastly out-numbered by non-Jews.' Is that a bad thing.? Who counted? And how can you tell the difference? Are we all supposed to wear yarmulkes, scull caps, to be identified? One more sentence 'In the long view, we believe their action to be profoundly mistaken.' *Nu gay mach*, literally, well go do, which means, what can one say? And what about *Die Zeit*? I'll paraphrase what the editor says, because he's written a long *geschicter*, story. He asks, what did the East End event show? And answers that a great fuss was made over about two thousand Fascists marching. Two thousand? There were at least five thousand! Another editor who can't count. What? Two thousand thugs are not enough? He also says that we were lucky that the march was stopped when it was, because as bad as the outcome was, it would have been a lot worse if it had been allowed to continue. Is that it? No. He thinks that Fascist agitation only serves the Communist cause. This fear of communism undermines the fight against Fascism and anti-Semitism. What I can't understand, said Rivka, is how he could have changed so much over the last few years. Three years ago, in 1933, he was asking us, no almost demanding us, to demonstrate against the Nazi treatment of Jews in Germany. Now that the problems are close at hand, he wants us to stay at home? Can anyone explain that? Perhaps it's because the anti-German boycott campaign failed and demonstrations, as successful as they may appear at the time, can achieve nothing unless supported by strong political action. And who is there here to support the Jews? Not the major parties, only the Communists and other fringe left wing parties. Some Jewish leaders think that Fascism is not a Jewish issue and they are afraid that they will be tarred with the revolutionary brush if they openly attack Fascism. Incidentally, the Yiddish newspaper also includes elsewhere a few snippets from the English press. Such as? Well, the Times talks about Communist and Fascist hooligans. Note which comes first. The Daily Telegraph says that the freedom of speech prevented the march from being banned earlier. What nonsense. Everyone knew that the march was a provocation and would cause a disturbance. That's putting it mildly. The Herald says that Fascism has no place in our society. Hear, hear! And listen to what the Manchester Guardian says. Well what? It would have been better to have stayed at home and let the Fascists march, thereby not giving them importance. What? Don't they know what the Fascists would do if unimpeded? They would have wreaked havoc. Look what happened the following week after the anti-Fascist march that followed the same route. The Fascists smashed windows and looted and even threw a Jewish man and a young girl through a shop window in Mile End. Fortunately the girl fell on the man and so wasn't badly hurt. The Mayor of Stepney has complained that Jews in some streets in the borough cannot sit in their front rooms because Fascist hooligans throw stones through their windows. We should be careful not to condemn all the Jewish leadership, after all there was that interesting letter to the Times from Basil Henriques who wrote about the Jewish dilemma. He said that had the Jews not joined in the opposition to the Fascist march they would have been considered cowards, and by joining they are being held to be the enemies of liberty and free speech. He also wrote that the Jews were being so terrorised by the Fascists that they were being forced into the ranks of Communism as the Communist Party is the only party militantly attacking Fascism. And look who took part in the anti-Fascist march of the following week. Well who? The Communists of course. Yes, but apart from them? There were the dockers, the Stepney Council for Democracy and Peace and the Furnishing Trades Association and other Trades' Unionists. There was also the meeting in Shoreditch of the Jewish Peoples Council that called for coordinated action by all sections of the community against Fascism.

One speaker there said that if Fascism reaches power in this country, there will be no question of discussing with the government about Jews. They will either be dead or in concentration camps. A Trade Union speaker pointed out that not only Jews were opposed to Fascism which was a threat to democracy and free speech. And the speaker from the Workers' Circle received a standing ovation when he gave his speech in Yiddish. That was truly refreshing. We all have much to lose, but the Yiddish speakers have the most to lose if the current trend continues.

Chapter 9

On the face of it Yulus did not have very much spare time. He was at school all day from Monday to Thursday and in the late afternoons, after school, he would come home, have some tea and then go to Christian Street *Talmud Torah* for a few hours to learn Hebrew and religious practices. Not that he learned too much there. The teachers were not too experienced in controlling boys who were not keen to attend the classes in the first place. Some teachers would rap boys over the knuckles with a ruler or pinch their cheeks or pull their ears as punishment for not paying attention, all of which made it less attractive to attend the following evening. Although truancy was generally high, Yulus always attended out of respect for his father. He did not always arrive on time, nor did he always don his *tsitit-confus*, the four-cornered undervest with a fringe at each of the four corners worn by pious Jews to remind them that God was ever present at all corners of the earth. The very orthodox wear this undergarment with the four long fringes hanging visibly outside their trousers. However, most orthodox Jews in Gentile societies, as distinct from the ultra-orthodox Jews, kept the fringes discreetly hidden from view. Every now and then, the Rabbi at the *Talmud Torah* would call for an inspection to see who was and who was not complying with religious practice. Stand on your seats, ordered the Rabbi, and let me see your *tsitses*, as he would call the undergarment. And where is yours? He would ask. In the laundry, Yulus would lie on those days when he had forgotten to, or decided not to, wear it. In the laundry? The Rabbi would roar, don't you know that you are supposed to have three *tsitses*, one on, one off and one in the laundry?

Leaving the *Talmud Torah* for home after classes was always an ordeal. Christian Street *Talmud Torah* was situated on the edge of the Jewish enclave and aggressive Christian boys would lie in waiting for the boys as they left Hebrew classes, so that they could call them Yids and throw stones and bottles at them and accuse them of killing Christ. Sometimes fights developed, but on most occasions, because these Christian boys were truly louts, discretion was thought to be the better part of valour, and the boys would scurry out of range.

One year, Yulus went on a short holiday trip arranged by the *Talmud Torah*. Jewish hygienic and religious practice has it that one is not to speak between saying the prayer for washing one's hands prior to a meal and saying the grace before meals. The hundred or so boys were all seated at the table for an evening meal together with the Rabbi, when one of the boys unpardonably spoke prior to grace. He was sent to wash his hands again. By the time he returned, another of the boys had spoken and he too was sent to the washroom. So it continued for what to the hungry Yulus seemed ages and ages, before finally the meal was served. Did you enjoy your trip? Rivka asked on his return home. I prefer eating at home, he replied.

On Fridays Yulus had to go to the public baths on his way home from school. And on Friday evenings he would go to *Shul* with his father. On Saturday mornings and late afternoons he would again go to *Shul* for *mincha* and *ma'ariv*, afternoon and evening Sabbath services. And on Sunday? Well, on Sunday mornings he would go to school for more Hebrew lessons and also to learn about Jewish history and Palestine. The Jews have had a long history of expulsion and wandering and in the nineteen thirties some Jews, including Yulus's uncle, were making a serious attempt to settle back into *Aretz Yisroel* (Jewish Palestine) and fulfil the aims of the 1917 Balfour Declaration which promised to establish a home for the Jews in Palestine. The school, and for that matter, the whole British Jewish community was somewhat ambivalent about Zionism. British Jews wanted to help their fellow Jews to settle in Palestine, but did not themselves generally wish to go there. Nor did they wish to give the impression that they had any loyalty other than that to Great Britain. And so, they salved their consciences by teaching about the rights of Jews to settle in Palestine and collected money to help others to settle there. One of the money collection methods was to issue cards on which was the outline of a tree with squares delineated on the branches. Stamps could be purchased for sticking onto those squares. The total of the value of the stamps on each card was enough to buy a tree for planting in *Aretz Yisroel* . Thus three aims could be fulfilled with one card, an affiliation with Zionism, assistance to fellow Jews and the ecological aim of draining malaria infested swamps while making the Palestinian desert bloom. While not appreciating all these sentiments at the time, Yulus nevertheless felt great satisfaction each time he handed in a completed card.

The main entrance to Jews' Free School is in Bell Lane. Yulus was very much aware of this, as recently he had met with an accident there. Not exactly athletic, the plump Yulus would, when he was not dawdling, run and play with the rest, or just run by himself. On this occasion he was running out of the school gates, hurrying to get somewhere or other, when he came into contact with a car travelling at some speed past the gate. Yulus was never sure whether he made contact with the car or whether the car came into contact with him. What he did know was, that there was a screech of brakes and he was flung to the ground. There he lay on the road beside the right front wheel of the car and there just close to his nose was the word 'Goodyear' embossed on the tyre. People crowded around. Are you alright? I think so. Can you get up? No. He can't get up, shouted one of the women who had come to help. Look what you have done, she turned on the driver, who shocked, was still sitting in his car. You should be ashamed of yourself. What? he said as he tried to open the door of his car. Don't do that, she shouted, do you want to hurt him again? Yulus's bottom was against the door. What? Is he hurt? Is he hurt badly? Asked the driver as he struggled to get out of the car from the passenger side. Well, he can't get up. The driver came round the front of the car. He bent over Yulus. Sorry son, I just didn't see you. Now, let me help you get up. I can't said Yulus. Back out of the way, shouted the school caretaker who had come to see what all the noise was about. Back out of the way, he shouted again yet louder, to the boys and women who were crowding around the car. Give the boy a chance to breathe. Now son, said the caretaker authoritatively, try to get up. I can't said Yulus again. Why not son? The caretaker's voice had softened, thinking of the brave boy and broken bones. Because my jacket is caught under the wheel. Get back into the car, ordered the caretaker to the driver, speaking to him as though he was just a naughty boy. Get back into the car, turn off the engine, which in all the excitement was still running. Put your gear into neutral. It is. Good. Now take off the hand brake and hold the steering wheel steady, and for goodness sake, close your door. Now, everyone get away from the back of the car. Away I said, stand aside. That's it. The caretaker seemed to be enjoying his moment of authority. Now, he said, you two big fellows, come here to the front of the car, and when I tell you, push the car backwards. Wait till I tell you and push slowly, I mean slowly. Right, are we all ready? Push!

His jacket freed, Yulus stood up of his own volition and started to dust himself down. You alright son? The caretaker asked. I think so. Then you were bloody lucky. Excuse my language he said turning to the attentive crowd. Anyhow, you had better go to the hospital for a check up. Is anyone meeting you here? No. Then you, he turned to the driver who, still somewhat shocked, had come to see what damage he had done. You had better take him to the hospital. You are prepared to do that, aren't you? Of course. I just didn't see him running out. He came out so fast. There ought to be a barrier there to stop kids running straight out into the road, said a bystander. We have made applications to the Council, but for some unknown reason, they keep refusing, explained the caretaker. Perhaps now, after this accident, which could have been a lot worse, they will at last agree. Who knows? Yulus got into the car. The doctor at the London Hospital checked him over, said he was fine and could go home. The driver sighed with relief. As Yulus emerged from the hospital, Rivka came running towards him panting. Yulus, she cried, are you alright? Friends had informed her of the accident and she had immediately come running. What are we to do with you? she cried smothering him with kisses. Are Goodyear tyres good tyres? He asked. Such questions, he asks me, how should I know?

Goodyear shmoodyear? From where do you get such questions? What I do know, she said, is that it was very foolish of you to run out into the road. Rivka rarely preached but when she did her words had bite. Perhaps now, she added, you will learn how dangerous it is to be foolish.

The rear entrance of Jews' Free School is in Middlesex Street, which is Petticoat Lane, known to locals simply as the Lane. On Sundays, the market encompasses the whole length of the street and adjoining streets. It is crowded and full of interesting things, so Yulus rarely went straight home. He would wander about the market and watch and listen to the predominantly Jewish stall holders making their pitches. Pitching is a form of auctioneering. It is basically a Dutch auction where the auctioneer, or pitcher, starts the price at the highest level and works his way down until he can find a buyer at that lower price. Yulus did not have the money to buy, but he liked to watch and listen. And there is so much to see and hear in the market, particularly on Sundays.

There is the man who can guess your weight, and if he is right, you have to pay him a penny. It is uncanny how accurate he is so much of the time, especially as the people are fully clothed with heavier or lighter garments. And who knows what heavy objects they have in their pockets? But nevertheless he is mostly accurate, perhaps he has some device on his portable scales that stops the arrow at, or close to, the number he calls out. He carries his scales with him, stands them on the ground and invites people to step on them. What have you got to lose? He shouts, if I'm wrong you get your weight for nothing. And if I'm right, don't I deserve a reward? With men, he makes a great show of feeling the calves of their legs through their trousers and then looking them up and down, he shouts out their weights before they step onto the scales. With the ladies he is more discreet, he touches their wrists and then whispers the weight into their ears. For the ladies, he shouts for all to hear, there is full confidentiality!

There is the poor artist who invites a small crowd around him as he demonstrates his art. With a lighted candle he blackens the white underside of a large dinner plate, a dramatic action that attracts onlookers. He then draws pictures through the soot with a match stick. The finished product may be a white on black portrait, or a town or country scene. This he does expertly and swiftly, chattering all the time so that he does not lose his immediate audience as he will soon go round the watching people with his cap to receive a few coppers. He then wipes off the sooty masterpiece and starts again. If only the past, he says philosophically, to those who remain for a second performance, could be wiped out so easily for life to start again on a clean plate.

There are the herbalists who can cure any ailment and who discourage onlookers from taking patent medicines other than their own. Look what happens in your stomach when you take aspirin and then a lemon drink when you have bad cold or flu, he shouts. Watch, he entreats, as he places a pill, supposedly an aspirin, on a plate and then squeezes the juice of a lemon onto the pill which begins to fizz busily as it dissolves. That is what you are doing to your intestines, whereas with my special formula, says he, holding up a small bottle of yellow, green or pink liquid, your problems will be solved swiftly and safely.

The escape artistes operate on the fringe of the market where there is a little more room. They will not start their performance before they have collected sufficient money from the crowd who have already been attracted by other preliminary tricks of their colleagues. These tricks include dramatically tearing up telephone directories that were probably previously baked in an oven to make them brittle, eating fire or broken gramophone records or pieces of coal or what appears to be broken glass. Lengths of chain are rattled and snaked along the ground by a muscular man, while another explains that this mighty man is about to be chained up with steel chains and secured with unopenable steel locks and then challenged to escape within five minutes. But first, first, some money has to be thrown into the ring. Thank you sir, he says, as one of his plants (a colleague planted in the crowd) throws a few coppers onto some sacking strategically placed to receive the offerings and to prevent the coins from rolling. Surely we can do better than that, he shouts as a second plant throws in a silver coin. Thank you indeed sir, now where are the other British sportsmen? Gradually, more and more coins appear on the sacking. The mighty man does a few dramatic exercises, flexes his muscles to the whistles of the watching men and giggles of the ladies. You will note, says the man winding the chain around the muscle man, that we are not using ropes that can expand with every movement of the body. Oh no. Here we are using steel chains. Once fastened securely, they cannot be moved. Here, you sir, step forward and see whether you can put your finger between the chain and this man's flesh. You see everyone, it's absolutely impossible, even Houdini, if he were here, couldn't and yet, ladies and gentlemen, within five minutes, this man, this unusual man, will free himself. But first, we need a few additional British sportsmen to throw a few more coins, preferably silver coins, into the ring to encourage this courageous man to do the impossible. After a moment or two of further cajoling and cries from some of the crowd, who had already made their contribution, for proceedings to start, the momentous struggle begins. Red in the face, muscles bulging, the upstanding giant, falls to the ground, grunts, twists, bends, flails his legs, and then appears to give up accompanied by sighs of disappointment from the crowd. But no, he has not surrendered. He makes one more tremendous effort and suddenly and miraculously, the chains begin to untangle and the great man is free to the cheers of those onlookers who have stayed for the full performance.

These are the same escape artistes, thought Yulus, who perform at Tower Hill, where the Socialist Reverend Donald Soper would speak to large crowds who either came specially to hear him or wandered over from their visit to the Tower of London. He would speak from his raised platform and preach a mixture of Christianity and Socialism which he claimed had much in common. He did not use a microphone, but his booming voice carried in all weathers and his repartee would generally demolish the comments of hecklers with whom he battled with relish. The essential thing, he said on one occasion when Yulus was present, was to remove evil from this world. A shrill heckler's voice floated across the crowd. Do you think we can do that before the next election? On this occasion the Reverend's retort was lost in the general laughter.

The pitchers of crockery in the lane are the greatest fun. They are full of humour as they sell their wares. Look, one will shout, this china is of the finest quality. Listen to it ring, he says as he flicks it with a metal knife. A full set of these cups and you have a full philharmonic orchestra. He enjoys the alliteration and emphasises the 'f' sound. A full fil-har-mon-ik orchestra, he repeats. But that's just the beginning. What I am going to sell you today, you will never before have seen in your lives. Never. Look, I am going to start with this centre large serving plate. On this I will place six dinner plates. Here they are, he says as he spreads them noisily onto the serving plate. On top of these, I will place six soup plates, pause, six dessert plates that he slots in under the soup plates, and six side plates that he somehow fits in under the dessert plates. Twenty five pieces in all, he shouts as he tosses the precarious pyramid in the air and catches the base plate in his secure hands with the other clattering plates miraculously remaining in place. Look at the beautiful design, he says. You might, if you are lucky, find such artistry in Selfridges up there in the West End, but at what a price, what a price! What is the price? Someone shouts from the crowd. Just a minute and I will tell you. But I haven't finished yet because, because, pause, Here Charlie, hang on to this lot, he says to his assistant as he hands him the precarious pyramid. Hang on while I show these kind patient people, what else they will get with this magnificent dinner service. Here, now hand me up that box. What you can't? I told you to hold on to the plates? Then put the plates down. Careful now. The crowd laughs. Now give me that box. No not that one, that one. Look what we have got here. It's the tea service that goes with the dinner service. Yes you remember, I showed you the cup at the beginning. You there, the gentleman with the blue tie, you thought I had forgotten it didn't you? You didn't? Well good for you. You've got a better memory than I have. Now where was I? Oh yes, he shouts as he unpacks the box, throws plates and saucers in the air, rattles them together, while never pausing for breath except when it is theatrically necessary, as he explains the virtue of buying from him and not from others. I am here today and here tomorrow. Everybody in this market knows me and those that don't soon will. And look at the shape of these cups. Just look at them. Look, I'll show you an example of what they are selling elsewhere. I won't say where because I don't want to malign anybody, but just look at the difference between these two cups. The one I am offering you is elegant. This other one, it seems to me, was designed as a gezunder, a chamber pot. My mother-in-law has got one exactly like it. More laughter. OK now, let's do some business. You want to know the price? OK here it is. What is it Charlie? Pause. Oh yes. I told you I had a bad memory, Charlie has just reminded me. Not only will you get a magnificent dinner service and an elegant tea service but I am throwing in, not literally you understand, I am throwing in this delightful condiment set, free and gratis. And I am not asking fifteen pounds that you would have to pay up west, no not fifteen pounds, not fourteen, not ten, not eight, not even six. Here it is, he slaps his hand on one of the boxes close to him, a giveaway, a real giveaway, the lot for five pounds ten. No, no wait a minute, here, I must be mad, here, the final, final price, a fiver. Have I got a buyer? You sir (probably a plant to start them off). Charlie, take the money and give him the goods. And so more hands with a five pound note are raised and the goods change hands.

Some people literally sell little or nothing. They call them surprise packages. The pitcher explains quite clearly that there is no guarantee that the package he is about to sell contains anything of value. There are some packages here which have a value at least four times that which I am asking. But the others are just rubbish. Caveat emptor, he says in the only Latin he knows, it's entirely up to you. You sir, you wish to take the chance? Good for you sir. No you have no need to open it now, he says to his plant. Well if you so wish. What did you get for your shilling? A vase? You were lucky, he says emhasising the "were". Then out come the shillings from expectant buyers, or rather suckers.

Once Yulus acted as a negative plant for his Socialist brother, who being out of work at the time, had decided to sell some books in the market. He couldn't set up a stall in the market because for that, one needed a license, so he obtained some books and sold them out of a suitcase. Among them, were books from The Left Book Club that produced a pocket educational series. One of the titles was on birth control. What do you know about birth control? His brother shouted to passers-by while Yulus stood conspicuously nearby. No not for you son, the Socialist cutter and designer, now bookseller, shouted. These books are for adults only. Go on, go away son, you're not old enough. That pitch was supposed to catch the attention of prospective customers who were to think that they were privileged buyers. Yulus only did this once as the ruse only sold two books. Yulus's face reddened a little as he thought of the book that he had managed to look through once, when no one was looking.

Yulus sometimes went with this brother to the Serpentine Lake in Hyde Park where they would hire a rowing boat for half an hour. It was fascinating to see grown Englishmen suddenly transformed into young boys as they stepped into the boats, sat down and grasped the oars. These same persons who would queue quietly for buses or cinema tickets and arrive on time for appointments would instantly lose all sense of time and orderliness as the oars touched the water. They dip the oar blades into the water to get the maximum push and then raise and twist the oars to feather, that is skim the water, making pretty patterns on the surface before dipping the oars once again to propel themselves swiftly away from the shore. The half hour allotted to them passes far too quickly and most of the oarsmen seem oblivious to the passing of time. Come in number forty two shouts a boatman through a megaphone from the shore, your time is up! OK, just one more time round, comes the shouted reply. No way, insists the boatman, a half hour is a half hour. Reluctantly and unhurriedly the oarsmen return to base.

It was great to escape the concrete jungle of the East End and to wander about that vast green area of Hyde Park, touching the old well-established trees whose leaves fluttered in the mild spring breeze. Yulus had been told once that Nietzche, the German philosopher had said that on a still day one can push and shove the trunk of a mighty tree with great force and the leaves will not move. But the gentlest of breezes will make every leaf flutter. It was true. He had tried pushing the great trees to no effect and now he was witnessing the all influential breeze. It is such a shame that a man who could disclose such wonders of nature should also have written things that have encouraged the Nazis to attack Jews. People were walking their dogs or throwing balls or pieces of wood for them to fetch. Some threw lumps of wood into the lake shouting fetch, fetch, and watched their pets dash madly into the water, grasp branches in their mouths and swim desperately for the shore, shaking off water from their fur onto unsuspecting passers-by. There seemed to be competition between dog owners as to who could throw their pieces of wood the furthest. On one occasion, as an exhausted dog emerged from the water after a long and desperate swim, another dog ran up and snatched the treasure from the poor dog's mouth. Pandemonium broke out as the hound robbed of its catch realised what had happened and scurried off barking after the thief, while the two dog-owners barked at each other and almost came to blows.

After some tea and buns in a cafe, the brothers would wander over to Speakers' Corner to join the crowds that gather there each Sunday. They come to listen to speakers who spout forth on various subjects, some of which are serious. Other speakers seemed to speak for the pleasure of listening to their own voices while yet others amuse and entertain. Religion and politics are taken seriously and members of the crowd heckle the speakers whenever possible. Revolutionary speakers are allowed to promote their revolutions at Speakers' Corner on the basis that they give their identities to the police who watch unobtrusively and almost disinterestedly from the sidelines. No revolutionary has ever been known to over excite the generally sceptical audience that attends the Sunday gatherings, although many heated arguments do ensue between audience and speaker and between members of the audience themselves. There are always preachers and someone insisting that a Prime Minister must go even though he may have only recently taken office. Certainly the government must go and as for the Trades Unions? And were the London Busmen right to go on strike and who said what about 1926, the year of the general strike? Did not everyone know that only in Russia have the workers got any rights or that the government had no right to ban volunteering to fight in the Spanish civil war or that the Fascist Mosley was right and foreigners were taking jobs away from deserving British workers or that after Guernica no town was safe from mad bombers. People would listen for a while to one speaker and then move on to another. There was always movement, with some people trying to get to the front of a crowd, while others were backing away, to go home or to find another interest.

One speaker announced that after much research he had discovered how it was that a brown cow eating green grass gave white milk. What is more, he would now divulge this momentous information to anyone prepared to listen. He then began detailing, with many digressions and using as many biological and scientific terms as he could muster, all the paths and processes through which the green grass passed before being transformed into that delicious and sustaining white liquid. Having portrayed all the terrifying experiences of the innocent weed he then exclaimed that it was no wonder that the milk was white. Who wouldn't be after such a horrendous process? says he, as his colleague comes round with a hat to receive some monetary contributions for the afternoon's entertainment.

Another speaker shouts his utter nonsense from a platform some little distance away. Everyone shouts as there are no microphones. A heckler, no doubt a friend planted in the crowd, calls out in relation to a peculiar statement just made by the speaker, "You must be mad". Just a minute retorts the speaker. Who said that? I did, comes the reply. I'm mad? says the speaker incredulously. I'm mad? Look, just a minute, look, he says as he takes a parchment out of his jacket pocket. Look at this document, he says, holding it up for all to see. I'll read it for you. It's from the Coney Hatch lunatic asylum, you know the loony bin. It says here that this is to certify that Mr. J. G. Tee, that's me, he says pointing at himself knowledgeably, that Mr. Tee is sane and fit to wander the streets of London or words to that effect. Much laughter. Has anyone else here got such a certificate of sanity? He asks. Of course not. The fact of the matter is that I, me, that is me, this person standing here before you, yes me, I am the only one here that has proof of sanity. A hat comes round to collect contributions for the speaker's supper.

A long-haired cynic, this time without a platform, explains walking to and fro, to a group of people who have encircled him at his bidding, that he has a friend who had become rich through some legitimate business deal. His neighbours started gossiping, suggesting that he had come by the money by nefarious means. The friend, rather concerned spoke to his priest and as a result he became a born-again Christian who believed sincerely what Jesus had preached and so gave away all his riches, retaining only the mere necessities of life. Very strange, said his neighbours, a man who gives away his money to the poor must be covering up something, and so they remained suspicious of him. What to do, thought the friend. Maybe I've gone too far, on the one hand by displaying my wealth too ostentatiously and on the other, making my poverty obvious to all. He decided to live a quiet, normal life whereby no one could raise a question as to his behaviour. This he did until he heard the local gossips. You know that man, he heard them say, nodding in his direction, he lives such an ordinary life that there is nothing, but nothing bad that can be said against him. He smiled contentedly until he heard the next comment. Very suspicious!

Yet another speaker was explaining that nowhere in the British Isles was there a housing shortage. Then why is it that there are so many people who haven't got a decent roof over their heads? questions one of the audience. That my friend is because they haven't got any money, not because there aren't any houses. Look, says the speaker, this is today's Sunday Times newspaper. I've turned to the real estate page. Here is an advertisement for a mansion with eighty rooms for sale with immediate occupation. So what's your problem? Where's your shortage. Not in housing is it? No. It's in your pocket. Who's ever heard of someone with money that can't find a place in which to live?

Yulus had few toys and as with most of his friends in the neighbourhood, he had to find his entertainment out of doors. He was once asked to describe the type of games he and his friends played in the streets. Oh! he exclaimed there are so, so many, I wouldn't know where to start. But the question intrigued him and one day he sat with his friends and together they compiled a list, albeit in haphazard order. The list read as follows:

Hopscotch, where squares with numbers are marked with chalk on the ground and one has to hop from one square to another in a certain order.

Hop and Barge, where boys hop and shoulder-barge each other to put the hopping opponent off-balance.

Walley, where a tennis ball is thrown against a brick wall. As the ball is thrown, the thrower calls out the name of the person who has to catch it.

Cutter, which is a form of leap-frog with two teams. One boy makes a back by bending forward and holding his legs behind his knees. The best jumper of one of the teams sets the mark from which boys have to leap to get over the back and the number of paces required before leaping.

Old Tin Can where a tin is placed on a marked spot. All but one have to run and hide when the can is kicked far away from its mark. The remaining person has to retrieve the can, replace it on its mark and then search for the others. When he sees one, he has to return to the tin, rattle it and call out the name of person he has seen who then has to come out of hiding and stand by the tin. Other hiders can release the 'prisoner' if they can get to the tin before being seen and then they can run away to hide again.

Knocking Down Ginger where a continuous cotton thread is attached to the front door knockers of houses on both sides of the street. One knocker at the end of the deserted street (this ruse can only be operated when the street is clear of people and traffic) is used to get the occupant to open the front door. That door pulls on the cotton thread that lifts all the other knockers that are activated as the thread breaks. Many occupants come to their doors, only to find that there is no-one there, except their frustrated neighbours.

Cricket played with one wicket and a tennis ball. Everyone knows how to play cricket, but how is a wicket made without stumps? The choice depends on the state of traffic in the streets. A wicket can be drawn in chalk on a warehouse wall, in which case there is no need for a wicket keeper, so even only two persons can play. It can be marked out on a lamppost. This requires a wicket keeper who has to watch for the ball from behind the post. When the ball hits the post, it tends to shoot off in all directions which adds to the excitement and frustration. Thirdly, a wicket can be delineated by three orange peels on the ground. The problem here is manifold. There are many arguments as to whether a ball, missed by a batsman, is too high or too wide for the batsman to be declared out. The decision often rests with the owner of the bat (there aren't too many bats available) who threatens to go home and so end the game if his decision is disputed. The wicket keeper also acts as traffic coordinator and warns of approaching vehicles.

Tennis is played without a net, or with a piece of string strung across the road.

Hi Jimmy Knacker is a tough game played with two teams of four or more boys. One boy stands with his back to a wall. A second boy makes a back by stooping with his head against the first boy's stomach. The third and fourth boys also make backs. Each places his head between the legs of the boy in front, gripping his thighs. The other team now jump on the elongated back of the first team with a view to making it collapse. This is done while shouting Hi Jimmy Knacker, one, two, three.

Many games with cigarette cards such as Pic-or-no where the cards are spun to the ground and when a picture falls on a picture the thrower gets those two cards or all the cards thrown up to that time. Some cards can be stood up against the wall while others are flicked at them from a distance. When a card is knocked down the person who flicked the card wins all the cards flicked to that time. This game is called Flickers which is also the name of a game where cards are flicked for the longest distance. Cigarette cards are collected from cigarette smokers. The streams of workers making their way home through the streets after a day's work are a rich source for collecting cards. Most people are congenial and often have cards at the ready to give the expectant collectors.

Hi-Li has a wooden bat with a rubber ball that is attached by elastic. The ball is hit and as it rebounds it is hit again. Some people become expert and can keep the ball going for a long time. Competitions have been arranged for this game.

Tops. There are two kinds. Spinning tops are pear shaped with a metal nail at the tip. They are made of ribbed wood around which string is wound, but not attached. The top is thrown to the ground while holding the string causing the top to spin. Many tricks can be done with these tops. They can be aimed accurately. They can be lifted with the looped string for the top to land on a shelf or on the hand, still spinning. They can be used to barge other tops. Then there are whipping tops that look like elongated mushrooms with the stalks coming to a point. The string of the whip is wound around the smooth stalk. The whip is whisked backwards causing the top to spin. It can be kept spinning by whipping and can be "taken for a walk."

Gamma is a game where articles such as keys or watch chains or pocket knives (closed) are to be placed in three pavement squares forming a triangle. The articles are thrown from the first square into the second and into the third and back to the first. Articles can be thrown at competing articles with a view to knocking them out of, or away from, the square to which they have to be aimed. The first to get round the triangle, wins.

Marbles.

Pesach (Passover) games with cob and hazel nuts as substitutes for marbles or for lucky throws into small square holes cut into matzo boxes. The holes are given different values to be won when nuts, that are thrown, enter them.

Cannon. Two or more short sticks are placed crosswise on the top of a very large cotton reel that is stood on end in a marked spot. The cotton reel is as large as a tin (say of beans) which can be used instead. There are two teams. A tennis ball is thrown by a member of one team at the cotton reel which will be upset and roll away and the sticks will fly in all directions. The second team has to reassemble the reel and sticks without being hit by the ball that is being thrown by the first team.

A coin is placed in the centre of a paving stone. One player throws a tennis ball at the coin in order to shift it out of the square. The ball is caught by the second player whose turn it then is to throw the ball for the same purpose. This game can be played by one person if the ball is bounced up against a wall.

Hoops are hit with a stick and kept rolling.

Matchsticks. A matchstick is held between forefinger and thumb to challenge another being held by a second person. The matchsticks are pressed against each other until one breaks. The victor adds the value of the opponent's victories to his own. So at first the matchstick becomes a oner and then a twoer and so on. If a twoer is beaten by a three'er, then the victor becomes a fiver and so on. Short Swan Vesta matchsticks are the strongest. Matches are not allowed to be artificially shortened and everyone is on his honour to tell the truth about the match's value before each contest..

Scooters, box-carts and wheelbarrows are made from orange boxes or other pieces of wood and small wheels are attached.

Diabalo is a game mainly played by girls. An inverted cone (it looks like two cones joined together at the tips) is balanced on a string fixed to two sticks that are held in the hands. The cone is tossed into the air, the higher the better, and caught back on the string. Experts can do many intricate tricks.

Skipping is mainly for girls.

Five stones that are thrown up and caught on the back of the hand.

Football (soccer, not rugby) played with any type off ball and makeshift goals. Goal posts are often marked by rolled up jackets or school satchels.

Rounders played with a tennis ball and a rounded bat. Similar to American Baseball.

Many other games including Yo-Yo, Tag, Hide and Seek and flipping coins.

Some boys had shop-made toys. One had a train set while another had a very large pedal car. One day, the pedal car owner and Yulus and another friend went together with the car to the Tower Hill Gardens. Two of the boys pushed while the third pedalled energetically through the streets and across the busy roads. Each took turns to sit in the car, even though they had to squeeze their way in, and propel it on its way. What fun they had pushing hard up slopes and running to keep up with the car as it ran down slopes faster than the driver could pedal.

What excitement when they at last reached the gates of the Tower Hill Gardens. Here, they thought, they could ride about unhindered by traffic and also be out of sight of the Beefeaters who patrolled the Tower grounds and chased the children off the grass. What the intrepid adventurers had not taken into account was the steepness of the path that leads into the gardens. This path drops down at a very steep angle to meet another that crosses it and forms a T-junction. On the far side of the main path is the old moat, that is no longer filled with water, but which is some thirty or more feet deep. The floor of the moat is covered in grass. Soldiers billeted at the Tower use it for recreation, often playing soccer there. The grey brick walls of the Tower itself rise imposingly on the other side of the moat. Heavy black painted iron railings, sharply pointed at the top, run along the side of the path to prevent and protect people from entering or falling into the moat. Such a fall is sure to result in multiple and serious injuries, if not death. Buttresses on the outer wall of the moat, that is the path side, enable the railings to form viewing recesses where embossed bronze tablets indicate, by outline, the various towers and the dates when they were built.

Not that the boys had come there that day for sightseeing. The car owner had the privilege to sit in the car as they entered the gardens. It looks very steep, he said. So, you two, instead of pushing, had better hang on to the back and act as brakes. OK? OK. The descent started cautiously. Yulus and his friend held tightly onto the back of the driver's seat as the driver tipped forward as the car moved downwards slowly as they themselves leaned backwards to take the strain. The car seemed suddenly to take on a motion of its own and the movement was faster. The boys heels scraped along the coarse grained asphalt path as they attempted to apply the 'brakes.' It's going too fast, shouted the driver. We know replied the boys who were now forced to run with the car rather than retard its progress. We are going to cra....., the driver screamed as the car slammed into the railings before he could finish the word, crash. At that same moment the two boys let go of the car, but their downward flight was so fast that they could not stop themselves and they fell, or rather, flew forward onto the unfortunate driver. They lay in that face down prone position for a moment or two, too shocked to move until they realised that the driver was underneath them, pushing and gasping for air. Some adult sightseers came to their assistance and helped them to their feet and extricated the driver from his squashed automobile. Miraculously, none of the boys was badly hurt, a graze here, a cut there and a nasty bruise somewhere else. The front of the car was buckled, one wheel was no longer straight, the steering column was somewhat twisted and one of the railings appeared to be a little bent. Do you think we did that? No, we couldn't have done. Look, the paint isn't chipped. That doesn't prove anything. What am I going to tell my dad about this car? asked the worried driver, hoping his friends would have some plausible answer, which they did not. Maybe we'll think of something on the way back. They carried the battered car up onto the wide main pavement adjoining the gardens and began pulling and pushing the front part of the chassis in an attempt to improve the appearance of the car. But for all their efforts and ingenuity they made little progress. They trundled home, carrying the car and feeling dejected and somewhat fearful of the reception awaiting them from the car owner's father. They told him the whole story saying at various intervals that it was not the driver's fault or anybody else's fault, it was a pure accident. Methinks you all protest too much, he said roughly but inwardly pleased with himself for quoting Shakespeare. You two had better go home and wash, you look like the ragamuffins that you are. And as for you, he said menacingly to the car owner, I'll deal with you inside. Perhaps you should choose your friends more carefully.

This last remark was familiar to Yulus, because the very friend with whom he had gone on this trek, is the friend that his family was urging him to drop. You will only get into mischief if you go about with him, they remonstrated. Look what happened the other day, he got caught stealing lemonade bottles from the sweet shop on the corner of North Tenter Street. They were empty bottles standing in crates outside the shop. So that makes a difference? Anyway he didn't want the bottles. What he wanted was to cash them in for the ha'penny deposit that the shopkeeper repays when the empty bottle is returned. So, this 'clever' friend of yours, took two empty bottles from outside the shop and then had the chutzpah to go into the shop and ask for the penny deposit. That's not just stealing, that's fraud! He doesn't do things like that when he is with me, protested Yulus, but to no avail. He's a bad influence. You are not to go about with him. Yulus was not easily dissuaded, because in his own mind he was sure that he was having a good influence on his friend and not vice versa. So he continued to associate with him despite the family protestations.

Some time later, Yulus's schoolmaster was consulted. Leave it to me, said the teacher, I'll try to dissuade him. Each morning for a week, the teacher asked Yulus whether he had been meeting his dishonoured friend. Each morning Yulus answered yes, whether he had or not, and each morning his hand was caned as a result. Disobeying a schoolmaster was almost always followed by the cane, despite the old adage that caning knocked nine devils out and ten devils in. Yulus explained the position to his friend and they agreed to part. He told this to his teacher and the caning stopped. You see, he said to his teacher, when my friend heard what was happening he, not me, suggested that we part. Not I, said the teacher automatically correcting the grammar of the last sentence. So you see, persisted Yulus, he wasn't such a bad friend, was he?

On some weekends Yulus would go to the cinema, more popularly known as the pictures or the flicks, with friends. There were many cinemas in the area, but even so, there were always queues of people waiting outside to enter before the next session started. This was the decade of the talkies which had now taken over from the silent films. Cinema was perhaps the most popular form of entertainment. It was relatively cheap and gave good value especially as children entered at half price. It was estimated that, in Britain, some twenty million people visited the cinema every week. There were few continuous shows. Most programmes consisted of a feature film, a shorter B film, a newsreel and some shorts or cartoons. There was an interval in which cigarettes, chocolates and ice cream could be bought from uniformed girls, who stood at the end of the aisles, with trays held at the waist supported by wide straps slung over neck and shoulders. In some of the so-called better cinemas that were also called picture palaces because of there ornate architecture, there were stage shows in the interval or the Wurlitzer organ would rise up majestically through a trapdoor on the stage with lights flashing and the organist already seated and playing some popular tune. At the end of the interval, the organ would slowly disappear descending to below stage with the trapdoors closing above. Other cinemas were dilapidated or converted basements and these were called flea pits in the vernacular. Films were graded into categories. Minors could enter unaccompanied to see U-films but they had to be accompanied by an adult to see an A-film. This meant that children often approached adults standing in the queues with the plea 'Please can you take me in Mister.' Most, if not all adults would agree. The children paid for themselves at the box office.

Some children would not leave the cinema at the end of the session, when generally, the hall emptied and staff cleaned up the auditorium before the next programme started. Instead, they would hide in the toilets and re-emerge to take their seats to see that fantastic Cowboy and Indian film again or the French Foreign Legion being saved from massacre for a second time without having to pay again. Ushers were aware of this ruse and would search the toilets and look for what they perceived to be guilty-looking unaccompanied children sitting in the hall. The culprits, who were unlucky enough to get caught, would be escorted off the premises. On one occasion, Yulus went with his brother who was four years his senior, to the Luxor cinema in Commercial Street. A U-film was showing and so they had no difficulty entering, although they had to stand in the queue for some time. Two halves, demanded the older boy as he paid for the tickets. The two boys sat down on seats near the aisle towards the front of the crowded auditorium which was full of chattering youngsters excitedly waiting for the programme to start. The lights dimmed and the children began to settle down to watch. Then, unexpectedly, the lights came on again and ushers were combing the hall to find any two-timing culprits. The two boys were sitting in their places quite innocently when an usher approached them and said. Come on you two, out! Why? asked Yulus. Because this is your second time round and you know that's not permissible. Other people are waiting to come in and it isn't fair for you to see the show twice. But we have only just come in, protested the brother. That's a likely story, I can always tell which of you has sneaked in again. But it's not true, the boys protested again and again. Don't you but me, said the usher aggressively. Are coming out or do I have to pull you out? We are going to speak to the manager. You do that, but not here, from the outside. And with that, he escorted the hard-done-by boys out of the cinema. We want to speak to the manager, said the boys to the uniformed door attendant. Do you? he said, well he ain't 'ear, so push orf. I'm never going to that place again, said the frustrated Yulus. Neither am I, the brother agreed.

Although one could not generally see silent films in the many cinemas, private clubs would show them to members. One such place was the Hutchinson House Club of which Yulus's athletic twenty one year old diamond mounter brother was a member. On some Saturday evenings, after *Shabbas*, his brother would take Yulus to a silent film show in Camperdown House in Half Moon Passage. The hall, that was utilised for all types of physical and social activities, had a polished wooden floor. One wall was lined with wall-bars up which athletes could climb and lift and stretch themselves in all directions. In one corner, a vaulting horse and other athletic equipment had been placed to clear the centre of the hall for rows of chairs and wooden benches. A cinema projector stood on a raised table at the back of the hall and the projectionist was focusing the strong white light onto the silver screen at the other end of the hall. The screen was secured by cords stretching from its four corners to two upright posts on either side. Classic silent films were shown. These included Charlie Chaplin, Our Gang, Buster Keaton, Harold Lloyd and other comedies, serious dramas, and Cowboy and Indian films. Sometimes there was a piano accompaniment but on most occasions the audience provided the music by singing whatever song they thought was appropriate for the scene being displayed. Members of the audience might shout out some comment at a crucial moment such as, Look out behind you, when a hero was being stalked by his enemy or make some amusing remark that would cause the audience to break out into laughter. In some ways silent films had an advantage over talkies, because going to the silents was like going to a social gathering. Friends could greet each other without disturbing the continuity of the film. At the silents, people could talk, while at the talkies, people had to be silent.

Rivka and Shulem sometimes went to the vibrant Yiddish Theatre. They rarely went to the cinema. because very few films were in Yiddish. When Rivka heard that the new Yiddish film, *Yid'l mitt'n Fiddle* was being shown at the Rivoli cinema in Whitechapel High Street, she decided to take Yulus to see it, as a treat for his ninth birthday. Generally, birthdays were not celebrated in any special way. There were too many of them in the family and parties and gifts were far too expensive. But the screening of this film happened to coincide with a birthday and so it was considered a birthday treat. The Rivoli cinema was truly a Picture Palace. There were five arched entrances side by side that led into the carpeted lobby where Rivka purchased the tickets for herself and her youngest son. Guided by the ushers, they walked up the carpeted stairs to the balcony seats which, unlike most other cinemas in the district, had ample leg room for people to get by without treading on the toes of those already seated, or forcing them to stand in order to pass. Rivka enjoyed the drama and jolly music in the film. It also reminded her of life in Poland and gave her further confirmation of how right she and Shulem had been to leave the *haim*, as the Polish homeland was referred to, and come to England, despite all the trials and tribulations of bringing up a family in straightened conditions. And, here beside her was her youngest, full of life, enjoying this unprecedented outing with his mother. She took much pleasure watching him laugh at the funny scenes and looking sad and anxious when things appeared not to go well for Yid'l. The actress Molly Picon, played the part of the young girl who sang and played the violin, and who had to pretend to be a boy, so that she and her father could join a musical travelling act and wander throughout Poland. That was a good film, wasn't it? said Rivka as they walked home hand-in-hand. Yulus nodded his agreement. There was a moral to it, you know, continued Rivka. There was? Yes. You remember at the beginning of the film when Yid'l was still a young girl and that Yokel wanted to dance with her? Yes. Well, you remember that when the dance was over he refused to pay the two Kopecks that he had promised to pay before the dance? Yes. So what happened then? Another man said to the one who wouldn't pay, *Du host getanced? Az b'tsool!*, You danced? So pay! Exactly. You know what that means? Rivka did not wait for an answer. It means that you should not take advantage of others. It means that if you take something, then you must pay for it. Nothing in life is free. If you get some benefit, then you must give back something of value in return, and certainly if you promise to do something, then you must do it.

Chapter 10

Yulus was sitting in the kitchen examining some of the many books that were always strewn around the house. One book that had caught his attention was an edition issued by the Left Book Club. It was entitled 'The Jewish Question.' Why, asked Yulus, of those family members who were present, is there such a thing as a Jewish question? *Alles vilt er vissen*, everything he wants to know, remarked Rivka. It's quite a legitimate question, said one of the brothers. If you think so, then you had better answer him. Well first of all, corrected another of the brothers, it is not 'a' Jewish question, but 'the' Jewish question. I would still like to know why? said Yulus. Well, just like the Jewish question itself, the question you raise is not an easy one to answer. The problem is this, the Socialist brother began in the manner in which he often addressed public meetings. But, as with public meetings, here at home too, his dissertation was soon interrupted by statements, questions and corrections.

The Jews are a distinct people who have had no land of their own since they were dispersed by the Romans almost two thousand years ago. That I am sure you have already learned at school. Of course. OK, but despite this long period of exile, the Jews have managed to retain their distinctive identity, which distinctive as it is, cannot be easily defined. Every Jew. Every Jew? Well, almost every Jew, knows that he or she is a Jew. And there are many Gentiles who think, quite often wrongly, that they can recognise a Jew when they see one. But ask any Jew or any Gentile to define who is a Jew and one will get a multitude of answers. Some say that a Jew is a person who believes in the Jewish religion. Others will say that he or she is part of the Jewish nation. Some will say that he or she is part of the Jewish race and yet others will say that a Jew is all three combined or neither one nor the other. Yet others, and these are the dangerous and prejudiced Gentiles, say that the Jews are just a misfit in the host society in which they happen to reside. What do you mean, host society? Does that mean that Jews are just guests in the countries in which they live? That is part of the major question and I will come to that, but just let us first try to define who is a Jew. Try, is the right verb.

Now, continued the Socialist brother who had once nearly attended a Yeshiva, a school of Jewish religious teaching, religious Jews define a Jew as a person who is born of a Jewish mother or who has converted *Halachicly* to Judaism. That means that he or she has adopted the tenets of the Jewish religion according to Jewish orthodox law. But this is not the whole story. It isn't? No, because while it is true that Jews who are accepted by the orthodox religious are also accepted by non-orthodox Jews, there are people who consider themselves to be Jews who are not accepted by the orthodoxy. This is because they have been converted to Judaism by non-orthodox Rabbis, or because only their fathers are Jewish or because they simply have been accepted into the Jewish community without any formality. However, paradoxically, there are Jews who do not practice the religion and who are even Atheists who are nevertheless still accepted by the orthodox as Jews because *Halachically* they were born of a Jewish mother. So, the question should not be Who is a Jew? in the singular, which has so many conflicting answers. It should be Who are the Jews? in the plural, a question that can be given a compounded, if complicated, answer. Like his youngest brother, he makes up his own questions, interjected Rivka. The brother continued, remaining serious, despite the laughter. Jews can be of any nationality and of any race as in fact they are. They are British, European, American, Asian, Chinese, Yemenite, Ethiopian or any other nationality. And Palestinian, added Yulus having learned his Sunday school lessons. Yes, that's true, but even here we have, or will have another paradox. Oh! What? Well, even if the Zionist Jews manage to establish a Jewish State in Palestine, will that change the definition of who is a Jew? Well, will it? In my opinion, no. No? How can it? All the Jews won't go to live there. There will still be millions of Jews living outside that yet to be created State, and so the position regarding definition will not have changed. It may even become more complicated. Is that possible?

Is the explanation over? No, of course not. Then let's continue. Right. OK. Gentiles, and particularly anti-Semites will define Jews as any one of the various categories we have just mentioned, persisted the Socialist. They will even trace back ancestries for several generations in order to prove that such persons are Jews. They will even continue to refer to persons who were born Jews but have since converted to another religion, as Jews. We Jews often do likewise, said one of the sisters. Take the example of Disraeli whose father converted him to Christianity at the age of thirteen. That's true, and what about Einstein? He didn't convert. Of course not. Then what about him? Well, do you remember what he said? Are you talking about Einstein the scientist or Eisenstein the sculptor. Eisenstein wasn't a sculptor, he was the Russian film director, Epstein was the sculptor. That's funny I thought Epstein was the cabinet maker round the corner. Are we quite finished with the jokes? OK, now, Einstein the scientist, that is the famous scientist, is reported to have said that if his theory of relativity was proven to be right, the Germans would refer to him as a German and the French would call him a Jew. However, if his theory was wrong, then the Germans would say he was a Jew and the French would say that he was a German. What has that has to do with the Jewish question especially as his theory has long since been proven right and the Nazi Germans have in any event

102

persecuted him as a Jew and forced him to leave Germany? The point is this, that while animosity between peoples or nations is not restricted to hatred of the Jews, the Jewish case, or question, is unique because of its universality.

Anti-Semitism is found all over the world, even where there are few Jews. One thing is clear, the Jews, whether they want to or not, have never been able to, nor allowed to assimilate within the host country in which they reside. Again he says host country. That's right. I say host country advisedly because Jews have never ever been fully accepted into any Gentile community even though they have, or should have the same rights as others within the same community. They have always suffered some form of restriction, whether legal or social, imposed or self-imposed. This has an advantage for the hosts, because dependent on the political or religious vagaries of the time, the Jews have been and can be held responsible for the ills of society. They are easy targets for the anti-Semites. Perhaps the question should not be the Jewish question, but rather the anti-Semitic question, because if there were no anti-Semites, then the Jewish question would not arise. And if there were no Jews? Then as some wit has already said, the Jews would be invented. There are Jews who think that the question or problem can only be solved by the Gentiles, because they feel that it is the Gentile attitudes that have to be changed. That, surely is wishful thinking. Maybe, but they too, have got a point.

Anti-Semitism may have originally stemmed from the teaching of the Church that claims that the Jews killed Christ. But there are those, like George Sacks, who wrote the booklet for the Left Book Club, who say that anti-Semitism always emerges during class struggles that have existed throughout the ages. They refer to the conflicts between the bourgeoisie and the land-owning feudal lords, including the Church, which was then one of the biggest landowners. The Jews were the link between the feudal lords and the peasants who were gradually being dispossessed of land. They were the link because the Jews could be neither landowners nor peasants. Later, the bourgeois French revolution gave Jews political rights that enabled them to become prominent in science, art, industry, commerce and social and political life. The current class struggle is between the bourgeoisie, that is, the middle- or trading- or entrepreneurial-classes who are in power in Britain and Europe and the working classes. In all the social conflicts, the Jews suffered from rabid anti-Semitism. So, Sacks and others, conclude that only in a classless society, where there is no class struggle, will anti-Semitism have no place. He is right of course, but where? And this is also a big question, where can we find a classless society? Certainly not in the Soviet Union, as he claims, because while there may be common ownership of the means of production in that country, they have managed to produce an elite management class through the Communist party. The people may have grasped power in the Russian revolution, but unfortunately their leaders have since abused it.

Some people think that the Jews themselves are responsible for anti-Semitism. Why is that? Because many of them are achievers and succeed. They work and study hard to achieve their goals. If people work hard, they are entitled to succeed, aren't they? The Jews in this area work hard, they don't seem to succeed. Look at the conditions in which they live, no bathrooms. That may be so but we have to admit that a relatively high percentage have succeeded in business, politics and the professions. There is another reason. Yes, what is that? Jews know the value of human rights which have been denied them over the centuries and so they are in the forefront of political protest movements. So they should be. Yes but what happens is that anti-Semites focus attention, not only on those Jews, but on we Jews in general which in turn makes us self-conscious and forces us to be on the defensive. Thus, the current Jewish leadership says that Jews should not attend anti-Fascist demonstrations, but should remain quiet and allow the fight against anti-Semitism to be fought in a gentlemanly and diplomatic way. As though Fascist louts are either gentlemanly or diplomatic. There are Jews too, even though they are bred and born here, who seem to think that we are not entitled by right, but only by privilege, to the rights of British citizenship. Rights that come naturally to our Gentile compatriots. What makes you say that? I will give two examples that were published in Yulus's school magazine that he brought home and gave us to read. I remember remarking about them at the time.

One item reported that the boys were assembled in the school hall in November to observe Armistice Day. They recited suitable prayers and kept the usual two minutes silence. What is wrong with that? Nothing so far, but then, it is stated that everyone sang God save the King fervently. So what is the point? The last word is the point. It appears that it is not sufficient to report simply that the National Anthem was sung. No, it has to be reported that the Jews sang it fervently, that is sincerely. You understand the point, loyalty has always to be proven. No-one should be left in doubt.

And the other example? The other item was an extract from an article published in The Times newspaper concerning Anthony De Rothschild's defence of Jewish youth. The extract stated that anti-Semitic speeches and attacks had left Jewish youth with a sense of grievance. That's putting it mildly. Maybe, but that is what it said. It also said that critics allege that all Jewish youth are Communistic while almost in the same breath, they accuse them, the Jews, of being hateful capitalists and conspiring international financiers. There doesn't appear to be anything wrong with that. No that's true, but the next part will illustrate my point. The extract then stated that the younger generation must accept the obligations no less than the privileges of their position, which is fine. But the speaker, himself a Jew, is then reported to have said, and this is the rub, that he was confident that the Jewish youth of this country would prove themselves worthy of their English citizenship. Now do you get the point. No matter how he may behave, the right of a Gentile to the citizenship of the country in which he is born is never questioned. But Jews born in this country, continuously have to prove themselves worthy of something that, not only should be, but actually is, their birthright. This, in my opinion, is the crux of the Jewish question.

I too have an example, said another brother. The English section of the Yiddish paper reported that the Anglo-Jewish community presented a loyal address to the King at Buckingham Palace. It included a statement to the effect that His Majesty's subjects of the Jewish faith yield to none in their sincerity, devotion and loyalty to the throne. Now why should the Jews specifically have to do this? I'll tell you why. Because they are a minority community within a Gentile community that too often, if not always, questions the right of Jews to reside within it, if you see what I mean. We all know that the rights of Jews are always open to question. That, in my opinion, is what is meant by the Jewish question and it is a question that remains unanswered.

It is my view, continued the Socialist, that whether the Jew is a capitalist or Communist or what have you, he cannot, and even if he could, he should not, hide the fact, that he is a Jew. What about us girls? interjected one of the sisters. You too, you too. Certainly he should not hide it from himself. Every person, Jew or otherwise, should evaluate himself or herself and know who and what he or she is. If he or she has any illusions, as did the German Jews, then sooner or later, someone, somewhere will remind him or her, in no uncertain way, just exactly who he or she is. That, I think, is the lesson we have to learn from all this. That, and the absolute necessity to fight for one's principles and one's rights and for the rights of one's fellow human beings. And certainly we must fight against any encroachment of our rights. We can do it and what is more we have done it. How? How? Let me give you some cases in point.

The truth is that we Jews have very little power. However, while we are in a democracy, we can exercise a certain amount of negative local power to combat Fascists and their supporters, that is, if we act in concert. This applies equally to Yiddish speaking immigrants who have as yet not been naturalised and are otherwise effectively disenfranchised because they do not have the vote. They joined with us in the demonstration that stopped the Fascists from marching through the East End of London in 1936. You mean the famous Battle of Cable Street. That's right. Following that battle, the authorities banned provocative marches through our East London Jewish quarter and also banned the Fascists from marching anywhere in their militaristic uniforms. That may be so, but it did not stop them from marching altogether. A year later, they tried to march through South London. Tried, is the operative word. Inspired by the earlier battle, people again put up the barricades and barred the route of the Fascists in what has been called the second Battle of Cable Street. Yes, I remember that well, over one hundred protesters were arrested.

Yiddish speaking Jews also joined in the boycott of local businesses that were believed to be supporting Fascism. What do you mean, joined in? They were probably the major players. They are the heads of almost all the households in this district and they determine where to spend their hard earned money. It was quite an effective campaign, while it lasted. When the Wickhams General Store in Mile End saw the level of sales falling, they had to put an advertisement in *Die Zeit*, the Yiddish daily newspaper, in order to deny publicly that they were, in any way, Fascist supporters. The United Milk Dairies also had to do the same thing in order to regain lost customers. The advertisements referred to what they called, a small section of the Jewish community believing that the companies had sympathies with anti-Jewish organisations. It clearly couldn't have been a small section, otherwise there would have been little reason to advertise a denial that they were in any way supporting Fascist and blackshirt organisations.

The importance of these actions by we East London Jews becomes clear when we see what dreadful things are happening in Europe. The Duke and Duchess of Windsor met with Hitler this year. Thank goodness, he didn't remain King of England. In Italy, Mussolini has told the Jews that they have to uphold Fascism or leave. In Danzig, the police have seized Jewish bank deposits. The Spanish civil war continues. The Germans have opened a concentration camp at Buchenwald to house enemies of the state. That is nothing new. They have been using concentration camps to confine Jews, Communists and others in primitive conditions for years now. And Hitler is talking again about Lebensraum, more living space.

Ganig, Ganig, enough, enough, said Rivka emerging from the scullery for the umpteenth time with extra cups of tea. Enough of Europe, the Nazis and Fascists and all that misery. Let's talk of some happier things. We had a Barmitzvah this year and we all enjoyed that, and soon, we are going to have more living space of our own. Why? are we moving? asked Yulus mischievously. No, silly, came the reply. Your sister and bother are moving out, because, in case any of you others have forgotten, we are having two weddings within the next two months. Yippee! Yulus exclaimed, does anyone want to buy a cot? It's in good condition, only been slept in for nine years and ten months..

Chapter 11

Celebrations and the organisation of the household were in Rivka's realm. Everything in the house moved around her. She organised the house from morning to night. She made the breakfast and other meals whether everybody ate together or not. She made up the beds, dusted and polished the furniture, cleaned the floors and washed the clothes. On Fridays, like clockwork, she whitened the square on the pavement outside the front door. Her fastidiousness set the standard for the family and the street. Shulem and the rest of the family knew that if they left anything untidy when they went off to work or to *Shul*, or to dance or play, or shop or meet friends, they knew, that all would be spick and span on their return. The house was an open house. Anyone could call in, and everyone did. When they arrived, in no matter what numbers, tea was always ready to be served. The kettle was always on the boil and Rivka was always on the go. Friends preferred to meet in Rivka's house rather than in their own. They were made welcome even if the member of the family they had come to see was not present. Oh! They would say, he or she is not here, then I'll come back later. No, No, Rivka would reply, sit awhile, have a cup of tea. No-one could refuse her. No-one wanted to refuse her, because she made them so welcome. Neighbours with some family or other problem would call in. She was always there for them. Come in, sit yourself down, have a cup of tea and tell me all about it. They came, even when they knew she could not possibly answer the questions they might have. They came just to talk and be revived by her hot cup of tea and even more so by her warm empathy.

She ruled the household with warmth, kindness and tolerance. She arbitrated in disputes between the sisters that generally arose over small matters that had developed out of all proportion. Whose stockings were those with the ladders? Who had used the wrong lipstick? Whose appointment was the more important and required priority use of the scullery sink to wash and prepare for the most momentous occasion? Rivka brought them down to reality. A button that had fallen off one of the boys' shirts at a critical moment would be sown on by her in a jiffy, even though all were capable of such a task. The speck of dust on the lapel or back of a jacket did not escape her eye and the garment had to be brushed to her satisfaction. She instilled common sense into her children from birth and occasionally supplemented her quiet entreaties with her famous *knip*, the sharp twist of the fleshy part of the arm between two bony knuckles. She was ever handy with a face cloth to clean up a dirty face or the dirty knees of her youngest sons when they arrived home from school or from playing in the streets. Importantly, she developed the modus vivendi between herself and her religious husband, Shulem, and also between Shulem and the rest of the family. She had lost some of her religious fervour over the years, while Shulem had retained most, if not all, of his. She kept a kosher house for him and she saw to it that the children and their friends did not openly contravene the religious laws in his presence. She and Shulem had a fine rapport, a fine love and respect for each other that they imparted to their children.

The East End London Jewish enclave was sometimes referred to as the ghetto because of its Yiddish speaking inhabitants who had brought with them, and retained, many of the customs and dietary habits from Eastern Europe. Synagogues abounded as did kosher butchers, a famous one being Bloom's, and grocers that sold foods unfamiliar to the English palate. This gave rise to the humorous verse that was sung to the tune of a popular song called Love in Bloom whose original lyrics were 'Can it be the breeze that fills the trees with a sweet and magic perfume? Oh, no, it isn't the breeze, it's love in bloom.' These lyrics were substituted by 'Can it be the *chrane* that fills Brick Lane with its sweet and magic perfume? Oh, no, it isn't the *chrane*, it's vursht from Bloom's.' *Chrane* is a sharp horseradish sauce reddened with beetroot and *vursht* is a sausage, similar to salami, with added garlic that provides the aroma.

The enclave was not immune from the influences of modern society. This was particularly so, because of the development of radio and cinema technology and because the children were being educated to become young English ladies and gentlemen. As the youngsters became adults, they participated in the social and political activities of the general society. The major political ideas of democracy and Socialism come into direct conflict with some of the tenets of orthodox religion. Liberalism and orthodoxy are entirely different concepts and reconciliation between the two is like trying to square the circle. And yet, it was essential that some form of tolerance on both sides be ever present for the orthodox and the liberal to live side by side in harmony. The older members of the family were fast moving away from their father's religious beliefs and yet they had sufficient respect for him, not to break the religious rules in his presence. The two elder brothers smoked heavily but not when in the house on *Shabbas* nor on High Holydays and never in Shulem's presence on such days. Shulem did not smoke at all, nor did he take snuff that was popular with the orthodox, partly because nicotine could be imbibed without striking a match, which is forbidden on the Sabbath. Yulus often noticed the yellow stained mustaches of some of the elders in the Synagogue that came from prolonged sniffing of the yellow powder kept in little snuff boxes extracted at intervals from waistcoat pockets. A little powder would be placed on the back of the hand, just above the thumb, and sniffed from there. Shulem preferred his sons not to smoke, remonstrating when one of them coughed. Not to worry, said the cougher, on one occasion, I'm smoking the Craven A brand which according to the advertisement of the cigarette manufacturer 'was made specially to prevent sore throats.' If you believe that, said Shulem, you ought also to believe in God. The adult members of the family might eat unkosher food in restaurants or eat milk and meat products together, contrary to Jewish dietary laws, but they would not break those laws in the house or bring *traif*, that is, unkosher food, into the home. The eldest daughter did this once, but only once. When Shulem discovered the sin, he broke the plate on which the *traif* had been placed and said a special prayer. Rivka was largely responsible for engendering the respect for Shulem. She was also responsible for getting Shulem to turn a blind eye to small infringements of ritual on the part of the children and for him not to insist that they all attend *Shul* regularly or keep their heads covered at all times once they had reached working age. The family had learned to combine pragmatism with principle.

It was the end of May 1937. Rivka sat in the ladies' balcony of Alie Street Synagogue together with her three daughters and her daughter-in-law to be, and her many friends to watch her thirteen year old son become Barmitzvah. She had brought with her bags of wrapped boiled sweets that she distributed among the ladies and girls who were all waiting in anticipation for the Barmitzvah boy to perform. The Synagogue was full. There was usually a good attendance on *Shabbas* mornings, but on those Saturdays when there was a Barmitzvah, the attendance increased and an atmosphere of gaiety and pleasure permeated the main hall and the gallery. Rivka anxiously watched from the gallery as the time for her son's Barmitzvah ceremony drew near. The gold embroidered blue curtains covering the doors of the *Aron Ha'kodesh*, the Holy Ark were drawn back. The polished wooden doors were opened to reveal several *Sifrei Torah*, Torah scrolls. They stood in the satin lined Ark, dressed in their embroidered velvet coverings with small openings at the top to allow for the two wooden scroll rods, known as the trees of life to extend through. The parchment scrolls are wound around these rods that were topped with *rimonim*, ornamental silver Torah finials. Silver chains, that hung from them, supported embossed silver shields or breastplates. The reader carefully removed a *Sefer Torah*, one of the Torah Scrolls, from the Ark and walked slowly to the raised *Bima*, platform, to the reader's desk. The *rimonim*, the chain, shield and the velvet coverings were removed to reveal a silk sash that binds the scroll. The sash too was removed before the scroll, now held by the lower ends of the wooden rods, was placed on the reader's desk. The desk faces the Holy Ark that is always on the eastern wall of the Synagogue so that the reader faces Jerusalem. Above the Holy Ark is the *Ne'r Tamid*, the Eternal Light and also the Hebrew declamation 'Know Ye Before Whom Ye Stand.' The *Sefer Torah* is unrolled by use of the wooden rods, as the parchment is not to be touched by hand. The week's portion is revealed. The handwritten Hebrew script contains no errors. The portion is divided into paragraphs that are read by the Cantor except for the section to be read by the Barmitzvah boy. The Reader calls out the names of persons who will say the blessings before and after each section is read. Firstly a Cohen, one of the ancient priestly community, will be called. Then a Levi, one of the priestly aides, and then the general Israelites. It is a *mitzvah*, an honour, to be called up to say the blessings for the Torah reading. The word *Barmitzvah* means the holding of the honour and obligation to uphold the Jewish tenets. Rivka heard Shulem being called, then her three elder sons and then her heart missed a beat when her young son's name was called. She watched him climb with confidence the few steps of the Bima to stand next to the Cantor. There he stood, a slim diminutive figure, looking straight ahead at the Holy Ark. He was wearing his new white *tallas*, prayer shawl, over his new suit that had long trousers, a sure sign that a young Jewish boy had reached religious maturity. He had watched his father and older brothers called up in turn to say the blessings prior to the Cantor reading various other portions of the law. Now here he was, ready to sing his part of the week's portion of the law from the Torah scrolls. A murmur passed through the Synagogue as people nudged and smiled at each other in anticipation of the great event in the boy's life. Now there was silence as the Barmitzvah boy sang, first the blessings and then the portion that he had rehearsed so many times. He followed the silver pointer, shaped at the end like a hand with an extended forefinger, that the Cantor held and guided gently over the Hebrew words. Above the script were small *neginot*, cantillation signs that indicated the required intonation. He did not really need this assistance as he knew the words and melody by heart. Shulem followed the reading of the Torah portion word by word, his pride increasing as his young son moved towards completion without fault. The elders of the Synagogue did not tolerate errors in reading from the Holy Torah. If an error was heard, they would shout out the correction and the reader would be obliged to repeat the word correctly or read the word he had inadvertently missed before proceeding. Rivka could see Shulem's pride by his body language. His head nodded in synchronisation with the melodic rendering of the budding tenor. She too, was proud and took pleasure in Shulem's pride. Yulus, as usual was sitting next to his father. He too waited in anticipation for his brother to complete his portion so that he could find a place next to his mother in the gallery and throw down sweets from there onto the Barmitzvah boy, a non-religious but enjoyable ritual. But even after his brother had finished and members of the congregation shouted *mazel tov* and *she'ko'ach*, good luck and be of strength, he still had to wait by his father's side. The proceedings had not yet ended.

The *Sefer Torah* was held up for all the congregation to see. The Barmitzvah boy then recited the *Haftorah*, a reading from the Prophets, during which time, the *Sefer Torah* was re-bound and re-dressed. Then it had to be returned to its place in the Holy Ark. The Rabbi had to say his piece. He had to present the Barmitzvah boy with a brand new *siddur*, prayer book, and speak directly to him about the duties of Jewish adulthood and state the importance of laying *tefillin*, putting on his phylacteries, that his father had purchased for him, each weekday. The Rabbi then remonstrated with those members of the congregation who did not come to the Synagogue as often as they should. Being twice-a-year Jews was not good enough. Coming to *Shul* for *simchas*, celebrations, was not enough. A remonstration that indicated the movement away from religious practice by the younger generation. Yulus had still to wait further until *mussef*, the additional *Shabbas* morning prayers, were completed, before he could get to the gallery and join with others in showering confectionery in all directions. Once thrown, he and other young boys then scrambled to collect the sweets from between the feet of chattering adults. They were congratulating the Barmitzvah boy and his father and brother and friends and each other. Another member of the community had become qualified to participate in a *minyon*, the Jewish quorum of ten persons required for certain religious prayers. They were also making their way to the lobby, where sweet red wine in small glasses and small cakes and biscuits had been set out to complete the morning's celebration. The real Barmitzvah party would take place on the next day at home.

The party was modest, but the front parlour came into use for such an important occasion. A white tablecloth was spread over the table. There were water biscuits with which to eat the *smaltz* herrings that had been cut into small slices or chopped finely. The chopped herring had been formed into a rounded shape and decorated with the crumbed yellow of a hard boiled egg. There were slices of sweet *chollar* bread that could be eaten with butter and jam. There were sweet biscuits and small cakes and of course the larger birthday cake. There were nuts and raisins, sweets and chocolate, and crisps to be eaten with soft beverages or wine. And there were cups of hot tea brought from the kitchen. This was Rivka's house, and everyone knew that the kettles would be on the boil and that Rivka's quality tea would be served. The Barmitzvah boy was congratulated on his performance the previous day. He received presents, that included the inevitable fountain pens. The current Barmitzvah joke centred around this particular gift by stating that the boy's speech of thanks would open with the words 'Today I am a fountain pen.' He also received small amounts of cash with the conflicting advice to buy yourself anything you would like or you should open a Post Office Savings account and watch the money grow. The Barmitzvah boy made his speech of thanks that had been written for him by his Hebrew teacher. It made no mention of fountain pens. He thanked everyone for coming, and stated his sincere intention to follow the instructions of the Ten Commandments of which he knew the full meaning. This he knew because of the thorough training he had received at the *Talmud Torah* Hebrew classes. He did not add how pleased he was, that he would now no longer have to attend those classes. There was a toast to Rivka, congratulating her on the festive spread. The toast to Shulem included a reminder that he had been absolved from carrying the sins of the Barmitzvah boy, who as an adult member of Jewish society, was now fully responsible for his own actions before God. Now, he had only to be concerned with the actions of Yulus, his youngest. Which was more than enough, came the jocular chorus.

One winter's morning, before leaving for work, the cutter and designer announced that, that very evening an eerie thriller play was to be broadcast on the radio. What's special about that? It's special. It's mystical and I recommend that we all listen to it together. You really think it's good? From what I've heard of it, it will be worth the listening. So much so, that I am forgoing my visit to the dog track tonight just to hear it. You're giving up the race track for a play?

The Racecourse Betting Control Board that regulated betting on horses, had its powers extended to cover greyhound dog racing in 1934. Since then, this popular pastime had become even more popular with over twenty million people passing through the turnstiles every year. Most went in with their pockets full and came out with them empty. It's the quickest way to lose money. They considered that the thirty seconds of concentrated excitement was worth every penny. And you never know, maybe this night will be the winning night. Gambling, like smoking, is an addiction. Starting is easy. Giving it up is difficult especially when the stakes appear to be low. The amount needed to bet on any race could be very low, but one loss encouraged another try on the next race and so on, until the accumulation of losses could be drastic. And in between, there was always the winning streak. Systems for winning at the races abounded. Some were even published, as though anyone who really knew how to beat the book would share that knowledge. What would happen to the bookies if everyone won all the time? Such questions were irrelevant, if a system worked some of the time, it had value. And when it started to go wrong it could always be discarded. Some people closed their eyes and placed a pin in the racing card to choose a winner. Some examined the dogs carefully as they were paraded before the race to see which looked the most lively, or the fittest. If its tail stands away from its behind, then fine. If it flops, then beware. Or vice versa. Some followed the big money. They watched as the odds being offered on a particular dog started to narrow just before the race. Then they would assume that heavy betting was taking place on that dog and they would rush to a bookmaker or to the tote and place their bets. Others studied form. They examined the racing history of the dog, its pedigree, the number of times it came first, or in the first three, from which track. If the chosen dog won, then it was clear that the method of choice was the way to fortune. If it lost, then, many a punter would insist that the system was not wrong, but that the dog failed in some way or was hindered. It failed to get out of the trap as fast as usual, or it was balked, bumped or checked at the first bend or the last bend. Somehow it faded in the finishing straight, or finished well but made its effort too late. Maybe it was in the wrong trap, or ate the wrong breakfast.

Yulus, even at his tender age, was once given the impossible task of trying to work out a system based on a mathematical formula. His brother explained the dilemma. There were six dogs in a race and eight races in an evening. This meant that one track or trap, at least, had to be the winning trap more than once in the evening. So the system had to be based on watching but not betting on the first race. The trap from which the winning dog emerged was to be noted. Say that trap number one produced the first winner, then that trap had the best chance of producing another winner that evening. So, bet on trap number one in the second race. If it wins, take your winnings and go home. If it doesn't, then bet on the two winning traps in the third race and so on until one of the traps produces a winner. Sounds easy. The trouble is that the odds offered on dogs in the various traps differ enormously. As the evening progresses, the winnings of any one dog were unlikely to cover the value of the bets placed in that, and previous, races. Still, said some, such a system was worth a try. Who knows? Maybe it will work in the first three races? Yulus's brother related the story of a man who claimed to have discovered the ideal system. A system that could not possibly fail. Nothing, but nothing could go wrong. There was only one problem. Just one flaw. The dogs would not conform! He would apply this anecdote in his political arguments against so-called ideal socio-political propositions. First, he would say, first, convince the people you are trying to systematise.

The family assembled in the kitchen that evening, after supper. It was dark outside. The radio had been switched on. The organising brother lit a candle and switched off the electric light. Why did you do that? For atmosphere, he said. The candle gave off a weak flickering yellow light that seemed to be arguing with the red flickering glow emanating from the coal fire that was burning low in the grate. Shoosh, listen, the play is about to start. The voice from the radio announced, The Monkey's Paw, by William Wymark Jacobs. A visitor arrived on a wet and windy night. He was a soldier whom the father had invited. In the course of conversation the father alluded to a monkey's paw to which the soldier had referred at a previous meeting. A monkey's paw? the

113

mother said curiously. What is special about it? asked the son. A holy man placed a spell on it in order to prove that fate ruled our lives and those who tried to change fate would be sorry. Three men could each have three wishes from it. I have had three, and the previous person's third wish was for death, the visitor said mysteriously. The manner in which the players said their lines and the ominous pauses and sound effects between sentences or words sent a shiver around the room. I told you it would be eerie. Shoosh. I was going to sell it, said the soldier, but it has already caused too much trouble, and with that he threw the paw on the fire. Despite remonstrations, the father pulled the paw from the fire. Let me wish, he said. I warn you, I cannot be responsible for the consequences said the soldier as he left the house. Make a wish, said the son to his father. The father held the paw in his outstretched hand and wished for two hundred pounds. The paw twisted in his hand and fell to the floor, but nothing else happened. I wonder what will happen? Will he get the money? Of course he will, but how? That's just it, shoosh and we'll soon hear how. The next day, another visitor called to say that unfortunately the son had been killed, caught in the machinery at work. Caught in the machinery, said someone, he must have been mangled. Shoosh. The company did not accept responsibility but were prepared to make a monetary payment in compensation. How much? asked the father in unison with the kitchen audience. Two hundred pounds. That's sad said someone. That's an understatement, said another. Shoosh. It's not over yet. The mother suddenly remembered that there were still two more wishes. Wish for our son to come back, she cried hysterically in the middle of the night. Are you mad? cried the father. Do it. Do it. She insisted. He made the second wish. The listeners sat transfixed as there came a knock at the door. Is that our door? No, silly, it's the play. Oh my God. Shoosh. The mother ran to the door, shouting, it's my boy, it's my boy. Don't let it in, pleaded the father. My God, exclaimed one of the listeners, he said it and not him. What state will he be in when he comes back? It was night-time, the door was locked. The knocking continued. She struggled to open the bolts and as she did the father made the third wish. The knocking stopped. When the door was opened, in came a gust of cold wind. No-one was there. Yulus did not sleep well that night.

Although economic conditions in the district had improved over the past year, rents were still inordinately high in relation to income. Many residential buildings were falling into neglect and living conditions were deteriorating. Many landlords insisted on collecting their rents while ignoring the complaints of their tenants and refusing to repair or maintain their properties. They argued that the rents needed to be increased for the properties to become economically viable. The situation had deteriorated to such a degree that some tenement buildings were neither worth repairing, nor fit to live in, and yet there was no substitute accommodation. In other buildings, tenants refused to pay their rents until repairs were executed. This situation led to some evictions and rent strikes. A Tenants' Defence League was established. Tenants in some large tenement buildings boarded themselves in to prevent rent collectors entering to collect rents and to stop the bailiffs from evicting tenants who had not paid their rents. Yulus came home one day quoting a notice he had seen in the window of one of the flats in the barricaded Brunswick Buildings in Goulston Street. Roses are red, he recited, violets are blue. We won't pay our rent and neither should you. The rent strikes lasted for many weeks until agreements were reached between landlords and tenants.

Conditions were not that bad in Newnham Street. All the adult members of the family, apart from Rivka, were working and making their contribution to the household coffers. Preparations for the coming weddings could now be faced without the awful prospect of going into deep debt. Rivka fussed about the clothes that the bride and her sisters needed but ignored her own requirements until almost the last moment. The bride made her own dress. Excellent seamstress that she was, she produced a stunning white silk bridal gown for herself and suitable dresses for her sisters. The hard working girl had built up a trousseau over the past year, so that with respect to clothing, she was all set for her honeymoon and future married life. Likewise, her brother who was getting married shortly after her wedding, was able to make his own suits, although he would rent his tails and top hat for the wedding day. Shulem would convert his *Shabbas* suit into a tuxedo by applying silk facings to the jacket lapels and a silk braid to the seams on his trouser legs. The young boys and their older brothers would all get new outfits. So what was left to do? Only Rivka's attire. Neither she, nor anyone else could remember when she last had a new dress. She could always manage with what she had. But now? For the wedding? She had to decide, but could not, so the girls decided for her. Something bright, black georgette with sequins, said the eldest daughter to a chorus of laughter. And black georgette it was. They busily measured her for size, purchased the material, designed a round neckline and studded it with sequins. The family, and Rivka too, were amazed how well that combination suited her.

Barmitzvahs took place on a *Shabbas* and weddings on Sundays. In orthodox synagogues, women sit separately from men. They sit in the gallery, in those Synagogues that have a gallery, while the men *doven*, pray, in the main hall. At wedding ceremonies, women too, occupy seats in the main hall, women on one side and men on the other. From this vantage point, they can see and applaud the bride as she walks up the aisle on her father's arm. Prior to the ceremony, the father of the bride visits the bridegroom's home while the mother of the bridegroom is present at the bride's home. The two fathers accompany the bridegroom to the synagogue and the two mothers accompany the bride making sure to arrive at the synagogue after the bridegroom. They travel in hired cars. No-one in Newnham Street owned a car and not often were cars seen in the street. Generally, only for weddings or funerals and at general election times when cars of supporters of parliamentary candidates roamed the streets with their loudspeakers offering to take voters to the polling stations. We fooled them, some voters would say gleefully, we were transported by the right but voted left. Expenditures relating to the wedding were divided between the families. The parents of the bride paid for the wedding celebrations, while the parents of the bridegroom supplied the transport. East End London Jews did not own the houses in which they lived. Rental was the order of the day. Young couples too, were rarely in a position to buy property. They either lived-in with one of the parents or rented separate accommodation. Both sets of parents often contributed towards furnishing the newly-weds' apartments.

The bride was radiant under the *Chuppah*, the wedding canopy, in the *Shul*. And Rivka too, was radiant as she stood next to the bride and watched, listened to, and participated in, the marriage ceremony. Her long greying hair had been combed with a parting to the left so that it fell with the gentlest of waves closer to her eye on the right side. Her long tresses were expertly twisted to form a bun at the back of her head, that was held in place by a modest decorative comb. She wore small earrings and a modest double pearl necklace.

A similar picture could be seen at her son's wedding a few weeks later. This time she stood next to the bride's mother. Rivka exuded the same warmth for her new daughter as she did for her own. She held back in her own modest way to enable the bride's mother to enjoy the limelight due to a mother seeing her radiant daughter being married. Everything about Rivka was modest, except her generosity to others and her warmth, pride and love for her immediate and now extended family. She would not hear of wearing a different dress for her son's wedding when the money could be more fruitfully used. There may be two weddings, but there was only one mother and, she insisted, one dress was enough.

Chapter 12

The weddings were over and the house seemed so much roomier and quieter in the absence of the newly-weds. Not that they were the noisiest. Far from it, but the reduction of occupants from ten to eight was significant. The two remaining girls each now had a separate bed and extra space in drawers and cupboards. Yulus had moved out of his parents' bedroom. They now had more room and privacy. The lodger had moved out and Rivka and Shulem had moved back to their old bedroom upstairs. Rivka did not yet have fewer daily chores, but the volume had reduced. Two less breakfasts. Less laundry. It was a *mechaya*, a delight and a foretaste of how much easier life would be when the other older children, too, were married and living in homes of their own. With the extra room, she could plan improvements. Perhaps extend the scullery to provide a bathroom and inside toilet, instead of the current cold toilet facilities outside in the yard. There was no need to heed the call to move out of the district to better living conditions, when improvements could be made at home within the warm Yiddisher, *haimisher*, homely, atmosphere of the East End.

The children had moved out of the district, one to Stoke Newington and the other to Clapton. Other younger couples and families were also moving out to these areas and even further afield to Hendon and Golders Green. It was good to see the younger generation improving their lot, especially as these and other similar areas could also be considered Jewish. They had sizable Jewish communities with established Synagogues, but, they were fast becoming anglicised and Yiddish was being heard less and less in those districts. Better for us Yiddish speakers, thought Rivka, to stay put and make improvements, gradually and sensibly. All our needs are here. Shops and schools are nearby. The main London market is within walking distance. The Tower of London and its gardens are not far away. The City of London and the West End are only short bus rides away and transport to any other part of London, and for that matter the country is within easy reach. So why move?

Yulus was happier now that he had escaped from his cot. It really was too long to have kept the boy in the cot, but what could we have done, thought Rivka, we had to wait until one of the older boys got married. Yulus doesn't sleep as well, yet, but he will get used to the disturbances that arise from the various movements associated with four people in a bed. They do not all go to bed at the same time, nor wake at the same hour. Not all sleep well every night and the bed cover tends to be pulled in one direction or another. These hardships are well balanced by the restoration of dignity. The boy is no longer a baby. He is a grown boy. This year he will take his Junior County examinations

117

that will determine whether he goes to Grammar School and perhaps even on to University. Just imagine that! Rivka continued her musing. He is a very bright boy. He was top of his infant's school and now, even though he is among the youngest in his class at the Junior school, his teacher says he works very well. All the other children have had to leave school at fourteen, even though they all had the potential to go further, but economic conditions always intervened. Perhaps now, with the youngest, better opportunities will arise. God willing.

It was difficult to be bored at the Jews' Free School. The school had the benefit of devoted teachers and enlightened head teachers. Its educational ethos outstretched the formal teaching of the three R's, reading, (w)riting and (a)rithmetic, by introducing physical and central themes around which these fundamentals could be taught and expanded. The girls' school catered for girls from the ages of eight to fourteen. It was a separate entity with its own headmistress. The boys' school was divided into Juniors aged 8 - 11, Seniors aged 11 - 14 and Central aged 11 -16 plus. One headmaster was responsible for the Juniors and Seniors and another for the Central School boys. The school catered essentially for the poor Jews of the East End of London. An indication of the poverty that still lingered in the East End could be gleaned from the fact that over two hundred children were fitted out with free shoes and clothing outfits in 1938 by a generous donor. There were many more poor families who were too proud to accept such charity. The JFS had, originally, to deal with an immigrant population that had a limited grasp of the English language. Although the school's pupils of the nineteen thirties had (with minor exceptions) all been born in England, many were the children of immigrants who, either did not speak the language or had little or no English education. Consequently, the teaching of the written and spoken English language always had a high priority and prizes were awarded for elocution. These 'electrocution' classes, as Yulus was wont to call them, were designed to eliminate both foreign and local vernacular accents from the everyday speech of pupils. The widened vocabulary of the newly nurtured English Jewish gentlemen helped further to distinguish them from their local non-Jewish counterparts whose street language was learned from their parents.

While the girls wore a uniform of a white blouse under a simple navy blue pinafore dress, the boys did not have a uniform. Instead they were distinguished by the school caps that they were obliged to wear and which indicated the student hierarchy within the school. The Juniors wore a navy blue peaked cap with a self-coloured blue button in the centre of the crown. Seniors had a gold button and the caps of the Central Schoolboys had a circular yellow band on the crown, which explains why they were nicknamed the 'beigel' boys. A beigel is a bread roll with a hole through the middle. Prefects had gold coloured braid added to the peaks of their caps. All the caps sported the JFS insignia on the centre front. Being fitted for these caps was an experience in itself. Each term, or as they outgrew their caps, the boys would troop up the stairs of the school's appointed hatter in Artillery Lane. The hatter would first shout, Hats off, then ask the size, which few pupils knew, and then generally ignore their reply if they did. He preferred to make a calculated guess, rather than measure the actual size, before retrieving a cap from a pile and pulling it firmly onto the head of a tousle-haired customer. Howzat? he would demand, rather than ask, and then say Perfect, answering his own question. If a boy objected, he either suggested that it would fit once the boy's hair was cut, or once it had grown. Only strong and persistent objections would get him to change a fitting of his choice.

A model house with all its furniture was built in the school by the boys. A planetarium with a thirteen foot world map on one wall, was constructed in one of the classrooms. A six inch reflecting telescope was built by the boys including its five foot long brass mountings. The boys also built a large aviary that was stocked with a variety of finches and other birds. Pupils witnessed the hatching of budgerigars and helped to rear them. The pool in the school garden was stocked with fish. There were pottery and typewriting classes and a printing press. The metalwork, woodwork and art classes all helped to build the tracks, bogie carriages, station and pastoral scenery for a miniature railway that ran around the large playground. A coal-fired miniature steam engine that had been donated to the school pulled schoolboy passengers sitting astride the bogie carriages around the playground. In the few months before he left the school, Yulus's brother, as the stationmaster, issued tickets and maintained some sort of order in the environs of the station. Maths and physics lessons referred to the physical existence of the miniature railway, so that students could relate their theoretical findings to reality. Likewise metalwork and woodwork projects had obvious goals. Because of the different activities within the school, boys could be placed in streams most relevant to their capabilities. The school also had a movie film projector and films of the boys' antics during school outings were shown after the events as well as travel documentaries. The school was effectively a forerunner of the later comprehensive schools. Yulus's only complaint was the excessive use of the cane or the constant threat of its use. Maybe teachers had little choice in this matter as caning was commonplace in the general educational system. Even now Yulus's school reports showed over forty children in a class and he had to admit that such a group, when over boisterous, was difficult to control, let alone teach.

Yulus had been doing quite well at the JFS Juniors. He could hardly have been expected to maintain his top position from the Infants school. On the strength of that exalted position, he had missed the first form of the new school and had been placed straight into the second form with boys one year older than he. He managed to stay in the top quarter of the class without too much of a problem. When he sat for the Junior County Examinations, to the surprise of his teachers, he failed to get a high enough pass that would enable him to go to a Grammar School. Admittedly, the teachers had noticed a growing apathy towards his schoolwork in the preceding few months, but it had not occurred to them that his apparent lackadaisical behaviour would prevent him from getting good marks in the examinations. They were disappointed and became somewhat concerned. On further enquiry, they discovered the reason for his untypical behaviour, which they now also felt was the cause of his relatively poor examination results.

It was early spring, but the winter had not fully given way to the new season. There were still some sharp frosts in the early mornings when Rivka made her daily walk to buy fresh bread and rolls from the baker in St. Mark Street. One morning, she stepped on some ice, slipped and fell heavily. Neighbours helped her up and escorted her home, but she could not stand. Her arm and side were badly bruised. Despite her remonstrations that it was nothing, Shulem could see she was in pain and she was taken to hospital for a check-up. There, they examined her obvious wounds. No bones were broken. The bruises would heal. But they saw something else that Rivka had shrugged off for some time. She was thinner than she should have been. She did not advertise the fact that her appetite had been waning. But the doctors guessed and so they kept her in hospital to undergo tests. They examined her thoroughly and discovered that her liver was malfunctioning. What does that mean? Can anything be done? We shall have to operate to see the extent of the damage, they said. Why hasn't Mama come home? asked Yulus. She is having some tests. Will she be long away? No, only a few days. What is the matter with her? Nothing serious. She fell and they are looking into it. There was consensus in the family. No point in worrying the boy. It took longer than a few days, and when she did come home, she was not the same Rivka. She was gaunt and so, so much thinner. She could not walk up the stairs. The back room was once again made into a bedroom, but this time just for her. What's the matter Mama? Yulus wanted to know. It's nothing, *boobela*, she lied, I will soon be better. Yulus could feel it was serious and could see the sadness on everyone's face. Friends came and whispered. Hot teas were served by the youngest daughter. Yulus overheard them talking. They operated on her. Opened her up. Saw what a mess there was in the liver. Closed her up again. She has got the *richteker crenk*, the real illness. They couldn't bring themselves to use the dreaded word, cancer. But Yulus had heard that word used too, in the past, in relation to other sick people. Will she be alright? Yes, the family lied to him. Somehow he knew it was a lie and yet he did not want to dispute it. Why should he? Maybe she will get better. But as the days and weeks went by, there was no such sign.

How is school? Rivka would ask him. Fine, he would say, also lying. School was school. He went through the daily motions. He dreaded going and leaving his sick mother and he dreaded coming home, in case...., he would not give expression to his fears. The examinations came and passed. How did they go? Fine, I think. He really didn't know, and when the results came through he wasn't really surprised. The teacher said it would be a pity for him to leave school at fourteen. He is capable and should get a higher education. A social worker came to the house and explained that Yulus could possibly be admitted to a Grammar School on the basis of what is known as a Free Place which is the equivalent to a scholarship in that no fees would be payable. These places are very limited, and failing that Yulus could probably be admitted to the Central School where he could stay until he was sixteen and even later if he took the external matriculation for which the school prepared its pupils. Shulem and Rivka agreed that the school should make the necessary enquiries. A free place in a Grammar School could not be found and some time later Shulem signed a declaration stating that he will send Yulus regularly and punctually to the Jews' Free Central School and encourage him to do any homework set. He also undertook to keep Yulus at the school for at least four years.

Rivka's condition deteriorated and in October she was taken back to hospital. Children under twelve years of age were not allowed to visit. Will Mama be there long? We don't know. Will she be coming home? We hope so. When? It's up to the doctors. Can I go to see her? Not yet. When? When? We will try to get you in. Maybe if I wear long trousers, you could say I was twelve? Maybe. We'll try. Did they say I can visit? No, but we will try again. Which day would you like to go? On Wednesday or Friday? On Friday, said Yulus. On the Wednesday, the second of November 1938, Yulus was called home from playing with a ball at the end of the street. We have something sad to tell you. Yes. Mama has died. They could hardly get the words out. But I was supposed to visit her on Friday. Yes, Yes I know. Tears flowed from everyone, but not from Yulus. He was frozen, numbed. Why did he say Friday? His mind was racing. He should have said Wednesday or now, now, not Friday! You too can cry, you know, they said as they embraced him. Yes he said. His cheeks puffed up and turned white, the tears built up inside but would not come out. It will be better if you cry. Yes, he murmured and turned away.

The funeral was the following day. Jewish funerals generally take place within twenty-four hours of death out of respect for the deceased and in compliance with biblical pronouncements. The *Chevrah Kadishah*, Holy Brotherhood, is responsible for preparing the body for burial and for the interment. They are employed by the Jewish Burial Society, which is under the auspices of the Synagogue authorities. Members of the *Chevrah Kadishah* had been informed and they made all the arrangements. They went to the hospital, washed and dressed Rivka in a simple white shroud according to tradition. They supplied the coffin and the hearse and the cars to take the mourners to the cemetery. They carried out the act of *Keriah*, the tearing of a garment, worn by each member of the immediate family while saying a special prayer. The hearse with the coffin arrived at the house. Women friends and neighbours from the street and further afield congregated inside and outside the house. There were so many that they could not all enter the house. All were silent and many were weeping. The men, heads bowed, got into the cars and the procession moved off slowly. The women did not go to the cemetery, but they paid Rivka a special honour not previously witnessed in the district. They requested that the hearse be driven slowly out of the immediate area so that they could walk behind it until it reached the main road where they stood in silence until it disappeared out of sight. Such a loss, they said, as they went back to the house to comfort the girls and prepare a light meal for the mourners.

The hearse and other cars arrive at the Streatham Jewish Cemetery. The coffin is carefully placed on a trolley that is wheeled into the anteroom. It is a cold, high ceilinged unheated room, with high double doors at each end, one for entry, one for exit. The Rabbi conducts a short funeral service from a small rostrum placed near the exit. The room is crowded with people, cousins, friends, fellow workers and acquaintances who have made their own way to the cemetery to honour Rivka, Shulem and their sons and daughters. All are silent. The Rabbi sings the prayer *El Malei Rachamim*, O Lord who is full of mercy, and includes Rivka's name. Sobbing can be heard at the mention of her name. Shulem and the boys stand closer to each other for support. The coffin is wheeled out of the anteroom into the cemetery proper, down the centre path, led by the Rabbi who continues with his prayers. The entourage stops and starts seven times according to tradition, before reaching the grave site. Seven is a symbolic biblical number. The grave has already been dug and pyramids of brown earth are piled on each side. The coffin is placed on two wooden planks that have been set across the grave. The gravedigger and his assistants hold on to the canvas straps that have been placed under the coffin. They slowly release the tension on the straps as the wooden planks are removed, allowing the coffin to be lowered gently into the grave. Shulem, his five sons and many, many others are crowded around the graveside. They watch the procedure with tearful eyes. May she come to her place in peace, recites the Rabbi as the coffin is lowered. The Rabbi picks up some earth and drops it on the coffin. The thud of contact signals a finality that sharply and sadly enters deeply into everyone's heart. Shulem shudders as he is handed a shovel. He pushes some earth into the grave. Can there be anything more final? One of the boys takes the implement from him and with determination adds another few shovelfuls of earth. Each brother in turn does likewise, including Yulus, who insists on participating fully. Others now take up the task of filling the grave and only then do the mourners return to the anteroom, washing their hands symbolically before entering. Additional prayers are said at the end of which Shulem and his sons recite *Kaddish*, the prayer for the dead. The first words come out haltingly and then more strongly as they recite *Yisgadal veyiskadesh shemai rabba*, may His great name be magnified and sanctified, and continue the prayer in unison to the end. The congregation responds at intervals and says a final Amen. The mourners' *Kaddish* will be said at every service where there is a *minyon*, a quorum, over the next eleven months when the memorial stone to Rivka will be consecrated. After that, the prayer will be recited on special memorial occasions during the High Holydays and other religious festivals and also on the anniversary of her death. Yulus was not yet of an age to qualify as a member of a *minyon*, but according to religious practice, he could recite *Kaddish* for his mother, as he was considered old enough to understand its meaning. There are esoteric explanations relating to the redemption of mankind, but *Kaddish* is commonly understood to help pave the way for the deceased to enter heaven. Mama is sure to go to heaven, isn't she? asked Yulus of Shulem. *Avadda*, of course, came the positive reply. Then why does mama need help to enter heaven? *Noor Gott ken doos clar machen unt fin Gott tzur mir nisht freigen*, only God can provide the explanation and God cannot be questioned, was Shulem's sad reply. His own belief seemed to have been somewhat shaken by the unfairness of Rivka's untimely demise. At the end of the short service, all people present in the anteroom file past the mourners to wish them a long life. Some just shake hands as they say the words, others embrace. All are lost for any other expression, because Rivka was a shining light for all who came into contact with her and she has gone. The mourners are driven back home by a different route from that in which they came. The soul of the departed must not be confused. It is left behind to find its own way to heaven.

The mourners arrive home to a house where friends have prepared a meal for the family and seen to it that all mirrors and photographs have been covered. It is not for mourners to prepare food or do the usual household chores, nor are they to concern themselves with their own or other peoples' appearance. The men will not shave and the girls will not use cosmetics for seven days. Shulem will not shave for thirty days as he will abide strictly by the religious practice. The members of the immediate family are to sit *Shiva*, the seven day mourning period, when they will sit on low stools supplied by the Burial Society and receive visitors. Visiting mourners is a *mitzvah*, an honour. Visitors bring food and do not expect any refreshments, but the daughter-in-law or friends make sure that those who have come a distance will receive hot tea and cakes or biscuits. The local *schnorrer*, the itinerant beggar, has found his place at the table. He munches whatever food comes within his reach and by tradition is not shooed out of the mourners' house. Indeed, he claims that he is not a beggar, but rather a *minyon macher*, a person who helps to make up the male quorum needed for afternoon and evening prayers that take place in the home and that enable the mourners to recite *Kaddish*. There is never a shortage of males to make up a *minyon* in Shulem's house, but Shulem would never dream of asking the *schnorrer* to leave. Visitors come to console, usually in the afternoons or evenings after work. They speak in low voices, extolling Rivka's many virtues and asking how they can help. What of the boy? they ask, referring to Yulus. Look how serious he looks, but have you noticed? he doesn't cry. The others are tearful, but him? I think he's in total shock. And the Barmitzvah boy? He's already fourteen. He left school earlier this year. He's a big boy now, he'll manage, And the others are self sufficient. Anyhow, the youngest girl will take over the household for a while until the problem is resolved. Poor girl, she's only nineteen. It's the time of life that she should be out and about enjoying herself. Why Rivka? Why Rivka? So young. So young. Only fifty-four, some murmured. And they say God is merciful?

The family had the house to themselves in the mornings. The two married members went to their own homes each evening and returned to sit with the others each morning. The *Shiva* period is therapeutic, it allows the family to mourn together. Emotions can be given expression. In the house of mourning, it is permissible to sit and reflect, to be sad, to be angry, to discuss the virtues and idiosyncrasies of the departed, and to commiserate and cry. Yes, men too can cry. Yulus, his brothers entreated him, Yulus, you too should cry. Yes, he said, but instead of coming out, his emotions dug deeper and deeper into his soul and the tears stuck behind his strained and reddened eyes. The lower lids of his eyes were naturally taut and he always had difficulty removing any grit that might find its way into, and get caught in, his eyelids. People suggested all sorts of remedies. Pull down the top lid. Make your eyes water. Some including pharmacists would pull the lower lid down with difficulty and gently brush it with lint. These remedies sometimes worked and sometimes made the condition worse. But Rivka had the remedy that always worked. *Loz mir zeyen*, let me look, she would say as she bent down to peer into the affected eye. Stay still, it will soon be better, she would add, as she rapidly but gently, oh so gently, passed the tip of her tongue across the affected area. *Nu, is es nisht shoin besser?* she would say, there, isn't that already better? No-one but a mother knows best how to treat her child. The family felt the absence of Rivka. The house was off balance. One of the stabilizing supports of the household had been removed. A bright light had gone out and a greyness had descended. Will they ever laugh again as they had in the past? They heard through a haze, the kind words of friends who came to visit. Time will heal, they said. Life would go on, it had to.

Outside politics could not be excluded from the discussions especially because of the persecution of the Jews in Germany. On the Wednesday following Rivka's death, friends reported that a reign of terror against the Jews had been instigated by the Nazis throughout Germany. Jews were beaten openly in the streets and many were killed while the authorities and German civilians stood by or gave encouragement to the organised hooligans. It was a modern pogrom. The windows of Jewish shops and houses were smashed. Thousands of the shops were looted and hundreds of Synagogues were burned down. So much glass was strewn about the streets, that the night was called Kristallnacht. This was the culmination of the many other events that had characterised the year 1938. Anthony Eden had resigned earlier in the year as Foreign Secretary, in protest against the appeasement policies of the government. In September, the Prime Minister, Mr. Chamberlain had returned from a meeting with Hitler in Munich waving a piece of paper that was supposed to ensure 'Peace in our Time.' The immediate price paid for this illusion was the delivery of Sudetenland to Nazi Germany, whose arrogant army marched unopposed into Czechoslovakia. The maltreatment of European Jews had become widespread. Rumania had stated that it wanted to expel five hundred thousand Jews. Goering had warned Jews to leave Austria, where Synagogues were being burned down and where Jews were being sent to the Dachau concentration camp. Sigmund Freud, now eighty two years of age, had to leave Vienna due to Nazi persecution. Mussolini had decided to expel all Jews who had entered Italy after 1918. In contrast, Britain considered itself generous in offering to settle a limited number of German Jews in the African colonies while explaining that the number of refugees Britain could accept was also limited. But on the other hand, Britain refused a request for ten thousand Jewish children to be allowed to enter Palestine. The British government abandoned the 1937 proposals for partitioning Palestine between the Arabs and Jews. It imposed martial law to pacify the country, where fighting had erupted between the Jews, Arabs and British forces. The Arabs seemed to be getting the upper hand. They certainly had the greater influence on Britain's restrictive policy regarding Jewish immigration.

Shulem had informed Rivka's sister in America of Rivka's death.. He had also written to his mother and sister in Poland and to his brothers in Germany, Danzig and Palestine. He had not heard from them for some time and so the events in Europe were even more disturbing. The cynical tragi-jocular expression *Es is schver tzu zeyen a yid*, it is hard to be a Jew, was losing its jocular connotation.

Chapter 13

The winter months were bleak. The house seemed empty and colder without the warming presence of Rivka. The family's first Englishman, the Socialist pacifist, had decided to leave the house and set up home in an apartment in the West End of London. He had developed an association with a non-Jewish girl whom he intended to marry. He decided to impart this news to Shulem and the family while sitting *shiva* as his girlfriend insisted on visiting him at home during the mourning period. He had refrained from introducing her previously as he did not want to create an upset in the family while Rivka was so ill. In common with many orthodox, she and Shulem had always hoped that their children would marry within the faith. Non-Jewish alliances were shunned and many family rifts had developed within the Jewish community over this fundamental issue. However the fears of a rift did not materialise. Instead, Shulem greeted her graciously on the principle of a friend of a friend is a friend of mine. His attitude had certainly softened. Perhaps, having just lost a wife, he did not want also to lose a son, although he did not attend the wedding that took place in a Registry Office. The following *Pesach*, Passover, the new daughter-in-law came to *Seder*, a sure sign that she had been accepted into the family. She understood that while she could visit and eat in Shulem's house, Shulem could not eat or drink in her home because of the religious dietary laws.

That winter too, Shulem learned that his brother, the Berliner had died and that because of the dreadful situation in Germany, his sister-in-law and her married daughter had decided to emigrate to the United States. One dark night a young woman and her husband called at the house. She was on her way to Chicago, where other relatives of her mother were living. Yulus had already gone to bed, but on hearing strange voices, came down the stairs in his pyjamas for a brief introduction to his first cousin. She was the first close relative he had ever met. Previously he had only heard stories of uncles, aunts and cousins in far away places. Some friends of his were also in the same predicament, while others had the good fortune to have such relatives and even grandparents close at hand whom they could visit. Fate, or whatever, had contrived to separate many people from their immediate families. He was struck by his cousin's blonde hair that sharply contrasted with the dark brunette of his sisters' hair. Apparently, her father had red hair. Strange how physical characteristics can vary so much within one family. And they say that all Jews look alike. The family heard at first hand, of the restrictions imposed on Jews in Germany, how it was now impossible for them to live a normal, let alone a decent, life in Germany. Her mother, the German aunt, as they would later come to call her, would also be coming to London, in due course, on her way to the USA. Yulus had become only too familiar with the frightening stories of refugee children who were now pupils at the JFS. A fellow student had recounted his story to the class. One day in Vienna, two uniformed men came to take his father away for no reason whatsoever other than that he was a Jew. Later all members of the family were told that they had to leave their house at very short notice. If they did not, their furniture would be thrown out into the street. Can that happen here? asked the boy. No way, said the teacher. What about Mosley? Yulus had called out. No politics in class, the teacher replied.

Yulus was on his way home from Hebrew lessons at Christian Street Talmud Torah. It was a dark winter's evening and the pavements and roads were wet from an earlier rainfall. They glistened from the reflected street lights. The wheels of vehicles swished as they passed him on the road. Windscreen wipers were still operating to remove the splattering spray whipped up when passing through puddles or by preceding vehicles. Yulus kept away from the kerbs to avoid being splashed. He had also to keep away from the grey brick walls when passing under the railway arch in Hooper Street, as they were dripping wet. They always seemed wet and steamy, even on dry days. As he turned into Leman Street, he could hear the sound of a brass band. There in the distance, marching along the wet road from the direction of Gardiner's Corner, he could now see a column of men silhouetted against the brighter lights of that junction. A group of people had congregated outside the headquarters of the Cooperative Wholesale Society whose main entrance was at 99 Leman Street. He joined the group as they all turned to greet the column of men marching towards them. Marching is perhaps too martial a term. True, the band was marching, but behind them came a motley crew of men, some in khaki uniforms and others in civilian clothes. All seemed bedraggled. Many were out of step, so that their heads bobbed up and down, totally out of unison. It was the British Battalion of the International Brigade. The volunteers were returning home, saddened by the success of Franco and his Fascist forces in the Spanish Civil War. They were saddened even more so by the loss of so many of their comrades in that bloody conflict. A car overtook the advancing column and came to a stop outside the CWS entrance. A small dapper figure stepped out of the now open rear door of the car and strode quickly into the building. That was Major Attlee, someone said. Another said that he must have come to greet the remnants of the Brigade. Yet another said that one Company had adopted his name after he visited the volunteers in Spain earlier in the war.

Yulus found himself standing next to a middle-aged man who was holding a photograph of a young man. As the first contingent of returning volunteers arrived at the entrance, its leader stood aside and directed the tired marchers into the building. The middle-aged man approached the leader and while showing him the photograph, said in a low voice, that it was his son. He mentioned his name and asked whether the leader had any knowledge of him, because he had not heard from his son for some time and was anxious as to his well-being. No, I'm afraid not, came the soft reply, try the next contingent. Yulus's curiosity was further aroused. He continued to stand by the man with the photograph as he approached one returning volunteer after another. Each gave a negative reply. How was it possible, said the man in desperation, for a person to disappear in this way? The volunteer to whom this question was addressed could only bow his head and shrug his shoulders. The crowd outside the building dispersed and Yulus made his way home, hoping against hope, that the father would be reunited with his son. Is it really possible for a person to disappear in this way? he asked when he got home. I'm afraid so, was the reply that he received. In war, anything can happen.

The school welfare officer came to the house during the *shiva* period to express her condolences and to enquire after Yulus. She understood the problems associated with the loss of a mother within a household, especially as it affected schoolchildren. She said that she would call again the day after the *shiva* ended to talk to Yulus and to see in what way she could be of any assistance. She said that Yulus should not go to school, but wait for her to call that morning. True to her word, a car drew up outside the house at the agreed hour of eleven thirty. The young woman in her lovat coloured matching tweed two-piece jacket and skirt and sensible brown shoes, came into the house. She had a brief word with Yulus's sister who had taken over the household duties and then invited Yulus to join her for lunch. Yulus had been primed for this event. His sister made sure that he was clean and tidy and in a motherly way had enjoined him to be on his best behaviour. Still, it was strange to ride in a motor car on his own, with a virtual stranger. Apart from the funeral ride that he preferred to forget, he had never before been in a car. He had travelled in buses, trams and coaches, but in a private car? This was a new experience for him. Yet another new experience awaited him. The welfare officer parked the car in a side street off Commercial Road and she and Yulus walked to Goide's fish restaurant. They sat at a table for two. It was decked with a white damask tablecloth. There were white cover plates with cutlery placed in position on either side of them and above. There were also glasses for water and wine and white damask serviettes folded in the form of fans. The waiter brought menus. What would you like to eat? Yulus was dumbfounded. There were too many choices. I know, said his sensible companion. I will order something simple for both of us. You like fried fish, do you not? Yulus nodded. Would you like a soup first? No thank you, he replied, remembering to say thank you. After that we can have tea and ice cream. How's that? Yulus could hardly believe his ears. Ice cream in the winter? That would be very nice, he said politely. The waiter took the order. He then took hold of one of the folded serviettes between forefinger and thumb. With a flourish of his arm in the manner of Sir Walter Raleigh, he opened the serviette and placed it gently on the lap of Yulus's companion. As he did likewise for Yulus, he whispered, ladies first, and smiled. This was Yulus's first introduction to gracious living.

The conversation, while stilted at first, grew more animated as the social worker expertly got Yulus to detail his daily life at school and at home. With difficulty, he explained that he felt guilty that he had not visited his mother in hospital on the day of her death. Instead of visiting he had been playing football at the end of the street. It was hardly your fault that the hospital rules do not allow young persons to visit, she said, attempting to console him. But they said they would try to get me in and asked me whether I would prefer to go on the Wednesday or the Friday. And I said Friday. Why didn't I say Wednesday? The tears rose to his eyes and could be heard in his voice, but they did not advance any further. You know what I think? she said, continuing softly without waiting for an answer. I think that the hospital would not have allowed you to visit on either of the days. I am sure that the family was trying to get you in, and I feel equally sure that the hospital would not have allowed it. It's a silly rule, said Yulus pouting in anger. I agree, she said, but you mustn't feel guilty about it. Promise me you won't, she requested earnestly. He nodded assent, but would not voice it in words, because he was sure that if he had been there, he would have got in to see his mother, somehow. After all, he used to dart behind the Beefeaters at the Tower of London to go down the stairs of the Bloody Tower to wander in and out of the dungeons. Nobody would have stopped him from visiting his mother. Have you cried since your mother died? she asked cautiously. No, he said. You should, you know. Yes, he said. Anyhow, about the future, she said in a lighter tone. I have arranged for you to have lunch-time meals at the school. That will help your sister to manage better at home and it will also ensure that you eat well. Now that you will be going to Central School, you will need to be fit and well. Remember too, that at age thirteen, you will have another opportunity to enter Grammar School through the supplementary examinations and for that you need to work hard. On the lighter side, you will also have more time to play during the lunch break, as you won't have to walk back and forth between home and school at midday. I don't suppose school dinners will be as posh as this meal, said Yulus. That I can guarantee, she said with a smile. Thank you, he said for the meal and your help. It's nothing, she said. In any case, she added tactfully, although it's part of my job, I enjoyed this meeting with you. The car journey home seemed shorter than the outward ride. Goodbye, she said as he was leaving the car, you can always contact me if you need me. Thank you, he said again, as he closed the car door and waved goodbye. Was the meal nice and did you say thank you? asked his sister correcting something that did not need correction. It was and yes, he replied, adding, please, please don't try to act like Mama.

1938 was supposed to have brought peace in our time, but from the very beginning of 1939, the media talk was of war and preparation for war. It was reported that the British navy was reorganising to boost its firepower while the Royal Air Force was taking delivery of hundreds of new aircraft each month. Even so, the British forces were lagging behind the German military build-up that included the launching of the battleship Bismarck. Civil defence commissioners were appointed and free air raid shelters were issued to London homes that had gardens and were most likely to be bombed. Hitler's army marched into Prague in the spring ignoring international protests. Prime Minister Chamberlain said that he was shocked as this was the first time Germany had occupied territory not inhabited by Germans. He also pledged that Britain and France would defend Poland against attack. Britain's response would not be half-hearted, said Hore-Belisha, the Secretary for War. In March it was announced that the territorial Army was to be doubled and in April the British government introduced conscription for men over twenty and plans to evacuate children from main conurbations. Italy's army occupied Albania on the specious pretext that Italian residents were being oppressed, and in May, Germany and Italy signed a military alliance. Britain stated it would support Poland if that country had to use force to defend Danzig against Germany. In August, the Soviet Union signed a non-aggression pact with Germany. Britain was surprised by this move as it had, together with France, been trying, since May, to negotiate an anti-aggression alliance with Stalin. Then at 5.45 a.m. on September first, German troops invaded Poland.

Although Fascist activity in London had not lessened, it had become less newsworthy as the critical events in Europe developed. Shulem, in common with other members of the Yiddish speaking community, followed these events from the outset with growing concern. The axis alliance between Nazi Germany and Fascist Italy and the other events taking place in central and eastern Europe, were not just international issues. They were real family issues as almost everyone in the Jewish community had close relatives in Europe whose lives and livelihoods were in immediate danger. Some, like Shulem, also had relatives in Palestine whose situation was being made more difficult due to British restrictions on Jewish immigration and a colonial policy that, in contradiction to the Balfour Declaration, favoured the Arabs. The Jews of Palestine were being prevented from providing a safe haven for Jewish refugees fleeing from Nazi persecution. The British government suspended the immigration quota of 75,000 over a five year period, claiming that illegal Jewish immigration had exceeded the quota for the year. Palestine, said the Colonial Secretary, could not solve the whole refugee problem. Where then, were persecuted Jews to go? No satisfactory answer was forthcoming. Britain had agreed to take in some 40,000 Jewish refugees in 1938/1939 in addition to the 10,000 or so who had already arrived. This was on the basis that the Jewish Board of Deputies had guaranteed that they would not be a burden on the public purse. However, when Hitler marched into Austria in March 1938, the Jewish Refugee Organisation said that it was not in a position to extend that guarantee to cover fully, further refugees coming into Britain. Most other countries in the world were limiting their intake of, or refusing to take in refugees. The USA had even refused to accept ten thousand Jewish children and a Canadian government official was reported to have said that one Jewish refugee would be one too many. Britain and Switzerland re-imposed visas for entry into their respective countries, an act that led to Germany stamping the letter 'J' into passports issued to German Jewish citizens. This was done to hinder Jewish travel and it effectively prevented many Jews from entering countries that had restrictive refugee policies.

Shulem's sister-in-law, the German aunt, arrived in England the day before Germany marched into Poland. She had escaped from Germany just in time. She had a transit visa and was allowed to stay with Shulem until transport could be arranged for her to travel on to America. His brother in Hamburg had remained in Germany and Shulem was worried as to what might happen to him and his wife and children. The fifteen-year old son of his brother in Danzig, had joined a Zionist group of people who had decided to emigrate to Palestine a few months before the German invasion of Poland. They travelled through Vienna to a Black Sea port in Rumania. From there, a ship named the Astir took them through the Bosphoros straits into the Sea of Marmara and then through the Dardanelles into the Aegean Sea, past Crete and Rhodes into the Mediterranean Sea and on past Cyprus to the Palestinian coast. The British navy prevented the ship from entering Haifa port and ordered the ship to sail out of the territorial waters. After some weeks of sailing in the Aegean Sea the ship entered a Greek port, where a motorised fishing smack was acquired. A new attempt was made to land in Palestine. It was night when the ship with the fishing smack in tow, arrived just outside the three mile limit. The 720 passengers crowded into the fishing smack to make a dash for the coast. The intention was to deceive the British into thinking that the passengers were still on the mother ship that sailed away. Unfortunately, the engine on the fishing smack failed and the boat drifted until morning when it was sighted by the British and towed into a Palestinian harbour. Some of the passengers had become ill from inhaling the fumes emanating from the faulty engine. All were interned and later released. Their number was deducted from the immigrant quota. There were many attempts by other Jewish refugees to enter Palestine. Some, too would disembark at night onto small boats that would take them to the beaches where Jewish settlers would be waiting to help them. Others came clandestinely over one of the Palestinian borders to be whisked away to the safety of nearby Kibbutzim. They became part of the *ma'apalim*, illegal Jewish immigrants about whom the British were complaining. Shulem was relieved to learn from his brother in Palestine, that despite the arduous journey, his nephew had finally arrived safely.

With war in the offing, some of the people who had been arguing against war for years were now having to make practical decisions. The growth of Nazi and Fascist power and aggression had weakened the anti-war movement that had reached its peak a few years earlier. There was the famous Oxford Union 'pacifist' resolution in February 1933 that stated 'that this house will in no circumstances fight for its king and country.' In the following year the Reverend Dick Shephard received over 100,000 postcards supporting a resolution that stated that 'We renounce war and never again, directly or indirectly, will we support or sanction another.' A Peace Pledge Union was established and an anti-war meeting was held in the Albert Hall. In 1935 a Peace Ballot was undertaken by the National Declaration Committee of the League of Nations. The Ballot asked five questions predicated on international agreement. Should Britain remain in the League? Should there be an all-round reduction of armaments? Should there be an all-round abolition of national military and naval aircraft? Should the manufacture and sale of armaments for private profit be prohibited? Should a nation that attacks another be compelled to stop by economic and non-military measures? or if necessary by military measures? Despite the objections of the Conservative Party and part of the press, more than eleven million people voted in favour of all the questions including seven million who voted for military measures, if necessary. The Women's Cooperative Guild sold white poppies for peace, instead of red poppies, on Armistice Day.

Now had come the time for *tachliss*, time for making real practical decisions. Most, including many who had supported the peace movements in the past, agreed with the government that the Germans had gone too far and had to be stopped by military means. A small minority of people were still against war in any circumstances and the British government gave them the opportunity to prove that their conscientious objections were genuine. Special tribunals were set up for the purpose. Yulus's Socialist pacifist brother was called upon to make his case. He pointed out that he had always been a pacifist, even in his schooldays and he produced essays to this effect that he had written as a boy. He also explained that he had joined the Socialist Party of Great Britain because he was both a Socialist and a pacifist. He produced printed statements that appeared in the Party's journal. They stated that the road to Socialism is the road of persuasion and of international democratic organisation. The Communists don't seem to believe that. Maybe, but my Socialist ideals are in conflict with them. That is why I am a member of the SPGB and not the Communist Party. War means death, maiming and disease for the working classes. Capitalists go to war for their own interests. But what about the Jewish question? he was asked. If this country were really concerned about the plight of the Jews, it would not restrict its intake of refugees here and in Palestine, would it? Is it not true that your younger brother has joined the army? Yes. Should you not support him? We have opposing views on this matter. You have an older brother too, do you not? Yes. What is his position? He is in a reserved occupation making army uniforms. I have friends too, who are engineers and in reserved occupations. They have been spared the necessity to explain their position. They have not been called upon to decide on principle as I have. Are you prepared to work on the land or in one of the auxiliary services, such as the Police or Fire services? Yes, I will support non-violently, the fight against Nazism and Fascism. He was granted exemption from serving in the armed forces.

Yulus realised the importance of the day when Shulem took time off work to accompany him to school on that fateful Friday morning, September 1, 1939. Shulem rarely if ever took time off from work, except of course for pressing religious activities. On weekdays, or rather workdays, he would have left home early in the morning for work, long before the schoolday began. On this day, however, the sixty-one year old walked hand-in-hand through the streets of the East End of London with Yulus, now eleven years of age. On this day, his youngest offspring was about to be evacuated with his Jewish school to somewhere in the English countryside. He knew not where but relied on the school to find a suitable haven. The government had decided on the wholesale evacuation of children from crowded conurbations in order to keep them safe from the impending aerial bombardments that could be expected should Great Britain declare war against Germany. Shulem was convinced that war was indeed imminent. That is why he had agreed that Yulus could be taken out of the intensive Jewish environment of his home and neighbourhood to live among the Gentiles in some obscure village, of which he knew not, several hours journey by train and coach from London. This was indeed a difficult decision for Shulem to make. Even in the relatively secure religious environs of the Jewish East End, the Christian, capitalistic, Socialist and Hellenistic influences of the general society were attracting young Jews away from traditional Judaism. Jewish parents, including Shulem, had agreed that their children be evacuated from their tight Jewish communities to totally strange Gentile environments, on the understanding that the Jewish schools would maintain their Jewishness and Jewish education. Preparations for evacuation of children had also taken place in the previous year at the time of the Munich crisis. Then the children had been equipped with the gas masks in brown cardboard boxes, the straps of which were now slung over their young shoulders. Rivka, God rest her soul, was alive then. She had given him the support he needed to make such a decision and the fact that she had agreed then to the evacuation supported him now. There had also been the thin hope that war might be averted and that Yulus would soon be home again. That hope had been expunged by the early morning news' broadcast. Hitler's Germany had attacked Poland that very morning.

Shulem and Yulus arrived at the Jews' Free School. Numerous other children, accompanied by one or two parents or other relatives, were streaming into the large playground. Teachers had previously instructed the pupils where to assemble. They now asked the adults to bid farewell to their children as the hour to proceed to Liverpool Street Railway Station had arrived. Shulem and Yulus embraced and said their words of farewell. Take care, said Shulem and be sure to write the moment you arrive. Yes *tatta*, father, said Yulus. And, said Shulem, keep a tight hold on your belongings. Remember what you have there is *diner gunsa farmaigance*, all your worldly goods. Shulem watched with sadness as his youngest took his place in line with his schoolmates. If only Rivka could see him now, he thought, looking so self assured, so clean and smartly dressed. Even his hair was in place and his socks had not fallen around his ankles.

Shulem waited to see the orderly lines of chattering schoolboys, shepherded by their masters, make their way out of the school grounds. They appeared to be unaware of the momentous changes that were about to take place in their young lives. He walked slowly and contemplatively towards his workplace. If the Germans marched into Poland that morning, he thought, then one of the important points of entry had to be Mlawa, the small Polish town on the border of East Prussia, where he was born and where his mother, sister and family were still living. He suddenly stopped in his tracks, and his heart missed a beat as a terrible realisation entered his thoughts. What a tragic, tragic irony. He had just waved goodbye to his son whom he was sending out of town to be safe from German attack. And on the very same morning in Poland, the lives of his mother, sister and family were being placed in the hands of the German Nazi murderers. And what of his brother and family who were still in Danzig? *Mein Gott, voos vill ziyen fon doos alles?* My God, what will be the outcome of all this?

134

Chapter 14

It was a strange beginning to the war. The immediate air bombardments on London that were expected, did not materialise although there were a few false alarms when people rushed to the air-raid shelters to which they had been allocated. Identity cards were issued to all British citizens. Shulem and many of his contemporaries still had their Alien Registration Cards that stated that they had to report to the police any change of address. Conscription of young men continued and British troops were sent to France. Together with the French army, they were going to face down the Germans. British troops were also sent to the Middle East. London had become quieter and less crowded. The children had been evacuated and the young men had been called-up to join the armed forces. All sorts of regulations were issued. There was a total black-out at night. There were no street lights and the windows of houses had to be covered with black or other suitable material so that not a chink of light could be seen at night. The most important duty of air-raid wardens who had been appointed at the outbreak of the war, appeared to be calling on householders to 'put that light out!' But at sea, the war had started in earnest. First a liner was sunk and then the battleship Royal Oak was torpedoed. Later there was some consolation when the German pocket battleship Graf Spee was scuttled by the German crew after having been trapped by British warships. There was no doubt that travelling by sea had become very dangerous.

The German aunt stayed for a few months. During that time she ignored most of the instructions that were included in the guide book issued to her on arrival in England by the Jewish Board of Deputies, ever concerned for its image. The booklet written in German and English was entitled Helpful Information and Guidance for Every Refugee while you are in England. She commented on each instruction as she read it out aloud to Shulem, translating into Yiddish where necessary. Number one, she read, spend your spare time immediately learning the English language and its correct pronunciation. I am not going to be here that long, she commented. Refrain from speaking German in the streets and in public conveyances and in public places. What else can I speak? Talk halting English rather than fluent German. Impossible! Do not talk in a loud voice. Do I talk in a loud voice? said she, raising her voice an octave or two. Do not read German newspapers in public. For me Germany is finished. I won't touch another German thing. Do not criticise any government regulations, nor the way things are done over here. Do not speak of how much better this or that is done in Germany. It may be true in some matters, but it weighs nothing against the sympathy and freedom and liberty of England which are now given to you. Never forget that point. Here, she said, they are right. I am grateful for being allowed to stay here, even if it is only for a short time. Do not join any political organisation or take part in any political activities. I won't, but why shouldn't someone who is going to stay here? She read on. Do not make yourself conspicuous by speaking loudly, nor by your manner or dress. *Noch ein mal?* once again? she complained, they are writing about speaking loudly. All the petit bourgeoisie, including the English, speak loudly. Don't they know that? It seems not. Listen. The Englishman greatly dislikes ostentation, loudness of dress or manner, or unconventionality of dress or manner. The Englishman attaches great importance to modesty, understatement in speech rather than overstatement, and quietness of dress and manner. He values good manners far more than he values the evidence of wealth. You will find that he says thank you for the smallest service, even for a penny bus ticket for which he has paid. Don't they know that we Germans, except for the Nazis, are even more polite? We say *bitte, danke, bitte*, please, thank you, please, every time. That's twice as many pleases as the polite Englishman. There is more, she said. Try to observe and follow the manners and customs of this country in social and business relations. *Ober kein politiks*, but no politics, she added. And listen, she continued, listen to this. It says here, do not spread the poison of it's bound to come to your country because the British Jew greatly objects to the planting of this craven thought. Listen, she said, if we had thought more about it years ago, perhaps this whole Nazi disaster may not have befallen us. We were ostriches. We put our heads in the sand and thought it couldn't happen here, in Germany I mean, even when it was happening. There is one more instruction. It says, above all please realise that the Jewish community is relying on you, on each and every one of you, to uphold in this country the highest Jewish qualities, to maintain dignity, and to help and serve others. What makes them think, she asked, that a refugee does not naturally want to live in dignity. Don't they understand that the refugees are just that, refugees, because they have been deprived of dignity? Thank God, Shulem, that there are still some like you who understand that dignity and service are not exclusively the values of English speakers. The German aunt set sail for America after a stay of a few months to join her daughter in Chicago. She said that she was prepared to take the risk of crossing the Atlantic ocean with all its wartime dangers. It was much more dangerous in Europe where the Nazis were carrying out their atrocities than on the high seas. Shulem had indeed become more and more worried about his family in Europe, especially after the British government had just issued a White Paper confirming that the treatment of inmates of the German Dachau and Buchenwald concentration camps was reminiscent of the darkest ages of the history of mankind. Jews were being flogged and tortured there by the Nazi guards. Why did the British government issue this disturbing report? The German Aunt had asked Shulem. Was is because they are concerned over the plight of the Jews in Germany? I wish it were so, answered Shulem. Then why? The government explains in its report that it was forced to make the revelations because of the shameless and unscrupulous German propaganda accusing Britain of atrocities in South Africa 40 years ago. Still, it is good that the report is out and that the world should know how those barbarians are treating Jews.

Shulem was in a state of constant consternation. He had lost contact with his relatives in Mlawa, Danzig and Hamburg. He had made enquiries through the Polish Jewish Refugee Committee who were coordinating with the International Red Cross, but so far had not received any positive information. Meanwhile the newspapers were reporting that the Jewish population was being expelled under most cruel conditions from a number of Polish towns, including Mlawa. Another report stated that tens of thousands of young Jews were to be concentrated in the town and district of Mlawa for subsequent deportation to labour camps in Eastern Prussia. The mere sight of the word Mlawa in the news' reports made his hair bristle on the back of his neck. He saw in his mind's eye, his old mother being humiliated while he, here in London, was unable to do anything, other than pray, to protect her. His sadness increased as he read of German and Austrian Jews being sent in cattle trucks to the Lublin reservation, as it was called, and of Jews being made to dig their own graves before being shot down in cold blood. Others were shot while being made to swim naked and yet others were being sent to Sachsenhausen, Buchenwald and Dachau concentration camps. Shechita, the Jewish ritual of killing animals to make them kosher, had now been banned in Poland, which meant that religious Jews could no longer eat meat. If only that were the worst of their troubles. In fact, in many places, the Jews had no food at all. One report stated that many had already died from starvation. By April 1940 over one and a half million Jews had been herded into concentration camps and two hundred were dying daily in Warsaw. On May 26, 1940, world Jewry held a day of prayer. Petticoat Lane did not open on that Sunday, such was the concern of East End London Jews for their fellow Jews in Europe. They joined in the cry published in his newspaper, Why? Why, is the world not paying attention to the suffering of the Jews in Poland?

Little, if anything, was being done to relieve the plight of the Jewish refugees. The British were not only maintaining their restrictions on immigration into Palestine, but had introduced restrictions on land sales to Jews there. Although the Jewish National Fund was still purchasing land, a new British White Paper had effectively imposed minority status on the Jews in Palestine. Some Jews did manage to escape from Europe and there were schemes afoot to settle small groups of Jews in remote places. But no solution was being offered to give sanctuary to the millions of European Jews who were facing annihilation by the Nazis. Life was full of contradictions. The Russians on the one hand were preventing Jews from crossing from German occupied Poland into Russian occupied Poland. On the other hand they were calling for Jews to go to Birobidzhan, the Jewish Autonomous Region set up by the USSR in 1928 on the northern borders of Manchuria. The US Secretary of the Interior was calling for the opening of Alaska to the refugees while the United States refused to accept ten thousand Jewish refugee children. But there was nothing contradictory about the Fascist attitude. An Italian newspaper advocated the transportation of all Jews from Europe and the rest of the world to the island of Madagascar where it was hoped they could all be forgotten. And the Nazis offered annihilation.

Anti-Semitism in England had not abated. Mosley and his blackshirts were still active in the East End of London. A leading British Fascist, William Joyce, emigrated to Germany. He became known as Lord Haw Haw because of the peculiar English accent that he used in his regular radio Nazi propaganda broadcasts to Britain. The anti-Semitic cry was that this was a Jew-war and their vile anti-Jewish propaganda was in conformity with Lord Haw Haw's view that the British government was under the control of the Jews. After all, the anti-Semites shouted, the British Secretary of State, Hore-Belisha was a Jew and as an early propaganda leaflet dropped by the Germans on London stated 'Jew Belisha means war.' Hore-Belisha resigned in January 1940. The Yiddish newspaper reported that the world wonders why, while the Nazis are happy. The resignation did not, however, stop the Germans from maintaining, in their broadcasts, that the British war aim was to return the Jews to the Reich and for them to control European finance. The Jewish Defence Committee had to issue statements to explain that England was not at war for the sake of the Jews. Nor was it at war solely for the sake of Poland, but to protect British interests and halt the consequences of Hitler's take-over of Austria and the Czech Republic. The so-called phoney war had been going for seven months with the allied armies in the Maginot Line facing the Germans in the Siegfried Line singing morale-boosting songs, while tragically, the only people being killed in substantial numbers were those who ventured on the high seas and the Jews of Europe. *Doos iz a meshigana velt*, this is a mad world, Shulem said to his friends and they nodded sadly in agreement.

London had emptied out of children when war was declared in September 1939, but with the advent of the phoney war, mothers were bringing their children back to the capital. Why should they be parted from their loved ones when there was no good reason and no obvious signs of danger? Bad enough that their older sons had been called up for the armed forces and were now away from home. Why should they leave their young ones in the care of strangers? Shulem, too had thoughts of bringing Yulus home, but what sort of a home was it for the boy now, without Rivka, without a mother? And why should he add to the burden of his younger daughter who had taken over the household duties since Rivka's death eighteen months ago? She should be going out and about, rather than be tied to the house attending to the family. How could he give her the added responsibility of a twelve-year-old? No, there was only one solution, a solution that would also help relieve the deeply sad loneliness that had stayed with him since Rivka had departed this life. He would have to remarry. He needed a Yiddish speaking companion of his own age. Once a new wife had settled in, and only then, could he seriously consider bringing the boy home to stay. *Erev Shabbas*, on the eve of the Sabbath, Friday, April 19, 1940, the week before *Pesach*, Shulem married Bertha in a quiet ceremony. She was called *Mema*, aunt, by the family. Shulem rarely used her given name and he too, soon joined with the others in calling her *Di Mema*. She was a cultured person, having come from a relatively wealthy family who had left the Black Sea port of Odessa in 1917 with the advent of the Russian revolution. In her early life she had been brought up with servants in her house and when she first married, her father had presented her with a library. However, her financial position had deteriorated over the years and after her husband had died she sought companionship and security. She had a pleasant enough personality and was immaculately clean in her personal habits. But a housewife she was not, and accordingly she could never meet the demands of the children of her new found family regarding cleanliness in the home or in the preparation of meals. Although, at no time did she attempt to usurp Rivka's place, some of the children felt a resentment to this new personality that had entered the household. Shulem though was content with his choice.

Yulus came home for the first *Pesach* of the war. He found it strange that the house was nearly empty. The three elder brothers were away. One was already married, one was working on the land and one was in the army. His married sister had been evacuated to a small town outside Cambridge where she had given birth to a daughter the previous December and had made Yulus an uncle and Shulem a grandfather. This was Shulem's first grandchild, an event of such importance, that he actually travelled by train to see the tiny addition to his family. His eyes shone as he spoke of her and became sad again as he thought how happy Rivka would have been to hold the newly born in her arms. It was not simple for Shulem to make that journey. He had the instructions written out clearly so that he could show the note to whomsoever, rather than ask directions in his halting English. He always joined in the laughter when previous misunderstandings relating to his limited English were related to friends. He had taken a bus ride to visit relatives. When the bus conductor asked, Where to? he had answered, For Stamford Hill, adding a polite 'plitz..' The conductor interpreted the directional 'for' as a numerical 'four' and presented Shulem with four tickets and after much argument insisted on payment. It was an expensive journey. On another occasion he had to change buses at a particular junction in order to reach his destination. Armed with his little note as to which bus he needed, he approached two men whom he saw talking animatedly to each other. As their hands were moving expressively, he assumed they must be Yiddish speakers. It is difficult to speak Yiddish without hand movements. To his surprise, he found that they were deaf and were speaking to each other in sign language. Shulem said that they were more than delighted that someone had come to them for help. They insisted on walking him to the very bus stop that he required and stood there until he boarded the vehicle. *In mein ganzer leben hob Ich nisht geve'en azoi git behundlt*, said Shulem, never in my life have I been treated so nicely! On this more distant journey to see his granddaughter, he had to take all his food and drink with him so that he did not break any of the Jewish dietary laws on the way. And as a registered alien he had to return home the same day. These problems had prevented him from visiting Yulus in the countryside, but a new offspring? Nothing could prevent him from making such a journey even if he had to fast all day.

The strangest thing of all for Yulus, was this unfamiliar person who was introduced to him as the *Mema*. He understood that she was his father's new wife and he felt no resentment. He did not allow this new factor to penetrate the wall of numbness that he had built around his emotions since his mother's demise. He never spoke of his mother unless he had to, and the *Mema's* presence was merely another strange element that had entered his young life over the past year or two. He was coping with evacuation. He could cope with this.

That *Pesach*, those who could attend the *Seder* night came. The *Mema* did her best to make a festive table, but the jollity of previous years was not there. The land worker was looking fit from his work in the fields, but he was desperately disappointed when he found that many of the conscientious objectors in his camp, were Fascists and anti-Semites. He had objected to the war on genuine moral and ethical grounds. They had objected because they did not want to fight the Germans, but had hidden behind moral arguments to obtain exclusion from service in the armed forces. He explained how, when he was hitch-hiking back to London, he was picked up by an army car. He was taken to some army barracks where he was interrogated for some hours before being allowed to continue his journey. There had been a scare that the

Germans had dropped agents on England by parachute. It seems that the army officer had suspected that this healthy looking hitch-hiker on a lonely country road, might be one of them. Later, when he arrived in London, he was often stopped by civilian or military policemen who would ask him to identify himself and explain why such a healthy specimen of humanity was not in uniform. He had now applied to be transferred to the Auxiliary Fire Service. At least, in that way, he could be of non-combatant service without being harassed at every street corner.

Yulus asked the four questions as usual in Hebrew, English and Yiddish and Shulem conducted the *Seder* service with more than his usual solemnity, reminding everyone of the hardships of the Jews in Europe. Some light relief was allowed when Yulus was obliged to search for, and find the hidden *Afikomen*, the half slice of Matzo that is eaten at the end of the meal. Shulem had hidden it according to tradition. As a prize, Yulus was given a volume of the book 'King Sol' that his soldier brother had written and that had recently been published. The book told of the difficult life in the East End of London and the unsuccessful attempt by one of its working class inhabitants to escape by becoming a boxing promoter. It graphically described the various influences in society and the political conflicts between the Fascist right and Communist left. Unfortunately the outbreak of the war seriously reduced the extent of the book's distribution. It had become an early casualty of the war. At least he can be certain of one reader, laughed Yulus as he proudly flipped over the pages. What I really need is a bicycle. Everyone in the countryside has one. Perhaps later in the year said Shulem, hoping against hope that the boy would be home permanently by then. Singing from next door could just be heard. In previous years the windows would have been wide open and the loud singing contest of the final *Pesach* hymns would have started. This year, the windows were not only shut, but were covered with black-out material to prevent even the smallest chink of light to escape. After all, no-one wanted to be shouted at by air-raid wardens to put that light out with the additional cry of don't you know there's a war on?

Chapter 15

If one asks an Englishman when the war started, what will he answer? He will say without hesitation, Sunday, September 3, 1939 because that was the day that Prime Minister Chamberlain stated in negative terms that Britain was now at war with Germany. If one asks a Pole, he will say without hesitation that the war started two days earlier on Friday September 1, the day that Germany positively blitzkrieged its way into Poland. Yulus was inclined to agree with the Pole as his war also started on that Friday morning.

Yulus remembered that day well. He had waved goodbye to his father as he and his schoolmates trooped out of the Jews' Free School playground towards Liverpool Street Station. He had his brown cardboard box containing his gas mask slung over his shoulder and he was clutching a bulging bagwash laundry bag as he marched along to, he knew not where. There was a peculiar air about the procession engendered by the realisation that this journey was not a holiday outing, but a real life adventure. Yulus held on to the bagwash bag tightly as instructed by his father. It contained his *gunsa farmaigance*, his worldly goods. The bag still showed the code markings, H 11, that identified the bag when deposited in the laundry for the weekly wash. On that day, it was being used as a travel bag.

The train arrived at Newmarket Station. Everyone off! shouted the teachers. Wooden trestle tables had been set up along the platform. Ladies of the Women's Volunteer Service were there to greet the schoolchildren and provide each with a brown carrier bag into which they placed 'iron' rations consisting of a tin of corned beef, a bar of milk chocolate and other emergency foods. Good luck! called the ladies as the boys trundled out of the station to board coaches that were to transport them to their final destinations. They still knew not where. Somewhere near Ely, someone said. It seemed to be a State secret and it added to the excitement of the moment.

The convoy of coaches in which Yulus was travelling, stopped outside the Conservative Club in the centre of the village called Soham. The boys were ushered into the main hall of the Club where they were offered drinks of tea and orange squash and asked to sit on chairs that had been set out in tidy rows. Yulus wondered what these conservatives would think if they knew the political colour of many of the evacuees. He thought how much his Socialist brother would be amused when he told him. Various officials and prospective foster parents moved about the hall, sometimes separately and sometimes with the teachers. After whispered discussions they would point at their chosen proteges who would give their names to the billeting officer and then proceed to their new abodes. Yulus and his friend with whom he had paired, were the last, left still seated in the hall after all the foster parents and their wards had departed. Yulus later said jokingly, that he and his friend chose to think that this was because they had been selected earlier by an official to be billeted with foster parents who could not be present in the hall, and not because of their political affiliations. Come on, you two, said an official jovially, it's your turn now. You've been left till last so that I can take you by car to your new lodgings.

The car sped through the High Street and on southwards, back along the route that the coaches had come. It passed open fields and turned right just after the windmill, into a lane called Downfields. The car stopped half way down the lane that had semi-detached cottages on one side and orchards on the other. The sun was shining and the fruit weighed heavily on the plum trees. That autumn produced a plentiful fruit harvest.

The foster parents came down the path to welcome the two boys. Welcome! they said in unison as they offered to take the boys' luggage. I can manage, said Yulus, remembering his father's instruction to hold on tight to his worldly goods. Food was ready on the table and the boys were offered tea and sandwiches which they readily ate. It had been a long time since breakfast. The boys were shown about the house and taken upstairs to the bedroom they were to share. It had one double bed and the necessary rudimentary furniture. We'll leave you to unpack, said the mother as she returned downstairs. The boys agreed between themselves which drawers were for their personal use and which side of the bed each would sleep. They looked around the room and noticed that there was no light switch and no light fitting on the walls or ceiling. That's strange, said Yulus, I wonder what we do at night. Let's ask when we go downstairs. How do we switch on the light upstairs? Yulus asked hesitantly. Oh, there are no lights upstairs, we use oil lamps up there at night, came the answer. She then added laughingly, I think the builder ran out of piping when he built these cottages last year. He seemed to have enough gas pipe to put gas lighting on the ground floor but not enough to go upstairs. He seems also not to have had enough water piping, because the water tap is on the wall of the outhouse. There is no water piped into the house itself. Oh yes, I should also explain to you that the outhouse toilet does not flush. It is a chemical system. The bucket is emptied each day into a pit at the end of the garden. At night, if you need to go, there is a chamber pot in your bedroom. You have to bring it down each morning and empty it into the toilet. You can rinse it out with the tap water. Be careful how you open the tap, as the water pressure is quite strong.

It was a lovely late summer's day and the boys wandered into the garden. They examined the outhouse and the two pits at the end of the garden. One was partially filled with the waste from the outhouse toilet while the second was just an open pit of similar depth to the other. I wonder why they have two pits, said Yulus. Just then they noticed two tousled heads appear from behind the outhouse and quickly disappear when the boys looked towards them. Hello! shouted Yulus two or three times. Eventually two boys emerged fully into view and cautiously approached. Are you evacuees? asked one. Yes. And you are going to stay in my house? This is your house? Yes. Are you Jews? the other boy asked querulously. We are, but why do you ask? Well, you don't look strange at all, in fact you look quite normal. Don't you have horns? No. Then why are you wearing caps? It's our religion. I bet the cap hides the horns, said the same village boy. It does not. Then take off your cap and let us see. The caps were removed and the heads examined at short range. I can't see any horns. Maybe they are hidden under the hair. No. There is nothing there. Of course not, said Yulus people don't have horns. That must be a silly old wives' tale. No it's not. We've seen pictures in books. Well, the pictures are not right. Maybe, the village boy said incredulously and then added to his friend, maybe they come out at night?

This place is strange for us, said Yulus. Where we live in the East End of London, the houses don't have gardens and trees are scarce. What, no gardens or trees? That certainly is strange. Why are there two pits? asked Yulus. Because as we put the waste into one pit we cover each layer with earth from the other pit. When one pit is filled the other is empty and ready for the waste to be put in it. And then you start another pit, said Yulus, pleased with his understanding. Of course. You two don't know anything about the countryside do you? No, but we're ready to learn. You are? Then come on, we'll show you something else. Off the two village boys ran, with the two Londoners close on their heels. Over the fence they went into the plum orchard where they had their first lesson in scrumping. You can take as many plums as you can eat, but no more. Otherwise you will be in real trouble. And you have to do it quickly and get out of the orchard as soon as possible. If you eat too many you'll get a sore tum, and if the farmer catches you, you'll soon have a sore bum.

The village of Soham is about eighteen miles north of the university town of Cambridge. The village lies on the main road between the horse-racing town of Newmarket and the cathedral city of Ely. Boys from the JFS Juniors and Seniors and girls from the JFS Girls School were evacuated to Ely which is about five miles from the village of Soham. The JFS Central boys were evacuated to Soham and also to the nearby villages of Isleham and Fordham. The postal address of what Yulus came to call 'his' village was Soham, Ely, Cambs, which Yulus would make into one word. In response to the question, where are you staying, he would say Sohamelycambs! It was a village with a long history, having been founded in Saxon times. It once had a cathedral of its own which the Danes destroyed in the year 870. The oldest part of the parish church was built in the twelfth century. The village which was situated in fen country had grown over the years. It had about five thousand inhabitants and some said it was the largest village in England. It certainly was the largest village in the area. Its Grammar School was the feed school for the University of Cambridge. The surrounding flat marshy lands had all been drained some years before to provide rich dark brown, sometimes called black, fertile soil that was ideal for growing sugar beet and potatoes.

Everyone listened to the radio at eleven o'clock on that Sunday in September 1939 when war was declared against Germany. Does that mean we will have to stay here until the war is over? It all depends was the stock answer. And how long will the war last? It all depends. No-one ever could say on what it did depend. For many months, the war did not seem like a war. There were some bombing scares but no bombs. There were no street lights because of black-out regulations. Everyone masked their windows at night to prevent chinks of light being seen from the sky by enemy bombers that didn't arrive. Ships were being sunk at sea and food rationing was introduced. So why continue the evacuation? Some mothers came to the village on a visit from London and found it impossible to part again with their offspring. So they took their children back to London. The mother of Yulus's friend was one such mother. Within a few months, his friend left for London.

Yulus had no mother and so he stayed in Soham throughout the phoney war and longer. First his youngest sister came on a visit for a day with a girl friend whose young cousin was billeted in the nearby village of Fordham. Village life seemed so attractive to them as that autumn was so summery and the countryside was so fresh. They came by bus from Newmarket and got off at Fordham to see the cousin first, before continuing on foot, the mile or so, to the southern end of Soham. They explained their plan to the bus driver who told them the time that the bus would return to Newmarket from the Soham windmill. They were a little late in getting to the appointed bus stop and were delighted to see that the bus had waited for them. Such a thing could never happen in London. Really, Yulus, you are lucky to be living in such surroundings and with such nice people.

Yulus's brother came on a visit for a day shortly before he joined the army. It was later in the year, the leaves had fallen from the trees and the day was dull. The countryside looked bleak. Are you happy here? he asked. It's alright, said Yulus. I don't know, said the brother, I'm not too happy about your staying here. I'll speak to father. And off he went home and then to the army.

Later still, Yulus's eldest sister came on a visit. She brought him the suitcase for which he had been asking and money to buy Wellington boots. She came by train to Soham Station where Yulus met her. There were no buses and so they walked the two miles to Downfields where Yulus was staying. It's quite a long walk, she said. I do it every day, said Yulus, as my school is in the centre of the village. I suppose it keeps you fit, she said. I need a bicycle, he said. I'll talk to father. She stayed for lunch, which she enjoyed. On the way back to the station, she remarked how tasty the chicken was that she had eaten just a little while before. That wasn't chicken, said Yulus. No? she said questioningly, but it was so nice. What was it? It was rabbit, we went out this morning to shoot it. Rabbit? she croaked as she stood by the side of the road trying to vomit.

Rabbit, it was. The father of the family worked in the sugar beet fields during the summer and in the sugar beet factory in some of the winter months, when the produce of the fields was turned into coarse-grained white sugar. That was his contribution to the war effort. At week-ends he would go rabbit shooting accompanied by his greyhound and sometimes with Yulus in tow. Occasionally he would shoot pigeons. Country folk could always supplement their food rations by hunting or by the plentiful produce of their vegetable gardens and fruit trees.

One of the strangest elements for Yulus had been the change in eating habits and the different odours that emanated from the kitchen. Instead of the smells of yeast and *smaltz*, rendered chicken fat, he had to get used to the smells of lard and fried bacon. A few days after the outbreak of war, the Chief Rabbi made an announcement that was broadcast on the BBC. It said that 'the Chief Rabbi has been informed that some difficulties have arisen as a result of the strong desire of Jewish children brought up in religious homes to carry out their observances in regard to food in their new surroundings. He wishes to draw the attention of all Jewish parents and children in the reception areas to the fact that in a national emergency such as the present, all that is required of them is to refrain from eating forbidden meats and shellfish.' The first morning that Yulus had breakfast in his new home, his foster mother had presented him with a plate of bacon and eggs. He and his friend were not sure as to what to do. They looked at each other and then saw the boy of the house tucking into the morning meal with relish. They began by eating the egg. The ever watchful foster mother could see their hesitation regarding the bacon. She asked quietly, don't you like bacon? Oh. Is that what it is, said Yulus. We are not supposed to eat bacon because it's not kosher. Yes, I heard about that from the billeting officer, but there is nothing kosher in this house, so what are you to do? You don't want to waste the food. Do you? The boys looked at each other and shrugged. Yulus said, please can we leave it this time so that we can ask our schoolmaster what to do?

They spoke to some of their schoolmates, some of whom had decided to eat only vegetables. But even they had to admit that potatoes fried in lard were also not kosher. They had always been taught that kosher was kosher and everything else was unkosher. Wasn't the old saying, that stated that one might as well be hung for a sheep as for a lamb, appropriate in their case? Their schoolmaster could give them no logical distinction between foods that were a little less, or a little more kosher. He did say, however, that as Jews we have always to remember that we ought to keep the dietary laws and that partial conformity would act as a constant reminder. On their way home, the boys discussed the matter between themselves and came to the conclusion that they had no choice but to eat whatever was offered. After all, the eggs they had eaten had been fried in bacon fat and the taste wasn't bad at all. They vowed always to remember that the dietary laws should be kept.

The Indian summer turned into a cold winter with heavy snowfalls. Yulus was pleased he had Wellington boots as he trudged the two miles to school. One day he stepped into a snow drift that was deeper than the height of his boots and the soft white snow entered his boots. He took them off, emptied them of the melting snow, as best he could, and put them back on, but his socks were already wet. He squelched the rest of the way to school. He had no opportunity to dry out during the day, so he squelched his way back home. The greyhound, who had become fond of Yulus over the months, saw the plodding figure turn into the lane and bounded along the lane to greet him. The force of the over-friendly greeting knocked Yulus off his feet into another snowdrift so that when he reached the house, he was wet and cold in all departments. You'll catch your death, chided his foster mother, and then what will I tell your father? She insisted he change his clothes and rubbed his feet with a rough towel to revive the circulation and prevent chilblains. She was a good woman.

No-one was fully prepared for the mass evacuation of schoolchildren. This was true even though plans had been made at the time of the Munich crisis, a year before the outbreak of the war. So, during the first few months of evacuation, the JFS Central schoolboys had to share the local Shade School building that was situated at the very north of the village. The locals used the school in the mornings and the evacuees used the building in the afternoons. Teachers had difficulty imposing discipline in those early days of confusion. Boys came late for school, or were not too attentive as any noise of an aeroplane was thought to be an enemy raid. One boy had trouble with his foster parents. Not all foster parents were pleasant. He caused damage to furniture in his billet. He was given two strokes of the cane and the incident was recorded in the Shade School Punishment Book. The boy reported to his friends that he had managed to get a glimpse of other entries in the book that dated back to 1907. One such entry amused Yulus. It said that a boy had received three strokes for doing nothing and shuffling his feet! Yulus's mind's eye could picture the incident. What were you doing said the master sternly to the boy who stood before him with his head bent. Nothing sir, the boy would have mumbled. Speak clearly boy and hold your head up. You say you did nothing? Roared the master. No sir, I mean, Yes sir, I did nothing, said the boy again, shuffling his feet. Right, said the master, three strokes.

The JFS boys attended the Conservative Club in the mornings for lectures while the local children used the Club in the afternoons until the end of November. The Vicar allowed the Church Hall to be used for Jewish religious services. From December 1939, the JFS Central School took over the Soham Conservative Club, which then became a school and recreation centre for the evacuees. It also became their Synagogue where religious services were held every Saturday morning and on the High Holy Days. Hebrew classes were held on Sunday mornings. Shulem was pleased to hear that Yulus's religious education was continuing . He was also proud to know that his son could, and did, continue to say *Kaddish*, the memorial prayer for the dead, regularly in memory of his mother.

When in London, the JFS Central School was divided into Commercial and Technical departments. In Soham and the adjoining villages of Isleham and Fordham, there was no longer such a distinction and the classes were combined. As there were no air raids on London there was a steady flow of children back to the Capital. Some masters also returned to London. By April 1940, the remaining boys in the village of Fordham were transferred to Soham and Isleham. Due to the shortage of facilities and teachers, such subjects as Chemistry, English Literature and Foreign Languages were abandoned. Matriculation studies now included restricted subjects such as Electricity, Magnetism and Hydrostatics. The evacuees had become wartime educational casualties. There was some compensation in that Londoners, inhabitants of the concrete jungle, now had an insight into life in the country. A half acre of land, together with two greenhouses was allocated to the school. The field was divided into smaller plots for individual boys to tend and grow their own produce. They learned the rudiments of 'Digging for Victory.' They were taught how to dig, sow, weed and reap and to recognise the difference between a Dutch and a swan-neck hoe and between a sickle and a scythe. Such opportunities rarely, if ever, presented themselves in the East End of London.

Yulus's married sister gave birth to a girl in December 1939 and Yulus at the grand age of eleven, nearly twelve, had become an uncle. He proudly made the announcement in class. Hooray! shouted some of the boys. That is an achievement said the teacher who was a pastmaster at sarcasm. Yulus was not the only student uncle in the school. There was another who was younger than his nephew who was also a pupil at the school. At times, when there was a friendly argument between the two relatives, the younger one would say, Don't you talk to your uncle like that! Everyone enjoyed the joke. It was nearly Christmas and there was a bazaar at the local Church. Yulus attended with one aim in view. He wanted to buy a gift for his niece. He searched among the many treasures on the trestle tables and could find nothing. What are you looking for son? asked a friendly buxom lady stall holder. Yulus explained that he wanted a gift for his newly born niece. You mean, your little sister, she said. No I don't, said Yulus positively and somewhat ruffled, I mean my niece. My, she said , you really are an uncle. How nice. Let me see, she said hesitantly, yes, I think I know just the thing. Come with me. She trundled off to another stall that was displaying knitwear. Listen dearie, she said to the stall holder, this young uncle needs a gift for his newly born niece. He's an uncle? exclaimed the woman in surprise. Yes, yes, said the buxom one who had just adopted Yulus and taken it upon herself to protect him from ridicule. Didn't I see a little baby's outfit on your stall earlier? Yes, here it is, she said holding up a minute pink woollen knitted jumper and leggings, and look she added, it has a bonnet and mittens that match, also pink with white edgings. It looks so small, said Yulus. The ladies laughed and assured him it was big enough for a baby up to six months. Really? he said disbelievingly,. It was his turn to be incredulous. Really, they said positively. He bought it at a bargain price, took it home, packed it neatly in brown paper, inserted a little note of welcome and congratulations, wrote the address clearly, tied the parcel and took it to the post office where he bought a stamp. All this he did on his own initiative and out of his own pocket money. What is it? asked the postmistress, a Christmas present? Yulus hesitated for a moment and then said Yes. He was not going through all those surprise theatrics again. He now knew how his eldest brother, who was twenty-three years his senior, felt when he, Yulus was born and was teased by his workmates.

Yulus's younger sister wrote telling him that Shulem was going to visit Yulus's married sister and the new baby. The village to which she had been evacuated was not too far from Soham. As father could not easily visit Soham, it was suggested that Yulus visit his sister the same day. In this way, he could see his father, sister and niece all at the same time. Early that Sunday morning he bade farewell to his foster parents and made his way to the railway station. There was only one train that day that went to Cambridge. When Yulus arrived at the station he saw the back end of a train leaving. How long till the Cambridge train? he asked the Station Master. Tomorrow, was the answer he received. Tomorrow? repeated Yulus in dismay. Yes, 'cos today's train has just left. That's it steaming away, he said pointing up the line. What am I to do? Yulus appealed to the official plaintively. I dunno son, but you won't get to Cambridge today. Yulus walked sullenly back home. His foster parents were more than surprised to see him so soon. What happened? They asked concernedly. There must have been some misunderstanding as to the time of the train, because I saw the back end of it leaving the station, just as I arrived. You know I left early. Did you dawdle? No. But if only I had walked a little faster, I would have been half way to Cambridge by now. I feel quite sick. Never mind, they said, you had better write letters right away to your sister and father to explain the position. They must be worried out of their skins. A few days later, letters arrived from his sister and from London. Both were in the same vein. Where were you? Are you alright? We were desperately worried. You must write to father, you must write to your sister. Did you make a mistake about the date? Their letters had crossed with his to them. After further correspondence, a new date for a visit to his sister was fixed. This time he made certain to catch the train. He looked at his sister and said, you don't look fat any more. No, she said, of course not. They laughed, because some months before he had asked naively why she was putting on weight. She looked closely at him. Your ears are dirty, she said. That's because I had my head out of the window all the way. That may explain one ear, she said, but what about the other. I looked out the window on both sides. That's a good story, she said, Can I see the baby, he said quickly changing the subject. Not with dirty ears, she said as she produced a wet flannel, Rivka style. You've grown, while I've got smaller, she said. You'll need a new suit when you go home for *Pesach*. I'll write to father. No, I won't mention your ears. He was delighted when he saw the baby wearing his knitted gift. It was ideal, she said. How are things at your billet? she asked. Fine he said.

On his return to Soham, his foster parents introduced Yulus to a man who had come to stay with them for a short while. It wasn't clear as to whether he was a friend or some distant cousin. At any event, there was no alternative but for the man to share the bed with him. Yulus was not too pleased with the idea, but what was he to do? He could hardly refuse. That night, he made sure to stay well on his side of the bed. Next morning he went off to school as usual. On his return home, he noticed that his foster mother had an unusually stern look about her. As soon as he entered the door, she confronted him. Yulus, she asked sternly, did you wet the bed last night? Yulus was flabbergasted. Me? No, he said, why? Well, when I went to make the bed this morning, it was wet. It wasn't me, said Yulus, I never wet the bed, you know that. Are you suggesting that a grown man did it? she asked, adding, there can always be a first time. The awfulness of the situation, suddenly dawned on Yulus. If he hadn't wet the bed then that man must have. Yulus's face went bright red. He was quite off his guard. He didn't know what to say. I'm not suggesting anything, he said. I only know that I didn't wet the bed. Well, if you did or you didn't, you mustn't do it again. Is that clear? She said. He couldn't quite follow this logic. Somehow, the atmosphere had changed overnight. The foster parents had to protect their guest and as a result,

Yulus felt that he was no longer trusted. What is more, the boy of the house started to make uncalled for remarks. Yulus consulted the school welfare officer who said she believed him, which was a great relief. She was aware that one of the problems associated with the evacuation of young people, was that when there was an upset in the household, for whatever reason, the evacuee was in difficulty. The foster parents had almost without exception to take the side of the family, so where was the young evacuee to find solace? After discussions with the foster parents it was amicably agreed that Yulus move to another billet.

The move took place a few months before the Easter and *Pesach* holidays. His new billet was more middle class and a little closer to the centre of the village. There was electric lighting throughout the house. There was a bathroom and the toilet was properly plumbed. The foster mother was eccentric. She did not like anyone to walk, while wearing shoes, on the carpet runner in the long hallway. She was always cleaning the carpet that also ran up the centre of the stairs. She said that she didn't want muddy marks on the carpet that she had just cleaned, which, of course, she had only just cleaned. One had to take off one's shoes prior to entering the house or walk with feet astride of the carpet runner. She didn't mind muddy marks on the lino, on either side of the carpet. Easier to clean, she said. Yulus found great amusement waddling up the hall and stairs, legs astride, to his bedroom where he could change his outdoor shoes for indoor plimsoles. Another idiosyncrasy of hers was that she had no fondness for children. All her affection seemed to be showered on to her sweet spoiled Scot's terrier dog that Yulus would often be obliged to take for walks. She had only accepted a young lodger for the monetary allowance given for fostering. Yulus was not too disappointed when, shortly before the school term ended for the summer break, she informed him and the billeting officer that he need not return to her house after the summer holidays. She had discovered that she could get a larger allowance for an adult lodger whose shoes were likely to be less muddy.

Chapter 16

The phoney war ended abruptly in April 1940. Hitler took the initiative and, using his blitzkrieg tactics, invaded Norway and Denmark. By the end of May Belgium and Holland had surrendered under the German army onslaught and by mid-June 1940 the Germans had marched into Paris. The French signed an armistice agreement before the month was out. The British managed, some say miraculously, to evacuate the bulk of their army from France through the port of Dunkirk at the beginning of June, leaving behind most of their equipment. Mussolini, seeing that Germany was now in control of the whole of Europe, east and west, brought Italy into the war, on the German side, naturally.

Britain now stood alone and braced itself for an expected German invasion. Winston Churchill who had taken over as Prime Minister in May 1940, made rousing speeches to uplift the morale of the British people. In July 1940 the Germans took over the Channel Islands and the British sank the French fleet.

The Fascist leader Mosley was interned together with other undesirables and later the British Union of Fascists was banned. The British government also interned German Jewish refugees, treating them as enemy aliens because of their German nationality. For some reason, the British authorities would not make any distinction between real enemies of the state and refugees who were clearly enemies of the enemy. These Jews suffered physically from attacks by Fascist anti-Semites with whom they were interned.

The Battle of Britain raged over the skies of Britain during the month of August. The Royal Air Force emerged victorious and Churchill made a speech saying that never before in the history of mankind has so much been owed by so many to so few. The Germans had failed to control the skies over Britain but the invasion threat remained and Churchill explained that he had nothing to offer but blood, tears, toil and sweat.

The Germans changed their tactics. Lord Haw Haw, otherwise known as William Joyce, the British Fascist turned German propagandist, broadcast from Germany to say that London would be hit hard by German bombers and that the Jewish quarter of the Borough of Stepney would be hit hardest of all. The Germans were true to their word. On the night of September 13, 1940, over three hundred German bombers attacked the East End of London and the Jewish Chronicle reported that bombing was severe in several, predominantly Jewish districts. Many Jews were killed and more injured. Whole Jewish families were wiped out. There was heavy property damage. The Jewish areas were among the first to be attacked and the Jewish death rate was above the average.

Shulem did not need to read these reports to know the extent of the damage and loss of life. The air-raid shelter allocated to the family and others in the street was situated in West Tenter Street. The authorities were so unprepared for the type and intensity of the air attack that they located the shelter in the basement of a cork factory adjacent to a petrol station. At the height of the air raid, Shulem and his fellow shelterers could hear the noise of battle taking place above them. They were shaken by the explosions of falling bombs and they could hear the continuous noise of anti-aircraft fire. What they did not know was that the whole area around them was ablaze and that instead of being in a shelter, they were actually in a fire trap. Fortunately a passing air-raid warden realised the danger. He called them out and escorted them through the burning streets, with bombs continuing to fall, to the safety of a larger and more suitable shelter.

The next morning Shulem discovered that the adjoining house to his had been completely gutted by fire from an incendiary bomb. Firemen did not have sufficient water to douse all the fires that were raging that night, so they soaked the adjoining buildings in order to contain the fires. Shulem's house, although damaged, remained habitable. It also formed the prop for the other terraced houses in the street that had been shaken by the force of nearby bomb blasts. Yulus's infant school had been destroyed that night and sadly, the young man who had accompanied him to the dairy some years earlier, was killed when the Buckle Street tenement buildings opposite the school, collapsed. He had joined the Auxiliary Fire Service at the outbreak of the war. His mother received a letter from the Fire Brigade Authorities stating that if it were not for the gallantry of men like him, there may well have been another great fire of London. After the raid, the Nazi's broadcast that Hitler had achieved his wish to rain bombs on Jews and that Nazi airmen had enjoyed the sight of the burning houses of the accursed Jews.

In October, the RAF retaliated by bombing Berlin and the Germans continued their attacks on British cities with renewed vigour. In November, the City of Coventry was devastated, and in December there was the fire blitz on the City of London, that also enveloped the East End. In September, Japan signed a ten year pact with Germany and Italy, and in November, Hungary and Slovakia joined the Axis. America remained sympathetic to the British cause, but neutral. The Germans had a non-aggression pact with the USSR that had recently encompassed the Baltic states of Latvia, Lithuania and Estonia. Britain stood alone against the Nazi might. Their only real ally at the time was the Jewish people who were prepared to fight to the death against the Nazis anywhere in the world. And yet the British did not treat them as such. German Jewish refugees were interned and in February 1941, many German Jewish refugees were even deported on the infamous Dunera ship to Australia. Immigration into Palestine was restricted and the call by the Jews for the establishment of a Jewish army was left unanswered. It was estimated that over 350,000 dedicated Jewish fighters could have been recruited worldwide for such an army that was never to be formed. Only in 1944, late, very late in the war was the Jewish Brigade of the British army established with mainly Palestinian Jewish recruits. It fought in the front line of the Italian campaign.

Anti-Semitism did not disappear from the English scene. Fascists continued to make contradictory attacks against the Jews of London. On the one hand they maintained that the Jews had taken for themselves all the best places on the deep underground railway platforms that had been opened up as shelters each night. On the other hand, they complained that the Jew-cowards had all fled from London to avoid the bombing. They provided no explanation as to how the Jews could be in two places at the same time.

Shulem experienced a measure of relief that Yulus had remained in the countryside during the German bombing onslaught, although he remained concerned that the boy's Jewish upbringing might be eroded while living in a Gentile environment. He therefore considered sending Yulus to stay with his aunt, Rivka's sister, in New York. America might be far away, but Yulus would be among relatives and in a Jewish environment. The American government had, ironically, agreed to accept the entry of ten thousand British children, in order that they should be safe from the German bombers. They had previously declined to accept a similar number of European Jewish refugee children. Shulem noted the distinction with a tinge of bitterness. British children - that's fine, Jewish refugee children - no way. It might also be ironic, thought Shulem sardonically, if some of the British children accepted by the Americans, were also Jewish. Yulus was due to sail to New York later that year. Fortunately for him, he missed sailing on the first 'childrens' ship as it was fully booked. In September 1940, the ship, the City of Benares was most unfortunate. It was sunk by the Germans on its way across the Atlantic ocean. Three hundred and six souls were lost including ninety children. The transfer of children across the Atlantic was then discontinued. The risks were considered too high. Yulus remained where he was for the time being, in Sohamelycambs.

In January 1941, Shulem received a letter from his brother who had escaped, together with his wife and daughter, from Danzig. In exchange for money the Nazis had allowed over five hundred Jews to leave the town in late August. They made their way by train to Bratislawa, the Slovakian Danube river port town. There, they boarded boats that took them down river to the Rumanian port of Tulcea. In mid-September his brother and family embarked with about nineteen hundred other refugees on the Atlantic, a 700 ton ship that took them across the Black Sea, through the Bosphorus and Dardanelles, and brought them to the port of Haifa on the Mediterranean coast of Palestine. It was a dreadful, slow journey that took two and one half months. They feared being sunk by the German navy throughout the journey and hung aloft perambulators to indicate to other ships that there were women and children aboard. The ship was overcrowded, people fell sick. There were cases of typhoid. About two hundred people died on the way and were buried at sea.

Two other small refugee ships, the Pacific and the Milos had already arrived in Haifa by the same route. The British had been turning ships away from Palestine, but now they had decided on a new policy. The refugees were to be deported to a distant British colony. The passengers of the two earlier ships had not been allowed to enter Palestine. They had been transferred to a 12,000 ton deportation ship called the Patria that was anchored in the Haifa port and waiting to receive the passengers from the Atlantic. No-one was anxious to go and Shulem's brother and family happily allowed others to go first. As some passengers left the ship, their own crowded condition suddenly improved. They actually had space to breathe. But all this was short-lived. As some of the Atlantic passengers approached the deportation ship, there was a large explosion and the Patria listed to one side and soon sank. Two hundred and sixty refugees drowned in that calamity. The Haggana, the Jewish underground organization, had intended to delay the sailing of the Patria by disabling the engine room and then to appeal to the international community to allow the exhausted refugees to stay in Palestine. Too much explosive was used and its positioning was wrong. The explosive device blew a gaping hole in the side of the ship that sank with tragic consequences.

This was only half the story. Those refugees who were actually on the Patria when it sank and managed to escape from the sinking ship, were allowed to stay in Palestine. Their number was deducted from the immigration quota. Those refugees who were on the Atlantic were interned for a short while in the Atlit Illegal Immigrant Detention Camp situated just outside Haifa. The women and children were held separately from the men. On Monday, December 9, 1940, British soldiers and the Palestine Police ordered the Atlantic refugees to leave their huts. They were to march to Haifa port and be deported that very day. Rumours of the deportation order had reached the refugees the previous day and they had devised a method to prevent their deportation. The British, it was said, were gentlemen. All that had to be done was for all of them to remove their clothes and be naked when the soldiers would come to take them. Shulem's brother explained that they were convinced that no British gentleman would force naked men women and children into the street. How mistaken we were, he wrote. A soldier came into the hut where the men were laying in their beds naked, covered with their blankets. Everybody out, he shouted. No-one moved. Come on you, he said to the nearest bed occupant, pulling off the blanket. Blimey! He exclaimed in surprise as the naked body was revealed, and retreated out of the hut. Everyone was delighted, certain that their ruse had succeeded. *Nechteke toog*, literally yesterday's day, which means, by no means at all. An officer came in with a sergeant and ordered all the people to be tipped out of their beds and forced outside. There was a mad scramble for underwear and trousers. The women's huts had similar experiences. Some sympathetic policemen threw blankets to the women to cover their nakedness. Blanket-covered, partly dressed, they were marched to the port where they boarded two ships that were to take them to they knew not where. Their destination could not be revealed for security reasons. When Shulem had read a newspaper report that one thousand five hundred Jews from the refugee ship Atlantic were being deported to an unnamed British colony, he had had no idea that his brother and family were among the deportees. When he received the news, he was alarmed at the way they had been treated, but relieved that they were alive and safe. Who would have thought that the British would behave so brutally? Or that they would have taken the trouble to divert much needed shipping in the middle of the war, to transport desperate, unfortunate refugees to some distant colony? What harm would have resulted if they had let them stay in Palestine? Later it was revealed that they had been deported to Mauritius, a little island in the Indian Ocean.

Chapter 17

Yulus settled down nicely in his new billet. His new foster parents were of an older generation, with a grandson of similar age to Yulus. He would visit his grandparents from time to time and even stay a while when he fell foul of his father's temper. Better out of harm's way, the grandmother would say. If he has been naughty then he deserves punishment, the grandfather would declaim. But mother and grandmother would have the best of the argument and the boy would stay 'out of harm's way' and free to pester his grandmother for money for sweets or the cinema. I wish I were punished that way when I was a boy, sighed the grandfather resignedly.

The grandfather was a cobbler of the old school. His shop was situated in the centre of the High Street. Living quarters were behind and above the shop. A hanging bell would be activated with the opening of the door from the High Street. The bell was rarely required to notify entry of a customer, because the cobbler was almost always at his bench facing the window that looked out on to the High Street. He seemed able to watch all the passers-by without it detracting from his immediate task of paring leather or hammering home nails. He had grey hair and his half lens spectacles balanced at the end of his nose. He needed the spectacles for close work only, he viewed his customers and passers-by over the top of the frames. He looked the spitting image of the cobbler in the advertisement for Phillips' patent soles that hung on one of the walls. If he were not at his bench, then he would be standing at the mechanical shoe polishing machine that he would allow Yulus to operate when he occasionally offered to be of some assistance. Yulus was fascinated by the dexterity with which the old man would wield his paring knife, as he cut away surplus leather around the edges of newly repaired shoes. He also watched with unabated awe, as the cobbler would place several small nails in a row between his lips and blow them with alacrity, one by one into the leather sole prior to hitting them home firmly into the leather with the flat peen of his hammer. The nails miraculously found their correct equidistant position around the rim of the sole of the shoe, more accurately than a professional darts player. How do you do it? Yulus asked. If I told you, you would be as wise as I am, was his reply. No, really? Yulus insisted. Experience, my boy, he said, and added quickly, don't you try or you might swallow them, and then what will I tell your father? The old man had soon gauged that Yulus's respect for his father and his father's opinion was a basic factor that determined much of his behaviour. What would your father say? he would ask, if Yulus ventured to do something that the old man considered was too adventurous. A rapport grew between the elderly cobbler and the young

Yulus. The old man would often defend him in arguments that developed with the grandson.

That autumn, the blackberries grew with profusion in the countryside hedgerows. Yulus has always, ever since that year, associated blackberries with *Yom Kippur*, the Jewish fast day that lasts twenty-five hours from dusk of one day until after dark of the next. Pre-Barmitzvah boys are under no obligation to fast, but their virility was often measured by the length of time they could maintain the fast. Hail to those who could fast for the whole period, no easy task for a twelve year-old. Yulus was determined to pass the test. He explained the importance of this day in the Jewish calendar to the grandmother. All Jews fast on this day, he said. It was good for the soul. He asked her to provide him with an early supper that night. She willingly complied with his request, not really believing that this plump short-trousered boy with socks falling about his ankles, would, or could go without food for such a long period even though it was good for the soul. That evening, when he returned home after the *Yom Kippur* eve *Kol Nidre* religious service in the Conservative Club Hall that was serving as a Synagogue, she offered him his usual hot cocoa drink. He politely refused, not tonight thank you, he said as he went upstairs to bed. Next morning he also refused breakfast. What, no breakfast? she exclaimed as he left the house for the Synagogue, but you will be home for lunch? Again he explained that the fast would last until dark that day. It doesn't seem right, she said, for a young boy to go without food or drink for such a long time. If that's his religion, said the grandfather, you should not interfere. Still, she said, twenty five hours is a long, long time. She was truly concerned and had visions of the boy collapsing in the street with all the other evacuees and being carted off to hospital. And then people would think the village hadn't been feeding the boys properly. Twenty-five hours without food, she kept repeating, nodding her head in disbelief.

After the morning service, the boys had free time before the combined afternoon and evening religious services began. They ventured out into the countryside. The sun was shining brightly even though autumn was in the air. The blackberries were as ripe as they would ever be. By the next day they would be overripe. Those deep, deep purple berries cried out to be eaten. This temptation of Satan had to be resisted, and yet...... The boys went into a huddled conference and came out with a decision. The blackberries could be picked, but not eaten until the fast was over. A basket was collected from one of the billets and soon filled to capacity. No-one, on his absolute honour, ate one berry. Not one even licked the purple juice from his fingers. They marched back to the Conservative Club and placed the basket in a vacant room, out of sight, although hardly out of mind. When the final religious service was over and darkness had fallen, the boys purchased a loaf of bread, sliced it and broke their fast with the most delicious blackberry sandwiches ever, ever tasted.

You must be starving, said the grandmother, when Yulus arrived home. Not really, he said, with the tell-tale purple signs of blackberry juice that he had omitted to wipe away, still visible around the edges of his mouth. I did it, he exclaimed triumphantly. I fasted for the whole twenty-five hours! I never thought it was possible, said the grandmother as she served Yulus with a hot supper. That's real food, she said relieved to find him still on his two feet. I expected you to be carried home, she said with a measure of awe at the power of religious practice and the resilience of the young.

In December, a parcel arrived from London for Yulus. It contained his brother's neatly folded *tallus*, prayer shawl, and his *tefillin*, phylacteries. The accompanying letter from his sister explained that the nasty Germans were still bombing London. Newnham Street and the surrounding area had suffered heavy damage. Electricity and water supplies had been restricted due to damage to power lines, equipment and pipelines. It was felt that it would be wiser for Yulus to stay in Soham over the *Hanukah* and Christmas holidays. Meantime, father felt that Yulus should practice laying *tefillin* in preparation for his Barmitzvah in March, when of course he would come to London. March was only a matter of weeks away and in any event, he would need to come a week or so earlier so that father could make him a new suit. In the present circumstances, it was not possible to obtain a new *tallus* or *tefillin* and so father had sent Yulus those of his sixteen-year old brother who had been evacuated to Scotland together with his eldest sister. The factory in which they both worked, as with many other factories, had been relocated out of London so that essential manufacturing processes would not be interrupted by the continuous aerial bombardment.

The JFS Central School set up a special class for those boys preparing for their Barmitzvah. Yulus had already been learning his *Parsha*, the text of the portion of the *Sefer Torah*, bible, that he would recite, or rather sing, in Synagogue on the specified day. Now, for each lesson, he would take with him the royal blue velvet bag containing the *tefillin*. First of all, said the teacher on the first occasion, first of all, he was fond of using that expression, you need to know why you are participating in this ritual. Does anyone here know why? he elongated the word why, to emphasise its importance. My father said I had to, said one boy, hoping to be provocative. Well, said the teacher, taking the response seriously, that in itself is not a bad reason. We should all remember the commandment that says that one should honour one's parents. But that is not the reason I'm looking for. I know, said another boy, it is to remind Jews that they are bound, both in mind and in heart, to God. Very good, said the master, and I would add that it is also a reminder that God released them from bondage in Egypt. Now that we know why, we can proceed to learn how. But first of all, you need to know that there are two perfectly square leather *beitim*, boxes, one with a long strap for your arm and the other with a shorter looped strap for your head. The boxes contain the texts of four portions of the *Torah*, two from the Book of Exodus and two from the Book of Deuteronomy. They have to be treated with care. I have asked one of the seniors to demonstrate the procedure and I will explain it as we go along. Each of you should carry out every action as it is explained.

First of all, take off your jackets and roll up your left shirt sleeves as high as possible. Yulus took only his left arm out of his jacket and then re-buttoned the jacket from under his arm, leaving the left sleeve hanging limply. His right arm remained in the sleeve of his jacket. That is how my father does it, said Yulus when the teacher looked at him questioningly. That's alright, said the teacher, as long as your left arm is bare. Now watch and then do. First of all, put on your *tallus*, prayer shawl. Right. And now, first of all, we deal with the box for the arm. This box has to be strapped tightly on the upper arm. Remember, it has to be placed on the top of the muscle. This produced a few giggles. Let me see your muscles, called out one wit, a comment that was entirely ignored by the master. It has to be fitted firmly, but not too tightly, he continued, so that it will be on the same level as your heart when you put your arm down. Now, wind the strap three times around the upper arm. See that it forms the Hebrew letter *Sh'in*. I'll explain why that is important in a moment. Next, wind the strap around the lower arm seven times, yes, and now around the palm of the hand three times to form the Hebrew letter *Daled*. Now stop and fix the strap there temporarily but firmly. Next, take the other box and place it in the centre of your forehead with your left hand and pull the looped strap over your head. Tighten the strap being sure to keep the knot of the strap at the nape of your neck. On the back of your head silly! called the master to one of the struggling boys. Now bring the ends of the strap over your shoulders. Good. Now finally, release the strap in the palm of your hand. No, not completely! You have to keep the letter *Daled* intact, that's better. Now, wind the strap three times around the middle finger to form the Hebrew letter *Yod*. Good. Secure the end of the strap into place under one of the bands. Very good. The three Hebrew letters you have formed, spell out the Hebrew word *Shaddai*, which is one of God's names, not to be taken lightly or in vain. The positioning of the *tefillin* on your forehead and next to your heart, also symbolises the coming together of heart and mind when saying prayers.

That's it, at this point you can start *Shachrit*, morning prayers, after which you take off the *tefillin* in the same order as you put them on. Remember to wrap the straps carefully around the four extended bases of the boxes and replace them carefully in your velvet bags. Try practicing for yourselves at home. We can't sir. Why not? They already think we Jews are a bit mad, wearing our hats at mealtimes and fasting all day on *Yom Kippur*. What will they think if they see us tying straps round our heads and arms? He saw the point. I suppose it would be a little difficult to explain, he said and then added, alright then, those of you who have problems can come in a little earlier to school to practice. He ignored the moans of protest. Next time, he announced, we will recite the appropriate prayers at each stage in the process.

The weeks soon passed and Yulus made his way home to London. His youngest sister met him at Liverpool Street Station and they made their way home, first into Middlesex Street in the direction of his school and then on the same route that Yulus used to take each day, to and from the school. But this was not the London that Yulus once knew. Bomb damage was evident on all sides. The JFS School premises had been hit shortly before his arrival and damaged beyond repair. They made a short diversion to look at Buckle Street where the frame of his infants' school stood, totally gutted. The site opposite, where tenement buildings once stood, was a huge pile of rubble. Is that where our friend from Bacon Street was killed fighting the fire last September? Yulus asked. Yes, said his sister sadly, and added, what a waste! They stood there in silence, in his honour, before continuing on their way. They passed Great Alie Street Synagogue. That's still standing, said Yulus. Yes, said his sister, but only by chance. It was hit by a bomb, luckily one of the smaller ones. The hole in its roof has been covered and most of the damage to the interior has been patched up. You can still have your *Barmitzvah* there. Thank goodness for that, said Yulus. Newnham Street was hardly recognisable. There were gaps where houses once stood. The plot next to his own house was empty. The walls of his own house and the one on the other side of the cleared site showed the blackened scars of the fire that had completely destroyed the home of the neighbours with whom he and his family had competed in song on Passover *Seder* nights. When could that have been? Surely not just the *Seder* before last? He was amazed that so much could have happened in such a short time. Luckily, said his sister, none of them was hurt, but they did lose all their possessions. That's luck? asked Yulus. In these days, if you remain unhurt, that is considered luck, she replied. She also explained that the authorities had cleared the site and intended to build a concrete emergency water supply reservoir there. So that is what those letters EWS stand for, he said. He had noticed them painted on a number of low walls, inside a white cross formed by diagonals. Yes, she said, the firemen do not want to be caught out again, as they were last year, by a water shortage.

Home was even stranger than the surrounding area. Father had not yet come home from work and only the *Mema* was there to greet him. Her welcome was warm enough, but where was the old homely atmosphere? Even in the evening, when Shulem did come home and they sat down for supper, the whole atmosphere seemed strange. There were only four of them and father seemed so much older. There was none of the usual banter. When he put his things in the upstairs front bedroom, Yulus realised that if he were to sleep in that bed that night, he would be sleeping on his own and not with his brothers. One was up in Scotland, one was somewhere in the army, one was working on the land and the eldest was, in any event, married and living elsewhere with his wife and her family. Shulem and family no longer slept at home. Instead they stayed the night in the basement of the building of the paper makers, Wiggins and Teape, in Mansell Street. The basement had been converted into an air raid shelter that served as a relatively safe nightly refuge for many people in the district. Each night people would take their bedding with them and each morning traipse back home with it, hoping against hope, that their houses were still standing.

Shulem measured Yulus for his new suit. He had already bought the material in the market. Later that week, he brought home the suit for a try-on. The jacket fitted well, except for the sleeves that were a little too long. *Nisht kein probleme*, that's no problem, said Shulem, *mir ken es bult recht machen*, we can soon fix that. But the trousers, the trousers! Yulus refused to put them on. They are short trousers, exclaimed Yulus excitedly, I'm not going to wear shorts for my *Barmitzvah*. Shulem was taken by surprise, he hadn't expected such a strong negative reaction. He took one look at that cringed up disappointed face and soon realised that the boy was right when he insisted, almost shouting, almost crying, that all *Barmitzvah* boys wore long trousers. It was true. The wearing of long trousers was one of the signs that indicated that a boy had grown to a certain stage of maturity. And he had grown so much in the past year. He had become a lot taller and slimmer since he had seen him the previous *Pesach*, Passover. The boy had truly grown, he seemed more serious and less boisterous. He should have known better than to have made shorts. He just hadn't thought of his youngest in long trousers. Tomorrow, he said to himself, I will get some more material. To Yulus, he said in a conciliatory voice, *Sha, sha, du bist rechtig, morgen vill Ich aheim brengen lunger hoisen*, you are right, tomorrow, I'll bring home long trousers. Yulus felt calmer as Shulem measured his inside leg. It was just a mistake, said his sister. Father simply didn't realise how big you had grown. He hasn't seen you for nearly a year and still thinks of you as his baby son. Next week, after he hears you sing your *Parsha* in *Shul*, he will know and see how much you have grown up. *Du duff nisht zorgen*, added the *Mema* in sympathy, *allus vill zeyen gut*, you need not worry, everything will be alright.

162

The great day arrived. Yulus, felt awkward in his new navy blue suit, clean white shirt and royal blue tie and yet comfortable and proud to be wearing long trousers for the first time. He walked beside Shulem as he had done in the past on many a Sabbath on their way to the nearby Great Alie Street Synagogue. At Shulem's behest, he had given his new black shoes an extra rub with a soft cloth to bring up the shine to the level of his father's well worn and well-rubbed shoes. Both pairs glinted in the cool early morning, early March, sunshine. Both father and son carried their velvet *tallus zackels*, prayer shawl bags, tucked under their left arms. Father and son of similar build, the son imitating his father's upright stance, both aware of the importance of the occasion, walked confidently through the war damaged streets. The *Mema* and his sister had embraced Yulus in turn as he left the house. They wished him good luck and promised to come to the *Shul* shortly after they had prepared the front parlour for the lunch-time party. They needed to take down the blackout material from the windows and set the table. Don't worry, we'll be there in good time, said his sister removing a speck of dust from his brand new suit and making a final adjustment to his tie and straightening his cap. She was surprised to see that he did not object. *Gay gezinteheit*, go in good health, said the *Mema*.

Shulem and Yulus entered the lobby of the *Shul* and through the already open big brown wooden double doors. Yulus noticed the deep untidy grooves that had been cut into the once well varnished doors by falling shrapnel and debris. They rinsed their hands at the ritual sink in the lobby and entered the main hall of the Synagogue. Instead of going straight to his usual seat, Shulem took Yulus by the arm, to re-introduce him to the Rabbi who was already seated next to the Holy Ark. The Rabbi shook his hand and said he remembered him from before the war. Didn't you once refuse to be blessed? he asked in order to confirm his recognition. Yulus blushed and remembered that it was always said of the old Rabbi, that he forgets nothing. Now he knew it to be true. Next he shook hands with the *Shammas*, the Sexton, who was an old friend of the family and knew Yulus well. He lived in the same street. *Gedenk tsu singen hoich und clar, und allus vill zeyen gutt, zer gutt*, remember to sing loud and clear and all will be well, very well, he said encouragingly.

The *Chazen*, Cantor, took his place on the *Bima*, platform, and the Sabbath morning service began. Yulus looked around the Synagogue hall. He noticed with pleasure that his brother-in-law who was now a special policeman had just come in. He had not been sure whether his duties would have allowed him to attend. He was wearing his uniform. Other than Shulem, he was the only male member of the family in attendance. How different from the *Barmitzvah* of his brother four years previously when the *Shul* had been full to capacity and all the family were present. Now there were only about thirty people in the congregation. He was told that this was much better than on a normal day when the attendance was barely enough to form a *minyon*, the quorum of ten persons required for certain prayers. Only one of his friends was there.

The population of London, as a whole, had diminished and that of East London more so than other areas due to the heavy bombing. At the height of the air raids, the population had dwindled to a quarter of its pre-war level. The young men were in the armed forces or evacuated with reserved occupation factories. Children had been evacuated with their schools and young mothers were evacuated with their babies. So who was left in London at this time, to take the brunt of the German aerial bombardment? Paradoxically, it was mainly the older generation and the middle-aged who stayed behind and were the air raid wardens and often the heroes of the day. In the Jewish quarter, it was the *alter Yidden*, the elderly Jews, and many of them had now been forced to move out of the area when their houses had been destroyed.

The ladies' gallery of the *Shul* was sparsely occupied. The *Mema* and his sister had arrived, as had his married sister who was leaning over the gallery rail smiling and waving to attract Yulus's attention. He waved back and also acknowledged the waves of some of his sisters' friends and the family of the *Shammas* who had come to give him support and encouragement.

The *Sefer Torah* was brought out from the Holy Ark and readings from it began. Soon it was Shulem's turn to stand by the Cantor and say the Blessings for a portion of the law. Some other members of the congregation also took their turns to say the Blessings as did the special policeman wearing his *tallus* over his uniform. Then Yulus's name was called and he ascended the *Bima* and stood between the Cantor and the *Shammas*. He looked up at the hole in the ceiling that had been covered with green tarpaulin. The Rabbi had explained to him that the hole was to his benefit, as his prayers would reach the ears of God without hindrance. Thus were the evils of war rationalised. Yulus sang the blessings that preceded the reading of his portion of the law, in full voice. The Cantor pointed to the text with his silver embossed pointer, shaped as a miniature hand with the index finger extended. The hall was hushed waiting for Yulus to continue. He took a deep breath, but before another note emerged from his now open mouth, the wail of an air raid siren filled the air. The loud raucous undulating warble indicated that an air raid was imminent. The congregation stirred, some started to move. The Rabbi sat up and raised his head. He took his eye off the copy of the text before him for a brief moment only, and then resumed his usual position, bent over his holy books. The cantor coughed. The ladies began to murmur and everyone, other than the Rabbi, looked at the *Shammas* for guidance. The *Shammas*, as usual, rose to the occasion. He slapped the palm of his hand down hard on the reading desk. It resounded like a clap of thunder and could be heard above the wailing noise of the siren. Ladies, he shouted in English in his ringing voice, *rabutai*, gentlemen, he roared in Yiddish, *loifen nisht, voos kon zeyen? Zatsen! Der Barmitzvah volt singen*, Don't run, what can happen? stay seated, the *Barmitzvah* wants to sing! The Rabbi nodded consent. The wail of the siren ceased and all in the congregation resumed their seats. Shush! Shush, admonished the *Shammas*, and soon the hall was silent again. The *Shammas* turned to the Cantor and said in Yiddish a *Barmitzvah* is a *Barmitzvah*. and to Yulus he quietly said, Yulus, *mach es geshvint*, Yulus, say it quickly.

The continuous wail of the all-clear siren was heard towards the end of the *Shabbas* service that was completed a little earlier than usual. A small concession that the religious allowed the threatening German bombers. But it did not end before the Rabbi gave his *drusha*, sermon, in which he explained that in these difficult and tragic times, it was even more important to initiate another responsible member of the community while so many Jews were being slaughtered by the barbaric Nazis. He congratulated Yulus on his performance and on his steadfastness in continuing with the reading of his portion of the *Torah* despite the uncalled-for interruption. He presented Yulus with a copy of the Authorised Daily Prayer Book in Hebrew and English popularly known as the Singer's Prayer Book after the compiler and translator. It was always said with humour that no East End London Jewish home was complete without the two Singers, the Singer's sewing machine and the Singer's Prayer Book. The Rabbi explained that every *Barmitzvah* boy received a brand new copy of the *Siddur*, but in the present circumstances no new books were available and so he had searched for a copy in the best possible condition and entered an inscription to make the *Siddur*, Yulus's own. Let us all be witnesses to better times, he concluded to shouts of Hear, Hear from the congregation.

At the appropriate time and in line with tradition, sweets were thrown from the gallery. Although they were few, they were of great value, as sweet rationing was in force and people had sacrificed part of their rations to make such a symbolic offering. Yulus and his friend gathered up the sweets after the service, before making for home where the table had been laid for the birthday party. It was a modest affair with sardine sandwiches and hot cups of tea being the main fare. Yulus's sister read out letters of congratulation that had been received from those who could not be present. The *Shammas* made a presentation of a copy of the Old Testament in Hebrew and English and a pocket size book of Grace and Blessings. The books, he said, could also not be new, but God's words would last forever. Shulem's cousin presented Yulus with a new Cyclopaedia that sported the flags of the British Empire and foreign countries. He said that, in contrast, he was not at all sure that all the countries represented would remain intact for too long but he did indeed hope that the accursed German flag with its swastika would soon be erased. It is about time the Jews had a flag of their own, someone said and everyone drank to that from the small wine glasses that had been half filled with sweet red wine. Yulus's friend presented him with an illustrated *Hagadah*, the book that contains the Passover service. This is no ordinary book, said his friend, because it contains a vital printing error in the English translation. Allow me to read the errata slip. Page 17, Para 2, line 3 should read "Unleavened." The significance of this correction was soon understood when it was realised that it referred to one of the four questions asked on *Seder* night. His friend now read out the passage. Why is this night different from all other nights? On all other nights we may eat leavened or unleavened while on this night only ..... He paused dramatically. Here, he said, they have printed the word "leavened" instead of "unleavened." Everyone roared with laughter. You must keep that book, said someone, it will truly be worth a lot in due course, like a misprint on stamps. Who knows? But it will always make a good talking point, said another. Yulus made a short speech, thanking everyone for coming and, prompted by his sister, expressed his appreciation for the presents he had received. He took advantage of the occasion to say that he would use the money gifts towards a bicycle that was so essential in rural England. Shulem took the hint and said that he would see what he could do on Yulus's next trip home, in the summer holidays.

When the family emerged from the air raid shelter the following morning, they found the usual tables set up by the emergency services at strategic points along the way. People were registering the known casualties and damage done by the night's very heavy bombing. They also found that Newnham Street had been cordoned off.. They were prohibited from entry because of an unexploded bomb that had fallen in the street. Find somewhere else to stay until we sort it out, said the official. Shulem, the *Mema*, Yulus and his sister traipsed through the rubble strewn streets to his married sister's apartment in Myrdle Street off Commercial Road. As luck would have it, she had returned to London with her baby a few months earlier only to be bombed out of her apartment shortly after her return. She, the baby and husband were not injured but had had to find refuge with Shulem until alternative accommodation could be found. She had moved away only a few weeks earlier and now ironically, Shulem and family would have to stay with her until their housing situation was sorted out. Yulus accompanied his brother-in-law to the house in Newnham Street in order to retrieve some essentials required for a stay over. The special police uniform provided an entry permit to the prohibited area. Yulus and the special policeman gingerly approached the crater in the road very near to the house and peered over to see the fins of a two thousand pound bomb pointing threateningly at them. It seems that Hitler also wanted to give you a birthday present, the brother-in-law said. They entered the house. It feels very rickety here, said Yulus. They hurriedly collected some belongings and made their way back to Myrdle Street.

The local officials later said that even if the bomb did not explode, the foundations of the house had been so badly damaged that it could no longer be occupied. The contents had to be removed before the house collapsed. The married sister's apartment was small and too cramped for all the family and so Yulus had to cut short his visit to London. He had hoped to stay over until after *Pesach*, Passover, but it was not to be and returned to Soham the next day. When we are settled, said Shulem, you will be able to come home for the summer holidays.

Why are you back so early? asked the grandmother, you are very welcome, but we were not expecting you for another week. Yulus explained the circumstances whereupon the cobbler said it looks as though Hitler has indeed been looking for you. Just after you left for London a parachute bomb fell only six hundred yards from the Shade school. Windows were broken and some ceilings were damaged from the blast. They weren't aiming at him, said the grandmother, taking her husband's remark seriously, they obviously just dropped part of their load as they were racing for home after attacking the nearby RAF base. Still, continued the cobbler in his avuncular tone, first they bombed his infant's school, then they bombed his school in London and nearly bombed the school near here. They bombed the Synagogue where he was being, you know, kind of confirmed, and then they dropped a bomb right near his father's house. What should we make of that? It's a good thing he keeps moving about, that's all I can say, he said laughing at is own wit, keeps them on their toes. Do be serious, his wife retorted. Serious? he queried, serious? he repeated, about what? this lousy war? If we can't raise a laugh now and again, where will we be? Don't you agree Yulus? Yulus nodded half-heartedly. He didn't think the war was funny. Anyhow, said the cobbler turning to Yulus, welcome home son. We're really glad to see you back and are truly sorry you had such a rough time.

Chapter 18

Shulem was offered by the local authorities, and in the circumstances had to accept, alternative accommodation in the adjoining Borough of Bethnal Green. He was distressed. His whole world had been upset. It had taken many years of struggle to establish himself in the Yiddish speaking area of the East End of London. He had become accustomed to his environment that was in many ways very convenient. His work was in walking distance of his home. His Synagogue was nearby. His Yiddish speaking friends were in the vicinity. Petticoat Lane and the stalls and shops in the surrounding streets were very close. Jewish shops abounded. There was no worry as to whether the food shops were kosher. All those that he and his family used were sanctioned by the Chief Rabbi's Office. The shopkeepers and stallholders in the area understood Yiddish even if they did not all speak it well. His children had had the opportunity to get a Jewish education and to live in a Jewish environment where there were Jewish Youth Clubs. The local libraries had a good selection of Yiddish books, even though he may have read most of them. Many of them were worth reading more than once. There was also the Yiddish Theatre and the Yiddish speaking club at the Workers' Circle. And in recent years there was the Polish poet Abraham Nahum Stencl, who after establishing himself in Berlin, had to flee the Nazis. He was one of the few more recent refugees who had chosen to settle in Whitechapel to be amongst the Yiddish speaking Jews. Shulem enjoyed reading his Yiddish booklets, *Leben und Loschen*, Language and Life, that he sold personally. Here was an immigrant who added to the character of the Yiddish speaking district, and brought hope for its future development.

Now, the war had come, this terrible, terrible war. The Germans, the Nazis, had wreaked havoc, first across the whole of Europe and now here in London. Some people tried to distinguish between the Germans and the Nazis. No, no, they would say, it's not the Germans, it's the Nazis. Shulem, for the life of him, could not accept the distinction. There would be no Nazis, if it were not for the Germans. God knows what had happened to his mother and his sister and her family since those barbarians invaded Poland. Those terrible reports in the paper about Jews being rounded up in his mother's town of Mlawa sent shivers down his spine and gave him restless nights. He knew nothing of the fate of his brother and family in Hamburg, news of whom he had not received from any source since the outbreak of war.

Shulem had decided some years ago that he did not want to move to a more salubrious area, as his eldest son was always encouraging him to do. What will I do there that I can't do here? he would ask. Where will I work? Why should I travel long distances to work? What about Yiddish and *Yiddishkeit?* the cultural ethos of Yiddish speaking Jews. Why should I re-establish somewhere else what I already have here? Oh! The bathroom? you say, well once some of you are married and living elsewhere, I will have room to improve the facilities here. He was steadfast in this view as were many of his Yiddish speaking friends. And Rivka, may her soul rest in peace, dear departed Rivka, had supported him in this stand. Now he had been forced to move to another working class area that could hardly be considered his, or his eldest son's, area of choice.

He now had a ground floor apartment in a recently erected estate of several residential buildings that had been designed to provide the minimum requirements for decent living. In terms of living accommodation it had the advantage over his previous house in that it had its own bathroom. It also had a separate toilet that was next to the small kitchen. Yulus once drew a sketch of the apartment in response to the master's request for a design of an ideal apartment, in an architectural lesson at school. The master took one look at the design and rejected it out of hand. Who would put a toilet close to a kitchen? he exclaimed. And this bedroom? Access is only through the parlour. That is totally unacceptable! But that is what we have got, protested Yulus. It cannot be, insisted the teacher, you must have got it wrong. The culprit is not me, protested Yulus, but rather the original architect. Clearly the apartment was not ideal from many angles, but one always had to remember that there was a war on and choices were not exactly plentiful.

The new address had a fine ring to it. During a lesson in elocution, a subject that continued to be taught at the JFS even during evacuation, Yulus was asked to state his home address. Pursing his lips so as to pronounce the words clearly without an East End London accent, Yulus carefully and slowly articulated his new address. Maitland House, Waterloo Gardens, Bishops Way, Bethnal Green, London East Two. A very nice address, said the master who had groaned when he heard the name of the district. Now repeat it, leaving out the words Bethnal Green. He too knew the snob value of a good address.

Waterloo Gardens was a misnomer. Apart from a narrow strip of grass that bordered the buildings, no gardens were to be found in that street. And as for Bishop's Way, many moons must have passed since a Bishop had ventured down that thoroughfare. The residential estate had, so far, escaped the bombing that had hit other sites in the area, and so could be considered a relatively safe abode. Although Jews lived in the area, it could not be considered a Jewish district. *Shabbas* was not like *Shabbas* in Newnham Street. The front doorsteps were not whitened on a Friday afternoon and there were no outward signs of welcome for the Jewish Sabbath. The nearest Synagogue was a goodly walk away, on the other side of Victoria Park. The park was the only real compensation to the dreariness of the area. It was not too far away and on sunny days it was a delight to stroll through the greenery and around the small boating lake. The magnificence of the trees could be admired and the birds could be heard and seen enjoying their freedom, flittering from branch to branch, unaware of the trials and tribulations of mankind. At dusk, an unsuspecting stroller, might be surprised by bushes that moved in response to muffled instructions. These were not supernatural happenings but rather camouflaged volunteers of the Home Guard who sometimes conducted practice exercises in the park in preparation for an expected German invasion.

Shulem now had to make use of his limited English. While he understood the language well enough to get by, his spoken English was truly limited. He had to travel by bus to work each day and he would now come into contact with Gentiles much more frequently in his new surroundings. At sixty-two it was no easy task for him to wrap his tongue around the English words and speak the language as it should be spoken. Umm speak perfect English, Umm speak, he would say laughingly to his friends, with a strong Yiddish accent. In time he came to accept the restrictions of his new circumstances. As he told his friends, *Ich hob nisht kein brerer*, I have no other option. He would add in consolation that his discomfort was as nothing when compared to the suffering of the Jews in Europe.

Shulem soon made friends with some Yiddish speaking Jews whom he met at the Synagogue that he now attended every Friday and Saturday. He would meet with these friends on Saturday afternoons at an appointed bench in the park where they formed, what he jokingly called, the Shadow Yiddisher Cabinet. He was dubbed the Foreign Secretary because he followed worldwide events so assiduously. He discussed with them the German takeover of Yugoslavia in mid-April 1941 and the fall of Greece a few weeks later. He complained about the French when they arrested a thousand Jews in Paris in May. He also berated the Vichy government for applying restrictions on Jews in June and arresting twelve thousand of them on the pretext that they were plotting to hinder Franco-German cooperation. What did the Vichy government expect of the Jews? Offer assistance to the Nazis? Betray their people as the Vichy French were doing? It was a good thing that the British, with the Free French troops had taken over Syria, especially after the anti-British revolt in Iraq. At least the Jews in Palestine would feel a little safer. It was not difficult to fathom the British government's attitude in this matter. It had obviously made the move for strategic purposes. Certainly not to protect the Jews. This was made quite clear by the real Foreign Secretary, Anthony Eden. His major policy speech on the Middle East in June made no reference whatsoever to the Jews. And what about Rudolph Hess, Hitler's emissary and rabid anti-Semite, who had landed in Scotland the previous month? What might he be offering the British government? Some sort of alliance? He will not get very far, was the general conclusion. After Munich, the British would have no truck with the perfidious Germans.

Members of the Yiddisher Cabinet did not need Shulem to tell them the significance of Hitler's invasion of the USSR on June 21, 1941. The news was startling and disconcerting. The Jewish press reported that there were now eight million Jews in the battle area, many of whom were being evacuated by the Russian forces. The British had now come to the conclusion that the Nazis were a greater menace than the Bolsheviks who had suddenly become their allies. The Jewish Chronicle reported that the General in charge of the Soviet Air Force was a Jew bearing the name Jacob Shmushkevitch. Perhaps now the Gentile world will understand that Jews were not lambs ready for slaughter, but fighters of the first order. The news of the early advances by the German forces was not at all encouraging. But everyone remembered Napoleon and hoped that Hitler's fate on the Russian steppes would not be less drastic than his famous French predecessor. At least now, Britain did not stand alone against the Nazi barbarians. And who knows? Maybe the Americans will join in the fight against the Germans. They were certainly friendly neutrals. They were helping with sorely needed supplies and also by sending troops to take over Iceland from the British who had occupied it earlier, to prevent the island from being occupied by the Germans. The British garrison in Iceland was thereby released for other wartime duties.

On the home front, the Yiddisher Cabinet examined the position. The German air force had chosen to rain bombs on London and especially on the Jews of the East End of London. Lord Haw Haw, the British Fascist who had defected to Germany, promised in his propaganda broadcasts in English, from Germany, that London would be hit hard, and the Borough of Stepney, where over seventy thousand Jews were living, would be hit hardest of all. His promise had been kept. The area was the first to be hit and was hit the hardest. The German bombs had taken Jewish lives and destroyed several Jewish schools and Synagogues and numerous houses in which Jews had lived. East London Jewry was not outside the orbit of Nazi terror.

The whole Jewish and Yiddish infrastructure in the area had been devastated. A great proportion of the Yiddish speaking population had already been forced, by the persistent and destructive bombing, to move out of the area. And if the bombing persisted, as it no doubt would, then the whole Yiddish infrastructure would be totally and irreparably destroyed. The result would be the end of the compact and comprehensive East End London Jewish community that derived its character from the Yiddish speakers.

The Anglicised and emancipated members of the Jewish community were already on their way out of the East End of London, prior to the outbreak of the war. Each found his or her way to escape as soon as economic conditions allowed. But the Yiddish speakers, cocooned in their religion and Yiddishkeit saw every reason to stay put, that is, until they were forced out by the deliberate targeting of the German bombers. There were some observers who said that the Jewish quarter was not a specific target, but had simply suffered damage because of its proximity to the London Docks. One might accept this argument if a few, or even several, stray bombs had hit the area, but not when both the extraordinary anti-Semitic obsession of the Nazis and the immense scale of bomb damage in the Jewish quarter is taken into account.

The adjacent St. Katherine Dock is an easy target to locate. It nestles in a loop of the River Thames, with the Tower of London and Tower Bridge acting as clear markers along the riverside. As Shulem, was wont to say, the German bomber crews did not need to look for Alie Street *Shul* to see whether they were in the vicinity of the docks. The bomber crews would use the river glistening in the moonlight as their guide to strategic targets, rather than blacked-out Aldgate High Street. In the light of these facts, it was clear that the Jewish East End of London was indeed a specific German Nazi target, not instead of, but in addition to, other more strategic London targets.

Chapter 19

Yulus came home to the new apartment in Waterloo Gardens for the summer holidays. Since the untimely death of his mother and the outbreak of the war, he had become somewhat inured to change. Even so, he was not too happy with the unfamiliar surroundings and the thought of starting again to find new friends. It was, therefore, a pleasant surprise to find that one of his schoolmates was already living on the estate. In Soham this boy, who was a little older than Yulus, had been but a casual acquaintance, but now the two boys struck up a closer friendship. They explored the area together and found the shortcut to Victoria park, past the wood yard where many tree trunks, while remaining whole in shape, had been sawn lengthwise, and rested on criss-cross wooden trestles. The boys had learned of the manner in which wood was seasoned in their woodwork class at school. They were now able to see the actual process at work. Small pieces of wood had been placed between the planks of the tree trunks to keep them apart. This allowed the air to circulate and hastened the natural drying process. It also took the oxygen out of the surrounding air and produced a pungent and all pervasive smell. It was difficult to breathe when in close proximity to the weathering planks. The boys held their breath and pinched their noses to take a closer look. Later, they found it best to run fast with mouths closed until, panting for breath, they left the wood yard behind on their way to the clean fresh air of the park.

The war created many shortages. Wood was one of them. The woodwork master was forever making them save every scrap of wood. Even sawdust had to be saved as though it were gold dust. It was used as filler when mixed with the smelly fish glue that they brewed on a stove in the workshop. Half-inch oak had to be sawn down the middle to make quarter-inch slats. These they glued to mahogany slats of the same width and thickness and then sawed them crosswise into strips of alternate light and dark brown squares to produce a chess board. It took ages and much elbow grease, to saw the oak strips. Care had to be taken not to deviate from the straight pencil line that had been drawn down the side. No wasting material now, declared the master, after all, there is a war on, you know.

After Hitler invaded the Soviet Union in June 1941 and the Russians became allies, people began to call each other Tovarich or comrade. The previously evil Russians were, after all, now on our side and could be looked upon with sympathy. The woodwork master was ever ready to make some quip about the dangers of misusing equipment. If you don't want to be sore, don't cut yourself with the saw! was one of his oft repeated expressions, pronouncing the word 'sore' as 'saw' to make his point. Now he found another way of issuing a warning. Don't stand astride the wood as you saw, he would say, otherwise we may have to call you by the name of that infamous Russian General, you know, comrade General Kutchyercokoff! He would guffaw, as he enjoyed his own joke.

Food, too, was a scarce commodity. It could no longer be imported easily because of the German U-boat attacks on British shipping. Dig for Victory became the slogan of the day. A large plot of land was allocated to the school. It was divided into allotments that were in turn allocated to the pupils for cultivation. Yulus soon learned how to dig, double dig, distinguish between a sickle and a scythe and between a Dutch and a swan-necked hoe, plant seeds and weed his allotment. When he wrote to say that he had succeeded in growing onions, he was urged to bring as many as possible home with him. He had also succeeded in growing cos lettuces that he wanted to take home to surprise his family. Two days before he was due to leave for London, he proudly reviewed the fresh green rows of lettuces that looked just right for harvesting. The next morning, to his dismay, the lettuces had all 'bolted.' Their stems had all shot up high and the lettuces had gone to seed, a condition that makes them bitter and inedible. No point in taking them with you said the gardening instructor. You can either dig them into the ground or give them away for pig swill. It happens to the best of us. That extra bit of rain followed by morning sunshine sends them shooting up to heaven. It looks as though your family will have to make do with the onions alone this time.

But Yulus knew that he also had lemons to take home. Special consignments of lemons were imported into Britain from time to time and their imminent arrival broadcast on the radio and in newspapers as a real news event. Each consignment would be distributed throughout the country. Country folk seemed to have less need of them than Londoners who snatched them up as soon as they appeared in the metropolis. Yulus had received an urgent letter from home, just before the holidays, urging him to buy as many lemons as possible, should they appear in the greengrocers in the village. They did appear and he bought many lemons that he packed together with his own grown onions and his clothing in his suitcase for his trip home for the holidays. The strong smell of onions permeated the train carriage. Yulus looked nonchalantly out of the carriage window when he noticed other passengers sniffing and wondering about the source of the intrusive odour.

At home his family was delighted, although his underwear had to be washed several times before the lingering smell of onions could be eradicated. People's noses will know you are coming well in advance, said his sister, as she rinsed and re-rinsed the offending clothes. She now had a boyfriend to whom she gave a parcel of onions and lemons to take as a gift to his parents. He reported that they thought that her father must be either rich or privileged to have such surplus produce in these trying times. Neither riches nor privileges, he explained, just a Barmitzvah boy who resides in the countryside and digs for victory. Maybe he can tend our garden too? queried the prospective father-in-law whose one eye twinkled whenever he felt mischievous. The boyfriend lived in Stoke Newington, a district of London that had grander houses. They sported front and back gardens whose flowers had been replaced by bean, tomato and other plants. The lawns of some had become chicken runs.

The prospective bridegroom was an engineer working in a reserved occupation, supporting the war effort by working six long days a week, and sometimes seven, maintaining British air power. He was also in the Home Guard and sometimes was part of the whispering bush brigade that moved around the park at night. Shulem called upon his engineering expertise to help Yulus find a bicycle to take back with him to Soham at the end of the holiday. The shortage of petrol had created a demand for bicycles that had become a preferred form of transport. Yulus accompanied the engineer from shop to shop in search of a suitable bike, within Shulem's budget limits. They had no success. The only thing to do, said the engineer, is to find parts and build a custom-made model.

The engineer's father was a metal spinner. He had a workshop in Clerkenwell among many other small engineering enterprises. We are sure to find something there, said the engineer, optimistically. They stopped over first, at his father's workshop where Yulus was introduced to a short, solid man with a twinkle in his one eye, the other being a glass insert that looked real but did not move. *Foor dir iz es a gesheft*, for you it is OK, he said, shaking Yulus's hand with both of his in the friendliest of gestures. Yulus was fascinated as he watched this portly man at work. He took hold of a thick wooden pole that looked like a stave used by Big John in a Robin Hood film he had seen, although this person looked more like Friar Tuck. He tucked the stave under one arm and by use of his side and inner arm, pressed it firmly against a sheet of metal that had been attached to a fast spinning lathe. Under variable pressure, expertly applied, the pole moved back and forth along the face of the sheet, forcing it to take up the shape of the lignum-vitae wooden former previously affixed to the spindle of the lathe. Another component to help the war effort had been produced as Yulus stood and watched wide-eyed, before continuing his search for a bicycle.

A bicycle frame was found in one workshop, handlebars and wheels in another, brakes and other accessories in yet another. The parts were assembled to produce a bicycle like no other. It had several special features. Instead of the sprung hand-brake grips being positioned, as was customary, at the ends of the handlebars, they were located near the centre spindle. Instead of being curved, as was customary, the handlebar on this model was straight. It was usual for the nuts and bolts to be of similar shapes and sizes, but in this model they formed an interesting variety. An exclusive model, said the engineer. It is more like a monstrosity, said Yulus. Only his adventurous spirit enabled him to mount the Heath-Robinson contraption and wobble uncomfortably along the street. His bicycle became a talking point wherever it was seen. He explained to curious onlookers that this was the only bike that continued to move directly forward even after turning the handlebars to the left, while right turns followed the usual pattern. Turning the spindle to the right, in some way tightened the retaining bolt, whereas the left turn tended to loosen it. Yulus learned to carry a spanner with him for safety's sake. He had to remember to give the offending bolt an extra turn before each journey.

The engineer was also a music lover and when listening to classical music recordings, was transported to another world. When he learned how sparse was Yulus's knowledge in this field, he became determined, war or no war, to add another dimension to his prospective brother-in-law's education. Two coincidental factors assisted in this process. Firstly, Walt Disney's animated classical music film, Fantasia, arrived in London. Secondly, but of no less importance, the Henry Wood classical promenade concerts had moved to the Albert Hall. Bombs may have rained on London, but culture never left the capital. Museums, theatres and cinemas stayed open whenever possible. In particular the Yiddish theatre continued to operate and the Whitechapel Art Gallery mounted exhibitions throughout the war, even though much of the surrounding district was devastated by the German bombing raids. The immediate area across the road from the Art Gallery was a complete rubble wasteland. The gutted Rivoli cinema, where Yulus was taken by his mother to see a Yiddish film, once stood there in all its glory.

Fantasia's combination of great classical music and ingenious animation left its mark indelibly on the formative mind of Yulus. As he sat in a plush seat in the darkened cinema hall of the New Gallery cinema in Regent Street, he watched and listened and listened and watched. The music swirled in his ears and the pictures imprinted themselves on his mind. He later related the experience in detail to his friend. He told how the opening bars of the Toccata and Fugue in D Minor by Bach were startling and unexpected after the quietly spoken introduction. How he found the Dance Chinois from the Nutcracker Suite by Tchaikovsky, that was danced by animated mushrooms, ingenious and very amusing. Beethoven's Pastoral Symphony was equally pleasant, although he was surprised to see that the many coloured centaurs were frightened by Thor, the god of thunder. He said that he really would never forget the image of the agonised twist of the head and neck of a dying dinosaur set dramatically against the burning sun. This was in Stravinky's Rite of Spring that was depicted as the evolutionary development of early life on earth. He could not but laugh as he tried to describe how funny Hippopotami looked wearing tutus and twirling in ballet shoes, in the Dance of the Hours by Ponchielli. And he found The Night on Bald Mountain by Moussorgsky eerie and frightening as the devil raised people from the dead, in the dead of night. In contrast, Schubert's Ave Maria was so, so peaceful. For Yulus, the highlight of the film was Mickey Mouse's appearance as the Sorcerer's Apprentice. Try as he may, Mickey could not stop straw bristled brooms from overfilling a well. They had, by Mickey's mischievous application of a magic formula, miraculously sprouted arms and hands that carried water buckets. Poor Mickey could not find the antidote. The animated actions of the characters were amazingly in line with the timing of the music by Paul Dukas. It was difficult to know what came first, the story, the music or the cartoonists' interpretation.

The visit to the Albert Hall was an altogether different experience. The hall was not darkened and the music was here and now. What he saw and heard was what there was. There were no graphic artists present to depict their own thoughts and visions of the meaning of the music. The hall was full. There were no seats in the centre of the hall. People stood throughout the performance enabling the entry price to be relatively low. They also stood in the gallery. Theoretically, the audience could walk about. That is why it was called a promenade concert. But in reality, people stood still whilst the music was played, although they might shuffle their feet from time to time. The raised stage enabled people to see the orchestra from all parts of the floor. The film Fantasia included eight items of music composed by eight different composers. Each piece was relatively short and none included a soloist. In contrast, the whole of this promenade concert was dedicated to the Czech composer Dvorak. The first half of the programme included an overture, his violin concerto in A minor and symphonic variations. The second half included an aria from Stabat Mater and his symphony number four. Yulus marvelled at the soloist, Ida Haendel, who played the violin without sheet music to guide her. The rest of the orchestra and the conductor had music to follow whereas she played the complicated melodies and variations by heart. That's how it is, explained the musical engineer. A few weeks ago she played Beethoven's violin concerto and in a few week's time she will play the violin concerto of Brahms. Doesn't seem at all fair, said Yulus, ever more impressed by the virtuosity of the talented artiste. At the end of each movement, Yulus thought the piece had come to an end and was about to applaud until he noticed that no-one else attempted to do so. Instead many people shuffled their feet, took handkerchiefs from their pockets and coughed or blew their noses into them. They all seemed to know when the piece did finish, as the great applause was immediate. There were shouts of bravo and encore that increased as the soloist returned to the stage. She took several bows and then reluctantly, so it seemed, played a short complex piece without the accompaniment of the orchestra to yet more applause.

Yulus watched the timpanist carefully during the performance of the symphony. He seemed to have little to do most of the time. He sat with arms crossed and sometimes with his eyes closed. Yulus wondered whether he would fall asleep and miss his cue. He almost wished that he would, so that he could report the incident to his friend. But no, a little before any critical moment, he would sit up alertly, bend forward, put his ear to the drum and tighten a screw here or there to increase the tension. He would then pick up his drum sticks and exactly on time, produce the very sound that the composer and conductor intended. Yulus wanted to know why people coughed between movements. An impossible question deserves an improbable answer, retorted the musical engineer. I suppose it is to let the orchestra know that the audience is still awake, he said laughingly.

As an additional treat, Yulus attended an old-time music hall night at the Unity Theatre, in King's Cross, with his sister and fiance. The Unity Theatre Company, that tended to put on serious, controversial left wing plays, occasionally let its hair down and mounted a raucous production of Victorian and first world war songs and comic cameos. The audience rose to the occasion, joining in the singing of familiar songs and heckling stand-up comics until called to order by the Master of Ceremonies who was positioned at the edge of the stage. The women artistes wore Victorian gowns, some with feather boas draped across their shoulders. All wore elaborate hats decorated with feathers and prettily coloured birds. When an artiste raised her long skirt to show an ankle, the crowd chorused, higher Maria. The male performers wore striped jackets with matching trousers of a length that revealed light coloured spats on the top of their shiny boots. Some carried canes and wore straw hats. The Master of Ceremonies was also appropriately dressed. He sported a large coloured handkerchief that he would wave demonstrably as he introduced each act with a flurry of alliterated words. He would emphasise the sibilant sound of the opening letter of each word and deliver the introduction without pausing for breath. This specially scintillating, sensual, sophisticated, significant, spectacular, singer will sing for you and you alone, soothing, sociological songs, sung so sweetly that some of you will be aroused from your (pause) somnolency. No such word, shouted someone from the audience. Yes there is, retorted the MC, look it up when you get home, that is if you have a dictionary at home. Who says he's got a home? shouted someone else from the gallery amid uproarious laughter.

Yulus returned to Soham with his unique bicycle and with a new set of cultural experiences to share with his friends.

Chapter 20

Shulem told his friends at one of their regular meetings in the park that he was sorry to see Yulus return to Soham, but he was convinced that it was for the best. London was still a major target for German bombers and further heavy air raids were expected. They all agreed that education in London was in a shambles because so many school premises had been destroyed and because recruitment into the armed forces had created a chronic shortage of teachers. Their newspapers had reported that some sixty percent of Jewish children in Britain were now receiving no religious education whatsoever. At least, in Soham, Yulus was both safer and still able to attend a Jewish school. His friends were impressed when Shulem told them that despite the difficult conditions prevailing in a totally Christian environment, every effort was being made to maintain more than a semblance of Jewish life and education in the evacuation area. They were particularly pleased to know that one of Yulus's schoolteachers had managed to provide the Jewish children with three kosher meals a day during the *Pesach*, Passover, period. He had help from his wife and from London. They were also gratified to know that Yulus and his schoolmates attended regular Hebrew classes and Sabbath services. It amused them to learn that the village Conservative Hall became a Synagogue every Saturday morning. It is hard to live a full kosher life in the country, said Shulem, but at least the boys are being continually reminded of their Jewish heritage.

We too, in London, have had to adapt our Jewish life to the conditions of war, said one of the friends. You mean because we can no longer live in a close knit Jewish society? Yes, but not only that, said the friend whose extended waistline revealed his interest in the availability and quality of food, we too have had to adjust our eating habits. You still eat kosher, don't you? Yes of course. It would take more than a war to get me to eat *treife*, unkosher food. No, what I am saying is that we can no longer buy kidneys, or rump steaks. That's because of food rationing. No it isn't. It's because of the arrangement that has been made with Gentile butchers. They get the hind quarters of animals while we Jews get the foreparts. Why is that? It's because our Jewish dietary laws not only require animals to be killed according to *Shechita*, religious ritual, but in addition, certain veins have to be porged (extracted) from the legs of cattle and sheep under the strict supervision of *Shomerim*, religious inspectors, before hind quarters can be considered kosher. The combination of the shortage of *Shomerim* due to recruitment into the armed forces and the necessity to avoid wasting any food, has resulted in the *Beth Din*, the Jewish Religious Court, issuing a ban on the sale of hind quarters in Jewish butcher shops. The meat in the Jewish butcher shops still comes from animals that are killed according to Jewish law, but only the foreparts of the animals are now kosher. The untreated hind quarters are sold to Gentile butchers. So you see, the Jewish cuisine has lost the benefit of kidneys and those meat cuts that are to be found only in the hind quarters of animals. *Alevai mir duffen oisshteyen noor doos,* if only that was all we had to suffer, said Shulem. Despite the fact that his own lifestyle had been shattered by the war and in particular by the German bombing, he applied this philosophy to all his deprivations. They are as nothing, he would say, compared to the untold suffering of fellow Jews in Europe.

The war in Europe was followed with the greatest concern and interest. Maps of Europe were hung on walls in houses and schools and coloured-headed pins were moved with regularity to mark the frightening progress of the German armies into the heartland of the Soviet Union. Newspapers published maps with arrows pointing from East Prussia, Poland and Rumania towards the important Soviet cities of Kiev, Smolensk, Leningrad and Moscow and even beyond. There were terrible headlines such as Nazi Noose Tightens Round Leningrad and Jubilant Hitler Nears Gates of Moscow. The Germans certainly had the upper hand in the summer and autumn of 1941. Nevertheless, the Allies were not entirely acquiescent. They took some positive action to forestall the Germans. British and Russian troops marched into Iran in a joint operation. The Arctic island of Spitzbergen was seized by Canadian, British and Norwegian troops to stop its coal stocks from falling into German hands. Towards the end of the year, the British and Commonwealth Eighth Army was having some success against the German and Italian forces in North Africa while the bitter cold Russian winter was slowing up the German advance on the Eastern front.

In December, the startling attack by the Japanese on the Americans at Pearl Harbour brought the Americans into the war and Britain declared war against Japan. The Axis powers maintained the initiative in the first half of 1942. The Japanese advanced into South East Asia. Within weeks, Hong Kong had fallen and British held Malaya and Singapore soon fell to the Japanese while the American held Philippine Islands were under full scale attack. In North Africa the Panzer tanks of the reinforced German Afrika Korps pushed the British forces back to El Alamein. Vidkun Quisling was appointed by the Germans as puppet Prime Minister of Norway. In his inaugural speech he declared that that this was not only Germany's war but also that of Norway, the Germanic people and Europe. It was a war against England, America, Russia and international Jewry. Shulem complained about this reference to international Jewry in one of his regular discussions of the current situation with his friends. Here we are sitting helplessly on a park bench in London while our brethren are being systematically murdered by the Nazis in Europe, and Quisling finds it necessary to declare war against us. At least said one of the friends, known for his biting sarcasm, at least he has placed us among illustrious partners. If only, responded Shulem, those partners would truly include the saving of Jewish lives in their objectives. The least they could do is to open their doors to receive those refugees who have managed to escape. In February, he reminded his friends, over seven hundred Jewish refugees drowned when their ship, the Struma, was sunk after being turned away from Palestine by the British authorities.

It was not until the late autumn of 1942 that the tide of war began to turn in favour of the allies. The British Eighth Army triumphed over the German Afrika Korps at El Alamein in North Africa while US troops landed in Algeria and Morocco. In Russia the Soviet army counterattacked and routed the Germans in the approaches to Stalingrad. The combined British, Commonwealth, American and Russian forces were proving to be a truly formidable force. But as Winston Churchill said in one of his impressive speeches, this favourable turn was not the end, not even the beginning of the end, but it was perhaps, the end of the beginning.

The end of the beginning for the allies, perhaps declared Shulem to his friends, but not for the Jews of Europe. The change in the war situation in favour of the allies was more than welcome, but it had come too late to stop the Nazi butchering of the Jews in Europe where, according to newspaper reports, two million Jews have already been murdered. Worse was yet to come and nothing physical was being done to alleviate the suffering of the Jews at the hands of the Nazis. There was talk, but no action even though the Nazi atrocities were publicised and well known. In the June debate in the House of Commons, Members of Parliament said that the horrible Nazi murders in Poland were not to be forgotten. And in July, a BBC broadcast in Yiddish on the European Service, reported the atrocities against the Jews in Poland. In that month, a New York newspaper printed a picture of Jewish children being publicly drowned in Warsaw. August 12, 1942, was declared a fast day by British Jews and the *shofar*, the ram's horn, was sounded in Synagogues where special prayers were offered for the lives of European Jewry. In September, the Telegraphic Agency received a desperate message that read, 'The Nazis have begun the extermination of Polish Jewry - Save us!'

Shulem and his friends attended a protest demonstration, against Nazi persecution of the Jews that was held in the Albert Hall on October 19, 1942. The Archbishop of Canterbury presided and Churchill sent a message. The BBC reported that it was an impressive meeting. There were no flags, stirring music or uniforms, just ordinary people in everyday clothes. British Jewry declared December 13, 1942, to be another fast day. The Nazi slaughter of Jews was condemned in declarations read simultaneously by the governments in

London, Washington and Moscow on December 17. The statements accused the Germans of carrying into effect Hitler's oft repeated intention to exterminate the Jewish people in Europe. It warned that those responsible for these crimes shall not escape retribution, hoping that such a declaration would act as a deterrent. On that day, Members of Parliament in the House of Commons, moved by the horror of Mr. Anthony Eden's recital of German atrocities against the Jews, stood silent for one minute in sympathy with the plight of European Jewry.

All this talk had no effect on the Germans who continued with their atrocities and their anti-Semitic propaganda. John Amery, a colleague of Lord Haw Haw, in a broadcast to Britain, told the British that only the Jew and his tools, namely the Bolshevik and American governments, stood between them and peace. Dr. Ley, the Nazi Labour Chief, declared that the Nazis would continue to wage the war until the Jews have been wiped off the face of the earth.

Frustration, sadness and feelings of helplessness concerning the plight of European Jewry grew during the year 1943, as bad news was followed by worse and the full extent of the Nazi bloodbath was revealed and confirmed. Tens of thousands of Jews were being murdered all over Europe and not only in the concentration camps. There were massacres in such towns as Kharkov, Rostov, Melitopol, Dniepropetovsk, Kiev, Smolensk, Viasma, Gomel, Kirovgrad and in every one of the larger towns of Eastern Europe. In April and May came the news of the Warsaw Ghetto uprising and the knowledge that despite the heroic battle against the German army, that lasted three bitter weeks, the Warsaw Ghetto was destroyed and the remaining sixty thousand Jews were either killed or transported to the Nazi death camps. Only a handful of Jews escaped through the sewers to join the Polish partisans. In August, the newspapers reported that Ilya Ehrenburg, the Russian writer, had stated that he could not remain silent and called upon writers, friends and champions of the truth to speak up. He made a clarion call to 'Let the blood of the Jewish children call to the conscience of the world'. In November 1943 came the chilling news that Polish Jewish children were no more. They had all been murdered by the Nazis.

British Jews were also very much aware of the dangers facing the Jews in Palestine. In August 1942, Shulem and his friends attended a mass rally in support of the *Yishuv*, the name given to Jewish community in Palestine. The meeting was held in Mile End while similar rallies were held in other parts of London and in Cardiff and Blackpool. The situation in Palestine and the attitude of the British government to Jewish refugees created a dilemma for British and Palestinian Jewry. On the one hand, the only real defence that the Palestinian Jews had against the Germans was the ability of the British to halt the advance of the German army in North Africa. On the other hand, a major obstacle to saving European Jewry from extermination was the obdurate refusal of the British to allow Jewish refugees free entry into Palestine. This conflicting role of the British brought about the declaration by David Ben-Gurion, the leader of the Jewish community in Palestine, that the *Yishuv* should fight the Germans as though there were no British White Paper that restricted Jewish immigration into Palestine and should fight against British immigration policy as though there was no war against the Germans.

Shulem and his friends were frustrated by the British government's dichotomy of thought and action that condemned the Nazi atrocities against the Jews while simultaneously refusing to give safe haven to the very same persecuted Jewish refugees. Britain had many opportunities to assist and yet refused to act even in a small way. In January 1943, a thousand Jewish children who were stranded in Teheran were refused entry into Palestine. Entry visas for French Jewish children to come to England from Vichy France were first denied and then reluctantly issued only after strong protests. Despite this, British Jewry wholeheartedly supported the British war effort in all spheres. In fact, in proportionate population terms, there were more Jews in the British armed forces than other denominations. Jewish communal centres in the East End of London were fully active in providing aid to homeless victims of German bombing raids, both Jews and Gentiles alike. Many Jews served in the Ambulance, Fire Fighting, Special Police and Air Raid Warden services along side their Gentile neighbours. Numerous Synagogues and Jewish schools had been destroyed in the raids and the London Jewish Hospital was badly damaged by fire caused by incendiary bombs.

Yet anti-Semitism continued to grow in Britain. So much so, that in March 1943, the Stepney Borough Council passed a resolution to make Jewbaiting a criminal offence. Anti-Semitic slogans appeared on doors of Jewish homes and on walls in the Borough proclaiming, 'Perish Judah', 'Bolshevism is Jewish', 'This war is a Jewish war' and 'Stop this Jews' war'. Advertisements in newspapers included the words 'Gentiles only' and 'No Jews'. The editorial in the local paper, the Hackney Gazette, was against such legislation claiming that it would mean more freedom for the minority by curtailing or suppressing the freedom of others. And as for the question of 'No Jews' it said that 'We have yet to learn that Britons have lost the right to decide whom they shall live with or employ'. 'The Englishman's home is still his castle!' In November 1943, the Fascist leader, Oswald Mosley was released from internment on the grounds of ill health. This was a bitter pill to take. A number of Trade Unions protested and statements were issued contrasting the government's treatment of this Fascist with that of other prisoners such as Ghandhi who had been arrested in India. He too was ill but not released. Shulem was among the thirty thousand people who demonstrated to demand Mosley's re-internment. An editorial in the Jewish Chronicle stated that it was now clear that the war was not a struggle against the Fascist-Nazi idea, but for British security. Debates were held in Parliament and one Gentile MP complained that while Britain entered the war in defence of Poland, it had not before, raised a finger in defence of the persecuted Jews of Germany. Shulem felt some consolation in the fact that the Trafalgar Square demonstration was not a Jewish or Communist affair but a genuine expression of the British people's hatred of Fascism, apparently not fully shared by the government. Following Mosley's release, anti-Semitic activity increased and again there were pernicious statements questioning Jewish loyalty. Jews have a certain double loyalty, it was said, a loyalty to the State and a loyalty to the Jewish people. And Christians and other religious denominations don't? asked Shulem.

Chapter 21

What is that contraption? asked the cobbler amiably, as Yulus rode up to the shop front, having returned to Soham from his summer holiday trip to war torn London. It's an excuse for a bicycle, retorted Yulus in the same vein. It has two wheels and more often than not, it goes in the direction in which it is steered. Better than nothing, everybody agreed.

Life in the country is so different from life in the metropolis. In town, one has to visit a park or travel some distance to enjoy the greenery of grass and trees. In the country, nature is one's continuous companion and often a partner that can make life both easy and difficult for man. Wartime conditions turned the countryside into one great food supplier. Fields that previously may have been left fallow were now in full production. Flower growers were now growing potatoes or other edible produce. The fenlands in the midst of which Soham was located, had a rich dark brown soil. Many years previously, the marshes had been drained to provide some of the most arable land in the country. The flat featureless landscape, interrupted only by a variety of trees and hedgerows planted by man to separate field from field, is ideal for agricultural development. The only hint that this land was once marshland where villages had to be approached by boats, can be found in the names of some of the neighbourhood hamlets, such as Isleham and the cathedral city of Ely which is in the so-called Isle of Ely.

In the spring, sugar-beet plants begin to sprout. The seeds had previously been planted in profusion in long straight rows in field after field. Each fresh green sprout, that had pushed itself up through the dark brown earth, represented a possible future fat juicy sugar-laden bulbous root that would be harvested later in the year. The plants were crowded one against the other and had to be thinned out to provide growing space for the bulbous roots. This laborious singling procedure was carried out by farm labourers and their young assistants recruited from the local schools. When the process was finished, there would be single plants in each row, equidistant from each other and almost exactly one hoe's width apart. Once the hoe heaving farm labourers got into their stride, they would cut out the surplus plants with amazing accuracy and consistency, sometimes leaving just one sprout in place. More often, a small cluster of plants would remain. The hoers started work early and renewed their energy half-way through the morning by drinking well-sweetened cold tea (without milk) that they poured from bottles they had brought from home and buried in the ground to keep cool.

Yulus joined his fellow schoolmates on singling expeditions. He crawled on his hands and knees in the wake of the rhythmic hoers, pulling out the surplus sprouts to leave the single healthiest sprout in place to grow in its own space. He had been pre-warned, by experienced singlers, to tie sacking around his knees to act as padded protection from the harsh earth and uninvited thistles that grew alongside the sprouting sugar-beets. Hands could not be protected nor backaches avoided, but aches and pains were soon forgotten when wages were received at the end of each half-day's toil.

Later in the year, Yulus was also recruited for potato lifting. Potato plants did not require singling like the sugar-beet. They were happy to grow crowded together to produce clusters of potatoes below ground that had to be lifted out of the earth into baskets that were then loaded onto carts. Two harvesting methods were employed. One was the traditional system of ploughing up the plants and then separating the potatoes from their root attachments by hand before placing them in baskets. The more modern method was to use a spiked spinning wheel that was pulled along each row of potato plants. As the wheel spun below ground level, the spiked protrusions would hit individual potatoes and propel them out of the ground. The potatoes would be caught by netting that prevented them from flying too far from their growing space. This faster process sometimes damaged potatoes that were hit too hard. The uprooted potatoes still had to be gathered by hand and placed in baskets.

Farmers generally shared out the physically hard work fairly between the boys, alternating jobs that were more difficult with less arduous tasks. One farmer, however, decided against work sharing. He picked out one boy to travel on the cart to receive the baskets that were handed to him by the potato lifters. As this was considered to be one of the less exhausting tasks, the boys thought that it ought to be shared between different boys during the working day. Yulus was part of the delegation that approached the farmer with the proposition that the work load should be more equitably shared. No, said the farmer. It's my farm and I allocate work as I see fit.

At mid-morning tea break, the boys discussed the matter and agreed not to continue working unless their reasonable request was met. Come on, said the farmer, time's up, let's get back to work. Will you share out the work fairly, as we requested? asked Yulus. No, repeated the farmer, so let's get on with it. The boys hesitated. Are you or are you not going to continue lifting? asked the farmer in a more militant tone. The boys looked at each other. There was a momentary pause. Yulus heard himself saying, Not unless we can share the work. In that case, shouted the farmer, his face now red with rage, you can all bloody-well get off my farm. This was Yulus's first lesson in labour relations. When the incident was reported to the schoolmaster who coordinated such work parties, he said that while he agreed to fair work-sharing arrangements, he was disappointed with the outcome. He added that this incident was not what he meant when he had asked the boys to be a striking example. He never missed an opportunity to pun.

On another farm, the kindly farmer had sown his potato crop in rows in a direction that ran to and from his stables. The cart-horse was the homely sort, weary of a lifetime of toil. He only wanted to go home to munch his hay in peace and quiet. The horse objected to pulling the cart away from the stables and had to be cajoled by the farmer to start his walk across the field of ploughed-up potatoes. Contrarily, once he got to the other end of the field and started his journey back, he tended to break into a trot and had to be restrained to wait for the potato lifters to pile their baskets into the cart. It was a comic performance at each turn. It was difficult to tell who was the more frustrated, the friendly farmer or the homely horse that objected to being pulled in one direction or pushed in the other. More comedy was added to the scene when one of the boys noticed that the farmer's heavy blue over-trousers had been split on the backside and were held together by what seemed to be a shoelace. Every time the farmer bent down, the boy would point at the offending split and make a funny face. The farmer would turn at the sound of laughter and ask what was the source. Just a private joke, the boy would say. How many private jokes can they have, mumbled the farmer as he once again renewed his struggle with the recalcitrant horse.

Yulus got on well with his foster parents. The cobbler and his wife were kindly people who came to understand the difficulties of a Jewish boy living in a Gentile environment. They made every effort to accommodate him in relation to his attendance at Sabbath services at the Conservative Hall on a Saturday, which was a normal working day for them. They also were very understanding, although still incredulous, when the young boy insisted on fasting for twenty-five hours on *Yom Kippur*. They also sympathised when Yulus told them of the persecution of Jews by the Nazis in Europe. They were especially sympathetic when he told them that, since the outbreak of the war, nothing had been heard of his grandmother, aunts, uncles and cousins who were under the Nazi yoke. They were also astounded to learn that, despite the war, Fascist anti-Semitic activity was intensifying in London. Their grandson did not share their sympathetic attitude. Perhaps he never understood the enormity of the tragic events in Europe. He had never reconciled himself to the presence of another young boy in his grandparent's household, one with whom he had to share his grandparent's attention. There was never a good chemistry between the two boys. When they quarrelled, the cobbler would often come to Yulus's defence. The arguments were generally petty and usually related to the grandson handling one of Yulus's possessions or invading his privacy. The quarrels were of no real significance until the grandson descended to using anti-Semitic language. This enraged Yulus. The boy ignored the protests of his grandparents. Such language is inappropriate to a guest in the house and is very hurtful, they said. The protestations were of no avail and the boy seemed to enjoy the fact that he could so easily rile and frustrate his adversary in this way. One day, when the grandson had been calling Yulus all sorts of names with the suffix Jew, Yulus lost all patience. He told the boy in the presence of his mother and grandmother that if he called him Jew Boy once more, he would have no alternative but to hit him hard. The boy began to chant 'Jew Boy' 'Jew Boy'. You had better stop him, said Yulus to the boy's mother. Stop it, she said firmly, what you are saying is not nice. Thinking that Yulus could not possibly carry out his threat in front of his mother and grandmother, the boy ignored the request, and continued his obnoxious chant. He was mistaken. Yulus, now fully enraged, landed one mighty blow with his right fist to the boy's stomach. The boy doubled up in pain and began to cry. What have you done? demanded the mother of Yulus, as the boy writhed on the floor. What I said I would, retorted Yulus defiantly. Disturbed by the noise, the cobbler left his last and came into the room to find out what had occurred. When he heard that the boy had been hit, he said it was about time. I am surprised that Yulus has waited so long. While this reaction gratified Yulus, the incident created a situation that could not be maintained. The grandparents could not bar their grandson from the house and they could not control his obstinacy, which would ensure more arguments whenever the two boys met. Once again during his sojourn in Soham, the only solution was for Yulus to change billets. In January 1943, he moved a few streets away to stay in a house with two gentle elderly ladies and a Pekinese dog. He would visit the cobbler in his shop from time to time.

Schooling at the JFS Central School was becoming more and more difficult. There were critical staff shortages. Teachers were being recruited into the armed forces and the remaining masters had to extend their teaching to subjects that were not naturally theirs. The student population was continually changing. Older students left when their courses were completed and some younger students were taken home by their parents during lulls in bombing raids on London. Some returned when bombing in London again increased in intensity. Other students moved to different evacuation areas to join their parents or siblings who had been evacuated with other schools. Likewise, new students would appear from other areas where schools had closed. One of the intakes into the JFS Central School, comprised evacuated schoolchildren from other London schools, who had been receiving tuition at the local Soham Shade School. That school, too, was suffering from lack of staff and had to restrict its teaching to local children only. Incoming students were of various ages and of differing levels of education. Some had to drop subjects they had been studying while others had to readjust themselves to the current curriculum. Students of this generation were wartime educational casualties. The constant movement of teachers and pupils created difficulties for the remaining teaching staff. Their devotion to the profession and their concern for the pupils in their charge was the only buffer to total educational chaos. It was this devotion that ensured that whatever was being taught at the JFS Central School was of the highest standard possible in the circumstances. The School's Soham branch had to close in December 1942 due to dwindling numbers of staff and pupils. Its remaining students had to cycle the four miles across the fens to the sole surviving branch in Isleham. While Yulus's eccentric bicycle stood up to the test, the School in Isleham did not. The continued erosion of staff and students, soon produced an impossible situation. Two masters were teaching four age groups at the same time, all seated in one room. Each group was distracted by the activities of the others. In July 1943, the last bastion of the JFS Central School closed its doors and Yulus returned to London in search of continued education.

The London school premises of the JFS Central School had been destroyed by bombing earlier in the war and the school was destined never again to reopen. Yulus applied for entry to Myrdle Street Central School the principal of which had previously been a teacher at JFS Central. The headmaster explained, that while he would be delighted to accept Yulus as a pupil, he did not think it wise because educational standards at the school had fallen way below those that Yulus had already achieved at the JFS. The extensive and continuous bombing had taken its toll of educational institutions and standards. Only now were serious steps being taken to revitalise and renew the educational system in London. Until now, Grammar Schools had had to give up their special status to be part of the general London Emergency Secondary School for Boys. This year the prewar status of Grammar Schools had been restored and they were the only immediate institutions that could provide the level of education required for matriculation students. Yulus was now fifteen years of age and needed to study intensively during the next school year if he wanted to take the matriculation examination. His best course would be to enter a Grammar School. It was his recommendation that Yulus apply to Parmiter's Grammar School that was only a short distance from his home in Waterloo Gardens.

The school secretary explained that, before any application could be considered, Central School students had to obtain permission for change of status from the London Educational Authority. Educational standards may have changed but bureaucrats had not given up any of theirs. Yulus, supported by his recently married sister, confidently entered the dark brown offices of the Local Educational Authority. Frustration was, however, not far away. Whoever heard of Central School boys taking matriculation? asked an officious clerk.

Yulus produced the letter of recommendation he had received from the JFS Central School headmaster. It stated that that he was a good student, reliable and conscientious. It also explained that he was a member of the School's Matriculation Class that had had four successes in the Reception Area. Only four? snorted the clerk, showing his ignorance of the extreme difficulties with which evacuated schools had had to deal. The rules are, he said, that Grammar School entrants have to pass the Junior County examinations at the age of ten plus or the supplementary exams at the age of thirteen. His mother died at the time he was taking the earlier exam, explained the sister, and because of the war, he did not have the opportunity to take the later exam. Two headmasters are recommending him for Grammar School education. Is that not enough? The clerk was adamant. No exam, no entry. Yulus and his sister were not satisfied. They appealed to the Myrdle Street headmaster. He spoke personally to the principals of the JFS Central and Parmiter's and also to a senior official at the Local Educational Authority. In time, it was agreed that if Yulus could pass an entrance test to Parmiter's, he could attend that school. Yulus took the test and passed.

On September 1, 1943, Shulem received a letter from the headmaster of Parmiter's which read 'I am willing to admit your son on the conditions I have explained to his sister and himself. He must, of course, accept the disadvantage of his new curriculum, but we will do our best to secure his passage through the School Certificate Examination.' *Voos maint doos?* What does that mean? asked Shulem. Yulus explained that in Soham, he had been studying English, Mathematics, French, Magnetism and Mechanics. Now he had to study some extra subjects. They were English Literature and History. He had also to study General Science that incorporated Magnetism and Mechanics to a lesser depth than he had been studying, but which included a wider range of subjects such as Biology and Chemistry, that he had not previously studied. All this he had to do within one year. *Doos iz oimyoisherdik*, this is hardly fair, said Shulem. *Vie const du tooyen doos?* How can you do it? *Ich vais nisht*, I do not know, answered Yulus in his halting Yiddish, *aber Ich vill tooyen voos Ich kan*, but I will do what I can. Four years away from home had severely reduced his ability to speak Yiddish, although his understanding did not seem to be impaired. Often, now, when he explained certain things to Shulem in his broken Yiddish, Shulem would say laughingly, *Yetz zug mir in plain English*, now tell me in plain English.

The principal of Myrdle Street Central was delighted when he heard the news. You know, he said, you are luckier than your own headmaster. He has also been looking for a school since he has returned to London. He has been less successful and has had to accept a temporary post. Yulus noted that headmasters too, can be wartime educational casualties.

190

Chapter 22

There was considerable improvement in the position of the Allies, on all the war fronts in the year 1943. The tide was turning in their favour. In the Pacific, the Americans recaptured important strategic islands from the Japanese. In Eastern Europe, the Russians had crushed some of the German forces, after massive tank battles. In North Africa, British and Commonwealth forces advanced westwards to link up with the Americans who had invaded Vichy-French held Morocco and Algeria. By May, the North African war was virtually over. At sea, new techniques were introduced to fight or avoid the German U Boats that still, however, remained a danger. Many German battleships were sunk. The Royal and American Air Forces were conducting heavy bombing raids on German cities. American and British troops invaded Sicily and then Italy. Mussolini was deposed and the Italians signed an armistice agreement with the Allies and later declared war against the Germans who were occupying Italy. But the war was far from over and London was still subject to bombing raids.

In March, over one hundred and seventy people were killed in the East End of London, in a tragic air raid shelter accident. An air raid alarm had been sounded and people were making their way towards the Bethnal Green underground railway station that was utilised as a deep and safe air raid shelter. While on their way, newly installed anti-aircraft rocket guns began firing from a nearby site. The unfamiliar deafening whoosh of the rockets created panic and caused the civilians to rush pell-mell into the station. A woman carrying her baby tripped and fell down a flight of stairs. An elderly man fell over her and others fell on top of him. People pushing from the street entrance created extra pressure. As a result, hundreds of people, struggling in vain against the pressure, were piled one on top of another and tragically crushed to death. Somehow, the woman who first fell, survived the disaster, but her baby did not. Why not the baby? asked Yulus of his father, when he heard the sad report. Shulem's face showed agitation as he replied in the manner of many religious people when confronted with inexplicable phenomena, *Fin Gott fraigt mir nisht*, One does not question God.

War stories are sometimes tinged with ironic humour. Many British soldiers were serving abroad, in North Africa, India, Burma and other spheres of conflict. Some had been away from home for years. Their young wives and sweethearts were left to guard the Home Front. Many American soldiers were serving abroad and their main European base was Britain where the Americans were very welcome. This concatenation of events led to many liaisons between handsome young foreign soldiers, laden with gifts, who spoke the same language, more or less, and lovely, lonely war weary young women. The amorous activities of American soldiers became legendary. So much so, that on the birthday of Princess Elizabeth, it was said that she was unique. She was seventeen and had not been kissed by an American soldier.

Not so humorous were the propaganda leaflets that the Germans showered on British troops in Italy. They were designed to demoralise the British soldiers while propagating the Nazi's favourite subject, anti-Semitism. One such leaflet read. 'You have a date with death. Your girl has a date with Sam Levy'. It continued 'At first she hesitated a bit about calling up Sam, the war profiteer. But then she said to herself that there is no point in waiting any longer for Joe to come back, the war seems endless, and the best years of my life are passing by....' Another leaflet asked the soldiers, 'Is it shameful to want to live?' It provided its own reply '..... it is more shameful to fight and kill to satisfy the greed for gold of a few Jews and capitalists. ..... there is no shame in becoming a prisoner of war.' Not for the first time, the Germans underestimated the fortitude of the British. One soldier, expressing his disgust while retaining his sense of humour, sent some leaflets to the Imperial War Museum, adding his own comment that the leaflets helped overcome the shortage of toilet paper.

Engine trouble caused an RAF plane to make a forced landing on the Italian Mediterranean Island of Lampedusa in June 1943. The tiny Island lies between Malta and the coast of Africa. The twenty-two year old Jewish tailor's cutter, turned Sergeant-Pilot, was quite taken aback when the commander of the Italian garrison immediately surrendered to him. Subsequently, his friends dubbed him 'King' of the island. Later in the year, a humorous Yiddish play about the incident was produced in the East End London Yiddish Theatre. It was very popular and ran for over two hundred performances, a fact that proved very disturbing to the Nazis. It prompted their irascible spokesman, Lord Haw Haw to state, in one of his broadcasts to Britain, that 'The Yids at the Grand Palais should not be laughing for much longer at the ridiculous play, The King of Lampedusa, because they are earmarked for a visit by the Luftwaffe.' His threat was made good. Air raids on the Jewish quarter of the East End of London were renewed and the play was later transferred to the provinces..

At the very end of 1943, the American General, Dwight D. Eisenhower was appointed the supreme commander of the Allied forces and the British General, Bernard Montgomery was appointed his field commander. The allied forces were preparing for the invasion of Western Europe. There were many who thought that this invasion should have been the first 'second front' rather than the last of the European fronts to be attacked. The Russians, Communists and others had been calling for the opening of that 'second front' for years. Shulem supported this view, as such an attack would relieve the pressure on the Eastern European front. It would divert German forces away from the then beleaguered Russians. It would also reduce the German resources in Eastern Europe where they were systematically murdering millions of Jews. Shulem attended rallies calling for the opening of the second front but he was not sure that it had been wise for his son-in-law, the engineer, and his Communist colleagues to paint large white 'Open the second Front Now' slogans on vacant sites throughout the town. The heavy casualties suffered by the allied forces in the abortive Dieppe raid in August 1942, had somewhat reduced the pressure for an immediate opening of the second front. After that fiasco, it was generally realised that full and careful preparation was needed for such an incursion. It became clear, in the beginning of 1944, that such preparations were being made. Britain was abuzz with activity and rumours. Everyone knew that something was afoot, but no-one knew what and those in the know, certainly were not going to reveal when or where an attack would take place. Instead, official news was focused on the allied victories in Italy, the Pacific, Burma and Russia. Invasion fever continued to grow. In March, Britain blockaded Eire and banned all travel between the British mainland and North and South Ireland, in order to prevent details of invasion preparation plans from reaching German spies known to be resident in Dublin. All thought that the invasion was imminent, but the days, weeks and months passed, filled with internal action, but no invasion

One night, at the beginning of June, one of the many ammunition trains made its ponderous way towards the south coast. As it passed through the village of Soham, where Yulus had spent four of his formative years, a spark from the steam engine set one of the wagons alight. The train's engine driver and fireman and the station signalman, recognised the inherent danger of the ten thousand tons of high explosives that the train was transporting. They worked bravely and furiously to uncouple the burning wagon and then used the locomotive to separate it from the rest of the train and pull it away from the village. On its way to a safer siding, the heat from the fire detonated the deadly cargo. The devastating blast killed the fireman and the signalman and badly injured the driver. The village station and domestic gas storage tank were totally destroyed and nearby buildings were severely damaged. Some six hundred homes in the village and the school suffered damage and Soham was left without a gas supply. A mobile kitchen was brought in to provide meals for the schoolchildren when the school was reopened. Coincidentally, the D Day invasion of Western Europe commenced on that momentous day of June the sixth 1944.

A week later, the Germans launched their first jet-propelled pilotless V-1 flying bomb, the Doodlebug. This was the miracle weapon that was supposed to win them the war. The very noisy aircraft was provided with just enough fuel to fly it to its main target, London. It flew at a low level and carried a ton of high explosives. Its engine stalled when the fuel ran out, whereupon the plane would, in one way or another, fall to the ground. The weather conditions were a major factor in determining the manner in which the Doodlebug descended. Sometimes it would fall like a stone, at other times it would glide, pushed this way or that, by the prevailing winds. Minutes could pass between the engine stalling and the plane hitting the ground or careering into some buildings. The bomb laden plane exploded on impact. It did not penetrate the ground, and so its explosive blast area was considerable. London's buildings whose foundations had already been shaken by the previous more conventional bombing raids, now shuddered and often collapsed under this new high explosive onslaught. By July, some one hundred to one hundred and fifty V-1 flying bombs were being launched daily. The East End of London received more than its fair share. The noisy engine heralded the approach of the murderous missile from afar and people felt relatively safe while they could hear its raucous roar. People were less sanguine during the eerie silence that followed the engine's final splutter. They waited tensely for the explosion that was sure to follow, now, soon, near to them, hopefully some distance away. They stopped doing whatever they may have been doing and awaited the big bang. The lucky ones would then carry on with their daily tasks or hurry anxiously to where the bomb had fallen to see whether relatives or friends had been hurt, or their property damaged. Many children were once again evacuated from London, but Yulus and most of his classmates remained. They were nearing their School Certificate examinations.

That school year had not been an easy one for Yulus who had had to make some difficult choices regarding his new school curriculum. On which subjects should he concentrate his studies? He reasoned that as his best subjects were English and Mathematics, he could neglect them somewhat, to concentrate on those new subjects of which he had little or no knowledge. He had been made aware that he could not possibly cover a five-year course in one school year and so he planned his work accordingly. He inquired as to the nature of the end of term examinations and did extra cramming prior to them. The system seemed to work. His first term report stated that his end-term History examination results were better than expected. His second term report stated that he was showing considerable promise in Physics while his English examination results were disappointing and that English and French needed attention. His third, and final, report was encouraging. It stated that he had worked hard and deserved success.

The school year had its humorous moments. Yulus became friendly with the boy with whom he shared a desk at the back of the class. They were often in trouble for talking in class and ordered to stay behind for an half hour or an hour after lessons, as punishment. They usually exploited that time to do some of their homework and so did not consider detention too much of a bind. Prefects were appointed from senior boys at the school to supervise these sessions, and also regular classes, when the master was called away from the classroom. Many students at the school were new, as the school had only recently been reorganised from a wartime emergency Secondary School into a regular Grammar School. Senior boys could not easily put a name to a face of a younger pupil at the school, as they might have done in the prewar days of continuity. Yulus and his friend exploited this deficiency. On one occasion, when a prefect called on one of them to come to the front of the class, the other went in his stead to the merriment of the other boys and the bewilderment of the prefect. I know you, he said to the friend, you are not Yulus. Yes I am, the friend insisted. Then show me your identity card, said the prefect. The British had an anathema to photographs. British identity cards issued during the war made no requirement for a photograph of the holder to be attached. Alien Registration Cards had to include photographs of the holders, but the holder's signature was all that was required of a British citizen. The friend searched in his pocket for the document that was to reveal his true identity. Here it is, he said as he handed over Yulus's identity card. The conspirators had anticipated the prefect's request and swapped cards. Let me see your card, demanded the flustered prefect of Yulus. Certainly said Yulus, producing his friend's card. Now, said the prefect, recovering his composure, sign here and let me see who is who. The game was up and the boys confessed. It was only a joke, they said. Joke or no joke, this will cost you another hour tomorrow. The friends were satisfied. The farce was worth the fine.

The day of the examination arrived. The examination could not take place in the classroom because of the threat of the flying bombs. There was a danger of flying glass that at worst, could cause injury or at best, disturbance, and examinees are not to be disturbed. Desks were arranged in the corridors. The glass fanlights above the classroom doors were boarded up to prevent shattered glass from falling on the students. Instructions were given, that if an air raid siren was sounded, the boys were to stay where they were and continue with their examination. They would be informed as to what to do in the event of an emergency. Heads down, the boys began their task of answering the intricate questions that were to determine their fitness for further education. Shortly after commencement, an air raid siren was sounded. The boys looked up. The supervising master, put a finger to his lips to indicate silence and then mimicked the underarm throwing of a football with both hands to indicate that the exam should continue. Yulus and his classmates were writing copious notes to show their erudition, when the ominous sickening sound of the

Doodlebug's engine could be heard getting louder and louder. Whenever a boy looked up anxiously, the master would repeat his miming actions. The engine noise grew very loud and then suddenly stopped. Simultaneously, the boys stopped writing. Each sat, with pen in hand, poised over the examination answer paper. Everyone sat frozen in place like a statue, or like the unfortunates who were inundated when the Vesuvius volcano erupted at Pompeii, waiting, waiting, waiting, for the explosion. The master too sat in statuesque silence, waiting. Then came the loud bang. The boards, protecting the glass fanlights, rattled, the master resumed his miming actions, and writing again began in earnest. Were they trying to bomb Yulus again?

Some weeks later, Yulus received a certificate that stated that he had been awarded the School Certificate of the University of London, having satisfied the examiners in the examination as a whole and having attained passes in English, English Literature, English and European History and credits in Written French, Mathematics and General Science. Yulus was both gratified and disappointed. He could hardly believe his eyes when he saw that he had received a 'credit' in his newly acquired subject of General Science, while he had received only the relatively lowly 'pass' in English. He had always wanted to be a writer. There is, unfortunately, no completely objective way of determining the quality of an English essay, and the subjective opinions of the examiner are active ingredients in his final assessment. These explanatory words from Yulus's headmaster did little to console him, as three credits were not enough to get him on to a University Course.

Stay with your mathematics, was the short advice he received from all quarters. Why not try Accountancy, where a degree can be obtained without attending a university? A five-year Accountancy course, involved entering into Articles for which a premium had to be paid. There was an alternative seven-year course during which a small wage could be earned and that required no premium nor Articles. Shulem's economic position ruled out the first alternative. On leaving school at sixteen, Yulus embarked on his seven-year stint to acquire an Accountancy degree.

Yulus's brother-in-law, the special policeman, had sometimes to fulfill night duties. He did not like to leave his wife and baby daughter alone in their apartment during the period of continuous bombing raids. On one occasion, Yulus readily agreed to stay overnight at his sister's apartment, to give her support in the event of an air raid. In the middle of the night, Yulus felt a tugging of his arm and a faint or distant calling of his name. With difficulty, he roused himself from his deep sleep to find that the calling of his name was neither faint nor distant. The bedroom was full of the noise of the firing of anti-aircraft guns and his sister's voice, that was now very high pitched. She and her baby were under his bed. She had come into his bedroom when the air raid siren had sounded with the express purpose of getting him to accompany her to the nearby air raid shelter. He was sound asleep and she could not awaken him. She shook him, pulled and pushed him to no avail. Bombs that started to explode in the vicinity, frightened her. Clutching her baby, she took refuge under the bed from where she had continued to call and tug. Bleary-eyed Yulus, looked surprised when he realised the situation. How long have you been there? he asked his sister. Too long, came her blistering reply. Yulus climbed out of bed. He pulled his trousers over his pyjamas and sleepily put on his socks and shoes. Come on then, let's go, he said, still half asleep, to his sister who had now emerged from under the bed. Go where? she asked. To the shelter, of course. She was furious. What now that the all clear siren has just been sounded? Later, she told her husband, Never again! I would have felt safer on my own. I'm sure that it would be easier to waken the dead than that lump of teenage humanity. Yulus, chagrined, apologised, ate his breakfast in silence and went home.

It was during the night of another of the air raids, that Shulem felt intuitively that a Doodlebug had fallen close to his youngest daughter's house. He was most concerned, because she was in her advanced months of pregnancy. She was due to go, that very morning, for a short visit to her fire-fighting brother's mother-in-law who lived in Pembroke Dock in South Wales. She needed a break from the continuous air raids. She had heard about Pembroke Dock from her younger brother, whom she hoped to meet there, as he was stationed in a nearby RAF base. He had been recruited into the armed forces, shortly after returning to London from Scotland. Next morning, Shulem asked Yulus to ride over to the house on his bicycle in order to allay his fears. *Ich vais nisht voos es is*, he said, *ober Ich vill vissen az zi hot avec gegungen tzu Wales gezinteheit*, I don't know what it is, he said, referring to his feelings, but I would like to know that she has got away safely to Wales.

As Yulus entered the street in which she lived and saw an ambulance speeding away at the other end, he realised that Shulem's concern was not misplaced. Groups of people were standing in the glass strewn street outside the house in which his sister was living. What has happened? he asked. The floors and ceilings of that house collapsed, one person said, pointing to his sister's abode. Two people living there have been taken to hospital by ambulance, said another. Yulus's heart fell to his stomach. Was one of them pregnant? he asked anxiously. Yes. Yulus felt sick. Was she badly hurt? No-one seemed to know. Was he hurt? Yes, said one, he had a head wound. Was he hurt badly? I really don't know, but he was bleeding profusely. To which hospital have they gone? Yulus asked, hardly waiting for an answer as he readied himself to ride away. Hackney Hospital, do you know where it is? Yes, yes, and thanks, Yulus shouted over his shoulder as he sped away.

He found his sister in the waiting room, somewhat shaken, but otherwise unhurt. And the baby? What about the baby? The baby too, will be fine, she said adding, How did you know I was here? Yulus told her of Shulem's premonition. What happened? Where is your spouse? Is he alright? he asked her without pause between questions. I'll answer the last questions first, she said. He was hit on the head by a tile and is having the cut stitched right now. They said it wasn't serious wound, but there was blood everywhere, she said stoically holding back her tears. Will they keep him in? They said no. Good, that means that it really can't be too serious. Bad enough, she said. Now, tell me what happened, he insisted. She explained that she was due to go to Pembroke Dock the next morning. Her suitcase was already packed. Normally, she slept in the upstairs flat, but not so on this occasion. The landlady had herself gone away for the weekend and had insisted that she sleep on the Ottoman sofa in the ground floor parlour. It will be safer there, she said, in case of an air raid. Father, is not the only one who has premonitions. At three in the morning she was awakened by an enormous bang. She felt there was some sort of dust on her face and something heavier on her legs. She wiped the dust away from her mouth and eyes and then realised that there was no ceiling above her. She pushed off part of the plaster ceiling that had landed on the blankets and sat up on the side of the sofa to find that her feet did not touch the floor. There was no floor except for the part on which the sofa stood. Such are the miracles of war. There's no floor, she shouted at her husband who had been sleeping beside her and who was brushing the white dust from his face and eyes with his hands. After removing some bricks, they climbed out of the house through the broken window frame. Luckily, the blackout material had protected them from being cut by the shattered glass window panes. She and her husband staggered down the moonlit street, still in their nightclothes, to his aunt's house that was relatively undamaged. The aunt, who lived in the same street, gave her tea and loaned her a dress. What about your husband? Wasn't he bleeding? No, not then she said, let me finish and you'll soon understand what happened. A little later, an air raid rescue man knocked on the door asking after a young pregnant woman. Thank goodness I've found you, he said, we thought you were buried under the rubble, but then someone said that they saw you walking down the street. I've knocked on the doors of half the houses in the street looking for you. Are you alright? Yes, she answered. Well, maybe you think so, he said and then insisted that she go for a check-up at a maternity hospital. The Matron at the hospital said she looked fine and that she should return in a few hours to see a doctor who could not then be disturbed because he had been up all night dealing with emergency cases. Yes, yes, said Yulus, but what about your spouse's head wound? That occurred later, she said. Having returned home from the second visit to the maternity hospital, he went into the house to retrieve some of their belongings, including her suitcase that was nowhere to be found. When he came out of the house, there was another explosion in an adjoining street. It dislodged tiles from the roofs of houses in the street, and one of them hit him on the head. An ambulance came and took him to this hospital. Did you go back to the maternity hospital? asked Yulus. Yes, of course, she said, I just told you so. And what did the doctor say? He said that the baby had moved and if I was going away to South Wales, I should stay there until after the baby was born. It would be safer that way, as the baby had been traumatised by the events of the night. So, is that what you are going to do? I'll see when I get there, she said. In the event, she did stay there and her daughter was born in a Welsh hospital.

Her suitcase had been blown out into the street. It had been picked up by one of the air raid site clearance teams that as usual were soon on the scene of bomb blasts. The dusty battered suitcase was later retrieved from the clerk at the casualty and damage desk to whom it had been handed. Such temporary desks are always quickly set up in areas where bomb damage has occurred. There, details are recorded of casualties and war damage to enable interested parties to find relatives or friends, or make war damage claims.

The engineer's injuries proved not to be serious, although the cut required six stitches. He always was hard-headed, said his father, whose one eye twinkled with obvious relief, when he heard the news. Yulus's sister was accompanied by her head-bandaged husband to Pembroke Dock, where he stayed for a few days before returning to the urgent war work in which he was employed. She telephoned her eldest brother, for him to inform Shulem, who did not have a telephone, that she had arrived safely and to tell him that her airman brother was now a sailor. She had not seen him, but he left her a note to say that he had been transferred from the RAF to the Fleet Air Arm of the Royal Navy. How does one make plans in these troubled times? she asked. Ask me, replied her eldest brother in exasperation. He too had problems. The workshop in which he was working had also been bombed, just the previous night. He needed her help. Could she find some lodgings for his wife and two young children in Pembroke Dock? He was concerned for their safety, if they were to stay in London at this dangerous time. She answered in the affirmative. She would be happy to have their company.

Shulem was delighted when he heard that his daughter and unborn baby were unhurt and that she had decided to stay for a while in South Wales. He thought, that after four years of continuous bombing, she deserved a floor under her feet and the chance to have her baby in peace and quiet

Yulus's school friend from Soham, decided to join the Merchant Navy. He was now over seventeen. His education had been disrupted by the war and he had found difficulty in finding a job suitable to his capabilities, because of the lack of supporting documentation. You were right to go to the Grammar School, he once said to Yulus. I should have done something like that when I came home from evacuation and I'm sorry now that I didn't. It was indeed a pity that this bright boy had not continued his education. He had a penchant for the Theatre. He knew the words of every one of Gilbert and Sullivan's comic operas and would happily sing any aria on request, and often without being asked. Why have you decided to join the Merchant Navy? asked Yulus. I just can't find permanent work, he explained. When I first left school, I was not at all sure what I wanted to do. I accepted all sorts of temporary jobs to see what type of work would suit my temperament and then, when I wanted to take up a career, I was told that there was no point in starting at seventeen plus, because I would be called up for the armed forces within a year. You might well change your mind when you are demobilised after a few years, they said, or you may have forgotten half of what you will have learned. So there is not much point in starting, is there? I am not sure they are right, he said, but there again, they might be. So, I thought that if I joined the services early, I might come out early and retrieve some of my lost years that way. Yulus wished him luck. But luck was not with him. On his first voyage to the Far East, he contracted some undefined disease and died on board his ship off the coast of India. He was an only son, and his parents were shattered by the news. Yulus was too embarrassed to meet with them. How can a lively young boy face bereaved parents? Yulus avoided them. They lived in the next block to him and when he caught sight of them, he would change course and sometimes walk twice the distance to his destination, rather than come face to face with them. One day, he was outmaneuvered by the father who purposely caught up with him. Yulus, said the father, I know you feel guilty that you are alive and your friend isn't. But you mustn't take this guilt upon yourself. It's not your fault. It's fate, only fate. Yulus listened in silence, his eyes lowered. You are alive, continued the father, and it's your right to live and live well and happily. The tears welled up in Yulus's eyes. He hadn't cried for his mother and he couldn't cry now, although he very much wanted to. How unfair can life be? he muttered as the father embraced him. Promise me you won't avoid us any more. I won't, whispered Yulus as they parted.

One early evening in the spring of 1944, Yulus approached the entrance to a square-built brick-faced three-storey building in Durward Street, a small street that runs parallel with Whitechapel Road. He was hesitant to enter. He stepped up slowly to the doorway. One of the double doors was open, latched back to an inner wall. He peered inside and then quickly stepped back. He felt like the character that Charlie Chaplin played in his film Easy Street when he made an effort to enter a police station in order to enlist in the police force. Charlie stepped forwards and backwards many times, in his own inimitable way, before finding the courage to enter. Yulus took a few extra steps forward. Now half his body was within the doorway. He was about to retreat yet again, when a friendly voice called to him. Can I help you? There was no going back now. Is this the Brady Boys' Club? His voice reflected the hesitancy of his body language. Yes, it is, said the young man, whose appearance now added form to the voice. Would you like to join? he asked and then recognising the uncertainty of the newcomer, immediately added, You don't have to give your answer now. Just come in and have a look around.

Yulus soon became an active member of the club that had been established in1896 as a social and recreative evening club for Jewish working boys. In those days, children began their working life at the age of thirteen, if not earlier. The club flourished and with the changing social conditions, included in its membership boys that were still at school. Yulus's writing skills were soon discovered and he was opted on to the editorial staff of the club magazine. Within a year he was appointed editor. A little later, he was voted Captain of the Club by popular vote.

Among other matters he edited for publication, letters received from previous members who were serving in the armed forces in Europe and in the Middle and Far East. Some were prisoners of war, held by the Germans and Japanese. Other members had unfortunately been reported as missing or killed in action. The Brady code included the phrase 'To serve God, King and Country.' By the end of the war, the lives of eighteen Bradians were lost fighting for this cause.

There was yet another group who had been recruited for work down the coal mines. They were among the ten percent of conscripts, called Bevin Boys, who were ordered by the Minister of Labour, to work in the coal mines because of the manpower shortage that had been created, ironically, when many young miners had volunteered to join the armed forces to get away from the pits. Working down the mines was hardly a recommended occupation. It did not attract volunteers. Wages were not high, and in March 1944, eighty-seven thousand Welsh miners came out on strike. They complained that a recent government wage's proposal did not make sufficient allowance for the more difficult Welsh seams.

The idea of a young fragile Jewish East End boy, discarding his tailored suit for a white singlet and digging away in the dark cavernous coal mines and then later emerging with blackened bulging muscles, was a source of great amusement, though hardly funny for the participant who shared the toil and dangers with the rest of the mining community. This image was possibly the source of the music hall joke that told of the Stakhanovite Bevin Boy who had received an award for personally extracting the most coal ever, in the period of one month. His award was a brand new gleaming steel coal-pick. What's that? asked the puzzled award winner. Why, it's a pick for digging out coal, came the reply. Why didn't you tell me about that before? exclaimed the newcomer to mining. Until now, I've been using my finger nails.

The club's activities included physical training, sports, first aid, dramatics, concert party, choir, arts and crafts including carpentry, table tennis, discussion groups, chess and other indoor games. In 1944, the club acquired, through a generous donation, the lease on a rundown country house at Skeet Hill, in the heart of Kent where week-ends could be spent away from London. The house and extensive grounds were later also to be used for summer camping, an activity that had been suspended because of the war. The house was renovated by club members and Yulus was among the first party to make use of its facilities. Bunk beds had been installed in the bedrooms, but mattresses had yet to arrive. On the first morning after arrival, the boys examined the criss-cross markings on each other's backs resulting from the wire bed mattress supports. In the evening, around the lounge fire, a ghost was created. An old house without a ghost was unthinkable. In that cosy atmosphere the legend of the ghostly Lady Cynthia was born.

Of the club's wide variety of activities, both physical and cultural, Yulus preferred the latter, although he did participate in team sporting activities, such as running, cricket and table tennis. In team races, he usually was last past the finishing line, puffing from the exertion and being willed on by his team mates. A completed run was worth a point. He was once invited to participate in a boxing class. The instructor was certain that Yulus's physique could withstand the inevitable blows to the head and body that boxers have to absorb. Yulus was not so sure. Nevertheless, on this occasion he was persuaded to enter the ring with a boy, whom the instructor assured him, was of similar weight and height. The comparison of ring experience was somehow omitted. The fight commenced. Yulus came out of his corner to the centre of the ring, his glove-covered fists raised in the traditional sparring position. His opponent started to side-step and bob up and down while Yulus turned on the spot to keep him in vision. The boy came close to him and Yulus flicked out a left jab, that, to his surprise, made contact with the other boy's nose. It proved to be a great mistake. This precipitous action annoyed his opponent who immediately reciprocated. Yulus's further jabs consistently missed their target while his bleeding nose managed to attract far too many blows for his liking. Thus ended his pugilistic career. His opponent, on the other hand, later became a professional boxer and then a boxing promoter.

Yulus lost his taste for calisthenics that some of his friends humorously described as grabbing hold of one's hair with one's right hand and holding oneself at arm's length. When asked, Yulus now claimed that he belonged to the less aggressive sporting community. He preferred playing chess for the club or taking part in general knowledge competitions and in the club's very active discussion group. He was particularly concerned with the democratic processes of management and government. He often came into conflict with the club leader, or Gaffer, who was autocratic in his manner of leadership. The Gaffer had come to the club at a critical time in its development and had successfully introduced various instruments of youth management. One of these was the cabinet that was comprised of members appointed by him and with himself as chairman. The boys voiced opinions relating to the running of the club and club activities, to which he listened, but his was the determining vote. Yulus accepted that most, possibly all, of the Gaffer's decisions were reasonable and based on a professional understanding of youth and their needs. But one important element was missing. The democratic right for youth to make its own decisions. He felt strongly that justice must not only be done, but be seen to be done. And he countered the argument that the ends can justify the means, with the opposing proposition that there are no ends, only means. He did, however, deviate from this last proposition, when he organised a democratic revolt when the leader was absent for a week. Elections for membership of the cabinet were held while he was away. All the previous cabinet members were elected plus Yulus, who had been considered too controversial to be appointed under the old autocratic system. Yulus attended the next cabinet meeting. What are you doing here? asked the Gaffer, unaware of the previous week's election results. I have been elected by the members, Yulus replied, fighting to keep his voice level and firm. Is this true? asked the leader incredulously. Yes, came a chorus of voices. The look of astonishment on the leader's face was a picture many would not forget. However, he was both wise enough and man enough to accept the situation. The election had effectively confirmed his wisdom of choice. It had also introduced the missing factor, the members' democratic rights of choice.

The club gave Yulus the opportunity to socialise with the opposite sex. The Brady Girls' Club had premises in nearby Hanbury Street. Twice a week, the boys were allowed to visit, to dance and fraternise with the girls, under the strictest supervision of the leader of the Girls' Club. The boys thought her somewhat tyrannical, but they soon came to regard her with considerable respect and affection. Yulus had attended modern ballroom and also folk dancing classes while at Soham. These social evenings at the Girls' Club, allowed him to show his prowess in dancing the light fantastic. He was not the best, but was far from the worst, ballroom dancer and, so he was told, his tango was a delight to watch. Yulus, for the first time in his life, took part in a fancy dress ball dressed as a stereotyped French artist. He borrowed a pair of black cycling tights from the manager cum racing cyclist, at the Accountancy firm, where he was working. He tied a black square cloth around his middle for an apron. He donned his sister's black blouse and her black beret, tied a red paisley scarf around his neck and voila, emerged as a genuine artist who failed to get a mention when the costumes were judged. Artists are rarely recognised during their lifetime.

Shulem had not arrived home from work one evening. He was usually home by seven. By eight o'clock Yulus and his stepmother were very concerned. They had no telephone and there was no way of communicating. It was very foggy that night. The sulphur saturated lime-green smog, a supreme 'pea souper' as it was called in the vernacular, had enveloped the town and it was difficult to see a hand in front of one's face. There were no street lights in case of enemy action. Buses only used their sidelights at night. He must be walking home, Yulus said to his stepmother, I'll go to the top of the road to see. I'll be back soon. Yulus walked out into the swirling green mist. At moments he could see just a little ahead, at others he could not see at all. He walked with hands outstretched, feeling for walls, corners, unlit lampposts and he felt with his feet for street junctions. As he reached the main road, he could just make out a shadowy bowler-hatted figure coming towards him. It was Shulem. They walked home together. We were getting worried, said Yulus, what happened, did you walk all the way home. Not quite, said Shulem. The bus driver lost his way. The bus driver? Yulus exclaimed in disbelief. It was always maintained that bus drivers know their route so well, that they could drive along it with their eyes closed. The fog was so thick, said Shulem, that he turned into the wrong road. He soon realised his mistake, but could not rectify the error. The conductor asked if anyone knew where they were, and apparently only Shulem with his halting English, could answer positively. They were parallel to the road they should have taken. Maybe then you can walk in front of the bus and guide him back to the route? asked the conductor. And so Shulem led the way to the junction at the end of his main road, which was the spot the bus should have reached by its usual route. Maybe I'll get a job with the bus company, said Shulem laughingly. Certainly, you should get a reward, said Yulus.

The war was still on when all these activities and incidents took place. Someone, somewhere, somehow, had promulgated that life was to be carried on as normal. What is normal? Normal is normal. In wartime normality means pretending that the war is not interfering with normal life as it was lived before hostilities interrupted that normality. It means that after a night of heavy bombing, when sleep was denied, people get up in the morning and go about their daily tasks in a routine way, denying that anything had disturbed them. Yes, talk about the bomb that fell nearby, the fact that a house or two had been declared unsafe to inhabit, but don't let such 'incidentals' interrupt the normality of existence. A friend was killed, a son was reported missing, two aircraft did not return from a sortie over enemy territory, the Germans have counterattacked, the Allies are advancing, everything is normal. School examinations were held in the corridors. What is abnormal about that? Yulus attended the party to celebrate the engagement of his demobilised brother to a red-headed nurse who lived in South London. In the evening after the party, he boarded a bus to take him back across the River Thames to Liverpool Street railway station, from where he would get another bus that would take him nearer home. Shortly after boarding the first bus, an air raid siren was sounded, no-one seemed to show concern. A little later, anti-aircraft guns began to fire and bombs could be heard exploding. The conductor informed the passengers, that the driver and he had decided to continue the journey. If passengers wanted to go to an air raid shelter, the bus would stop at a shelter along the way. They had only to say. No-one made such a request. Let's keep going they said. The bus stopped at its usual bus stops. Some people got off and some others got on. The noise of battle got worse as the bus crossed the Thames. Still no-one showed concern. This is normal behaviour. The all clear siren was sounded. People sighed with relief. That too was normal.

Chapter 23

Shulem followed the progress of the war with hope and trepidation. The joy he felt with every advance, or battle won, by the Allies, was tempered by additional adverse news of the plight of yet more European Jews. In January 1944 the Russians broke the siege of Leningrad. In February they had routed the German troops near Kiev. In March the Germans took control of their erstwhile ally Hungary where some eight hundred thousand Jews had lived in comparative safety. Now they were in mortal danger as Adolph Eichmann, the Nazi responsible for sending Jews to the Auschwitz and other concentration camps, began organizing the deportation of Hungarian Jews. In April, the Russians swept through the Crimea and captured the Black Sea port of Odessa. In May, British and American forces advanced through Italy and in June, Rome was captured just a few days before D Day, when the Allies invaded Western Europe. In July the Germans were driven out of Normandy and in August the Free French General, Charles de Gaulle led the Allied troops triumphantly into Paris. The French people were jubilant, and rightly so, but in that same month the news from Poland was sickening. The horrors of the Majdenek concentration camp were revealed. In September, the Allies had marched through Belgium. There was a setback in Holland where many allied soldiers were lost in an abortive attempt to capture the town of Arnhem.

In the same month, the Germans launched their V-2 long-range rockets against London. They carried one-ton warheads, but unlike the V-1 flying bombs that were still reaching the capital, these rockets were silent emissaries of death and destruction. They gave no prior warning of their arrival as they descended from a height of fifty miles at a speed faster than sound. They penetrated the ground and destroyed the foundations of buildings as the warheads exploded. In October, the Russians entered Czechoslovakia and the Allied forces crossed the Western border of Germany itself. The British landed in Greece and the Red Army entered Yugoslavia. The British Home Guard was disbanded in November, their war was over. Not so, the war in Europe. In December, the Germans mounted a major counterattack in the Ardennes. It took the Allies by surprise. Three bitter weeks were required to contain and defeat the Germans in what was called the Battle of the Bulge. .

In January 1945, the concentration camp at Auschwitz and the death camp at Treblinka were captured by the Russians. Now the full awful truth of the reported horrors of these and many other so-called labour camps was revealed. Many millions of people, primarily Jews, were slaughtered there in every conceivable barbarous way. Men, women and children were starved, shot, worked to death, battered to death, mutilated in ghastly medical experiments, gassed in specially constructed chambers and cremated in continuously burning ovens. Six million Jews, including one million five hundred thousand children, were murdered by the Nazis and their underlings. Their sadistic anti-Semitic obsession caused them to continue the dastardly process even when the Russian and Allied troops were in close proximity. This devilish work took priority over concentrating efforts to retard the advance of enemy troops. At the very last minute, the Nazis and their underlings fled, leaving great heaps of naked rotting emaciated corpses awaiting cremation. Thousands of survivors were so emaciated from starvation, typhoid and typhus, that they too, died soon after liberation. Shulem said that all through the war there had been a glimmer, a flicker of hope. Now, he said, it was the time to weep. Yulus shared his father's distress and felt a heaviness in his heart that he was sure was representative of the suffering of all his fellow Jews. He penned a poem that seemed to flow outwards from his inner self and yet expressed more than his own personal feelings.

I was not there
And yet I was
We were not there
And yet we were

We, the lucky ones
Whose forbears flew the European nest
Before the black and blackened German eagle pounced

We were not there
But our Grandmothers were
And our grief and anger remain unabated
At the bestial manner in which they were humiliated

The atrocities echo across the nation and time
Reawakening the would-be deaf
Reopening the unhealed wounds
Reamplifying the unheard cries
Reinforcing the resolve to never ever
Endure such miseries again

Who said the Jews should suffer because they are Jews?
Or man should suffer for his views?

Was it God who has long forsaken mankind?
Or mankind that has forsaken God?

A thousand miles away
A thousand years away
The stench of the stinking Nazi cesspool
Will forever permeate the thinking Jewish soul

One need not be near the gas chambers
To smell the foul gas
One need not see the acrid smoke of the crematorium
To know it symbolises the Nazi German emporium

The universe, so the scientists say
Is dotted with black holes
Their energy draws into its very centre
All within its range

So with the Holocaust
It is the black hole of the Jewish collective soul
It draws and will continue to draw us in
For generations to come

The Jew knows in his heart
That the past will never pass
It is with us forever

Shulem kept in touch with his brother in Mauritius where internment
conditions were indeed difficult. In December 1944, the British government
issued a bland official report concerning the Jewish internees on the island in
the Indian Ocean. It reported that there were 1,400 inmates, and that there had
been 57 marriages,12 births and 17 deaths in the half-year to September 1943.
It said that the general buildings included two Synagogues, one Orthodox and
one Liberal, that there had been four Barmitzvahs and eight circumcisions. It
reported that two hundred artisans were employed in motor repair workshops,
that underclothing and jams were produced by the refugees and that Hebrew
and English were taught in the schools.

In contrast, an account by a refugee on conditions on the island, reported in
the Jewish Chronicle, stated that the men were housed in a penitentiary dating
from Napoleonic times. There were two large stone buildings containing four

hundred solitary cells. The men were separated from the women and children who were housed in corrugated huts. There was hardly any schooling and little chance of vocational training. Only a few men were allowed to work and earn money outside of the camp. The two hundred men working in the camp were unpaid at first and then lowly paid. Food consisted chiefly of tropical vegetables and only those who received remittances from relatives abroad were able to preserve their health. Most prisoners suffered from under-nourishment, scurvy and malaria that was endemic on the island. Up to one hundred and eighty persons were always in hospital, a twenty-minute walk away. Often, the sick, with high fever, had to walk that distance or be taken in a food cart. Over the years, 104 people had died, 50 from typhus. In 1943, eighty Austrian Jewish internee volunteers, joined the British Army Pioneer Corps and another two hundred volunteers joined the Czech Army stationed in Britain. An indignant letter to the Jewish Chronicle in January 1945, compared the harsh way the Jewish refugees were being treated in Mauritius with the cosy treatment the Nazi, Rudolph Hess, was receiving as an internee in Britain. Hess was treated like an honoured guest, being taken for daily motor rides and provided with the best food available.

In February 1945, Shulem received letters from Mauritius, from his brother and his niece. She complained of the monotony of life on the island which was only alleviated by her learning French and Hebrew and by the fact that, once a fortnight, she was allowed to go to town where there were Indian and Chinese shops. She wrote about the strong cyclone that had recently hit the island. It did a lot of damage, uprooting very big trees and lifting the roof off the hut in which she and her mother lived. When the cyclone reached the island, the women were transferred to the men's brick-built quarters for safety. They returned to their huts as soon as they were repaired. A wit who had enjoyed the temporary female company, remarked at the time, that it would be nice if they could have more cyclones.

His brother thanked Shulem for the money that he, together with one of his cousins, had sent to the island. It had been most helpful. He lived in hope that the terrible war would soon be over and that he would be allowed to enter Palestine and lead a sane and normal life again. His son, who at fifteen, had succeeded in reaching Palestine, was now a soldier in the Jewish Brigade serving with the British Army in Italy. He had been wounded in action and was now recovering in an Army hospital. He had written to the King of England explaining that he was serving in the British forces while his parents and sister were interned on Mauritius. The British authorities had replied, stating that his family would be allowed entry into Palestine after the war.

The letter also contained a very sad note. There had, regretfully, been no news of their mother and sister and family who had remained in Mlawa.

Shulem had made extensive enquiries about them and about his other brother and family who had not left Hamburg in Germany before the outbreak of the war. He could get no specific details, but it became clear that they had all perished in the Nazi Holocaust. Reports from Mlawa survivors stated that the Jews of the area who were assembled in the Mlawa ghetto were transported to the death camps in 1942, if not previously murdered. The elderly and children were sent to the Treblinka gas chambers for immediate annihilation while the able-bodied were transported to Auschwitz, where they were worked, starved and then gassed to death. In June 1944, Goebbels had declared that there was no longer a Jewish problem in the Reich. Germany was Judenrein. Germany was cleared of Jews.

What a strange world, thought Shulem. The war in Europe was now over and yet not over. It was over for the Gentiles but not for the Jews, especially not for the displaced Jewish survivors of the Holocaust. Where were they to go? Who would accept them? Some had gone back to their home towns to find their homes occupied by Gentiles who had never expected them to return. Some were even killed, on their return, in a pogrom in Poland. In any event, who would want to live amongst the people who, at worst had murdered their loved ones or collaborated with the killers, and at best had done nothing to prevent the catastrophe? The Western countries would take a limited quota of refugees, tokens to salve their consciences, but where were the rest to go? Palestine, which was the natural place for them to go, was still closed to the majority of Jews. The British government had once promised to provide a national home for the Jews in Palestine, but had since reneged on that promise. The British parliament had stood in silence for a minute to record its antipathy to the sadistic Nazi persecution of the Jews, but where was the real practical expression of sympathy? Gunboats that turned displaced persons away from their only safe haven? Internment camps in Cyprus? Displaced persons' camps in Europe? The Allies, the British in particular, seem not to want to even help solve the problems of the displaced Jews. Instead their policies were exacerbating the problem and encouraging illegal actions on the part of those desperate displaced Jewish Holocaust survivors who want to emigrate to Palestine. It provoked violence on the part of the Jews in Palestine against a restrictive authority. No, for them, the war was not yet over.

What a strange and unjust world thought Shulem. He had survived the war, but his mother had not. She had been gassed in the Nazi Treblinka death camp. What had that dear, dear innocent woman done to deserve such a fate? His sister, brother-in-law and their children too, what had they done? And his brother and family in Hamburg? What was their crime? That they did not leave the Reich before the Nazis could murder them? Shulem remembered that his

210

brothers had scoffed at him in the pre-war days when they were prospering in Europe while he was living in relative poverty in London. Now it has transpired that he was the wise one. But who could say that those early geographical choices were made out of wisdom? They had also scoffed about the religious faith that he had maintained and they had abandoned. Would religion have improved their lot? Had it improved his?

What a strange and unfathomable world. The disgusting Nazi concentration camps were liberated and there was much joy in that. The unimaginable suffering of those incarcerated Jews had ceased. Unimaginable to decent thinking people, though regular daily fare for the Nazi perpetrators and their victims. Those abominations had ceased and Jews in London were rejoicing that the European war was almost over when, once again, tragedy struck the East End London Jewish community. At the end of March, the very last German V-2 rocket to fall on London crashed into Hughes Mansions, a block of flats in Valance Road, Stepney. One hundred and thirty people were instantly killed. Whole families of Jewish people were wiped out in this last devastating early morning blow. Twenty-one of the young people who lost their lives in this tragic incident, were members of the Brady Clubs of which Yulus too, was a member. He was terribly upset and wrote an article to their memory in his club magazine. He wrote that his generation would fight to see that the evil forces that brought so much death and misery would never rise again. Amen, but when Yulus asks me, where was God in all this? What answer do I have? The only one I know. *Fin Gott fraigt mir nisht*, One doesn't question God.

What a strange and idiotic world. Shulem continued with his thoughts. He had survived the war but his East London Yiddish speaking community had not. Its infrastructure had been deliberately and completely destroyed by the German bombing raids. Yes, there could be little doubt on this matter. It was deliberately targeted for destruction together with the Jews who lived there. Lord Haw Haw had said that London would be hit hard by German bombers and that the Borough of Stepney, where the Jews live, would be hit hardest of all, and that is what happened. One third of all the housing in the Borough was either destroyed or made unfit for habitation and for what? To satisfy a sadistic anti-Semitic obsession? The post-war population of the Borough was now less than half of what it was before the war. Many *Shuls*, Synagogues, and Jewish schools had been destroyed while others were badly damaged. Most of the individuals who made up the community had survived, but they had been dispersed throughout London or even further. Yiddish and *Yiddishkeit* in London had suffered a heavy blow from which it was unlikely to recover. The *Shabbas droshes*, Sabbath sermons, at the *Shul*, that he now attended, were delivered in English with perhaps the odd Yiddish word thrown in for the sake of nostalgia. Shulem sadly envisaged in his thoughts that his grandchildren would grow up almost, if not completely, ignorant of Yiddish. It will be an obscure and long lost language that even history books will ignore and *Yiddishkeit*, the communal way of life of Yiddish speaking people, will be even more obscure.

It was late autumn 1945. It was *Yom Kippur*, the Jewish Fast Day and Day of Atonement. Yulus did not accompany Shulem to *Shul* that year. He told his father that he would attend the special service being held at the Brady Girls' Club. He explained that the club hall had been made into a temporary Synagogue. The special service was to commemorate the victims of the last V-2 rocket to fall on London and those club members who had been in the British armed forces and had given their lives fighting the enemy. Yulus assured Shulem that he would say *Kaddish*, the memorial prayer for the dead, for his long departed mother and now also for his grandmother and other relatives who had died in the Holocaust.

During the break between the morning service and the resumption of prayers in the afternoon, Yulus and his friends walked along the war torn streets of the East End of London. They viewed the utter mad wasteful destruction that the war had left in its wake. Yulus was not the only one to ask, Where was God in all this? And in the other multitude of calamities that had occurred during the war? The Holocaust was uppermost in their minds, but they were also very disturbed by the wholesale loss of life when the Japanese towns of Hiroshima and Nagasaki were obliterated by the two atom bombs dropped by the American Air Force. It shortened the Far Eastern War, said one. Yes, but at what a price, said another. What I cannot understand, said Yulus, is why two bombs? Wasn't one enough? No-one was qualified to answer.

They walked past the bomb site that was once the Rivoli Cinema. We saw some good films in there in our time, said one of the friends pointing at the pile of rubble. We did indeed, said another, and then each tried to remember the titles of the films they had seen and enjoyed and the actors and actresses who starred in them. They did not always agree as to the quality of the films or the ability of the actors or directors.

They continued their walk and discussion. Churchill must have been surprised with the size of Labour's massive victory in the recent General Elections. Maybe, he was a fine war leader, but he was still a Conservative and was never really in touch with the masses when it came to social and domestic matters. The people's memories proved to be longer than his, and they voted on the basis of his, and his party's performances prior to the war. That is also why a Communist was elected to represent the Borough of Stepney. He was in the forefront of the fight against the Fascists in the pre-war days. He's not likely to have much influence in Parliament though. There is only one other Communist there and he comes from Scotland. Still, it does no harm to have a dissenting voice in the corridors of power. You should know, one said to Yulus, you're always disagreeing with somebody or other. Only on matters of principle, he retorted, defending himself.

The discussion moved to other more important personalities. Would the Attlee government be more sympathetic to the plight of the displaced Jews in Europe?. Will it let them into Palestine? Let's hope so, but with that anti-Semite, Ernest Bevin in the post of Foreign Secretary, it seems most unlikely. So what will happen now? There will be a struggle and more people will be killed and maimed before a solution is found. That's for sure.

Why are we fasting? Someone suddenly asked the question out of the blue. Didn't you go to *Talmud Torah*, Jewish religious classes? I know the reason for *Yom Kippur*, that's not what I meant. I mean, why are we, you and I, fasting? Is it because we believe in God? Who can believe in God after the Holocaust and that last rocket? asked Yulus. Some do. Well, I don't. Then why? I suppose, it is out of respect for my father. Is that good enough? It depends on the father. In my case, yes, it's more than good enough. Respect for one's parents who deserve it, is one of the Ten Commandments well worth keeping.

They walked all the way to Tower Hill, sat for a while on one of the benches in the garden adjacent to the Tower of London and then began to make their way back to the Club for the afternoon and evening services. Didn't you live near here? said one of the boys to Yulus. Yes, he replied, but according to the Local Authorities, the whole street is due for demolition and no new housing will be built there. Let's make a short detour and have a look. They stood in West Tenter Street, outside the damaged Temporary Shelter for Jewish Refugees and viewed the bomb damaged mess that was once Newnham Street. In pre-war *Yom Kippur* days, as on the eves of the Sabbath and other High Holydays, the street would have looked spick and span. Every front door would have had the square paving in front of it, whitened to perfection. If houses are not to be built here, what will be? They say that a Catholic School will occupy the whole site. What does your father say about that? He bemoans the fact. He is convinced that the destruction of the infrastructure caused by the German bombing of this and other streets and the many Jewish institutions in this district, spells out the end of the Yiddish speaking community that once thrived here and I am inclined to agree with him.

They stood there for some time, looking sadly and in silence at the desolate site. Yulus mulled over in his mind the momentous events of the recent past that had so affected his and his father's life and lifestyle. If, at some future time, he were to bring some complete strangers to this spot and tell them what had happened, how would he answer the question that they would surely ask? You say that this street and this East End District of London was inhabited by a thriving Yiddish speaking community. You have told us that they were here, but you have not told us to where these Yiddish speaking people have gone or what has happened to them. Can you tell us that? How would he answer? How should he answer? Sadly, only one answer continued to revolve around his brain. My friends, he would say sadly and deliberately, my friends, he would say, though strangers they may be, my friends, They have gone from here to obscurity.

THE END

Epilogue

Shulem died in June 1951 aged seventy two.

Yulus, aged twenty three, took Shulem's Alien Registration Card to the Bethnal Green Police Station and presented it to the police officer on duty. My father died, explained Yulus, and in accordance with the regulations printed on the card, I wish to report this sad fact. The police officer looked at the photograph stapled to the card and then at Yulus. He's your father, is he? he asked. He was, said Yulus, but he died last week. He's dead is he? responded the police officer, as though trying to grasp hold of the situation. Yes, said Yulus. And you are his son? Yes, said Yulus. Well, he won't need this any more, said the police officer as he tore the card into pieces and threw it into the wastepaper basket by his side. He then turned away as if to deal with some other matter. Yulus stood in shock, silently, for a few minutes and then said, Excuse me officer, aren't you going to record the fact that my father died and that I handed in his Alien Registration Card? No, that won't be necessary, his death has been registered at the Registry of Births and Deaths, hasn't it? Yes, said Yulus. So nothing else needs to be done, said the police officer. You can go. He again turned away. Excuse me one moment, said Yulus, if that is what you are going to do with the card, Yulus pointed at the wastepaper basket, do you think I might have the photo? Certainly, said the police officer, if that is what you want. He scrummaged through the wastepaper basket and produced the photograph of Shulem which was miraculously intact. The staples had somehow protected it from being torn. Thank you, said Yulus, as he looked at the serious soft-featured face and balding head of Shulem. He turned the photograph over. Boldly printed on the reverse side was, Certificate of R, the rest of the word had been torn away. Below, in smaller print, it stated that You may not be absent fro (torn) address between the hours of (torn). Yulus did not need to read any more. He thanked the police officer and asked, Is this all that is left of a human being?

The police officer shrugged.